Meet Me
in
Paradise

Meet Me in Paradise

in

Paradise

~

Libby Hubscher

JOVE
NEW YORK

A JOVE BOOK
Published by Berkley
An imprint of Penguin Random House LLC
penguinrandomhouse.com

LIBRARY OF CONGRESS CATALOGING-IN-PUBLICATION DATA
Names: Hubscher, Libby, author.
Title: Meet me in paradise / Libby Hubscher.
Description: First edition. | New York: Jove, 2021.
Identifiers: LCCN 2020035715 (print) | LCCN 2020035716 (ebook) |
ISBN 9780593199428 (trade paperback) | ISBN 9780593199435 (ebook)
Subjects: GSAFD: Love stories.
Classification: LCC PS3608.U2524 M44 2021 (print) | LCC PS3608.U2524 (ebook) |
DDC 813/.6—dc23
LC record available at https://lccn.loc.gov/2020035715
LC ebook record available at https://lccn.loc.gov/2020035716

First Edition: March 2021

Printed in the United States of America
10 9 8 7 6 5 4 3 2 1

Cover art and design by Vikki Chu

For my family,
who taught me to be careful
and inspired me to be brave,
in (mostly) equal measure

Listen, are you breathing just a little, and calling it a life?
—Mary Oliver, "Have You Ever Tried to Enter the Long
Black Branches"

One

MARIN

AT OUR MOTHER'S FUNERAL, I lost Sadie. One moment she was beside me, shaking hands with strangers who had come to tell us how sorry they were and wax poetic about our mother's appetite for life, the next she was gone. Sadie was like that, in perpetual motion. It never bothered me until that moment, because she hadn't been my responsibility before, but in that cathedral my mother would have detested with all those people who didn't really know us, I suddenly realized that I was the only person Sadie had left. I endured several endless moments in a silent panic, until her shoe struck me on the top of my head. I looked up and found her sitting on one of the oak rafters thirty feet above the crowd of mourners, swinging her legs back and forth like a child on a park bench. I said nothing. I wasn't about to climb up there and, besides, it would have been no use. Sadie didn't march to her own drummer . . . she was a regular one-girl Mannheim Steamroller, and she wouldn't come down until she was good and ready or she became so exhausted she lost consciousness and fell. Until then, all I could do was return to the awkward handshakes and hugs and worries.

That was twelve years ago. I'm thirty now, all grown up and a world-class professional worrier. I don't mind. Not really. For all her antics, Sadie is like the sun, warm and bright and singular. Anxiety is simply the price I pay to orbit around someone like her, someone amazing, who is constantly running off to climb some untamed mountain or photograph a never-before-seen tribe in a remote jungle. She feeds off adventure. I prefer fingernails, nibbling mine down to the quick while I wait for her to come back. Without her, I slog away the days, writing single-line advertising slogans for pet food companies and organic tampons all week. At night, I come home to our empty house and eat salad alone at the kitchen table, then I watch reruns until I fall asleep on the couch.

Don't get me wrong. Being Sadie's sister has its upsides, like her sharp wit, her unconditional love, and that wonderful balloon feeling I get in my chest when I know her plane has landed back here in Chattanooga and I could just float away or burst from relief. It's why I always pick her up at the airport, despite her protests. I crave that moment, the one where Sadie's searchlight smile shines through the crowd and finds me. I never go anywhere, but in that moment, it's like I've come home instead of her. And she has no idea. She's too busy trying to keep those unruly blonde curls of hers out of her face as she practically dances her way toward the baggage claim to notice. I lived for that high. And I needed a fix now.

Sadie'd been in China for three months—actually ninety-two days, seventeen hours, and forty-one minutes, according to my watch—and I had lost my cuticles and much of my will to live. I'd gotten to the airport earlier than usual, a good forty minutes before her flight was due to arrive, but now an hour had passed and the digital display over the baggage claim showed her flight number. People filtered past me, picked up luggage from the conveyer belt, but Sadie didn't appear. I half expected her to put her hands over my eyes and pretend to be some sort of intriguing stranger like she sometimes had done when I was in college and studying at the library. I checked my phone for the eight hundredth time.

"Too busy sexting to notice your own sister?"

Sadie. I wrapped my arms around her. "Hey, wild one. I was worried you were never going to get here."

"*You* worried? I can't believe it." She batted her eyelashes at me. "You of all people should know I love a dramatic entrance. Too bad you spoiled the whole thing by staring at your phone." I drew in a relieved breath. Sadie sounded like Sadie. A little hoarse from the dry air on the plane, maybe, but her sense of humor was intact. I stepped back and looked at her. She'd felt strange in my arms, like part of her was still on the plane, and now I saw why. She was thinner. Her usually cherubic face looked drawn.

"Jesus, Sadie, did you not eat or sleep in China? You look like shit."

"Wow, thanks, Marin. You're so kind. You look fantastic too, by the way." She snatched up one of my hands and examined it. "I love this new manicure you're rocking. What's it called, the Anxious Gnaw?"

I reclaimed my hand. "Point taken. I thought you were going to some sacred temple to take pictures of monks. What was it called again?"

"Guangzhou Fuda."

"Right. That was it. I guess I just didn't realize you'd be roughing it this trip."

"That's one way of putting it."

"You can tell me more about it later. Let's grab your bag and get you home. Nothing a nap and a good meal won't fix, right?"

Sadie gave me a tight-lipped smile and nodded. "Right."

In the passenger seat, Sadie dozed off minutes into our ride home. I tried to remember how she looked after she'd climbed Kangchenjunga for that eco-extreme feature last year. Probably the same. When we got to the house, I carried her duffel bag inside for her while she slept in the driveway.

"Sadie," I said, and unbuckled her seat belt. "We're home."

She rubbed her eyes. "Sorry. My body clock is totally off. What time is it anyway?"

"Noon."

"It's one a.m. in China right now."

"I forgot about the time difference. I thought maybe you were coming down with something."

Sadie shook her head and yawned. She followed me into the house and dropped onto the couch.

"Home sweet home."

"I put your bag in the laundry room. There's some take-out menus on the coffee table. I was thinking barbecue, but you can pick."

Sadie touched the menus, but she didn't pick them up. "I'm not really hungry. To me, it's still the middle of the night."

I snatched the Dave's BBQ menu up and headed toward the phone. Sure, her stomach was on Shanghai time or whatever, but knowing Sadie, there was no way she was going to turn down ribs when they were sitting right in front of her.

"I get it," I told her as I dialed. "Do you mind if I eat, though? I had to go into the office early to finish up a pitch for a new luxury pet accessory brand and skipped breakfast. I'm starving."

When the food arrived thirty minutes later, I arranged it like a Tennessee wedding banquet on the coffee table. I even got out Mom's good china that we only used for special occasions. The ribs were still steaming, sending sweet, spicy scented notes into the air. I eyed Sadie, waiting for the telltale nostril flare that would happen right before she grabbed the entire Styrofoam box and claimed it as her own, like some kind of ravenous alpha she-wolf.

"I'll be back," she said, and climbed off the couch.

"Where are you going?" I asked. Sadie was walking away from ribs?

"Bathroom."

I sat on the couch in front of enough food to feed a football team, perplexed. Sadie never turned down Dave's. Not at noon, not at midnight. Never. We always joked that she had multiple stomachs. One was always on call. I remembered reading something while I was on one of my insomnia-driven research binges, that in China you have to drink boiled or bottled water. Maybe she hadn't followed that rule? Next to me, Sadie's phone buzzed on the cushion. I picked it up. A text message flashed across the screen. It was from Jessica, the senior editor at the magazine. I didn't mean to read it, but Sadie and I didn't have secrets. Jessica had kept it short. Her text read: Let me know if there's anything I can do.

Weird. Anything she could do, what was that all about? I stared at the screen for a moment. "Maybe I'll have some of that brisket," Sadie said.

I dropped the phone. "Great." I picked up her computer and put it down in the middle of the buffet. "I charged your laptop—how about a Sadie Slideshow while we eat?" The screen came on and there was a picture of a man. He was bald, with tan, shriveled skin. Still, he was smiling.

"Maybe later," Sadie said, closing the laptop. "I haven't had a chance to cull yet." She grasped a small piece of brisket between her fingers and placed it on her tongue. "What? I had my hands full."

"Was he one of the monks?"

"He was someone I met at Fuda." I waited for her to elaborate. She always had such great stories about her subjects, but she was too busy dissecting another piece of meat with her fingertips.

"Are you sure everything's okay?" I said.

"No. Everything is not okay. There's not even close to enough barbecue sauce on this. Dave's off his game."

"I meant with you."

She waved a hand at me before dumping an entire container of barbecue sauce over the meat in front of her. "You worry too much."

"I know I do. It's just one of the areas in which I excel," I said. My anxiety was almost a running joke between us, except when it wasn't. I turned my attention to the tub of coleslaw and started making a mountain on my plate. "Did something happen in China? You can tell me. I promise not to freak out."

"Nope," she said. "Nada. Zilch. *Méi Shì*. I picked up a little Mandarin, does that count? Turns out you're not the only brainiac in the family."

"That's great." I smushed the coleslaw mountain with my fork. "I just wonder if you could use a little break from all this crazy travel and these hard-core assignments."

She shrugged. "I love that stuff."

"I know you do. But you've been on the road all year . . . Peru, then Canada, now China for months. You barely had time to call, and when you did, it was like five minutes. And"—I chose my words carefully—"you have to admit you look a little run-down."

"You've got me there. I am a little tired. And I'm sorry. I love my work, but I love you too. And I missed you, Mar, even if I'm a shit who doesn't video call as often as I should to let you know that." Sadie was quiet for a long time. She poked at the brisket on her plate. "Tell you what, let's take a long weekend somewhere warm and beautiful and relaxing, just you and me. We'll finally put that emergency passport of yours to use. We can get massages and bankrupt the all-you-can-eat buffets. I'm thinking froufrou drinks on a beach and meaningless sex with pool boys."

"Since when have you ever known me to do any of those things?" I asked.

She gave me a look. "Please. I know you and Ted used to get it on. It's a small house. Good acoustics." She gave an exaggerated gasp. "Is it possible that it's been so long you've forgotten?"

"Not all of us are as libidinous as you. And besides, Ted and I were in a serious relationship. It wasn't meaningless."

"Fine. Come with me and have *meaningful* sex with pool boys. It's just what the doctor ordered . . . Or, Jessica had said something about another assignment for me. What was it . . . hmm . . . Russia maybe, no . . ." Sadie tipped her head to the side. She was really milking this. She tapped her forehead. "Not Venezuela. Oh! I remember now, Papua New Guinea. You know, small island near Australia. Ever heard of it?"

"You're messing with me."

Sadie shook her head. "Would I do that? Nope. Three months with a tribe in the highlands. And snakes. Lots of bad ones there. So much venom."

Maybe it was envisioning Sadie surrounded by a slew of venomous jungle creatures, but I caved, faster than I'd like to admit. "Fine."

She flashed me one of her famous exaggerated expressions; this one I titled "complete shock plus palpitations" based on the drop of her jaw and the hand on her heart. "Marin Cole," she said. "Did you just agree to a beach trip?"

"What can I say?" I told her as I put my arm around her shoulder and pulled her toward me. "You are a force that is futile to resist, Sis."

She bumped me with her shoulder and said, "Don't you worry about a thing. It's going to be perfect. Just leave the whole thing to me."

I didn't know what I'd been thinking earlier; she was the same old Sadie. The mischievous glint was back in her eyes. "Famous last words," I said. "Pass the hush puppies."

Two

SADIE

I GUESS I SHOULD start with why did I plan this? I'll tell you a story. One time, when I was in high school, our house caught on fire. I can't remember what caused the fire exactly—a faulty wire, a shorted-out kitchen appliance, me leaving a pot of my famous sauerkraut soup cooking on the stove overnight—it's not important. My older sister, Marin, woke up to the shriek of the alarm and a smoke-filled hallway. She's always been a light sleeper. I, on the other hand, could sleep through the apocalypse. It's practically a superpower of mine. My memory of the fire is just shreds of moments, tiny recollections here and there. Pain in my arms. Marin's upside-down face streaked with black. Her robe on my cheek. How cold the air was outside. Flashes of red light. The things we had to throw away because of the water and smoke damage, pictures of Mom that we couldn't replace. We never talked about it. For Marin, talking about her death made it more real. I only knew what happened because a firefighter told me. I slept through the whole thing. If Marin hadn't gotten me out, I wouldn't have made it.

She saved me.

I was asleep and in trouble and she dragged me out.

All this to say, this is my way of dragging her out. Marin's been sleeping for a long time, and our house is on fire.

Three

MARIN

THE ENTIRE POPULATION OF Tennessee seemed to be at the Nashville airport, everyone, that is, except for Sadie. In classic form, something had come up at the last minute and she'd promised to get a ride with a friend. For the past half hour, I'd been scanning the crowd, tapping my boarding pass in my hand, and checking the time on my phone on repeat—in that order. And now, our flight was due to start boarding any minute. This wasn't fashionably late, this was missing-the-flight-without-a-miracle late. Of course, I'd insisted on being at the airport the recommended two and a half hours early. Sadie, on the other hand, still hadn't completely unpacked from China. None of this was surprising. She was the spontaneous, carefree yang to my admittedly uptight yin. Somebody had to keep shit together.

I took my phone out and tapped off a quick message. If being a pain in the ass was a sport, you'd be a gold medalist. Where the hell are you? You're going to miss the trip, you know, the one you insisted we take!

Then I remembered that the whole reason I agreed to this last-minute sisters' getaway was to spend time with her. That and I'd come up with a plan to convince her to quit the magazine and come work with me at the advertising firm where I was employed—we needed a photographer, she was a photographer . . . it was perfect.

A couple of Bahama Mamas, a little pool boy flirtation, and Sadie would be putty in my hands. *Play nice,* I told myself. Delete. Delete.

Where the heck are you??????

Not quite there. I tweaked the verbiage the way I did for my ad campaigns. Think about the target consumer, what do you want them to feel? How will you make them want to buy what you're selling? Sadie wasn't a customer, exactly, but it was the same idea. I needed Sadie in a good mood so she'd finally take my advice to find a more stable job in town.

Where are you, Sis? Hope everything is okay. ☺

It wasn't perfect, but if I took any longer our nonrefundable tickets would be worthless. I hit send.

A voice crackled over the airport loudspeaker. I couldn't make out what the gate attendant was saying, so I turned to a woman nearby who was tucking a magazine into her purse.

"Sorry. Could you hear that announcement? I missed it."

"Oh yeah, totally. It said, Island Air to St. Maarten, first-class passenger boarding. I only know 'cause I'm going there for my honeymoon. As soon as my husband gets out of the bathroom, I've got a glass of champagne with my name on it. How about you?"

"Oh, um, yeah. Same. Well, not the honeymoon or husband part. Just a quick getaway . . . with my sister." Who still had not shown up. And had not yet bothered to respond to my text. Basically the opposite of a husband. For a brief moment, I let myself wallow a little in the memory of my ex-boyfriend, Ted—the closest I'd come to a husband, a college boyfriend who . . . well, we'd really liked each other, even if it wasn't meant to be. It's funny the things that you remember. He had a great laugh. I missed that. And he could wear the heck out of a baseball hat.

The woman's husband arrived then, wearing a white hoodie with *Mr. Right* emblazoned across the chest in shiny gold script. She stood and revealed her own coordinated sweatshirt, a very pale pink with the same gold script *Mrs. Right* across the chest.

"Here he is!" the woman said, grinning, and then grabbed a fist-ful of that hideous sweatshirt to pull him in for a kiss. They were sort of cute in their coordinated outfits, if not slightly vomit-inducing. Heat rose in my cheeks and I wondered momentarily if it would be super rude to flee. Instead, I did what everyone does in those un-comfortable situations and took out my phone again. I started a new text to Sadie, and this time, I decided not to sugarcoat the situation.

> Do I need to remind you that sisters' trip is plural? The plane is boarding. You'd better be through security soon or you won't make it.

No answer.

Next to me, the couple was still going at it. It was impressive, actually—they didn't seem to need air. Mrs. Right threw a pink-tracksuit-clad leg over Mr. Right's. *Okay, you're in love. You're on your honeymoon, we get it.* I picked up my leather carry-on. As I walked away, I started to feel a little bad for my mental tirade.

"Congratulations!" I called back, but it sounded awkward, even to me.

On the other side of the carpeted waiting area, I found a spot against a large pillar near the line that was forming beside the Jetway entrance. From where I stood, I couldn't see the Rights, but I would be able to spot Sadie and her trademark bouncing curls as soon as she got through security. *If* she got through security. I smoothed a hand over the sleeveless emerald silk blouse I was wear-ing. I'd felt good putting it on this morning, but it suddenly seemed like a stupid choice for the trip. *Don't wear your usual business stuff,*

Sadie had said. *You know, the kind that makes you look like a high school principal. Wear something cute. Green. You look great in green. Now let's talk about underwear*, Sadie'd gone on. I'd told myself that I was going to go along with her suggestions until I had her back in Tennessee for good, but I'd had to cut her off there with a promise that I'd buy some new clothes. The blouse had been a compromise, along with a pair of linen pants. Ann Taylor was the right look in any situation, wasn't it? I glanced down at the pants. Did anyone actually wear linen in real life? Why was it a thing? They were wrinkled already, and though I was fighting an irresistible urge to buy an iron in the airport and fix them, I understood their plight. I was starting to feel a bit wrinkled myself.

My phone dinged. Finally, Sadie had texted me back.

> I'm close, but if I don't make it, I'll get the next one. Go ahead without me. XO

Go ahead without me? Just like that, like it was no big deal, like I did it all the time. Was this Sadie's idea of a sick joke? I took an intentionally deep breath. While Sadie'd been in China these past few months, I'd downloaded a meditation app and started using it. In-two-three-four. Out-two-three-four. Nope, Sadie was not kidding. Unlike me, the big fraidy-cat who'd never left the state, much less the country, solo international travel was a regular old day at the office for Sadie. It was practically her trademark move. I let the facts sink in. Sadie had planned an entire international girls' weekend and then was going to miss the damn flight. I closed my eyes. I wanted to be mad, I really did. I picked up my bag and started looking for the exit. Sadie might have been cool jetting off to some random tropical island on her own, but not me. I was putting an end to this fiasco and going home.

My phone dinged again.

Don't even think about coming back to this house, you
pansy-ass. I used all my miles for your first-class ticket.

I glared at my phone. That little mind-reading punk. A second
later, Sadie sent one more text. No worries, Sissy. I'll be right behind
you. You've got this. Have a drink on the plane for me.

I'd like to say that I decided to go ahead and get in line to board
the flight because I'm a badass. Or even because I was fully com-
mitted to my plan to convince Sadie to join the firm so she could
stay home with me. But really, she goaded me into it. Just like she
could goad me into anything. I would show her just how big of a
pansy-ass I wasn't. Ha. Of course, when it came to picking up my
carry-on and actually walking over to the line, my indignant resolve
faded fast. Heaving a sigh, I leaned over to grip the handle of
the carry-on. Why the heck was I doing this again? I'd never even
left Tennessee. I hated airplanes. I was afraid of heights. Sadie's
voice popped into my head. *Shut up and get your shit together, Mar.
You're supposed to be the adult here.* I straightened up. That's right. I
was the one who had taken care of her all these years since Mom
passed, not the other way around. Back then, I'd had no idea what
I was doing either. I'd been seventeen, terrified, heartbroken, unsure
of anything. And we'd made it through. This was nothing, right? I
could totally get on this plane.

Another announcement came across the loudspeaker and everyone in the waiting area rushed to form a new line. I hung back for
a moment. Sadie might still make it. I turned back to face the on-
coming traffic from security and scanned the queue one more time.

"Ladies and gentlemen, this is the last call for Island Air flight
292 to St. Maarten. Please make your way to the gate for immediate
and on-time departure."

I reluctantly joined the end of the line.

"Welcome to Island Air," a steward said as he took my ticket. He was dressed in a navy-blue uniform accented with gold embroidery that flashed only about half as brightly as his huge smile.

"Thanks."

"Two-A. That's a window. Lucky you."

"Lucky me." My attempt to sound upbeat fell flat. In trying to recall historic moments of personal strength, I'd also recalled a horrifying fact—Sadie was the one bringing me some Ativan she'd gotten "from a friend" for the flight. Sadie always had something that she'd gotten "from a friend." I was pretty sure her thing now was weed. She smelled like patchouli-flavored peanut butter. When I'd asked her about it, she'd shrugged. "It's legal," she'd said.

"Not in Tennessee."

"What's the saying? It's legal somewhere."

"That's not the saying," I objected.

I hadn't objected to the suspiciously obtained antianxiety pills that I would now have to go without. Cold sweat prickled on the back of my neck. Strike two in the clothing department. Not only was I wearing wrinkled pants, but now my fear of flying was going to ruin my new silk blouse with stress sweat stains.

The steward made a face. I hesitated, looking down at my phone. I didn't want to get on this plane without my sister. Honestly, I didn't want to get on this plane at all. What if something happened? What if the plane dropped out of the sky or an engine exploded? I couldn't leave Sadie alone. She was a mess—burned out, skinny, always running from one dangerous assignment to the next. At this point, even a visit to a temple in China had worn her out. She needed stability. She needed me. That was the whole point of this trip, I reminded myself. Plus, Sadie'd been so excited about this sister trip. Sadie—the girl who never planned a thing—had made a binder. She'd been adorable, insisting on doing everything herself.

We both needed a break, she claimed. I couldn't argue with that logic. I'd just finished a huge campaign for a new language-learning AI company, and Sadie, who normally was bouncing up and down with energy like Tigger, was having trouble shaking the jet lag. A weekend of tropical relaxation had seemed like a great idea. Quality time together. So we weren't off to the best start here, but I could breathe my way through it and just start our girls' weekend at the spa on my own until Sadie got there.

The toothy vulture in the uniform was looking at me expectantly.

"Sorry," I said.

"Tick-tock," he said. "Paradise is waiting."

It was now or never. I took a deep breath, then I handed him my ticket and passport.

"Enjoy your trip!" he called after me.

I stepped past the podium and glanced back one last time, a final hopeful check for Sadie. Which was why I didn't see the bump in the Jetway carpet, caught the toe of my high heel, and fell face-first onto the jet bridge.

Four

THE PLANE WAS A small airliner, but the first-class section featured eight spacious blue leather seats. I placed my carry-on bag into the open compartment and sank into my seat, appreciating that it was more comfortable than I'd expected. Everyone always complained about the seats. My spirits lifted. Maybe this wouldn't be so bad after all. A row all to myself.

I turned my gaze to the small oval window. Couldn't I get sucked out of this thing if it broke? I didn't see any cracks, but still. I'd been on the plane less than five minutes and I was in full pansy-ass mode. Maybe it was a good thing that Sadie wasn't here to witness it.

On the bustling tarmac below, small figures in orange vests moved about, loading bags and completing final checks on the aircraft. I just needed to keep breathing. People flew all the time without getting sucked out of windows. It was supposed to be safer than car travel. I took a pillow from the flight attendant, propped it against the window, and nestled into it. This would all be okay. I'd simply put on my headphones and play some good music, take a little nap, have some kind of drink in a coconut or something at the airport in St. Maarten, and then Sadie would meet me.

A softly accented female voice came over the aircraft's sound system. "Ladies and gentlemen, we are just waiting for one more passenger. Then we will be on our way to your destination, the beautiful Caribbean island of St. Maarten. Thank you for your patience."

I perked up in my seat and leaned over to try to see the plane's entrance and center aisle. Sadie must've worked one of her famous miracles and made it in time after all. That little punk. Several minutes passed and the passengers grew restless. Across from me, a middle-aged man in a neon-green golf shirt called the attendant. "I have an appointment I need to get to on the island. Why the hell aren't we taking off?"

"Your patience is much appreciated," the attendant said. "May I get you a complimentary beverage while you wait? It should only be a few more moments."

"It better be."

Hurry up, Sadie, before this becomes one of those stuck-at-the-gate horror stories where the passengers turn Lord of the Flies *and start death fights over packages of pretzels.* I hadn't even considered that in my list of things that could go horribly wrong when flying. I abandoned my eager stakeout of the walkway and sank down in my seat. At the sound of footsteps and a bag brushing against one of the seats, I popped up again. Sadie! Thank goodness. I could almost feel the calm from my sister and her borrowed antianxiety meds washing over me. But instead of my favorite (only) tardy sibling, my gaze settled on a man. A tall, angular hunk of a man. He was so attractive, I thought for a moment that the stress of the impending flight had caused me to hallucinate. It's entirely possible that I did some sort of extremely obvious double take. He practically radiated confident nonchalance, from his slightly worn khaki pants and linen—yes, linen, of course his wasn't wrinkled—button-down shirt, open just enough to give everyone a hint of his chest, which was irritatingly perfect, to the disheveled black hair that managed to look like he'd either just woken up or stepped off a freaking runway. And the pièce de résistance? Mirrored aviator sunglasses he'd left on inside the cabin. Who did that? Oh, I knew who . . . some celebrity, probably. Sadie would've eaten this up. She was always texting me snapshots of famous people she'd seen on planes. At the thought, my spirit lifted, just a tad. Perhaps by some miracle Sadie would show up, breathless and beaming. But no. Without a word, the man plopped down into the seat next to me and shoved his satchel under the seat in front of him. I eyed him warily out of the corner of my eye. This was too much. I had a limit and it had been exceeded. I cleared my throat.

"Excuse me." I touched his shirtsleeve to get his attention. He turned, pulling his sunglasses down. Up close, he was distractingly handsome. He had smooth tan skin, clear brown eyes, and a strong jaw. His eyes had fine lines bracketing them, suggesting that he either smiled or squinted often. One of his dark eyebrows raised slightly in an expression somewhere between irritation and mild amusement. "I think maybe you've got the wrong seat," I said. "That one's taken." I nodded toward the seat he was occupying.

"That's right. Taken by me." His voice was deep with an intriguing accent I couldn't quite place.

"No . . ." I said slowly. "It belongs to my sister, Sadie."

The man looked around with feigned dramatics, then settled back into his seat and began pulling out his headphones. "Don't see her."

"She's running late. She'll be here." *She has to be here.*

"I'm sorry," he said harshly. "They held the plane for me. I'm the last one on."

"But—"

"And this is my seat." He held a ticket clearly marked with 2B in front of his face, just below his self-satisfied smile, and flicked it with a finger.

I tried to think of something to say—words were my business, for God's sake—but came up with nothing. How could this have happened? Sadie had told me our seats were next to each other in first class. She'd used her mountain of air miles to get them. Had the airline given away Sadie's seat? Oh God, she really wasn't coming, and I'd just made a complete fool of myself. To make matters worse, he'd rendered me speechless, sitting there, mouth open like a fish out of water, trying and failing to come up with a witty retort. I was many things, but I was never speechless.

I leaned forward and reached up to increase the fan's output. The guy seized the opportunity to stretch out his long legs, slid down in his seat a bit, and commandeered the entirety of our shared armrest—he wasn't subtle about it either. Then, before I had a chance to ask if he'd mind giving me just a tiny bit of room, he donned a pair of noise-canceling headphones. I shot off a quick message to Sadie:

> Would a pansy-ass confront a celebrity on a plane?
> Asking for a friend.

Sadie wrote back immediately. Ooh, details.

Me: Forget it, I'm projecting. You left me on my own and now there's a random guy manspreading in your seat. I think he might be famous AND I was accidentally rude to him.

Sadie: Ah, anxiety is a cruel mistress. Try to enjoy the view.

Me: Ha! When you get here, you owe me an extra drink.

When she didn't respond right away, I opened my meditation app. The blossom I was supposed to breathe in unison with had just opened when the flight attendant stopped next to our row.

"Ma'am, I'm going to need you to turn off your electronic device for takeoff."

I put the phone into airplane mode. "You'll need to power your smartphone off and stow it," she said, not nearly as nicely as the first time.

"Fine, fine," I said, following the attendant's instructions. "There, it's stowed."

Turning away, I fluffed my pillow aggressively and then mashed my head into it. I'd planned on using the app to stay calm during the flight. My heart rate was already elevated. On to plan B. Try to fall asleep. Think about a beverage in a coconut, Sadie, massages, never having to see another airport again once this trip was over.

The jolt of the plane starting its push from the gate onto the runway startled me. It was rougher than I'd expected. Did that mean something was wrong with the landing gear? Before this, I'd been too preoccupied with the sexy seat-stealer to remember that I was about to hurtle into the sky in a metal can full of flammable substances. I pressed my hand against the wall, leaning to peer out the window. I should have taken my chance back at the Jetway to escape. It was too late now. The plane had already backed away from the terminal, and now the airport looked so small. I wished I was still in there—or better yet, at home—instead of in this projectile. The ground transformed into a blur as the aircraft accelerated. I gulped. Looking out the window had been a mistake. I knew what was coming—the takeoff. Any moment now. My whole body tensed with dread, my pounding heart thrummed in my ears, and then my stomach lurched as the jet lifted into the air and banked toward the ocean. I scrunched my eyes shut and gripped the armrests as hard as I could.

"That hurts," the man next to me groaned. He snatched his hand away and shook it.

Fire burned in my cheeks. I'd accidentally grabbed his arm in my death grip. "Oh no, I'm sorry," I said. "I'm not normally like this. I don't *grab* people. My sister—you know, the one who was supposed to be where you are sitting—had my Ativan."

"Oh," he said, but that was it. As unsatisfying an answer as you could get. But he did let me have the armrest. Maybe I'd misjudged him.

After several horrifying moments, the ride smoothed out and I started to feel a little better. I felt brave enough to peek out the window again. The world below appeared to shrink and then disappeared beneath the clouds. Finally feeling more relaxed, I smiled.

The clouds around us were thick and white, not the kind that came with storms.

I glanced over at my rowmate, who had put his sunglasses back on, before I settled back into my seat and closed my eyes. An announcement came across that we could now use our electronic devices, so I got out my earbuds and turned on the self-hypnosis app, the one with the soothing music and calm voice that told me to close my eyes, breathe deeply, slowly, and visualize the air coming in through my fingertips as I let the smooth motion and constant low hum of the airliner lull me to sleep.

Five

SADIE

I KNOW, I KNOW. Stranding your uptight sister alone in the Caribbean seems a bit harsh, and perhaps not the best way to start off a transformative adventure. Blame the drugs. I'm going to.

Our mom always said, the first step is the hardest one—whether you're walking into a roomful of people or jumping out of a plane, it's the same raw deal. So this is me, standing at the open door, fuselage a few feet away, wind in my face, trying to figure out how to take my big, hard step.

Marin needs this. She's carrying around a suitcase full of unresolved issues beyond her obvious adventure avoidance disorder—me, our mom, the somewhat adorable ex-boyfriend she can't quite seem to get over—and she needs closure. A fresh start. A stint in paradise orchestrated by her little sister.

The first thing you should know is that as soon as my fabulous, mega-control-freak, best big sister a girl could ask for has the chance, she will be on the first plane back to Tennessee, if she gets on the plane in the first place.

She has to make it to Saba. My plan won't work any other way—and it has to work.

She'll be the brunette knockout dressed like she's about to scold a student for talking in the library. She should be wearing green and probably a pair of uncomfortable shoes with a heel, along with an expression of poorly disguised panic and extreme irritation (my fault).

Don't let her fool you—she's wonderful.

Six

MARIN

THE LOUD DING OF the seat belt alert startled me awake. I pulled myself up straight in my seat and adjusted my limbs as they came back to life. How long had I been sleeping? The cabin was bright, and out the window the clouds were thick and gray. Ominous, maybe. No—foreboding. I glanced over at the man next to me and he caught me. Just great. I reached for the SkyMall catalog sticking out of the seat pocket in front of me.

The plane lurched. It propelled me forward, hard. My head smacked the tray table and the seat belt dug into my core. I hadn't been flung completely out of my seat, thankfully, but I had to grab the armrest and pull myself back. My head stung.

Over the speakers a woman's voice sounded. "Ladies and gentlemen, we are experiencing some turbulence. Please remain in your seats with your seat belts securely fastened around you."

Turbulence? Even the word had a bad feeling to it.

Another tremor shuddered through the aircraft. That must be the turbulence, I thought. I fumbled for the seat belt strap and yanked to tighten it. I took another peek at my neighbor. He didn't seem fazed at all.

"Anxious flier?" he said. He took a long gulp of his drink and didn't spill any of it.

He was teasing me. "No," I shot back.

"Right," he said, eyeing me. I liked him better with the sunglasses on. It was bad enough to have to endure this flight, but to be mocked by a stranger, that was beyond tolerable. He gestured toward my head while still holding his drink. "You've got a bit of a goose egg there."

I didn't want to let go of the seat to check for a lump, but my forehead was throbbing. I wondered if I had a concussion. I was clearly impaired if I couldn't even respond to a simple statement like that. I loosened my grip on the armrest to touch the tender spot, but at that exact moment the plane seemed to plummet down in space; my seat was suddenly gone and my stomach lurched. This was it. I knew this would happen. This was what I got for taking an irresponsible vacation when I should have stayed at home. This was what I got for following Sadie, who hadn't even made it to the airport on time. I was about to die in a plane crash or be stranded on some bizarre island like in that show *Lost* that I couldn't bear watching. I slammed back down into my seat. Quickly, my fingers grappled for my seat belt to check that it was fastened as tight as I could get it.

A voice crackled over the speaker. "This is your pilot, Captain James Pope, speaking. No need to panic. What you just experienced was an air pocket. We've flown into some bad air near a large storm system. I'm going to try to reroute around it, but it will undoubtedly be quite rough for a while. Hang tight and stay in your seats, folks."

I swallowed hard. My heart started to race. I could feel a light sheen springing up along my hairline. What would Sadie do right now if she were here? She'd probably laugh and tell me to enjoy the ride. I closed my eyes and tried to subtly wipe the moisture with the back of my hand while I took slow, even breaths. The plane shuddered a little, but then the ride smoothed out.

"Just out of curiosity," I said, now that I was breathing regularly again. "What exactly is bad air?"

As soon as the words came out of my mouth, the plane started to shake, hard, as if I'd willed it to happen by speaking.

"This," he said, but I barely noticed. I'd glanced down at my seat belt with the intent to cinch it until it was practically part of my body, and found that in my desperate attempt to tighten it earlier, I'd somehow managed to disengage it.

"Shit," I muttered under my breath.

The guy turned toward me. "What?" he asked.

"It came undone."

My hands were shaking so badly that I couldn't fit the end of the buckle into the clasp. "Can you help me?" I asked, trying to keep the rising terror out of my voice. The plane jerked again.

"Sure. It's okay," he said. Then he reached over and took the buckle from me. "I've got it." His hands brushed over the top of my thigh and I waited for the audible click. At that moment, the plane jerked violently from side to side with a force so great that several overhead compartments exploded open and luggage rained down. I was thrown sideways out of my seat toward the center of the aircraft. Something dug into my waist and wrist and then I slammed down onto a hard object. My side throbbed. I squeezed my eyes shut. This was it. The plane shuddered a few more times and then the vibrations subsided.

I forced my eyes open. There, an inch away from me, my traveling companion stared at me. I'd landed squarely on his lap. He was so close, I felt his warm breath on my skin. He smelled like whiskey and salt and clean laundry. I was about to scramble off his lap, but the plane shuddered again. Without thinking, I threw my arms around his neck. It was a reflex. He didn't push me off, but he didn't cling to me either. When the shaking stopped, I pulled away. He looked totally unfazed. I couldn't get off his lap fast enough. Which would have been great, ideal even, except that in my haste, I accidentally placed my hand down right on his crotch.

"Oh, come the fuck on," I said aloud. My cheeks burned, and I did the worst thing possible. I froze. "I'm sorry," I stammered. "I didn't mean you. God. This is why I never travel." I'd calculated all the risks before I'd agreed to this trip. Landing gear malfunction. Bermuda Triangle. Engine failure. Water landing. But bad air and my hand on some random guy's crotch, that was some next-level danger I hadn't even fathomed. So yeah, forget the plane crash, I was clearly meant to die of mortification. Dammit, Sadie. I could've been at work, sitting in my cubicle with my salad and my stupid slogans, safe and sound.

He reached down and curled his fingers slowly around my hand. As he relocated it to his thigh, he said, "Let me help you with that."

I struggled ungracefully to regain my balance and whacked my head on the bulkhead. My cheeks stung hot with humiliation. I wasn't even sure where my seat was anymore. I wanted to cry, but that was not something I did. Ever. So I just stood there, hunched over like an idiot. He reached out and grabbed high on my waist.

"Wait. What are—"

Before I could finish speaking, he'd pushed me roughly into my seat. I was still staring at him, mouth open, trying to muster a phrase to express my gratitude, when a loud boom rang out and the aircraft seized. The noise was followed by a blinding flash and then all the cabin lights went out. I screamed. I did. I'll admit it. Perhaps there was some truth in Sadie's calling me a pansy-ass. But I wasn't the only one. The man in neon yelled, "It's just supposed to be a sales trip! Oh God." A collective cry came from the back of the plane. Around me, people were starting to buzz with worry and fear, or sheer terror, in my case. We all expected those scary yellow masks to drop down from the ceiling at any moment. I turned to my seatmate. He seemed like the only one on the plane who wasn't panicking.

"What's going on?" I tried to control my voice, but it came out as a shriek. "Were we hit by lightning?"

"Hard to say. Probably not."

"How can you tell?" I tried to press myself into the seat leather, hoping it would just swallow me up and this nightmare would end.

"We're not on fire."

That was it. The tenuous grasp I'd had on my panic escaped me. "Oh my God!" I screeched. "We could be on fire? Are we on fire?" I grabbed his arm. "What happens if we're on fire?"

"Listen . . . what's your name?"

"Marin Cole."

He nodded. "Marin Cole, I'm Lucas Tsai. Relax, okay? This is going to be fine."

"That's it? It's fine?" I asked. "This doesn't bother you."

"No," he said, his voice flat.

"How is that possible? Do you know the pilot or something?"

He nodded. A gesture I wasn't sure how to interpret. "It's smoothing out." He was right. The plane was no longer shaking. I released my grip on the armrest a smidgen. "We're out of the worst of it now."

"You're sure?"

"Few things are certain in this world, except that nothing is."

The captain's voice came over the loudspeaker again. "Folks, we've managed to get around the storm, but the system was larger than we originally thought, so we've been rerouted and diverted to Captain Auguste George Airport on Anegada. Our team at the airport will help you to get to your final destinations upon arrival, but you should expect significant delays until this system moves through."

"That's just great," I muttered.

"Problem?"

He was eyeing me so intensely, I broke down. "I was supposed to go to Saba for the weekend with my little sister, then she missed the flight. That's why I was so snippy with you about the seat earlier. I have no idea how I'm going to get to Saba now . . . our flight was from St. Maarten, I think. I don't travel, so my Caribbean geography is, well, nonexistent. She's the adventurer in the family and she made all the plans. You could say I'm sort of lost without her."

"You got stood up?" He shook his head, then raised his glass to take a swig of his drink. I caught a hint of a smile. It was the first time I'd seen any emotion on his face at all. He had a nice smile, even if the fact that he seemed to find my misery amusing made me want to punch him a little. He held the glass out to me. "Here. You need this more than I do."

I had to uncurl my fist to take it from him. The strong scent of the liquor washed over me and I almost handed the glass back. But I figured I could use something to dull my shot nerves. I swallowed it in one gulp and tried to keep my face neutral while it burned down my throat.

"Thanks." He was nicer than I'd thought.

He nodded. He shifted his body in his seat, then turned back to face me. "What will you do?"

"Go home, I guess. Surely this plane will go back to the States, right?"

"Not in this weather."

I let my head fall back against the headrest. Tears were flooding my eyes, but I squeezed my eyelids hard.

It was the altitude—I'd read it was easier to get drunk at higher altitudes—and I was definitely drunk. Because it sounded like the guy said he'd take me to Saba.

"Huh?" I said.

"I'll take you to Saba."

"You want to help me? I've maimed you twice already and my sister tells me I'm a bit of a nightmare when I'm stressed. I wouldn't want to trouble you."

"You're not. I'm going there myself."

The plane's wheels hit the runway. The jarring impact was followed by a screech and sharp deceleration that flung me forward in my seat again. I was so thankful to be alive that I almost forgot about his offer.

Seven

SADIE

I PROBABLY SHOULD HAVE mentioned earlier—Marin is afraid to fly. She'd have a better word, that's kind of her thing, but maybe *terrified* is closer. Let's just say she's not your normal anxious flier.

It's because of our mom. Lydia Cole. She was a reporter, a pretty killer one. She won a Pulitzer when we were kids . . . and then somebody shot the helicopter she was riding in out of the sky.

I think about it sometimes myself, when I get on a plane. But I figure we're all going down sooner or later. Marin is more practical than me and chooses to keep her feet on the ground.

Would it have been better if I had packed her some medicine for the flight? I'm still a little mad at her for thinking she could use this trip to pin me to the same kind of job that has snuffed out every spark of creative genius and inspiration she ever had. Me, at an office. I shudder to think of the blasphemy. I guess I just think that it's better to rip the Band-Aid off when it comes to fear.

Eight

MARIN

THE RUBBER TIRES SCREECHED as the plane touched down at the small airport in Anegada. The landing was a bit rough—though the sky had cleared, strong gusts of wind cut across the open fields, bending the palm trees in the distance.

When the plane finally stopped, I took several deep breaths. I'd survived. I gathered my bottle of water and my bag onto my lap while I waited to deplane. Between the turbulence and hitting my head and drinking most of Lucas Tsai's drink, I was feeling a little woozy. I took my phone out of airplane mode and checked my messages. Nothing from Sadie. Eight new messages from work, all about the new advertising and PR campaign for T Group, Unlimited. It was probably the most important pitch I'd ever worked on—other than the one I planned on using to get Sadie to change her life trajectory. If we got it, the ad campaign for the international conglomerate would be worth more than fifty percent of the firm's total income for the year. I reminded myself not to stress. Before I'd left I'd triple-checked that everything was done, from storyboards to mock-ups. The only thing any of my coworkers should've been doing was polishing and perfecting.

I glanced at the emails and shot back quick responses to the questions. Font, Frutiger. Color, maroon. The first tagline. Not a comma, a period. Condé Nast. The pressure on the inside of my skull was mounting—a sure sign of a major headache ahead. Lucas had stepped out into the aisle already and was waiting. I slid my phone into my pocket and reached for the overhead compartment where I'd stowed my carry-on, but it was empty. The image of the luggage flying through the air during the violent turbulence flashed in my mind. I surveyed the aisle quickly and finally rested my gaze on a horrifying sight. There, in the middle of the aisle, was my bag. The impact must've popped the latch open, because there was the perennially unfinished copy of *Ulysses* I'd packed—much to Sadie's chagrin—sitting among clothes strewn about the first-class cabin. A heroic flight attendant dashed toward a particularly lacy pair of black panties.

"I'll just get these things," she said as she lunged.

That was odd. It was my bag, but I hadn't packed black underwear. I didn't even own any black underwear. I knew someone who did, though. Someone who had underwear in every color of the rainbow. Those lacy specimens had Sadie written all over them. So did the sad excuse for a bikini top that was dangling from a footrest. I stumbled toward the bag, tripping over someone's protruding briefcase, and managed to snatch up a silk camisole and the book before regaining my footing. I stuffed them back into my suitcase and slammed it shut.

I used my free hand to tuck my hair behind my ears while I clutched my damaged suitcase in front of me with the other. Lucas was still standing next to his seat. I was about to reach past him for my purse when the red silk thong dangling from his finger caught my eye. Now I was sure this was Sadie's handiwork—I'd never worn a red thong in my life. In fact, back when Ted and I were together, Sadie had bought me one and called it a Valentine's Day present to him. I'd promptly put the thing into the donation box in the Food Lion parking lot. Even so, I snatched the thong out of Lucas's hand and walked off, hoping no one would notice my cheeks trying their best to match the color of the lingerie that I'd just stuffed into my purse.

The airport was bursting with displaced tourists; flowing caftans and Hawaiian shirts abounded. Beyond immigration, there was a small desk with a stack of brochures and one man trying very hard and failing to serve the long line of stranded, disgruntled passengers. After the customs agent stamped my passport, I took my place at the end of the line, which was clearly moving on some sort of beach time, if there was such a thing. The weekend would probably be over before I made it to the front. Someone bumped into me and I stumbled into the neon-shirt guy from the plane. He was beet red, yelling at a woman in a uniform holding a clipboard. He paused long enough to shoot me a searing glare and then restarted his tirade.

"I'm sorry, sir," she said. "We're doing our best, but no outbound air traffic is allowed right now. We will let you know more as soon as conditions change."

"You've got to be fucking kidding me!" the man said. "Do you have any idea how much this detour is costing me in business right now?"

"Again, I apologize. We are just a small airport. We'll do our best to assist you."

"What are you doing?" There was Lucas Tsai again. I tried to hide my face behind a brochure.

"What's it look like?" the other man snapped. "I'm waiting like everybody else to find a way out of here."

"I was talking to her," Lucas said, holding out a hand like a bad-ass crossing guard. I had to admit, I wish I'd had his chill. He caught me peeking at him and hooked a finger over the top of the brochure to push it down.

"I told you I have my own transportation."

"That's nice," I said, and returned my attention to the brochure.

"You won't accept my help?"

"You just mortified me," I whispered.

"Red is an auspicious color."

"You're a pervert."

He leaned in. "I'm not the one who left my underwear all over a plane."

And to think, I'd thought he was *nice*. In stunned silence I watched as he extracted the aviator shades from his pocket and slid them on. Then he grasped the handle of my smashed roller bag like he was daring me to say something. Which I did not, because he looked like James Bond, and I was too busy trying to figure out if I felt like Moneypenny— And while I was at it, why were all the James Bonds white dudes? That seemed very much like a travesty.

The woman with the clipboard stopped next to us. "Mr. Tsai!" she said. "I'm so sorry I didn't come to you first. I didn't realize you were on one of the affected flights. Please tell me what I can do for you."

The neon-clad man turned even redder—he looked like a Christmas elf. "What you can do," he snarled, "is help *this* guy!" He poked a finger into his own chest. That was going to leave a mark. He wasn't done. "I'm the one who needs helping here, not this guy, whoever the hell he is. You should be figuring out how to assist me, you stupid idiot."

"But, sir, don't you know who—"

Lucas held his hand up again. "Don't speak to her like that."

Bond. James Bond.

Several people had already distanced themselves from the agitated man. Some of them clapped, but Lucas didn't seem to notice. The veins on the man's neck bulged. He turned a sick shade of purple and opened his mouth (to spill more vitriol, no doubt). Lucas shook his head. It was so subtle I almost didn't notice it. The man grumbled but ended up grabbing his bag and storming off. The employee leaned toward him. "Mr. Tsai—" she began.

"Please don't worry about me; my team's already made arrangements. Try to help the other passengers, okay? It's fine." He gave her a warm nod, which she returned before she hurried off with her clipboard.

"You need a taxi?" a guy in a uniform asked me. I'd been so engrossed in the exchange that I hadn't noticed him approaching.

"Yes . . . No." I was still processing what had just happened. I wasn't the kind of woman who took rides with men she'd just met, especially ones who held up her underwear for all the world to see, but the way he'd stood up for the airport worker gave me pause. "I need a sec," I told the transportation assistant. I swiveled back around to where Lucas had been standing moments earlier, but he was already striding through the automatic doors with my suitcase in tow. The airport was busy; travelers and taxis littered a small street lined by palm trees and oleander and bougainvillea in large clay pots. I had to dodge around them to try and keep up. I lost him for a moment in a rush of people trying to make a bus that was about to leave. Fortunately, his onyx-black hair, tall lean frame, and that cocky walk made it impossible for him to not stand out in a crowd. There he was, sauntering along about fifty feet in front of me, one hand in his pocket, one hand on my bag. He appeared to be enjoying the scenery, just taking a relaxing stroll. I picked up my pace. My feet protested while I worked hard to close the distance. If it hadn't already been ruined, the silk shirt was toast now. I was completely soaked with sweat.

"Hey! Come back with my bag!" I trotted behind, full of regret over the stilettos I'd chosen for the trip. I stopped and stooped down for a moment to catch my breath, then picked up pursuit again. "I need that!"

This guy was infuriating. He had slowed considerably, as if he was toying with me. I pointed a finger at him while sucking in breaths. I managed to yell, "Thief!"

He turned around then. "Thief?" he said. "That characterization seems a bit unjust."

"You stole my suitcase!"

"I believe in most parts of the world this is called being a gentleman." He raised a hand casually. "My car's over there."

My brow furrowed. "Your car? How do you have a car here?"

"I have cars in lots of places."

He took off again at a fast clip. I hobbled along after him. He was heading toward a private VIP lot that was a couple of football fields away. I sighed. The skin on the back of my ankles had rubbed raw and the balls of my feet were throbbing. I struggled to keep up, wincing with each step.

"Ooh, ouch," I said, under my breath.

Lucas stopped. I nearly bumped into him. When he turned around, the distance between us was so small that I had to lean back so my face didn't slam into his neck. When I looked up, I saw myself reflected in his sunglasses. What I saw there was a hot mess. My hair was all disheveled and my light traveling makeup had melted off in the heat. I reached up to smooth my hair back and tucked it behind my ears. That's when Lucas made his move. He ducked down and grabbed me around my legs before I could do anything to avoid it, and threw me over his shoulder.

"What are you—"

"Let me help you. The bad weather is moving toward this island. We don't have time to wait for you and your silly shoes."

"Put me down. I can walk fine on my own."

"Your suffering was obvious."

"I don't need your help," I said. This whole scene was completely ridiculous. I had an urge to kick my legs so he'd have to put me down, but he was already on the move and I had a feeling that fighting him wasn't worth the effort. And even though he was clearly an entitled ass with a huge ego, he had been kind to the woman working in the airport. Besides, I had to admit I was hugely relieved not to have to walk in these shoes anymore. *Sadie's never going to believe this,* I thought.

"You're not a pool boy, are you?" I asked, thinking aloud.

"No. But I employ a few at my hotel, if that's your thing."

Nine

JUST BREATHE. STAY CALM. While I sat in the passenger seat and Lucas drove, I pictured the motivational mantra that sat in a frame on my desk where everyone else had a picture of their spouse. Fine by me. A younger sister was enough trouble. And after Ted had chosen adventure over a life in Tennessee, the romance ship had sailed. I inhaled a cleansing breath. What the framed print actually said was *Keep Calm and Kick Ass* in bright green and my signature hot pink (thank you, Lilly Pulitzer), but I'd trimmed that bottom part off. What would clients think? I kept it right next to the picture of Sadie in a tank top and cargo shorts, on the top of some peak somewhere. Sadie. I was so furious at her I wanted to scream, but mostly I was mad at myself—I should have known better than to let her take charge of the trip. Now instead of a relaxing time with my sister at a spa, I was stuck with this arrogant . . . hotelier, and about to take yet another form of dangerous transportation. I didn't have much of a choice. Lucas had parked the SUV in a small gravel lot, taken my bag out of the trunk, and was heading toward what looked like a pier. Just ahead of us, white boats of various sizes bobbed on the most striking blue water I'd ever seen.

"Don't have any problems with seasickness, do you?" Lucas called back to me.

"I don't know."

He stopped. "What do you mean? Usually it's pretty obvious if you get seasick. You'd know."

I shrugged. "I've never been on a boat."

"Surely you've been to the ocean."

"I didn't say I'd never been to an ocean."

"But you haven't."

I looked away. My existence back in Tennessee was starting to feel embarrassingly small. "It never interested me," I said.

He appeared to think this over for a beat. "Huh." He nodded toward the harbor. "Well, if you do get seasick, we'll find out pretty fast. Looks a bit choppy out there, and my guy at the resort tells me there's a storm rolling in."

"You know, you probably don't want a strange woman getting sick all over your boat. I think I'll go back and try my luck at getting on another flight. Thanks anyway."

"I'll take my chances."

"It's fine. I should probably just go home."

"In this weather? They're already grounding flights for later in the day."

"So you're telling me that if I wanted to go back to the airport and fly home . . ."

"You'd be there awhile."

I nodded. "Wonderful." The alcohol I'd had on the plane had worn off and, combined with the heat, was starting to give me a throbbing headache. *Cleansing breath.* Ahead of me, Lucas had stopped at a jetty next to one of the bigger boats. I knew next to nothing about watercraft, but I figured this thing fell squarely under the definition of a yacht. It was glistening white, with a sharp bow that made it look like it was built for speed; black windows sliced along the hull, out of which rose two visible levels above the water, with rich wood decks. Along one side, its name was scrawled in crimson and gold cursive—*Sea Dragon*.

"This one's mine," Lucas said, and walked across a small ramp onto the vessel.

"Why a dragon?"

"*Sìhǎi Lóngwáng* is the dragon king of the West Sea. You should feel secure; he helps keep ships safe on the water."

I checked his expression to see if he was toying with me, but his face was serious. "C'mon," he said.

I took another look at the yacht and those privacy-glassed windows that seemed to be grinning at me with a degree of menace that I did not like. What did I really know about this guy, other than the fact that he seemed to be rich and overly confident? I glanced over my shoulder in the direction of the airport but was met only with giant storm clouds that seemed to be swirling toward us at an alarming rate. What other option did I have? I stepped quickly across the gangplank and onto the deck.

On closer inspection, the word *yacht* sort of under-described the vessel. Small cruise ship. The main deck boasted not only a custom table with chairs but a hot tub. If ever there was a time when I needed a soak in a hot tub, it was right now.

"Feel free," Lucas said, catching me.

As if. He was still grinning at me with that same stupid look he'd had when he'd dangled the underwear—That. Was. Not. Mine.—in front of the entire airline cabin. I glared at him before dropping into one of the chairs. He busied himself with boat stuff and I got out my phone. I needed to get in touch with Sadie and figure out just what the hell was going on. I'd thought that she was ready to settle down—she'd seemed so worn out with all the traveling for work, and then just last week it even seemed like maybe there were troubles at the magazine. I'd run into one of Sadie's friends from work in town and he'd acted so strange when I said she was still off in China on assignment. He'd said if she needed anything, to give him a call. Had Sadie been fired? Maybe the China trip wasn't for *Wild World*. But Sadie hadn't said a word about it when she got back and I didn't want to ask. Besides, she was totally engrossed in planning this trip we had to take together. My sister, the girl who never planned a thing in her life. I took it as a sign that this trip would be the perfect time to figure out what had happened. She'd seemed different, calmer somehow, more grown-up, and I thought that meant she might be ready to hear my suggestion. But no, Sadie was still as immature and irresponsible as ever.

The yacht's engine rumbled to life and Lucas pushed it to what felt like full speed in mere moments. The force lurched me back in my seat and the horrible disquiet in my stomach returned with a vengeance.

"It's not that far," Lucas yelled over the noise of the engine. "Just want to beat out this storm." He gestured to the left side of the boat where thick, threatening clouds had gathered.

"What happens if we don't beat the storm?" I asked.

He didn't answer. He'd taken off his sunglasses and fixed his gaze on the horizon. He reached into a bin, pulled out a bright orange life vest, and handed it to me. I put it on—safety first—but I was fairly certain that it looked like a creature forming a symbiosis with me. My hair was tangled around my face. I tried to tuck it back as I wobbled over to Lucas.

"We still have farther to go," he said.

I nodded. "Actually, I—"

"You're not sick, are you? These waves are pretty big."

"No. My stomach's fine. I was wondering if you could take a picture of me."

"Now?"

My face flushed. "I realize it seems like a very silly, tourist thing to do, but Sadie would be so surprised that I'm on a boat on the ocean. I wanted to send her a picture."

"The sister whose seat I took?"

"The very one. Consider yourself lucky she didn't show up. She's littler than me, but she's extremely scrappy."

"Why not," he said, taking my phone. "One, two, three." Lucas took several shots and handed the phone back. "Are the two of you close?" he asked.

"You could say that." I tugged on one strap on my life vest. "I feel like this thing is choking me."

Rain started to fall around us. Lucas reached over and unclipped the belt buckle. "Why don't you go belowdecks where you can take that off? There's a large guest suite you can use to freshen up if you'd like. There's even a small movie room with snacks."

"It *is* getting a little wet up here," I admitted, rubbing my bare arms. "And I wouldn't mind some snacks. Thanks."

I headed toward the stairs, taking slow, cautious steps. The boat pitched in the waves. I slipped on the wet decking but recovered my footing. "I'm okay," I called.

Lucas didn't answer. He appeared totally focused behind the wheel. Behind him, the sky was black and the rain was coming down in sheets. The storm had caught up with us.

Ten

DON'T FREAK OUT. Don't freak out. Rain slammed into the tinted windows that lined the stateroom. The floor tilted beneath my feet as the boat pitched from side to side. I knew getting on this boat had been a terrible idea. Yes, the taste of salt on my lips, the fresh air, the sheer massiveness of the sea had been breathtaking. I'd felt a strange swelling sensation in my chest, but now my whole body was tense with dread. Before me my suitcase was splayed open on the bed. Actually, not mine, I realized at the sight of the oh-so-subtle *Just Married* see-through negligee atop the heap of clothes. Mrs. Right and I must have had identical carry-ons, because, aside from my book, the contents of this bag were definitely not mine. I'd thought maybe I could find something suitable to change into, but that was before the bed started rocking like some kind of giant torture cradle.

Lucas seemed to know what he was doing, I reminded myself. He'd taken several pictures of me, decent pictures, I realized as I scrolled through them, trying to decide which one I should send to Sadie before the boat capsized and sank to the bottom of the ocean. I'd seen *Titanic*. I knew how these kinds of things went. I copied the picture into a text and typed *I saw the ocean!* I didn't mention the part about how I was probably going to drown.

The last thing Sadie needed right now was more stress, since she was clearly going through her own personal crisis, whatever that crisis was. I was the one who was supposed to be her rock. Not that this would stress her out. Sadie loved this kind of terrifying stuff, called them power-ups.

My phone dinged. We were too far out to get a signal, so the text had bounced back. I was truly on my own. A piece of me wondered what Sadie would do in this kind of situation. Maybe if I could channel her nature, I wouldn't have to feel so petrified, but every thought I tried on seemed to make me feel worse instead of better. My sister might love chaos, but it wasn't my brand of comfort. I liked plans. Lists calmed me. Sure, bad things were inevitable, but then again, good things could be manifested if one took the time and energy to make a solid plan. I took a small notebook out of my purse and started writing.

1. Survive storm
2. Arrive in Saba
3. Sadie arrives
4. Convince Sadie to take the job
5. Go home

I took a deep breath and closed the notebook. The boat didn't seem to be moving around quite as much as it had earlier, so I chanced a peek out the windows. Rain still slicked across the surface, but the sky seemed lighter than before. Maybe that was a good sign. Now that I could walk without tipping over, I seized the opportunity to investigate the space. The room was beautiful, with the kind of bedding you'd expect in a luxury hotel, but it was cold and impersonal. There were no pictures or personal items anywhere. The art consisted of abstract paintings with splashes of color in gold, persimmon, and scarlet. I'd headed straight for the room earlier, but I thought it might be safe to step back out now. Besides, there wasn't anything in the suitcase that I could put on. Too bad. Between my bare arms and the wet silk shirt stuck to my torso, I was so cold that

I briefly contemplated wearing the velour bride tracksuit that Mrs. Right had packed.

There was another door outside the cabin I'd entered. It looked the same, but it had a medallion hanging from a red ribbon on it. I hesitated, hand on the doorknob. Was this Lucas's room? I probably shouldn't. The boat rocked and I lost my balance. I crumpled into the door and in the process, the door unlatched and I tumbled inside.

This room was nothing like the last one. It wasn't cluttered, but there was a definite feeling that the space belonged to someone. I picked up one of the framed photos on the shelf. Lucas standing next to an older man in front of what looked like a tropical rain forest. Lucas wore a white linen shirt and a big smile. The man was shorter than him, deep wrinkles etched on his face. They didn't look similar, except for their smiles. Twin sets of lips curling up, revealing perfect teeth. But that wasn't the part I noticed. It was their eyes. Their eyes smiled more than their mouths, making them look like they were so happy their faces could barely contain the joy. It was the way Sadie smiled when she was really happy, like if she were one iota happier she might just burst.

Below the shelf that showed the picture of Lucas and the smiling older man were other photos. Lucas on a beach with three other guys. The tallest had kind eyes, dark brown skin, and black hair, trimmed close to his head. He'd slung his arms around the two next to him, leaning down to close the distance between them. There was Lucas, looking younger in board shorts and a V-neck T-shirt. He was tanner than now, his hair was longer and lighter, more of an auburn than black, but he was otherwise the same. Beside him stood an Asian man with a black pompadour and a Hawaiian-style shirt, a beer bottle dangling from one hand. He was flanked by a deeply tan guy in a wet suit, with a board tucked under his arm. They were all laughing about something, not looking at the camera exactly. They looked like the best of friends.

Underneath the photo, books were neatly stacked. I ran a finger along the spines. The edges of some were frayed, broken, as if they'd been read many times. Strange. Lucas hadn't struck me as the kind of man who read books over and over again, returning to them like old friends. I thought of the bookshelf in the den of my house back in Tennessee, where each one had earned its place over the years. I could find them in the dark if I had to. When I was younger, I'd always pictured displaying the books I would write there, but I'd shelved that dream a long time ago. On a bedside table, there was one other photo in a simple frame. I crouched down to inspect it. There was a young boy in it. His face was fuller, the shape of his jaw rounder, but the nose and eyes gave Lucas away. He was with a woman on what looked like the seat of a boat. They were both in bathing suits, their hair damp, broad smiles on their faces. I turned it toward the light. I guessed that must have been Lucas's mother? She was lovely. I caught a glimpse of my own reflection in the glass, superimposed over the image of Lucas and the woman. I looked like a drowned rodent.

I found a bathroom next to a closet that was bigger than mine at home. Even the flattering lighting that ringed the mirror didn't do much to help my appearance. Other than my blue-hazel eyes and a sprinkle of freckles that seemed like a mandatory Cole family trait, I had not been blessed with Mom's looks like Sadie had. I'd missed out on the gorgeous blonde curls, delicate features, and petite frame Sadie'd inherited—I must've taken after our dad—but my chestnut-brown waves were usually one of my best features. Just not today. I used my fingers to comb through my hair and smooth it down. It wasn't good, but it would have to do.

I didn't know how long I'd been in Lucas's room, but I figured that it would be a good idea to see what was going on with the storm. I ducked back out into the hallway and climbed the stairs carefully.

Lucas was in the same spot where I'd left him, except he'd

donned a black Gore-Tex jacket at some point. His wet hair was slicked back. He lifted his chin when he saw me. I let go of the handrail to wave and nearly lost my balance. The rain had eased down to a sprinkle. In some spaces between the clouds, the sun broke through. I stepped into a swathe of light on the deck, hoping that it might be a little warmer there.

"Did the storm pass?" I asked.

"I headed southwest and that took us out of the path of the system. It might have added a little time onto our trip, but we should be there soon."

"And when we get to the island, is it a long trip to the resort?"

He laughed. "You really didn't plan this trip," he said.

I shook my head. Rookie mistake, but yes. I forced a smile.

"Saba is only five square miles."

Oh. "So it should be easy for Sadie to find me, then."

He looked down at the instrument panel. "Should be."

I turned around to look at the view ahead of us. The sea was bluer now that the storm was clearing—not the turquoise blue I'd expected but a richer navy. "It's so dark," I said. "It doesn't look like the pictures."

"It will change. It's dark because the water is deep here. Wait until we get to Saba, which is . . . there," he said, and pointed past me.

I rubbed my arms while I strained to see what he was pointing to.

"Are you cold?" he asked.

I shook my head.

He unzipped his jacket and handed it to me. If I'd had any sort of brief vision of him draping it gently over my shoulders—which I did not—the reality would have been disappointing.

I looked down at the high-tech jacket with *Arc'teryx* emblazoned on the chest. "I'm okay," I said.

"Put it on."

Begrudgingly, I donned the jacket. He was right. It blocked the wind and I instantly stopped shivering. I let my eyes search the horizon until I spotted the dot that he was pointing to. It was still a fair ways off, but I could see the rich green sprouting from the ocean.

"That's it," I said. "That's Saba?"

I waited for him to say something, but he merely nodded. I walked to the bow of the ship and pressed against the railing. Below me, water frothed around the hull as the boat sliced through the ocean. I lifted my face to the warm sun, which was growing stronger. In the distance, Saba appeared, verdant and alive, like a spring bud, stretching up from thawing soil. I hadn't realized it would be so mountainous. Lucas took us closer, and I could make out new details—the red-orange roofs of white houses nestled in the valleys.

"That's the resort over there to the right," he said.

I squinted. Between two massive hills, there was a large white building with shutters and the same clay roof I'd seen on other buildings. From my vantage point, I could make out the tiny dots of color, what I guessed were tropical plants blooming everywhere, on decks, around windows. It was beautiful.

"That's your place?" I said.

"What do you think?"

I turned back to look at him, half expecting him to be wearing some sort of smug expression, but I wasn't prepared for his appearance. His brow was deeply furrowed, his lips pressed together. If I didn't know better, I would've thought he looked troubled, sad even.

"I've never seen anything like it."

Eleven

SADIE

MARIN ALWAYS SAYS I never think things through. Can you imagine the irony? I mean, I got her to go to a tropical island alone. I have accomplices! I even have a surprise guest. More on that later.

I have to admit, not being able to gloat is killing me.

There's a piece of me that wishes I was with Marin on Saba. I'd love to see Marin's expression when she sees the island. As much as she would want to remain unmoved, I know she won't be able to resist it. A very reliable source once told me that it's magical. Anyway, I want to see my sister crusted with salt and magic and all lit up from the inside. But since I can't share this with her, I hope there's pictures. Lots of them. Pictures are kind of my thing, after all.

Twelve

MARIN

I WOULD NEVER ADMIT this to Sadie, but by the time I'd set my feet on the pebbled beach on Saba, I'd already forgiven her. Had she royally messed up missing the flight? Definitely. But it's not like she could control the weather. Staying mad at Sadie always had been an exercise in futility anyway. Frothy waves lapped at my feet, soaking the bottom of my pants, washing away any irritation I felt. I bent down to roll them up to my knees.

On either side of me, rocky cliffs rose up, blue-gray speckled with lush green. Everything was in technicolor here. Even the breeze seemed to hold a full spectrum. Some birds I hadn't seen before, brightly colored, with big wings, swooped overhead and disappeared into the trees.

"This way," Lucas called to me. He was dragging my suitcase along a wooden walkway toward a winding road that was barely visible through the brush. Over the gentle heartbeat rhythm of the waves, a car horn beeped twice. "Our ride," Lucas said.

I picked my heels up from where I'd dropped them on the pebbles and tossed them into my bag.

"Coming," I called, and headed toward the walkway. It seemed an odd thing to have on a beach until I noticed that the sand quickly gave way to dark rocks. At the road line, palm trees bowed in the wind.

I managed to catch up with Lucas before we reached the road.

"I need to say thank you. It wasn't pretty, but I definitely wouldn't have made it here on my own."

He looked at me but only gave a subtle nod. That was it. I'd planned on saying more, but given his response, I decided it wasn't necessary.

Lucas set my suitcase in the back of a forest-green SUV, and a man whom I recognized from one of the pictures on the boat closed the hatch. He gave me a small wave.

"You can sit up front," Lucas said.

I climbed into the car, pausing to brush off my feet.

"Don't worry about it," the man said, eyeing me. He was already in the driver's seat. "Sand is a part of life here. It's unavoidable."

I reached for my seat belt. I'd forgotten that I was still wearing Lucas's jacket, but it was too late now to take it off.

"I'm Ken. Whatever Lucas told you about me, it's not true."

"Marin Cole," I said. "He didn't mention you."

Ken glanced in the rearview mirror. "Harsh, buddy."

"We didn't have much of a chance to talk on the way over. I spent most of the ride below deck," I said. "There was a lot of rain." I plucked at the sleeve of Lucas's raincoat.

"It rained a little here too. But on Saba the sun never stays covered for too long. It's one of many things to love about our unspoiled jewel." He eased the SUV off the shoulder and accelerated around a curve. I grabbed onto the handle above the window. Sadie called them oh-shit handles, not that she ever needed one when I was driving, and I suddenly understood why. I also wished I were behind the wheel instead of Ken.

The windows were down, and over the rush of the wind, he shouted, "So what do you think of our Saba, Marin?"

"It's unlike anything I've ever seen," I said.

"Marin's from Tennessee," Lucas piped up from the back seat. "She doesn't get out much."

Ken checked the rearview mirror. "And you've traveled the globe and probably would still admit that not much rivals Saba."

I liked this guy. He cast a glance my way and smiled. He was warmer than Lucas, with softer features, a round face, and a big open smile. He would never wear sunglasses on a plane, I bet.

"How booked up are we this week?" Lucas asked.

"About seventy-five percent."

"Good. Anything else I should know?"

"The advertising firm is coming by in a few days to shoot some footage for the new campaign. Other than that, it's a quiet week, so you can relax and take some time for yourself, *Lǎobǎn*."

I looked over my shoulder at Lucas. He seemed fine, if a bit obnoxious. He was definitely not the poster child of someone needing self-care. At the thought, I pulled out my phone to try Sadie again. After the sixth ring, I hung up.

"Still can't reach your sister?" Lucas asked.

"What's that?" Ken said.

"I was supposed to be here with my younger sister. Between her missing the flight and the weather, well, the trip's sort of turned into a disaster so far. I even picked up the wrong luggage and ended up with a newlywed's suitcase. Murphy's Law, I guess."

"How so?"

"I finally take a vacation and it's more stressful than my job."

"Talk to me tomorrow," Ken said. "I doubt you'll be feeling stressed."

"You're that confident?"

"Yeah." He glanced at Lucas again. "It's virtually impossible to feel stressed at Paradise Resort."

"And you agree with this?" I asked Lucas.

"See for yourself," he said, turning his attention out his window.

While we'd talked, Ken had pulled up to a tall iron gate painted white with ornate scrollwork. To one side was a large wooden sign surrounded by lush, colorful plants. It read PARADISE RESORT, BY

THE TSAI GROUP. Tsai . . . as in Lucas Tsai. So he wasn't just a humble single-hotel owner after all. I resisted the urge to ask him just what the Tsai Group entailed. I had a pretty good idea—I'd seen the resort website.

Ken drove the SUV through the automatic gates and then pulled up in front of a white building, like the one I'd seen from the boat. Up close, there was more detail on the shutters and window boxes than I'd expected. The flowers were waxy and fluorescent, so exotic they almost looked like they couldn't have been real, but the man watering them carefully while balancing on a ladder ruined that notion. A bellhop came out and took our bags.

"Mr. Tsai," he said. "It's good to have you back. How are you holding up, sir?"

Lucas patted his breast pocket. It wasn't the first time I'd seen him do it in the few short hours we'd spent together. "I'm fine, thank you, Reginald. How's your wife doing? The baby's due in a few weeks, right?"

The man's face changed, his polite smile evolving into a beaming grin. "Three, sir! We're all doing just fine."

"Good to hear." He patted the man on the shoulder. "If you're free for a few minutes, Reginald, could you bring this bag down to Villa One? It's open, right, Ken?"

Ken nodded.

"Great. That'll be it, then."

When the man had gone, Lucas leaned close to Ken. In low tones, I heard him say something in a language I couldn't understand. The exchange continued for a few moments, during which I tried my best not to look like the awkward eavesdropper I was. I turned a full circle to take in my surroundings.

"Marin," Lucas said. "I have to go see to a few things. Ken will show you where you'll be staying. You'll like the villa; it's right on the water. I'll stop by a little later to make sure you're settled."

"Oh." I tucked a strand of hair behind my ear. "I think we reserved a double with a garden view? I don't think oceanfront is in my budget."

"Don't worry about it."

"You don't have to do that."

He nodded. "I never do anything I don't want to do. It's your first time traveling and so far your experience has been less than ideal. I'd like to offer you our best villa to make up for all the misadventures."

"That's nice, but I—"

Ken leaned toward me. "Just say yes."

"Okay . . . yes," I said, trying not to think of how much I already felt in Lucas's debt for all his help. "Thanks."

When Lucas was inside, I turned to Ken. "What were you two talking about just now?"

He laughed. "He was telling me to send that guy Reginald home when we got to your villa."

"Was he in trouble?"

Ken shook his head. "Lucas isn't that kind of boss."

"Huh," I said. Then, realizing he was giving me a look, I added, "It's nothing. He's a hard one to read, whereas you instantly come across as nice."

"I am the nicest one. Remember that." He laughed. "We were speaking Mandarin. He told me to let Reggie go home early to take care of his family."

Several guests passed by us, outfitted in casual clothes with backpacks. "I can't wait to see the volcano," a woman said.

"Volcano?" I asked Ken.

"No worries." He gestured to a cobbled path that disappeared into a grove of palm trees. "Your villa's this way," he said.

We walked a short distance through what seemed like an enchanted tropical rain forest. Birds chirped from their perches. Thick banana plant leaves marked the edges of the path like flags. Finally the forest opened and there, nestled among the rocks, was a small pool surrounded by a gray stone patio. At the end of the patio sat a white cottage that looked like a smaller replica of the main house. The French doors were open and long gauze curtains fluttered in the breeze. I stepped inside to admire the spacious main room, with glistening wood floors and high ceilings. It was appointed with rich, tropical-style furnishings. Beyond that there were several doors.

"Main bedroom, guest room, bathroom," Ken said, indicating each door in turn. I peeked into each new space, trying to remain collected. I pressed my lips together to suppress a grin as I checked out the larger bedroom. In the middle of the space, there was a giant four-poster bed with mosquito netting around it. The accent tables scattered about the room all had vases filled with fresh flowers. Doors opened onto a veranda that gave a view down the secluded hill to the ocean below. Sadie was not going to believe this when I snapped the pictures and sent them to her with an *I got us an upgrade* caption as soon as Ken left.

Reginald set my bags down in the bedroom, and while I was digging around in my wallet for some cash, Ken pressed some bills into his hand. Reginald whooped with delight. "Thank you! You tell Mr. Tsai thank you from me too," he said, pumping Ken's hand before he left.

"You didn't have to do that," I said. "I was going to tip him."

Ken shook his head. "Don't worry about it."

"Let me pay you back, then."

He held up a hand. "Not necessary."

"I want to. How much did you give him?"

"A thousand."

"In Saba money? I only have US dollars."

"We use US dollars here."

My eyes widened. What kind of place was this? I didn't even have that much cash for the entire trip.

"I think it's a lot too," Ken said. "I just do what Lucas tells me. The CEO of Tsai Group can afford it."

I raised my eyebrows. I'd seen flashes of Lucas's generous nature, but also when he wasn't mildly amused by my misfortunes, he seemed aloof. I couldn't quite figure him out. It was a strange thing to wrap my head around. "Sorry, I'm not sure what that means. I don't know what the Tsai Group is . . . That's Lucas's family's company?"

"Just his now. You seriously haven't heard of it? They own the airline you guys flew in on, among other things."

So that's why they'd held the plane and given him Sadie's seat. Those were some of the perks that that kind of mind-blowing wealth bought you.

"So, Marin Cole, what's your story?"

"Mine?" I set my purse on the silk brocade accent chair and eyed a piece of fruit. "I don't have one. Why?"

"No reason. Most women would be pretty stoked to have Lucas Tsai escort them personally to Paradise, but you're not."

Well, he's probably used to women throwing themselves at him. So now he just expects it. I hate to break it to your big, important Mr. Tsai, but I will never throw myself at an arrogant guy who holds my underwear up for an entire cabin of people to see . . . philanthropist or not, I thought about saying, but instead what came out was, "I don't travel much. At all, actually. I was supposed to be traveling with my sister—but we got separated. I do appreciate Lucas helping me, and I probably should have told him that. Today has taken a lot out of me."

"Hmm. Well, there's a first time for everything."

"You know, he wasn't exactly a delightful traveling companion. He's kind of a cold fish." Putting it lightly.

"Lucas, a cold fish? You're kidding. He's a saint." He gave me a look. "You've got a tense energy about you. Maybe it's you. I mean, if the shoe fits . . ." He picked up the shoes that had macerated my feet earlier. "These look painful."

"You're not helping," I said. But Ken's good-natured teasing had reminded me of Sadie, and like my frustratingly sweet sister, I was finding it very difficult to be mad at him.

He picked up the phone on the table. "Call the main house if you need anything."

After Ken had gone, I took stock of my surroundings. I texted Sadie, ate what might have been the world's most delicious orange, peeled off my stained, damp clothing, and took a long soak in the garden tub. *How bad could this be?* I thought. This place really was Paradise. Afterward, I donned an incredibly soft robe with the resort crest embroidered on it and checked out the resort guide on the nightstand. There was a botanical garden teeming with orchids that looked amazing. Sunrise yoga, maybe. Cliffside. Or not. A pool that looked like a lagoon and had its very own waterfall—now, that I had to check out. A little sun, a relaxing swim, and a day passed on a chaise lounge, finally finishing *Ulysses* while sipping one of those drinks with an umbrella and a maraschino cherry; that was exactly what I needed.

Thirteen

SADIE

PEOPLE WHO KNOW MARIN now would swear she was born forty-five years old. They'd be wrong. There was a time—it doesn't seem all that long ago—when she drank in the world, when she thirsted for it. When she wasn't afraid, she was fucking fun. Okay, she wasn't a nut like me who wanted to get on top of everything, but she had adventures and dreams. I still remember, but I'm afraid she's forgotten how she used to be.

We all have history, and ours starts with our mom. She was hard core and amazing and she's gone. What can I say, life's a bitch. That kind of loss—it changes you, for better or worse. I went wild and Marin turned careful. Safe and sound and in one piece, that's what Mom promised us every time she went away. So I guess it's not a shocker that Marin basically took it as a freaking manifesto for her whole life. She didn't have much of a choice.

When my Mom died, I was only in eighth grade and my favorite pastime was climbing buildings and hanging out on the roof until some security guy threatened to call the cops. I mean, there were still at least eighty people left in the line at our mother's funeral when I decided to pull that stunt and sneak off to sit on a rafter. I didn't have a good reason. I don't usually have a good reason for doing the things I do. I just couldn't stand there anymore, listening to people reduce our mom, the parent who was like a god to me, to

an anecdote. I had to wear a dress that Marin picked out for me—
it itched. I didn't have the right shoes, so I picked a pair of Mom's,
but that wasn't right either. Marin told me to take them off, but I
wore them anyway. I probably should have listened. She was right
that time. She's right a lot of the time. They were too big and gave
me blisters.

Who knows what would have happened if she hadn't become an
adult in an instant? And she's so good at it—she's even got the soul-
sucking big job and pantsuits to prove it. Marin's dry cleaning gets
delivered not once but twice a week, and she uses one of those meal
services where they send her a recipe and the ingredients and she
cooks it at home for all meals except breakfast—two hard-boiled
eggs, yolks discarded, and a kale smoothie—and weekday lunches,
which her company orders in from an organic, farm-based sandwich
shop each day. I like croissants. In fact, I am a connoisseur of
croissants and maybe even food in general, or I used to be. I don't
enjoy it now the way I once did. Marin does not eat for enjoyment.
Food is fuel, she always says. So practical, my darling sister. I don't
think she owns any fancy underwear . . . nope, she's control-top all
the way, whether or not she needs it. Don't ask when the last time
was that my dear sister got laid. A guy wearing a backward baseball
cap and an actual mixtape were probably involved.

I made a list of some of the things I have done that Marin would
never do. In fact, the very idea of them would appall her or send her
into a panic spiral.

1. Flown on a plane
2. Traveled to a foreign country solo
3. Gone skinny-dipping
4. Met a dictator
5. Climbed a mountain
6. Spent the night with a stranger
7. Held a real treasure in my hands

8. Looked death in the eye and screamed in its face
10. Fallen in love

I think I missed one, but who fucking cares, right? Ahhhh!!!!

Maybe number ten is a bit unfair. Marin and her college boyfriend, Ted, might have been in love. Can you love someone who probably leaves his favorite baseball hat on during sex? I'm not sure . . . it would have had to have been pretty phenomenal. All I know is Marin wouldn't know fun if it came up and slapped her right on the ass. Marin thinks she has to protect me, that I'm a mess, but she's wrong. Life is messy. And amazing. And I've coated myself with that messiness. I want Marin to get messy now. I want her to have all those things she missed out on because of me. She is so loyal, so dependable. Never was there a woman who took such good care of others, even at her own expense. Next to the dictionary definition of *Obliger Tendency*, there should be a picture of her. See also *anal retentive* and *uptight*. Here's the truth: my sister and I aren't so different from each other. I'd do anything for that girl. I'd let her remove my heart from my body and squeeze it in her hands if she had to. I've been called a rebel, and while I'm not big on labels, I would say it's true. Everything I do is full-out. I don't hold back—not my heart, not my body, nothing. If I'm doing it—and let's face it, I probably am—I am 110 percent in. Squeeze, Marin, squeeze hard.

Marin has a reserve that I don't understand, but I still admire her. My big sister kicks ass and takes names. In the rat race, Marin is one superfast rat in practical panties. The thing is, I am positive she doesn't know what it's like to feel her heart beat in her throat while adrenaline courses through her blood, or that when a firefly almost lands in your hand, its wings make a gentle breeze on your skin. She doesn't know what it feels like to swim naked in ocean water that glows with tiny, almost-magical algae, or to nearly explode from the heat of a passionate love affair. Marin lives like a nanny. She swims in a one-piece bathing suit. One-piece. She's forgotten how to catch fireflies and go wild.

There is nothing wrong with any of this.

It's just that sometimes I wonder how Marin breathes without air.

I tried it once, on Everest, but I couldn't go on without oxygen. This plan is an oxygen tank. Not just for Marin, but for me. Put on your own oxygen mask before helping those around you. Live so you don't have any regrets.

Fourteen

MARIN

I WOKE UP THE next morning with one hell of a headache and Lucas Tsai banging on my villa door in rhythm to the pounding in my head. I dragged myself to the window and leaned out. "Some people are sleeping," I said.

"It's time for your massage."

I shook my head. "I don't have a massage booked."

"Yeah, you do. It's the least I can do after your rough travel experience," he said. "Besides, it's part of your honeymoon package."

"Funny," I said. "I'm not really into being touched by strangers."

"It's just a massage, Marin, not a marriage."

So what if after Sadie showed me the resort website, I personally had every intention of taking full advantage of every service the spa had to offer? Deep-tissue massage? Check. Hot-stone treatment? Check. Seaweed wrap? Yes, please. I might be a little uptight, but I'm not a robot. But this felt different. Sadie wasn't here, and Lucas Tsai was offering me a free massage on the beach. My spasming shoulders screamed at me. The real problem was not the professional masseuse stranger, it was the other stranger . . . the one I couldn't quite get a read on, but who was starting to intrigue me.

"If you're worried about being by yourself, I'll stay. I could use a massage too." He rubbed his neck.

Nope. No way was I getting naked under some sort of sheet with him anywhere in the vicinity. But, oh man, a massage was exactly what my sore muscles needed.

"Are you sure you aren't interested?" Lucas asked.

I hesitated. "Yeah. Not this time. I should probably try to call Sadie again. She was supposed to let me know when she got her new flight squared away."

"At least come see the beach? We have our own private beach. I'll show you the way."

A short walk to the beach and back surely wouldn't be a problem. I met him outside and followed him down the path that eventually emerged onto a small semicircle of smooth pebbles and gentle waves washing over them.

Up ahead of us, there was a pavilion that matched the gingerbread-cottage style of the rest of the resort, with ornate fretwork, green shutters, and a red tiled roof. Thin curtains of gauze lining the edges fluttered in the breeze. I rubbed a hand over my neck. A knot of tension had settled there and run down my spine and parked itself between my shoulder blades. It was roughly the size of my absentee sister.

"Okay," he said. "Do what you want. It's your vacation. I'm going to go get my massage."

He kicked off his flip-flops and picked them up before he started off toward the pavilion. I watched him, half expecting him to turn around one last time, but he didn't. In the distance, Lucas stepped through the curtain into the pavilion. I could just make out the silhouettes of two women who stood in between two tables. It was a couples massage, I realized. The two masseuses were already there waiting. I rubbed my neck. I couldn't very well leave the extra masseuse standing there. She'd come all the way out to the beach, after all. I pulled off my shoes and jogged toward the pavilion.

"I'm coming," I called.

I'd like to say I did not scope out Lucas while he was getting ready for his massage. It's possible I caught a few glances while I was wriggling out of my stupid cutoff jeans under the safety of my blanket.

"You have a lot of tension," my masseuse said to me a few minutes later while she set to work kneading my tight muscles into blissful submission.

I'm pretty sure Lucas stifled a laugh.

"I was traveling all day on my own yesterday. I guess you could say I'm a little stressed."

"The appointment said couples massage, honeymoon. You're not on your honeymoon?"

"Nope."

"He's not your new husband?"

I turned my head to glance at Lucas. He appeared to be sleeping. His eyes were closed and he didn't move. "Not my anything," I said. I turned my head back to center.

"That's fine," the masseuse said. "You don't need a husband."

I took a very deep breath and let it out. "Now you're relaxing," she said. "Good."

She might have said more, but I didn't remember. I drifted off into some sort of magical massage-induced sleep. At the end, she gently woke me with the sound of her voice. "How do you feel?" I felt amazing. Slack and relaxed and wonderful. Lucas was sitting on his table wrapped in his blanket.

"Thank you," he said.

"Yes, thank you so much," I said.

The two women exchanged a glance before dissolving into giggles. "We knew he wasn't your husband," they said between breaths. "Like we don't know Mr. Tsai! Imagine that! Everybody knows Mr. Tsai."

I opened my mouth to say something, but they each gave a little bow and then left before I could pull my blanket up around me. "Did they just mess with me?" I asked.

"Yeah, they did. You must seem fun to mess with."

I rotated my neck. Had he been messing with me too? Until that moment, I hadn't realized how stiff my neck had been. Messed with or not, the tension had melted away. "It's beautiful here," I said.

Lucas nodded. "I think I'm going to go for a swim," he said. "Would you want to join me?"

"I don't have my bathing suit."

"Your point?"

"Wonderful," I said. "Well, have fun, I guess."

He tipped his head to the side and eyed me. I pulled the sheet up a little higher on my shoulders. "C'mon. We could just get dressed in this heat and go about the rest of our day, or we could take advantage of the fact that most of the resort guests are on an excursion to Quill National Park over on Sint Eustatius, leaving this beach practically deserted, and go get in that inviting blue ocean and cool off." His eyes were locked on mine. For my part, I was trying very hard not to stare at his perfectly muscled torso. "Your choice."

My choice, as it turned out, was to stand in the pavilion like a mummy in my sheet, watching him as he strode down the beach to the waterline, unwrapped his sheet, and waded into the water. I had to hold on to the massage table for support. He stopped when the water was waist-deep, ducked under a wave, and came up shaking salt water out of his hair. It looked as if he were in slow motion. I gulped. Seeing him like that, glistening in the sun like a damn Poseidon reigning over his aquatic kingdom, I had to admit that maybe there was a shred of me that regretted my decision. A microscopic thread. A kind of turned-on thread. But the rest of me was quite happy to be not naked and on dry land, especially considering the fact that the practically deserted beach Lucas referred to actually had several guests on it playing badminton about twenty-five yards away from us.

"You're unusual for an American, Marin," Lucas hollered at me. "I didn't think Americans were so . . . repressed."

"I am *not* repressed."

"Okay, maybe that's not the right word. That happens to me sometimes . . . I speak several languages, and sometimes I need to search for the right word. Let me try again. Uptight?"

I glared at him.

"Scaredy-cat? Prissy?"

"Real hilarious."

"I don't think I've ever met someone so uptight they needed a bathing suit to dip a toe into the ocean. Let me guess, you're a one-piece kind of a girl."

That was it. He was definitely messing with me.

I cannot explain what came over me. Maybe it was the fact that the massage had made me just a little too relaxed, or that the water was a postcard shade of turquoise. Sweat *was* accumulating in places that just shouldn't sweat, but when it came down to it I really didn't like being called prissy. One-pieces could be super hot. Hadn't he seen that picture of Halima Aden in a burkini in the *Sports Illustrated* Swimsuit edition? She looked amazing.

I narrowed my eyes and grasped the sheet around myself tightly, then I started toward the water. The soft rhythmic shush of the ocean's waves invited me closer. Clear water flooded over my feet. This wasn't so bad. I lifted my face to the sun. And then it happened. While my eyes were closed and the golden warmth washed over my cheeks, a rogue wave came along and knocked into me. The force of it threw me off balance, and as I tried to keep from falling down in the surf, I lost my grip on the sheet. The ocean snatched it right out of my hand. It happened so fast. One moment, I was enjoying the sensation of freedom, damp sand squishing beneath my feet, warm, refreshing waves lapping at my skin. The next, I was standing in thigh-deep water, totally naked. I whirled around, searching desperately, grasping to find the sheet, but it had already floated out of reach.

"Don't look at me," I yelled, and dropped to the ocean floor. I held my breath and let the waves crash over my head until I ran out of air. Had Lucas seen everything? Who was I kidding? Of course he had. This was why women over the age of eighteen did not go skinny-dipping. It was humiliating and horrifying. I had no idea why Sadie thought swimming naked was such a freeing experience except that she was addicted to adrenaline and was probably an exhibitionist. She enjoyed putting herself through torturous mountain climbs and facing imminent doom. She was a masochist. I, on the other hand, was mortified. When I surfaced, Lucas waded over to me.

"Are you okay?" he asked.

"No!" I tried to contain my panic. I grabbed a tangle of floating kelp and held it front of myself. "I am most definitely not okay. Could you please get me my clothes or your sheet . . . please?"

He headed back to the beach. I figured he'd stop for the sheet, but he didn't. He walked all the way up to the pavilion, grabbed our clothes, and brought them back. He pulled on his Bermuda shorts. "You do realize that you'll have to come out of there to get dressed," he said.

I waddled in a crouch, like some ridiculous, nude sand crab, until I was close to the shoreline. "No way," I said. "Throw me my shirt."

The tank top arced through the air and landed in my hands. I quickly pulled it over my head.

"Shorts."

Lucas had a good arm. The shorts hit me in the face. I held them while I figured out how I was going to do this. The waves were coming in fast; I struggled to stay on my feet. I had two options: come out of the water, like Lucas had said, proving him right and possibly exposing myself even more, or taking my chances with the ocean.

I chose option two.

Ever tried to wrangle yourself into another woman's Daisy Dukes underwater? I don't recommend it.

Fifteen

A STRANGER SAW ME naked, okay?" I growled at Sadie's voice mail. "I'm a woman on the edge. So you had better call me back and tell me that you'll be here in the next twenty-four hours."

I hadn't even set the phone down when it buzzed.

"Sadie?"

"Hi, Sis."

"Oh, thank God. I've been going crazy. I had a massage on the beach and lost my bag and went swimming in the ocean, then I lost my sheet . . ."

"You lost what? The connection's not good. You lost your shit?"

"My sheet. I—Forget it, it doesn't matter. Where are you? Did you get a flight? Are you close?" The questions rattled out of my mouth, but I stopped myself. This was like one of those moments at airport arrivals, when she was coming around the corner by the baggage claim and all the missing her and the worrying, the angst, was about to end. I wanted to savor her response.

"Uh . . ."

There is nothing delicious in "Uh." I had a feeling that this moment was not going to be an airport-arrival moment after all. "Is it the storm system? Did you have to get a later flight?"

"No," she said. I counted the seconds—four—before she answered. "Please don't hate me."

I closed my eyes. Over the years, I'd learned that *Please don't hate me* was Sadie's lead-up to a major bomb deployment. On me. *I'm going to be an international photojournalist.* Boom. *I'm going to free-climb El Capitan.* Boom. *They want me to photograph this guerrilla resistance group.* Boom. I braced for impact. "I'm not coming," she said.

"Ha!" The sound was out before I had a chance to register what she'd said. "Of course you are. That's hilarious. Like I'd believe that."

"Believe it," she said. I could not stop laughing. My sides were already beginning to ache. "I'm serious, Marin," I heard her say through my laughter. "I'm not coming."

"Sisters' getaway, that's what you called it. Sisters. Plural. You can't have a sisters' getaway with one sister," I said. "You have to come."

"Listen, I've been everywhere, and I'm tired. You were right about that. I just figured you're always at home. I wanted you to have a chance to get away, to explore, to relax and take care of you for once. See things for yourself. Do whatever you want to do."

I tried to pull in a few calming breaths, but it didn't work.

"Can't you just take this free trip and enjoy a few days in paradise?"

"You have no idea what the last day and a half has been like for me. I lost my bag and ended up with someone else's suitcase. Some newlywed who dresses like a cross between a stripper and a sorority house vice president. And I don't feel like myself."

"That doesn't sound so bad. You could stand to step outside of your safe, stifling comfort zone for once."

"This isn't funny, Sadie."

"You were laughing your ass off a minute ago."

"That was a stress response!" I countered. "I fell into the ocean wearing a sheet."

"Oh, was that when you lost your shit?" she said. "I'm loving Island Marin. I've been trying to get you to go skinny-dipping for years."

"Yeah, except I'm sure in your fantasy of my letting loose I didn't end up mortified, wearing a kelp bikini top."

"Seriously?" She laughed again. "Classic!"

"Okay, giggles, real funny. We can talk about this more when I get back."

"I can't wait to hear about your amazing trip."

"I hardly think two days' worth of fiascos constitutes an amazing trip, but whatever you say."

"What do you mean, two days? I paid for a whole week. With my own money. So no backsies."

I shook my head. "Did you just 'no backsies' me? Are you eight?"

"It's the law, Marin. You know it and I know it. Marin Cole upholds the 'no backsies' rule until the end of time, because without rules, the world would descend into chaos."

"That was the old Marin," I said. "Island Marin is going home."

Sadie was still protesting, loudly, when I ended the call. I abandoned the robe and pulled on the longest skirt I could find and a sweatshirt that said *Mrs. Hot Stuff*. Because why not, right? Mrs. Hot Stuff probably loved skinny-dipping. I jammed everything else back into the suitcase and closed it shut, catching the soft fleshy part of my thumb in the process. Sadie had put me through a lot over the years, but this had to be by far the most ludicrous, insensitive, harebrained scheme she'd ever attempted. And that included the time she threw a beach party that involved flooding the first floor of our house while I happened to be away on my first—and only—overnight business trip. Who knew what she was doing at home right now? She'd probably turned the place into some sort of Coachella while I'd been schlepping around Saba in newlywed-chic. I was in the middle of trying to decide which would be faster, calling the airline and booking a flight or taking my chances at the airport, when someone knocked on the door.

"I thought I'd see if you wanted to have dinner." Lucas.

I crossed my arms across my chest. Was he looking at me with a weird expression? This was because he'd seen me naked earlier. Dinner was some sort of olive branch for my accidental exposure.

"You have other plans?" he asked.

"Yes, as a matter of fact. But if you wanted to atone for the beach, you could help me with something," I said.

"Sure," he said. "What do you need?"

"I need a ride to the airport. I'm already packed." I did a quick inventory. Random suitcase. Wallet. Oh no. No, no, no, no, no.

"What's wrong?" Lucas asked.

I buried my face in my hands and groaned.

"That's one language I don't speak," Lucas said. "What's going on?"

I looked up at him. "My passport isn't in my purse."

He stepped over and looked at all my stuff. "It's got to be around here somewhere," he said. "Didn't you have anything else with you?"

I blew out a loud breath. "No. This is everything." I surveyed the stuff I'd laid out. The newlywed's bag with all its hideous sparkle and lace content. The shoes that hurt my feet. My purse. Wallet. ChapStick. Lint roller. The outfit that I'd worn on the plane, wrinkled and stained. There was even a small tear in the pants pocket. The pocket where I'd put my passport. Just great.

My passport was probably floating around somewhere on Anegada or at the bottom of the ocean at this point. At any rate, the exact location didn't matter, because it wasn't with me, and I apparently was staying right here.

Sixteen

SADIE

THE DAY I GOT the diagnosis, I got drunk. Not just your normal drunk, but like Felix-had-to-carry-me-home-from-the-bar blitzed. Because sometimes, when everything is going wrong and you don't know what to do, you just want all the tequila. Marin always told me too much alcohol was bad for my health. Hilarious, right? Maybe she's right. I'd be lying if I said there wasn't at least a moment after the doctor told me when I wondered if maybe I was being punished for living just a little too big. But then again, sometimes a few glasses of some good liquor is just what the doctor ordered. It's not going to solve your problems. When you wake up, everything still sucks and you have a hangover. But for a few brief hours of obliteration, you get to forget. And maybe that's enough.

Once Marin got to Saba, I had to make sure she stayed there. I should probably feel a little guilty, but honestly, I'm proud of my slightly Machiavellian capabilities. She probably didn't even notice the bump and snag at the airport.

Anyway, knowing Marin, she's in a panic spiral right about now. That's where the booze comes in. She's going to need to pour herself a glass . . . or four.

Seventeen

MARIN

SOMEONE ONCE TOLD ME when things go wrong, sometimes the best thing to do is drink heavily," Lucas said.

"Drinking's bad for your health."

He raised an eyebrow at me. "I guess you could always do a little light reading," he said, holding up my copy of *Ulysses*. "I couldn't get through this myself."

"I've been attempting to read it since college," I admitted.

"Maybe James Joyce isn't for you. I seem to remember a professor said Joyce used alcohol to cope with life's misfortunes."

"Makes sense. Maybe that's why I can't seem to get into it—I'm not much of a drinker," I mumbled.

He shrugged. "Me either. There's a first time for everything, I guess." He walked over to a wooden stand beneath the window and extracted a bottle. "Do you like peaches?"

"What's that?" I asked. The bottle was clear with an intricate red design on the glass and a large matching red cap. It was unlike any liquor I'd ever seen. Living in Tennessee and having no social life to speak of had pretty much limited my hard-alcohol knowledge to the familiar black label of Jack Daniel's.

"Kinmen Kaoliang, three years," Lucas said. He pulled off the cap and filled two tumblers with ice. "It's from Taiwan. Very smooth."

I took a glass from his hand and took a tentative sip. It was as he described, smooth, but I could tell straightaway it was strong. Lucas picked up his glass and the bottle and headed outside. There was a little stone patio there with two chairs and a small table.

I paused in the doorway, considering if I should follow him. Already, the alcohol had warmed my cheeks and softened the edges of the scene. The air was still slightly warm and tinged with humidity, but there was also the scent of some kind of night-blooming flower. Lucas turned on a hanging lantern that swayed gently in the breeze. I took a seat across from him.

"It's resplendent out here," I said.

Lucas took a long sip of his drink and then nodded.

I don't know what I'd been expecting; some sort of cutting remark about how most people would want to stay in a place like this forever, not run away the first chance they got, maybe. I grew uncomfortable in the silence and emptied my glass. I was finding the Kinmen a little too drinkable. Lucas poured me another.

"Ba's favorite drink," he said, turning his glass. "We keep one bottle in every villa. What do you think of it?"

I squinted at him. "It's nice. But it doesn't solve my problem."

He nodded slowly. "The passport."

"Getting home."

"Is it so bad here?"

"It's not that. I'm really more comfortable at home. And I was hoping to spend time with Sadie—"

"You mentioned that."

"I know what you're thinking. My sister sets me up on a surprise luxury trip in paradise. I should be jumping for joy. I probably seem like a lunatic, right?"

"You seem like a person who doesn't like not being in control."

"Exactly," I said, lifting my glass. I had to give it to Lucas Tsai— he had a side of brains to go with that beauty. He'd called me exactly. Some of the Kinmen spilled out onto my hand. "But it's more than that. I wanted to spend time with her. I don't care about fancy bathrobes and ocean views. Nothing is more important than family. And my sister needs me."

"She planned all this. She seems pretty self-sufficient."

"You don't know Sadie. She's like one of those fires that burns so hot and bright it burns itself out. She needs someone to take care of her and make sure she doesn't do anything too crazy."

"Sounds like a big job."

"Don't you run some sort of business empire?"

He shrugged. "It practically runs itself. And anyway, I don't have any siblings to take care of. It seems like having one is a lot of work."

"Not really. I'd do anything for her and she'd do anything for me. We're family."

"You say you'd do anything for her . . . Maybe you should do this."

"You're drunk."

"Perhaps." He leaned back in his seat. "I could also be right. It's like this place. It was all Ba. He wanted a resort on Saba to add to our holdings. I didn't get it. We've got hotels all over the world. Airlines. We didn't need anything else. It seemed silly to put a resort on a tiny island; even worse, sentimental. Ba was a businessman. But I guess he knew that Saba was something I needed. I hadn't been back since we'd moved to Taipei when I was ten. You know, Ba actually had the resort built around our old house; it's where I live now when I'm on the island. Anyway, I reconnected with friends I'd made when I was a kid. I was able to remember some times with my mother. And it brought me and my father closer together, which was . . . I'll always be grateful that I went along with his plan, even if I didn't agree with it at the time. Now I come here whenever I can. It's more home at this point than Taipei. Somehow he knew I needed this place, even when I didn't."

"Your father sounds like a smart man."

"Mm." Lucas nodded. "He was stubborn too. Once he got an idea in his head, he wouldn't stop until he'd made it happen. Like this resort. His latest obsession was making all our properties eco-friendly. Sounds great, right? But Ba, he took everything to an extreme. He acquired an entire solar-power company and the plant that makes the glass and panel components. Everything."

I smiled. Sadie was always going on about the fate of the world. She'd have loved this. "So he's wise and tenacious."

"He was."

"I'm sorry," I said. "Losing a parent is . . . well, it leaves a gaping hole."

He gave a short nod.

"I lost my mom in high school. It's been twelve years and I still miss her just as much. Not as often, but as much."

Lucas drained his glass and poured himself another. "You know, he wanted this huge funeral. Hundreds of mourners with white envelopes instead of red. They put paper flowers on the coffin lid and the lawn—yellow lotus blossoms everywhere. They're supposed to fend off the demons that might try to stop him from reaching the afterlife. We even had professional mourners. One was a beautiful girl in one of those white ceremonial shrouds. Ba would have loved it. It was awful. She crawled on her knees toward the coffin, wailing. She didn't even know him. I remember these details. I hear the Buddhist prayers we all chanted in Mandarin. The ghost money we burned. It was what he wanted, but it felt so . . . wrong."

I thought back to Mom's funeral. All those strangers. Sadie sitting above us all, looking down at the awful scene. How I wished I'd been able to escape it.

"My mom's funeral was like that. All these people who knew her work, but not her. Sadie climbed up onto the church rafter and scared the heck out of me. That and she left me down there to face them by myself. I was so mad at her."

"That sounds awful." Lucas took a long drink from his glass and filled it again. I offered my glass for a refill. "You were just a kid."

"I was almost eighteen. And anyway, I grew up fast."

He was quiet for a long time. "I haven't talked much about this with people. No one seems to know what to say, including me."

I nodded. "It's hard to understand unless you've been through it."

"I just want to honor him and I have no idea how. But it's more than that." Finally, he said in a voice so low I almost didn't hear him, "I'm already having a hard time picturing his face."

My mother's face had done the same disappearing act from my memory. "I used to pull out the binders of my mom's article clippings just to see the picture that ran next to her byline. I still do it sometimes, even now."

"She was a journalist?"

"Yes. She traveled all over the world. People used to say there was nowhere she wouldn't go. I was going to be just like her . . ."

"Not anymore?"

"I'm still a writer, I guess, except I write catchy slogans about bespoke vitamins and raw pet food instead of the important stories I always planned on."

"Why?"

"It's not worth getting killed over." The stars were starting to blur in front of me. "But try telling that to Sadie. No go. She probably sent me down here so she could do that story on the rival clans in Papua New Guinea." I turned to Lucas. "Now do you get why I need to go home?" My mouth felt sticky.

"I'm getting the picture," he said, taking the glass from me. The skin on his fingertips seared against my hand.

"You're so hot," I said.

"Why don't I get you some water?"

"You don't have to take care of me." As I registered my own words, they sounded strange and singsong. A fog was settling over me, warm and liquor-flavored. I laughed. "I'm completely fine."

The island seemed to be slowly turning sideways. Lucas reached for me. *Completely fine,* I hummed to myself. And then I slumped down in my chair and the lights went out.

Eighteen

IN MY LIQUOR-SOAKED SLEEP, I dreamed of that day. The one I had danced around when I was talking to Lucas. The one I wished had been erased from my mind instead of the memory of my mother's face. But there it was, in full color, as if I were back there again. Every detail unmistakable. The warmth of the room as the school's ancient air conditioning struggled against a late-May heatwave. The antiseptic smell. My teacher's pleated skirt swishing as she entered the chorus room and walked toward me. She let us finish the song we were singing before she spoke.

"Marin? They need to see you in the principal's office."

"Did they say why?" I asked, gathering up my book bag.

Ms. Anderson shook her head. "I'm sure it's nothing to worry about." She smiled. "Here's your final essay, by the way. Wonderful, really wonderful work. You must take after your mom."

I glanced down at the bloodred A in big, fat marker, the smiley face next to it; it wasn't much compared to Mom's Pulitzer last year for her work reporting on the humanitarian crisis in Ethiopia, but maybe it would make her proud. Sadie beat me when it came to being brave, but I could write, and those two things were Mom's whole reason for living. Words and adrenaline, she always said, now that's living.

The hallways were empty since the bell wouldn't ring for another ten minutes, so I walked down them clutching my A-paper, an essay about American interference and corruption in Nicaragua told through the story of a family of female weavers, to my chest. I knew

I hadn't done anything wrong, so I wasn't too concerned about being called to the principal's office. Sometimes when Mom was away, Dr. Dawson would check in with me to make sure that Sadie and I were doing okay. This happened more after Grandpa George passed away. He'd always stayed with us while Mom traveled, but he'd gotten some kind of cancer—stomach maybe, I can't remember—and died when I was sixteen. After that, Dr. Dawson kept an eye on us both. Other times, she let me know that Sadie had done some crazy stunt during gym class and was in the health office holding someone's discarded T-shirt to her nose. I wondered what Sadie had done this time. At the rate she was going, she'd probably climbed onto the roof during free period to retrieve all the lost items that mysteriously ended up stuck there during the school year and fashion them into some sort of political-statement sculpture. I squinted at the glass double doors to see if I could make out a fire engine that would no doubt have been summoned to get her down, but there wasn't one. A police cruiser was parked in its place. I could tell by the familiar design on the door, our city crest surrounded by *Protect and Serve*. My stomach tightened. Had I not thought big enough? The police were here, so it had to have been more than her usual antics of climbing the field house roof.

I let myself into the office. The reception desk was empty, so I sat down in one of the chairs to wait. I reread the first lines of my essay to distract myself from the anxious thoughts that were starting to bubble up. *Anielka Ortega comes from a long line of female artisans. From her modest home in the heart of the biggest tropical rain forest after the Amazon basin, she weaves by the light that filters through the canopy.*

I'd probably have to call Mom on the station's sat phone and let her know. If Sadie had really gotten in major trouble, Mom'd have to come home earlier than next Tuesday, when she was due. That wasn't such a bad thing. Maybe Sadie was actually an eighth-grade genius.

"It's just such a shame," a muffled male voice said.

I looked up from my paper. A door creaked and the light from one of the administrative offices leaked out into the dim hallway that led back from reception.

"She always was a risk taker."

My palms grew damp. I wiped them on my pants and stood up. They were talking about Sadie. I took a step toward the hall.

"But can you imagine, Leanne, going to a place like the Sudan with two young girls at home depending on you? It's not like we don't have a newspaper here. She could have worked there, found a nice guy—what about Bob, that podiatrist, wasn't he always interested in her?—to settle down with. Then those girls would have had a father, and goodness knows that Sadie could use one." They were talking about Sadie again, and Mom. The woman who was speaking had a sharp tone, Mrs. Hughes maybe, the health teacher. I walked as quietly as I could, pressing my body against the wall so no one would see me. The voices were lower now. I could barely make out a word here and there. I leaned toward the door, straining to hear what these people were saying about my family.

"It's a shame," a man said.

"Irresponsible, is what it is. Who's going to take care of those girls now?"

Maybe I'd leaned too far, or maybe the weight of those words, their implications, threw me off-balance, because before I understood what was happening, I was pitching forward past the open doorway.

"Oh my God," the woman who'd just spoken cried out. Her voice was unmistakable. Even in the dream, I could feel the bile rising in my throat.

"Marin," Dr. Dawson said. I saw her face. It was turned sideways as I careened toward the floor, but I could still read her red-rimmed eyes, the concern in her expression. "Oh, honey." There was a police officer next to her. Behind them I saw Laura, the receptionist, and the school psychologist.

I didn't feel the impact when my cheek slammed into the floor. I had a bruise of the pattern, a diamond with a small fleur-de-lis in the middle, for weeks. Mom always called bruises battle scars, a thing to be revered, she said. Scars and bruises, any kind of wound really, are proof that you're alive. I'd always thought she was so badass. My mom, Lydia Cole, Pulitzer Prize–winning badass. But now I knew different. Wounds, like the kind you get when someone shoots your helicopter out of the sky with an RPG, don't prove you're alive. They kill you.

My mother was dead. And she was full of shit too. Every time she went off on an assignment, she'd take my face between her hands and kiss my forehead, and then she'd promise me, "Safe and sound and in one piece." She even made me repeat it back to her, like an oath we took to each other. She was going to go off and live, and I would make sure that when she got back Sadie was still kicking, with no major injuries. I'd always thought she was so brave and amazing, the way she charged into all those war-torn landscapes to do her meaningful work. She was a hero. She was *my* hero. But she was gone. She was never coming back.

Someone at the station had arranged a grand memorial service for her with all these important people, industry bigwigs and politicians who kept talking at me, telling stories of how fearless, how singular my mother was, how even though her life was short, it was so big. I nodded politely, trying not to look like a robot, while I clutched Sadie's hand. She couldn't stop crying. She cried from the moment she'd practically tripped over me on the floor of the principal's office that day to the funeral. She cried and drank water and cried more. She climbed to the top of the garage and sat up there, crying and swilling water long after dark. And now she leaned against me and cried.

"Your mom was so full of life. There was no challenge she wouldn't take on," the man before me was saying. He had blond hair and the tan, prematurely aged skin of someone who spent a lot of time in the field. "I just can't believe she's gone."

I wanted to ask him, really, if it was that unbelievable that she would have died when she was traipsing around a wilderness where multiple terrorist regimes and governments were warring with each other. Didn't he know how risky that was? My mother must have known how risky it was, and she'd gone anyway. Even though it was so dangerous and irresponsible. Even though Sadie and I were alone in the world now. But I wasn't like her. I wasn't adventurous or brave. I was a writer, like my mom, but even that connection to her wasn't something I wanted to have now. I glanced over at Sadie, who was blowing her nose, loudly, on the man's handkerchief. Her eyes were nearly swollen shut. I squeezed her hand and managed to curve my lips into a semblance of a smile for her. I wanted her to know that we had each other and I would never let anything touch us. I would never let either of us go through this kind of pain again. It was that instant exactly when she wriggled out of my grasp. More mourners came through with their war stories that were supposed to make me feel proud of my mother, make me see that her life had had meaning. Then there were my teachers. Dr. Dawson, who hugged me a little too tight and a little too long. She squeezed the air out of my lungs. My AP English teacher said I could call her for anything and slipped me her cell number on a small piece of paper she'd torn from the program. Then the health teacher.

"I'm so sorry, Marin, for your loss. If only your mother hadn't gone to that terrible place. It's such a tragedy." I was about to say something—thank you, maybe, or fuck off—but instead I got whacked on the head. After several stunned seconds, I saw the offending object on the floor—one of Mom's shoes, the ones I'd told Sadie not to wear. I looked up, and there she was, sitting on one of the cathedral's great stone rafters, swinging her legs as if she were merely hanging out on the top of the monkey bars. The remaining shoe dangled from her foot. I willed it to land on the health teacher's head.

No one had seen Sadie climb up there. It was as if she'd flown.

"Oh good Lord," the teacher exclaimed, covering her head with her hands. "Sadie Cole, you get down right now. Haven't we all lost enough?"

Sadie's face contorted, and then she opened her mouth and roared. I'd never heard a sound like that, except maybe in a nature documentary. The teacher's eyes grew wide and she opened her mouth to speak, but only a few breathy syllables came out before she stomped off.

Nineteen

I WOKE UP IN the morning with one hell of a hangover. I didn't have a plan or a passport. What I had was the world's worst headache. Fortunately, over the years I'd had plenty of experience handling the aftermath of Sadie's antics. I didn't know much about dealing with a missing passport, but I figured between the internet and the concierge desk, I could be heading back to Tennessee in the next twenty-four hours. Still wearing the same clothes as the night before, I pulled my hair into a messy bun and headed to the jungle path that led back to the main part of the resort.

I hadn't explored the main house before. At the end of the path there was a garden area with a flagstone patio. Lush tropical plants of every hue abounded. A few teak chairs with thick cushions were set below dangling string lights. It looked like the perfect place to sit with a glass of—definitely not what I'd drunk last night. Kombucha, maybe. A few of the seats were occupied by guests sipping hot beverages; the rich aroma of coffee filled my senses. Double French doors led to a large lobby that had an understated elegance, and more fresh flowers everywhere. I scanned the area for reception and headed toward a dark wood desk where the man who had picked me and Lucas up was sitting, eating a doughnut.

"Good morning," he said. "Enjoying your stay?"

"Ken, right?" I said. "It's great. Actually, I need some help with something."

"You came to the right place," he said. "What'll it be? I can book a restaurant reservation, another massage, scuba—whatever you want, I can get. Your wish is my command."

"How do I get to the US consulate?"

He raised his eyebrows. "Important diplomatic business?" he asked.

"Lost passport. And I need to get home, so, well, you can imagine that's kind of a problem. I did a little research on the internet and it says I can get an emergency passport at the consulate."

"Absolutely. No problem. I can make the travel arrangements."

"I thought I could walk there. The island's pretty small, right?"

"Right," said Ken, stretching out the word.

I waited. Was everyone here on some sort of island slow-motion? I flashed an expectant smile.

"Ah, yeah, it's just that Saba doesn't have its own US consulate. There is one in Curaçao, though. That's the one Americans on Saba use."

"Fine. How far is Curaçao?" How far could it be, right? Twenty minutes by boat? A half hour at most.

He cleared his throat. "It's seven hundred kilometers," he said.

I closed my eyes.

"Are you freaking out?" he asked.

"Not at all," I said, and pulled a calming breath in through my nose. "Why would you say that?"

"Because you look sort of like you're freaking out. Your face is really red and kind of scrunched up. Are you shaking? Look, don't worry, I can help you. There are flights to Curaçao. We'll get you on one of those."

"Wouldn't I need a passport for that?"

"Good point. In that case, we should probably ask Lucas. He's better in a crisis. Plus, he travels all the time, so he'd know."

Yes, that's a great idea, I thought. We'd ask Lucas—Lucas, whose idea of handling my emergency was getting me drunk on some kind of Taiwanese liquor last night—clearly the *perfect* solution. Wonderful. I'd probably have better luck as a stowaway. I started to tell Ken this, but he was already on the phone, rambling away in what I guessed was Mandarin because I could make out, like, three words: *hi*, *sorry*, and *bye*, the last of which was almost exactly like English only admittedly cooler. I liked the way it sounded.

"He's already on it. He's got people searching the airport as we speak. Anything else I can do for you in the meantime? Have you had breakfast?"

"You know, I'm really not hungry. But thanks." I gave a half-hearted wave and walked away.

Sadie picked up on the fourth ring. She sounded like I'd just woken her from the Mariana Trench of sleep. "Hello?"

"Hello to you."

"Who's this?"

"I've only been a castaway for two days and my own sister has already forgotten me. What will become of me?"

"Everything."

"Huh?" I said. Must have been some dream. "Look, Sadie. I get it. I was being too overbearing so you thought I needed to relax. I got the message. I'm relaxed and ready to come home."

"Did you get laid?"

"Are you drunk?" I said.

"I wish. Are you? If you're not, you should be."

"Listen, as fun as this bizarre conversation is, we could totally do this on the couch in the living room. But I can't get there because my passport is gone. You have to help me. They don't even have a consulate here. The nearest one is seven hundred kilometers away."

Sadie burst out laughing. Did I mention that my sister laughs like a nine-month-old angel? Her laugh could be the world's most powerful weapon. I couldn't even get mad at her. The corners of my mouth started to lift.

"Stay on topic here, Sadie. Help me."

"Okay, I'll help. I know exactly how to solve this problem. I'm going to give you some advice that's perfect for this situation. Are you ready?"

"I'm all ears."

"When things go wrong . . ." I waited. "Go crazy!"

"That's it?" I tried to keep the annoyance out of my voice.

"You're not getting out of my trap that easily, Mar. You've got two options: figure it out yourself, or start having some fun. If you can show me that you are really taking advantage of this trip—and I mean full-fledged photographic evidence—then I will have my contact in the State Department overnight you a new passport."

"You have a contact in the State Department?"

"Desmond Brown? Oh yeah, I had *a lot* of contact with him." She laughed. "Don't get your boxer briefs in a twist, Felix. You know you're the only man I'd still like even at twenty thousand feet when you smell like a goat."

"Felix is there?"

"Like I said, when things go wrong, go crazy," Sadie said.

"Wait—"

"I gotta go, Sissy. He's made me a smoothie, and I just can't resist a man with a blended beverage."

She hung up.

I stood in the middle of the patio that was now drenched in warm morning sun, taking deep breaths of the fragrant air, trying to process what the hell had just happened.

My phone rang. "I forgot to tell you," Sadie said, sounding out of breath, "Post the proof on Instagram. Hashtag Project Paradise. No proof, no passport."

I opened my mouth to respond.

"Get over here, you magnificent Yeti," Sadie said, sounding far away.

Oh my God. I shook my head and ended the call. I didn't want to leave the line open—what I'd heard already was more than enough. Way more. I dropped into one of the chairs to consider my options. Struggle through a voyage to Curaçao and whatever unknown red tape waited at the consulate, or take a few pictures, post them on Instagram, and get Sadie's ex–sex friend, Desmond, to express me a brand-new passport. Another sea voyage. I thought back to the storm clouds and the pitching of the yacht in the waves when I'd come here with Lucas. Nope. Pictures. Definitely pictures. People staged stuff for the internet all the time, made their lives look perfect, majestic, wrinkle-free. All it took was a little lighting, the right camera angle, and filters. I could do that. Hell, I worked in advertising. I could even write the copy in my sleep.

"Two can play at this game," I said aloud.

"I like games."

Cheeks burning, I swiveled in my chair. There was Ken, smirking, walking toward me with Lucas beside him. It's important to note that Lucas did not look hungover. He looked, well, not like a hot sex Yeti, but pretty damn fine. I took this in while noting that I probably looked about as bad as I felt, and for an instant I contemplated diving into a thicket of Mexican petunias and hiding among the dark-green stalks and large purple blooms.

"You like games too, right, Lucas?"

I tried to read his expression, but he was wearing those damn aviator shades, the ones that made him look like a movie star, yet again. He shrugged and settled into a chair.

"I'll speak for my friend," Ken said. "He's a little under the weather this morning."

Serves him right.

Ken continued. "Lucas's people didn't turn up your passport. It looks like someone may have taken it. We may have to start the process of getting you a new one." I looked at Lucas and then Ken. Lucas was a complete enigma; Ken looked a little afraid of me. I plastered a smile on, picked a piece of lint off my sweatshirt.

"No problem," I said, my voice like sugary syrup. Time to set my plan in action. "I've got it handled. Maybe you could help me with something else though, Ken? While I'm here, I'd really like to see the island."

"Sure. We offer tours, or there's—"

"I'll take you," Lucas said.

"That's okay, I'm sure you've got more important things to do."

"Let's go," he said. He stood, and in the same motion he grabbed my hand and dragged me after him. It was so abrupt, I almost dropped my phone. His grip on my hand was firm. I didn't see the point in pulling away. I needed someone to take me to some good locations for the pictures I needed to satisfy Sadie, and besides, I was almost certain that he would look great on camera. Behind us, Ken said, "See, I knew you liked games, man."

"So where are we headed?" I asked.

"You tell me," Lucas said. "It seems like you might have some thoughts."

I turned to him. "Actually, I do. I want to take some pictures to send home. Apparently, my sister thinks that I am not capable of having any fun. She can get me a passport overnight through a connection, but she said she won't until I prove that I got something out of her little stunt."

"Seriously?" Ken called. His hearing was amazing.

I turned around. "She created a hashtag. Project Paradise. I'm supposed to post my adventures on Instagram. No pictures, no passport—her words."

"Oh, she's devious. I think I like your sister," Ken said. "I wish she'd come with you."

"You and me both."

"I know some spots," Lucas said. "Let's go."

Twenty

EVEN THOUGH I WASN'T a writer anymore, not the kind I'd planned on being anyway, I still liked to sort through adjectives for the perfect one to describe everything. It was a little game I played sometimes. I'd see a dog walking down the street and decide—was it menacing and mangy or jocular or salubrious? I observed Lucas sitting beside me in the Jeep. He wasn't sullen exactly. Pensive maybe. Quiet? Definitely. I smoothed my hands over the folds of my skirt.

"So, what's this place where we're going?" I asked.

"The Ladder."

I waited for him to elaborate. He did not. Instead, he tightened his grip on the steering wheel. His knuckles turned pale and then recolored again when he relaxed his hands.

"What's the Ladder?" I asked. "Do I have to climb something? Because I'm not really into climbing."

"You'll be fine. It's just stairs. But if you want to see Saba, you have to go to Ladder Bay," he said. We made brief eye contact and I tried to make sure that my not-into-climbing position was clear. Lucas exhaled. "It's a great place to take pictures."

I mulled this over for a moment as we passed a sign that pointed toward Wells Bay and then took a left at a gazebo onto an unmarked road. Lucas slowed the Jeep and pulled to the side of the road.

"We're here," he said. "The trail's just over there." He gestured with a slight nod of his chin.

I followed his gaze across the road where there was a small opening in the tropical forest. On either side there was a small white-and-green sign that read, simply, THE LADDER, with an arrow pointing toward the forest. The trees stretched toward the sun. Beneath the canopy, there were giant leaves that I envisioned drinking rainwater from, like Swiss Family Robinson. While it didn't look like anything special, it also didn't look particularly treacherous.

"All right," I said. "Let's check it out."

Lucas nodded.

He pulled a backpack from the rear of the Jeep, threw a couple of bottled waters inside, and headed across the road. I nipped along behind him. If a snake or some other creature dropped from one of those trees that seemed straight out of an Indiana Jones movie, he could deal with fangs in his face.

The light dimmed as we went deeper into the forest. To my great relief, there was a narrow trail, worn down by lots of tourists, I imagined. The dirt was hard-packed and smooth. Still, I watched my step. Beneath me, the terrain changed. The steps were modern at first, right angles and concrete. I relaxed. Why had I been nervous? This was going to be a piece of cake. Lucas had gotten my message. As we descended deeper into the forest, the nice even steps gave way to more haphazard ones created by round gray cobblestones pressed into the soft earth. We started down them at a steady pace. Lucas checked my progress over his shoulder as the grade got steeper. Once he even extended his hand to me when we reached a step that had lost several stones. He let go before I did. I was too busy analyzing that to notice he had stopped dead on the steps. I slammed hand-first into his back. Actually, it was his ass. I admit it. And maybe Sadie and I aren't as different as I like to believe, because for one split second I did not think about the fact that we were climbing down steps that were probably going to come out on the side of a cliff, and that because I'd knocked Lucas off-balance we both were potentially going to plummet off said cliff face. I was too busy really just enjoying the fact that I'd touched a cute man's ass. I'd enjoyed it a little too much. Lucas regained his footing and swiveled around to look at me. He cleared his throat. I removed my hand and used it to shield my eyes. We'd emerged from the forest and were now standing in the open on what felt like the edge of the earth. There was that headache again, throbbing in my temples.

"Photogenic location number one," Lucas said. "Over there."

My cheeks burned. "Great."

Beside us, there was a square, one-story building that looked like it might have had one room inside. The outside had been painted white, but was made out of some kind of stone or concrete material that could stand up to the harsh elements here on this cliff above the ocean. A stiff breeze tousled my skirt. I used my hands to hold it down and took a tentative step toward the house.

"What is this place? Does someone live here?" I asked.

Lucas shook his head. "It's abandoned. It used to be a customs house. The Ladder continues from here all the way down to the ocean. If you look down, you can see there's a bay. People used to bring all the supplies to the island this way."

Against my better judgment, I stepped close to him and peeked over the edge. The view was dizzying. We were hundreds of feet up the side of a mountain. Below us, there was a beach covered with thousands of tiny boulders. The steps did indeed continue a snaking path down the side of the cliff face. There was no handrail and nothing to stop a fall. By the time our bodies reached the beach, they'd be smashed to smithereens.

"You're not going to fall," Lucas said. "Give me your phone."

"Why?"

"You need pictures, right?"

"Oh, yeah," I said, rummaging through my small purse. I took it out.

Lucas took in the scene for a few moments before he directed me to stand in front of the house. "How about one of you standing here?"

He snapped a couple of pictures and showed them to me. Other than the stupid shirt and a bit of a hair situation, I looked okay. But it wasn't exciting. The little building could have been anywhere. "It's nice," I said, "it's just . . ."

"What?"

"There's no element of danger." I sat down on the steps. "Sadie's a hard-core adventure person. She wanted to see me step out of my comfort zone. I don't think this is going to cut it."

I stood and brushed off my skirt.

"What if I stayed up here and you went down the steps and I shot straight down? That would give her an idea of the whole picture," he suggested.

My stomach turned. "You want me to climb down by myself?"

"Yeah."

I shook my head. "How about you lie down and shoot from the ground so it looks like I'm up high?"

He made a face. "Didn't you say your sister was a photographer?"

"You're right, that would never fool her."

"Climb down. You can do it."

"I'm not that brave," I said.

"My friend's four-year-old climbed the Ladder last summer."

I narrowed my eyes. Lucas Tsai couldn't have possibly known about my very proud, very competitive Achilles' heel. But somehow he had just poked that sore spot with a four-year-old's very brave, very adventurous little finger. I swallowed a little bile and headed toward the steps.

"Fine," I said over my shoulder. "You better get a good shot, because I am not doing this more than once."

"Got it."

Irritation got me down the first couple of steps without too much trouble, but then I made the mistake of looking down. I've never been a fan of heights (that was Sadie's thing, not mine), but I hadn't realized until that moment that I was afraid of heights. And not just a tiny bit afraid, but full-fledged, heart-racing afraid. I froze.

"You looked down, didn't you?" Lucas's voice was calm.

"How else am I supposed to keep my footing?" I shouted back. I didn't know what to do. Turning around to head back up seemed like a bad idea. The narrow stone stairs pitched straight down the rocky face to the ocean below. What if I lost my balance? I couldn't keep going. Puking seemed like a very real option.

"Take a deep breath," he said. "You're okay."

I drew air in through my nose and blew it out slowly. Once. Twice. Three times. My heart started to slow.

"Now, find the horizon."

I lifted my gaze from my dusty shoes to the sky in a quick arc. I'd done it too fast and now I was disoriented. My body swayed a little. I thought Lucas might grab on to me—his voice was closer than when he first spoke—but he didn't. After a moment, my body found an equilibrium.

"Better?" he asked.

"Yeah," I said, and surprisingly I meant it. I *did* feel better. The sun was shimmering on the water's surface. In front of me, the sky was a shade of azure that didn't seem to exist in Tennessee. The fresh air on my face filled me with energy. My heart was still beating faster than normal, but energy coursed through me. I wanted to keep going. I pushed my foot out a little, feeling for the edge of the step. I stepped down. To a witness, I probably would have looked ridiculous, feeling the stone steps with my toes, testing each one before I put my weight on it, but I didn't care. I took my time, one step at a time.

"Stop," Lucas said.

"What's wrong?" I asked, glancing back at him.

He was holding up my phone and smiling at the screen. "Nothing."

Twenty-One

ON THE BEACH AT Ladder Bay, Lucas showed me the pictures he'd taken of my climb while we lounged on a volcanic rock, baking ourselves in the late-morning sun and waiting for one of Lucas's friends, Ronaldo, to pick us up in his boat.

"I like this one," I said, studying an image of myself. In it, I had one arm up, bent over my head like a model. I'd just turned around when the wind had kicked up and blown my hair everywhere. I'd had to put my arm there to pin it away from my face. I was grinning back at Lucas, and before me the stairs snaked down to the sea. In the next photo, I stood on the treacherous stairs about halfway up with my arms out wide. After the first shot, Lucas had expertly scaled down the rocks next to the stairs and crouched down ahead of me so that in the shot, I looked like I was way higher than I was.

"These are great," I told him.

He nodded. I tried to discern what he was looking at on the vast sea in front of us but saw nothing.

"I actually look like I'm having a good time."

Lucas started to say something, but a ship's horn interrupted him. He hopped off the rock and jogged toward the water's edge. "Ronaldo!" he called out. "Good to see you."

A man with a broad smile and warm brown skin jumped over the edge of a small boat. He was tall with thin legs and long arms that he wrapped around Lucas with gusto. "Good to see you too, Tsai. You been gone too long this time."

Lucas nodded.

"You doin' okay? Laurentina and me heard about your dad. That's a shame. Everybody liked him."

"Thank you," Lucas said. "It was hard, but I hope he has made it to a good place now." Lucas waved me over. "Ronaldo, this is my . . . special guest, Marin."

"Nice to meet you, Marin," Ronaldo said, extending a hand.

I shook it and he smiled.

"You have a good handshake," he said. "I like that. People with weak handshakes are suspicious, if you ask me."

"Thank you," I said. "My mother always said a good handshake was the first step to making a new friend."

"Sounds like a smart lady."

Ronaldo grinned and elbowed Lucas. "We're friends now," he said. "You friends with her too?"

"Not yet," I said.

Ronaldo laughed. "What's funny?" Lucas asked.

"Nothing," Ronaldo said. He held out a hand and helped me into the boat. "It's just that Ken told me that you'd already seen each other naked so I figured you were at least friends. At least."

From my new spot on the narrow bench, I glared at Lucas, my mouth agape. He shrugged. "What? Ken has a big mouth."

"You're not exactly the pinnacle of discretion," I said. "Who told Ken? It sure as heck wasn't me."

"Somebody had to review the video footage, with your passport missing."

I twisted my torso away from him and turned my attention to the water around us. It was so clear I could make out the rocky bottom and some colorful fish swimming around the edge. I dipped my hand into the water.

"I wouldn't do that if I were you," Ronaldo said.

I pulled my hand back. "Why?"

Lucas didn't look at me. "Piranhas," he said, deadpan.

There was a puff of smoke and then the roar of the outboard motor drowned out Ronaldo's infectious rumble of laughter. "Piranhas," he howled. He steered the boat out of the shallow waters and skirted the edge of the island. The air felt cool on my cheeks, which I was sure had freckled and started to turn pink. Still, I couldn't help lifting my face to the sky again. I watched the island, green and black, surging from the sea, speed past us. In the distance, brown birds unlike anything I'd seen at home swooped and soared. One plunged into the ocean and came up with a fish wriggling in its break. Before long, buildings loomed in the distance. There was a long sort of concrete pier and a large boat parked there, its flags whipping in the wind.

"What's that?" I asked Ronaldo.

"Ferry terminal. One of a few places you can drop anchor and get onto the island without a climb like you two just did. I leave my boat around here sometimes, and my truck's just there." He gestured toward the road where an old blue pickup with a rusted hood was parked. "I'll take you to my place," he said. "Ken moved the Jeep over there for you."

Ronaldo maneuvered the boat next to the pier and he and Lucas helped me out. I watched as he dropped anchor and made a leap to a small ladder that was embedded into the side of the pier. "We live close," Ronaldo said. The truck was small, with only a driver's and a passenger's seat. I paused by the passenger-side door. How was that going to work? Lucas hopped into the back.

"You sit up front," he said.

Like all the other roads on Saba so far, the one that led away from the ferry terminal was steep, a ruthless climb that looked straight out of the Tour de France or something. At one point, Ronaldo's car made a chugging sound and I wasn't sure we were going to make it. "Don't worry," Ronaldo said. "Imelda's never let me down."

"Imelda?"

"Of course I had to give her a woman's name. She looks a little rough but she's tough and dependable. Plus, she's fun to ride." There was that amazing laugh again. My sunburned cheeks got a little hotter, but I found myself laughing along too. "You've got to meet my wife," Ronaldo said. "She'll like you."

"That would be great," I said. "I was supposed to come with my sister, but she was unexpectedly detained. Since then, my girls' trip has been me surrounded by men."

"I can't lie and say I would be complaining about the reverse situation," he said, and turned the wheel hard to the left. My shoulder slammed into the window, but before I had a chance to recover, Imelda came to an abrupt stop and I was flung forward almost into the dashboard.

"Still driving that truck like a maniac, I see," a woman called from the driveway. Her dark hair was piled high on her head and she was wearing a colorful skirt and a peasant blouse. "Lucas!" She flung her arms open and practically pulled him out of the truck. "So glad to see you. You holding up okay? We've been thinking about you nonstop since you went home to be with your dad. I heard you were back already, but I didn't believe it."

She caught sight of me over his shoulder and released him. "I'm Laurentina," she said. I held out my hand to shake hers, but she hugged me instead. "I've got tea. C'mon inside out of this heat." She called back, "You let this poor thing get burned, Lucas. It's fine. I've got something for that."

Their cottage was small, but light flooded every inch and made it feel much bigger than it had appeared from the outside. The wood floor was worn smooth and shiny. All the walls were painted white, but brightly colored artwork hung everywhere. In one corner there was a chair with a small table that was strewn with fabric. I started toward it, but Laurentina, who had been digging around in a cabinet, called me over. She handed me a small jar of something milky.

"Aloe, lavender, and coconut cream. Very soothing. Here . . ." She unscrewed the cap and dipped her fingers in, then gently applied some to the back of my hand. "Feels better, doesn't it?"

I nodded.

"Let me get you that tea," she said.

While she got glasses, I roamed around the room, taking in the beautiful artwork. "It feels like a gallery in here," I said. "Did you paint these?"

"Those are Ronaldo's, believe it or not. He's a man of many talents. Paint isn't my medium." She handed me a cool mason jar. "We have many artists on Saba. It's quite an inspiring place. Though I was born here, so I have no comparisons to make."

"This is the first time I've left where I was born too. I like Tennessee, but this is different. It's like a dream."

"Saba or Lucas Tsai?" she said, and burst out laughing.

"Definitely Saba." I hid my face behind the mason jar and took a slow sip of tea. It was delicious.

"Now don't be shy, Miss Tennessee, I already heard you two got naked together and played in the ocean."

What kind of hellscape gossip island was this? It seemed like everyone knew about the after-massage incident. "It was not like that. I just lost my grip on— Forget it," I said. "You said paint wasn't your medium. Are you an artist too?"

From another room, a baby cried. "Mm-hmm," Laurentina said. "I make lace."

My gaze drifted to the table piled high with intricate fabrics. The baby howled again. Laurentina stood up and put her empty mason jar in the sink. "Sounds like Jonathan is up from his nap. I ought to go get him."

Just then, Lucas poked his head in the door. "Marin, are you ready to head out? I've got something I have to handle at the resort."

"You should come for dinner. I want to talk some more with you," Laurentina said.

"I'd like that. Will you tell me more about the lace?" I asked.

"I can do better than that. I'll show you how I do it." She turned to Lucas. "Bring her back for dinner. Ronaldo's got a charter tomorrow. How about the day after? I'll send him out for some fish to fry up and we'll have a nice meal."

"That's Sabaoke," Lucas said.

"How could I forget? The next evening, then," she said.

"Sounds great," he said. "Okay with you?"

I hesitated for a moment, torn. "Yes, I'd love that," I said. "It was so nice to meet you."

Laurentina was still wearing a broad smile. She gave me a gracious nod, but the baby cried again and she disappeared through a doorway to go get him.

I followed Lucas outside. "You're sure you won't be too busy flagging down a passing cruise ship for your escape plan to have dinner?" he asked.

I tried to think of a witty comeback but came up with nothing. As much as I was desperate to get back to Tennessee, I also really wanted to go to that dinner.

"She makes lace," I said. "How amazing is that?"

"It's kind of a big deal on Saba. The island's famous for it." He opened the Jeep's door for me.

"I had no idea. Do you know if they use patterns, or is it spontaneous, like jazz?"

He glanced at me. "You're really interested in this," he said.

He was surprised. Even I was surprised at how intrigued I was. In fact, the moment that Laurentina had mentioned dinner, I was already picturing whether I should bring a notebook or use my phone to record our conversation. The lede was coming together in my mind. It was the strangest thing, the way that creative process started up again as if I'd been writing essays only yesterday. As if I hadn't stopped writing them the day my mother died, and spent the

last too many years writing things like *Food pets love, from the peo*
who love pets and *Make "looking your age" a compliment.*

"I guess I am. Laurentina seems like a very special person. I'm
not used to people being so open and welcoming . . . except for
Sadie," I admitted. "Have you known them long?"

"Everyone knows everyone on Saba. There's only maybe two
thousand people on the island and lots of those are medical stu-
dents, so the rest of us, we're a tight group. I've known Laurentina
and Ronaldo since I was a kid. And you're right, they're special."

I nodded. While Laurentina and I had talked inside, the guys
had taken the top off the Jeep. The wind whipped at my hair as Lucas took the winding trail everyone called The Road around the
perimeter of the island. I tried not to look out my window at the
cliff below. "Why do you call this The Road?" I asked, trying to
distract myself.

"We're a literal people. It is the road. The only real road."

"I'm not a fan of The Road. In fact, I'm sort of glad there's only
one. I don't think I could take more like this one." I grabbed the roll
bar over my head as we went around a particularly sharp curve.

"You should try our runway," he said. "It's the shortest runway
in the world."

"No thanks," I said.

"Okay, shortest runway's off the list. What adventure's next for
your photo project, then?"

I shrugged.

"Parasailing? Hanggliding?"

I looked at Lucas, who appeared to be having a little too much
fun teasing me with activities suited for adrenaline junkies or people with a death wish. "Honestly," I said, "I'm pretty sure my next
adventure involves a bed."

Lucas raised an eyebrow and instantly my cheeks flushed as I
contemplated flinging myself out of the moving vehicle.

_wo_

I WAS UP LATE staring at my pictures on Instagram, waiting for Sadie to call or text me to let me know that she'd made a deal with her government booty call to procure my passport. Everything was working out great. The pictures Lucas had taken were surprisingly good. I looked like a tourist who wasn't afraid of heights and things other people knew as fun. My face was a little red and freckly, but I looked happy. That should satisfy Sadie. That was what she wanted—for me to have fun in the sun, to do something out of my comfort zone. Well, I'd held up my end of the bargain. With any luck, I'd be holding my passport in my hot little hands in a day or two and I'd be able to go home a little tanner, and most important, be able to leave this strange place (as beautiful as it was) where I was constantly uncomfortable and everyone knew I'd lost my sheet in the ocean. I'd have dinner with Laurentina and maybe try some of that fresh fried fish and learn about lace. I couldn't explain why, but my soul was ravenous for the story of Laurentina and her lace. Who needed sleep when your soul was hungry?

I woke in the morning to the ding of a new text message on my phone. A message from Sadie that read: Nice pictures. BUT. You can do better than that, Sissy.

I glared at the message and then shuffled into the bathroom to splash some cold water on my face. Better than that? I'd almost fallen off a cliff face trying to get that picture. In fact, I remembered with discomfort, I'd grabbed Lucas's ass and nearly shoved him off the island at one point. Oh God. I took a calming breath. I headed to the front door and opened it. The sun was already golden and warm. Birds chirped in the trees beside the villa and there was a gentle breeze that smelled sweet, like some exotic island bloom. I left the door open.

The Ladder hadn't been extreme enough for Sadie, I figured. Of course not, the girl was used to climbing K2 for fun.

I typed back: Have you forgotten who you're dealing with?

She said: That's kind of my point. You need to break out of your boring life, Marin. I want more. More sun, more surf, more sexy. Capiche?

I brushed my teeth more aggressively than I should have. Mouth full of foam, I bit my toothbrush to hold it in place and typed out, Fine.

☹

"Ugh," I said aloud, and spit a mouthful of toothpaste foam into the sink.

"Yeah, our toothpaste isn't the best," a familiar voice said.

I swiveled around to find Ken standing in the main room behind me, dressed in board shorts and a thin hoodie. "The door was open," he said.

"I have to do more stuff today," I said.

"So you liked the Ladder?" he asked. "Lucas gave me the impression that it freaked you out. I tried to tell him you didn't seem like you scare easily. I think he was actually worried."

"Did I like it? Not exactly. It was horrifying." And invigorating, awe-inspiring. I could feel my heart beat in every cell of my body during that experience.

"That's going to peel," he said, cringing at the sight of my sunburned nose in the mirror.

"Believe it or not, it looked worse last night." I headed back to the bedroom and Ken followed. "Is Lucas busy today?" I asked.

"He sent me to fetch you," he said. So he was busy. That was fine. His pictures had been nice, but they hadn't convinced Sadie. I had a feeling Ken was the kind of guy who would go the extra mile.

"Here's the deal," I told him. "I need to take some pictures doing extreme stuff, things that would impress my adrenaline-junkie sister. Are you someone who can make that happen?"

He was pushing clothes around in my suitcase. "Seems doable," he said. He pulled out an iridescent silver thong bikini bottom. "Is this your only bathing suit?"

It was not, thank goodness. I found a slightly more modest hot-pink number with red hearts all over it, and while it was not my style, it seemed upon quick inspection like a good percentage of my ass and one hundred percent of my nipples would be provided coverage. I headed into the bathroom to change.

"What do I need a swimsuit for, anyway?" I asked, double-knotting the halter top behind my neck.

"You'll see," he said, and handed me a pair of flip-flops.

I followed Ken through the resort grounds, past the pool where several guests were already relaxing on lounge chairs. A few others were in the water, swimming laps or splashing in the waterfall. I stopped to picture myself with this group instead of having to face whatever frightening fate lay ahead.

"Come on, Marin," Ken called. "I was a little late picking you up and we still need to make a stop on the way."

The stop turned out to be a dive shop with a big red-and-white flag hanging from the front porch. Inside, there were masks and snorkels everywhere, large fins of different colors hanging on the wall, and racks of black wet suits. I ran my finger over the neoprene.

"Good call," I said to Ken. "This will definitely be more convincing."

Ken handed me a wet suit with teal panels on the legs and arms. "Try this one on," he told me.

It took a couple of minutes for me to wrestle into the suit. I examined myself in the full-length mirror. The good news was that the suit provided complete coverage. The bad news was that it was squeezing the life out of me and now I had to pee.

"What do you think?" I asked Ken.

"It works. I got the rest of your gear. You may want to take the top part off and let it hang so you don't overheat on your way to the dive site," he said.

"Wait, what?"

Ken waved to the man behind the counter and left without paying. He steered the car back to The Road and continued driving for a few minutes. His driving was horrifying. The previous day, I'd thought Lucas's driving had been reckless. I now realized that while Lucas had maneuvered the Jeep around The Road's twists and turns without much trouble, Ken seemed like a thirteen-year-old who had stolen his dad's car and taken it for a joyride. Was that the tires screeching? When he finally slammed into a concrete parking space marker, I was ready to fling myself out of the car and kiss the ground. We were back at the pier where we'd met Ronaldo the day before. I followed Ken toward the water, where several small motorboats were moored. I searched them for Lucas and found him stooped on the deck of one, sorting through a pile of tubes and tanks.

"*Lǎobǎn!*" Ken called. "Look what I found. Scuba Barbie! You know, except not blonde. Anyway, we're all set to go."

Go where? I wondered. But instead I said, "You're coming?"

Ken nodded.

"Don't you need one of these numbers?" I asked, lifting the wet suit fabric.

"Nah. I'm hard core, VIP. Jump down."

I looked down at the boat, bobbing on the waves, and shook my head. "I'm not sure this is a great idea," I said. "I've never done this."

"It's pretty easy," Ken said. "You just jump. Tsai will catch you."

"That's not what I meant." I crouched down. "I've never done scuba before. I don't know how to do it."

Lucas grabbed my waist and put me in the boat. I thought I would be more annoyed. Normally, I would have. But it was kind of nice not to have to figure out how to hit a moving target. The only trouble was that I was feeling less sure that I actually wanted to be in that boat. Lucas was wearing a similar wet suit. Like mine, the top half of his was folded down, revealing that fantastic carved-from-travertine torso. I crossed my arms across my chest.

"I'm a master diver," Lucas explained. "You don't have to worry. It's a shallow dive. Think of it as advanced snorkeling."

"I've never been snorkeling," I said. "No ocean in Tennessee."

Lucas looked thoughtful. He said, "Well, then—"

"This is going to blow your mind," Ken finished. "Let's go." He untied the line and threw it into the boat. Then he started the engine and pointed the bow away from the pier where it'd been tied off. "You might want to hang on to something," he said. I had a millisecond to grab some kind of metal handle before Ken opened the throttle and sent me slamming into the seat behind me.

"Where are we going?" I shouted to Lucas over the wind and the roar of the boat's engine.

"Torrens Point. It's calm there and bottoms out around fifteen meters max, so it's a good beginner dive. You'll still see a lot of fish and other sea life." He reached out. "Hand me your phone."

I pulled it out of my bag and gave it to him. "Why exactly do you want it?"

"Posterity," he said, and snapped a picture of me. "A speedboat counts as adventure, right? You said you'd never done anything like this before."

"Good point. And I'm wearing neoprene."

"Yes you are." There was something about the way he said it that made me feel like I wasn't wearing a wet suit at all. I shivered and pulled the top half of the wet suit in front of me. Lucas looked back out at the horizon. He said something to Ken. It was hard to hear over the other noise.

"How come Ken doesn't need a wet suit? Doesn't he get cold?"

Lucas laughed and shook his head. That laugh was so rare, I felt a little proud to have caused it even though I had no idea what was so amusing about my question.

"He's not coming."

The boat slowed and the engine's roar turned to a subtle purr. Ken tossed an anchor over the side that had a buoy with a flag on it that looked like the red-and-white one we'd seen by the dive shop. "That lets other boats know that there are people in the water," Lucas explained.

Ken walked over to us and handed me the other equipment we'd picked out at the shop. "Did I hear laughter back here? What was so funny?"

"Tā yǐwéi nǐ yào hé wǒmen yīqǐ qù qiánshuǐ."

"Zhēn de? Nǐ zhēn ài shuō xiaò!" Ken said.

"Sorry," Lucas said, seeing my confusion. "I just told him that you thought he was diving with us, which is funny because Ken is completely terrified of diving. The last time we tried to go, he cried and Ronaldo had to fish him out with a pole." My eyes widened. Lucas put up a hand. "Don't worry. Scuba isn't scary. He's claustrophobic."

"Like really claustrophobic," Ken said. "You're not claustrophobic, are you, VIP?"

I thought of the little house that I had lived in my whole life. The twenty-mile radius I hadn't left since Mom died. "Am I afraid of small spaces?" Now that was laughable. "No. That's the one thing I'm not afraid of."

"Good," Lucas said. "Let's get you suited up."

We both pulled our wet suits up and I wrestled myself back into mine. The zipper pull had a long piece of fabric attached to it that I guessed was put there to make zipping up a wet suit by yourself easier. And it would have been if I could get a hold of it, but despite bending myself into a human pretzel, I still hadn't managed to grab it. Something brushed my hair off my neck and over my shoulder. "I've got it," Lucas said. He slowly slid the zipper up my spine, careful not to pinch my skin or the hair at the nape of my neck. He was gentle. I spun around to thank him, but the boat pitched as I turned and I bumped into him. He looked down at me. I looked up at him. Was this a moment? Were we having a moment? No. Couldn't be. I didn't have moments with people—not since Ted. Moments led to messier things. But we were still staring at each other and his hand was on my arm.

"Classic," Ken said, shaking his head. "Tank check time."

Lucas showed me how to breathe through my regulator, how to clear my ears, and how to control my descent and ascent. It was intimidating, but he was so calm and confident that I didn't feel all that nervous. The day was warm, and ours was the only boat bobbing gently on what seemed to be calm seas. The edge of the island wasn't far off.

"You're sure this is safe," I said.

Lucas nodded. "I'll make sure you're safe," he said. There was something about the way he said it; I believed him. He checked my oxygen tank and his own. Then he stepped up to the edge of the boat. "Ken, take a picture of Marin before we go in."

Ken grabbed my phone. "Ready!" he said.

I took a tentative step toward Lucas. My fins made me feel like a clumsy penguin. "Put your regulator in your mouth," Lucas said. I did. "Mask on."

I nodded and pulled my mask over my eyes and nose. "One hand on your mask. And remember, we're going to take one big step off the boat."

I shook my head. My heart was racing. I wanted to tell him I'd changed my mind, but the regulator in my mouth stopped me. Lucas put his own regulator in his mouth and took my hand.

"Three, two, one, go!" Ken called from beside us. I saw a flash go off and then I was in the water, rising to the surface. My mask was still on and I could feel oxygen flowing with each breath I took. I opened my eyes. Lucas waved one arm over his head twice, signaling the all clear to Ken. He swam over to me and took out his regulator. "See? It's easy," he said. "You ready to go below? Let's try to control your buoyancy a bit first. Remember how I showed you on the boat? It's just like that here." I nodded, trying to ignore the sound of my heart pounding in my own ears. "We're not going very deep, but at the end of the dive, we'll stop about halfway up and stay for a few minutes. It's just safe practice to do a decompression stop. It lets all the nitrogen off-gas and it also helps make sure we have a controlled ascent." I nodded. "I'll be right with you the whole time," he said.

He wasn't kidding, because he took my hand again and we slowly let air out of our buoyancy compensators, which Lucas referred to as BCs, to make us sink. Little by little we descended, his hand gripping mine. The pressure in my ears grew. I watched him plug his nose to make his ears pop, something he'd called clearing his ears. I did the same. Immediately I felt relief. He flashed me an okay sign and I returned it with my free hand. He pointed down and I nodded. We let more air out of our BCs and went down. I looked around me past Lucas and the bubbles that spewed from his regulator every time he exhaled. It was darker down here than closer to the surface, but what the scenery lacked in light was made up for in color. A shimmering school of electric-blue fish swam by. *Blue tangs,* Lucas wrote on his dive board. He signaled for me to follow him and I did, waving my fins slowly. He took hold of my hand again, and I was glad. He was checking his dive computer, looking at the direction we were going, keeping track of all the technical details, and now and then he would point things out to me and identify them on his board. The parrotfish was amazing; its head and beak looked just like the birds that flew around the cloud forest near the resort. We swam through tunnels and one dark cave. I gripped Lucas's hand tightly. It was like being in another world completely. I could feel the history of the island bubbling up as liquid rock from the ocean. Around us, spires emerged from the ocean floor. We skirted along the bottom, finding sponges and more fish, a squid, patches of coral, even something Lucas wrote was a flamingo tongue snail. The bottom was littered with shells. Lucas produced a mesh bag, and we put some interesting ones into it. An unbroken conch that looked like a sunset inside. A closed shell that looked like a clam. Finally, Lucas checked his wrist. He signaled that it was time to go up. Gradually, we added air to our BCs and let the air help us move toward the surface. Before we went all the way up, Lucas tugged on my hand and signaled for us to stop. We bobbed below the waterline, breathing slowly, for five minutes. It felt like an eternity. Up there, it was just me and him. No fish. No squid. Just the two of us in the whole world, in that whole vast ocean. We looked at each other. He still hung on to my hand. Finally, he gave me the okay sign and the thumbs-up and we slowly swam to the surface.

When we finally broke through, I could hardly believe I was alive. A strange kind of energy was rushing through me. Must have been all the extra oxygen. I pulled off my mask and dipped my hair back in the water to smooth it out. Then I swam toward the boat's ladder, where Ken was standing with my phone.

"What'd you think?" he asked, extending a hand to help me back into the boat.

"That," I said, "blew my mind." I grinned.

We sat on the deck eating sandwiches and drinking cold ginger ales from bottles while Lucas and I told Ken what we'd seen.

"This is great. It's like going myself, except without the suffocation. Your descriptions are choice, Marin."

"Thanks."

"How'd the reef look?" Ken asked.

"Not great," Lucas said. "It's definitely not as healthy as last year this time."

Sadie'd done a story on the health of the ocean a few years ago. Between floating trash islands and dying coral, what I remembered was not optimistic. "Is there anything you can do?" I asked.

Lucas nodded. "Honestly, we don't have a big reef here like other places. And Saba is pretty pristine. But the same principles as other places apply. Reduce pollution. Responsible diving and fishing; definitely no touching. Even using the right sunscreen can help. But that bleaching? It's global warming, so really only lowering our carbon output will help."

"Like using solar power."

"That's the idea. Small changes are great. But big change is what we really need."

"Maybe if Tsai Group leads, other large companies will follow," I said.

"That's what Ba said."

"Sounds like a pretty good legacy to me," I said. "You know, saving the world and all that."

Lucas was quiet for a bit after that, staring out at the horizon, and I hoped I hadn't overstepped. Ken fell asleep on one of the benches. The heat was tiring, but I'd never felt more energized.

"Are you glad you went?" Lucas asked, opening another ginger ale.

"Yeah. I was nervous," I said. "But it helped that you held on to me." I realized how that sounded, and I looked away. "I wonder what kind of shells we got," I added, and grabbed the mesh bag we'd filled. We sorted through what we'd found on the deck.

"I did it for safety," Lucas said.

"Huh? What's this one?"

"Inexperienced divers can have uncontrolled ascents. That's dangerous. If I'm holding you, I can compensate to prevent that."

"Good to know." A girl might get the wrong idea. I ran a hand over the closed shell I'd found.

"That's a big oyster," Lucas said. "Should we see what's inside?" He pulled out his dive knife and ran it along the edge and then used the blade to pry the shell open. Something glistened in the sun. Lucas smiled.

"What is it?" I asked.

"I can't believe it," he said. I looked into the palm of his hand. A small sphere, shining white and perfect, rested on his skin. I'd found a pearl.

Twenty-Three

ACCORDING TO LUCAS, THE odds of finding a pearl in an oyster are something like twelve thousand to one. He told me this while we returned the oyster and some of the other shells we found that contained living creatures to the ocean. Ken was snoring in the same spot on the bench. Lucas and I put a towel over him and Lucas drove the boat back to shore.

We sprayed off the dive equipment and left the Jeep for Ken. It wasn't hard to get another ride around here, Lucas explained, as we stood on the side of The Road. After a few minutes, a small van stopped beside us.

"Hey, Lucas," the woman inside said. "You need a ride back to the resort?"

"Yeah, we were out at Torrens Point and Ken fell asleep on the boat. We thought we'd be nice and leave him the Jeep."

"You're too nice. I would have thrown him overboard." She waved her arm. "Climb on in. I'm Elisabet."

"I'm Marin," I said. "Thanks for the ride."

"Oh, we all give each other rides around here," she said. "It's no trouble."

Elisabet's van was full of produce. It turned out that she was the owner of a small restaurant on the Windwardside of the island. "You should come by sometime before you go," she suggested. "We have music most nights and the food's not too bad."

"She's too humble," Lucas said. "Elisabet is very talented."

They exchanged a smile, and I suddenly felt very left out. "Have you seen my phone?" I asked. "I need to post the pictures from today."

"Marin's working on an adventure photojournalism project right now," Lucas explained.

"Neat," Elisabet said. "Like *National Geographic*?"

I shook my head. Maybe Sadie, but not me. "It's a personal thing. Not work. I'm not a journalist. The rest of my family is, but not me. I'm the boring one."

Lucas frowned. "You're not boring. You found a pearl today."

"No way," Elisabet said. "I've lived on Saba my whole life and all I found was a Taiwanese expat with commitment issues."

I looked out the window. "It's no big deal," I said. "Tell me about your restaurant. What kind of food do you serve?"

"Fresh island fare. At least that's what the tourism magazines say. I just try to serve good food, satisfy the hunger and the heart." She pulled off the road and parked just outside the resort gate. "Here we are. I'd love to talk more, but I gotta run," she said. "My fish guy stops by around three."

Lucas climbed out and opened my door for me. Through the open window, Elisabet said, "Don't tell *Cheng-Han* I said hi."

"I'll make sure he knows he missed out."

"I bet. It was nice meeting you, Marin," she said.

"You too. Thanks for the ride."

We walked back to the main house in silence. "Are you tired?" Lucas asked.

I shrugged. "I'm fine."

"You're quiet." He grabbed my wrist and shifted me back toward him.

I stiffened. He was examining me, and I worried that if he looked hard enough he would read between the lines of my expression. "What are you doing?" I asked.

"Are you feeling all right?" he said. He looked down for a second and then at his watch. "That was a shallow dive, you shouldn't be having any problems. Are you sure you're feeling okay? Not dizzy or having any pain?"

"I'm fine. I just want to get back to my room so I can look at the pictures and maybe read a couple of chapters of my book."

He dropped my wrist.

"Thanks for taking me diving," I said. I started toward the path.

"Wait, what about the pearl?" he asked.

I closed my eyes for a second. "You should keep it," I said.

The walk to the villa was torturous. Lucas had told me the symptoms of decompression syndrome—pain in the joints and muscles, confusion, and a bunch of other unpleasant things—but I knew that wasn't my problem. My ego, on the other hand, was having a hard time. It didn't help matters that I followed a couple who I guessed, based on the number of times they stopped on the narrow path to grope each other, was either on their honeymoon or having some kind of tryst. Either way, they were having a better time than I was. *Idiot,* I thought, and pushed a giant elephant ear out of my face. Of course someone like Lucas Tsai had a beautiful girlfriend on the island. Someone worldly and talented, a chef. She probably surfed. She looked like someone who surfed. And then he seemed so concerned about me. How embarrassing. What had I even expected—that I'd hang out on the island and take some pictures for a few days and he'd fall for me just in time for me to head back to Tennessee and never see him again?

Back in my room, I sat down and thumbed through the day's pictures. Me and Lucas getting ready to step off the boat, his hand holding mine. Next. There we were bobbing beside each other in the water. Him helping me take off my mask. His hand pulling the zipper of my wet suit after we were out of the water. I stopped on the last one. He'd been pushing a strand of wet hair away from my face. God, what did Ken think he was—a paparazzo? I didn't look particularly adventurous in any of them except for the one of me and Lucas in midair, stepping from the boat into the ocean. I opened Instagram and hashtagged it #ProjectParadise. For added measure I put *Scuba!* as a caption. Then I called Sadie.

"Hey, Sis," she said, her voice thick, like pouring molasses.

"Were you sleeping?" I asked. "It's the middle of the day. I hope you weren't out all night partying with Felix."

"You know me."

"Any progress on the passport?" I asked. "I made another post."

"Let's see," she said. "Oh, you look hot in a wet suit. Neoprene, where have you been all my life? And is that the resort guy? Isn't he a tall ocean of water? Looks like fun. Question is, did you actually dive?"

"I saw a freaking parrotfish, okay?"

"You could've googled that."

"I have proof. I found a pearl."

"Interesting."

"Sadie," I said. "You know I love you. I know you mean well, but I'm tired. This isn't my thing. I tried."

"I know, Marin. Just one more post, okay? I'll call him tomorrow. That'll give you time to hit it with that resort owner."

"You're so gross."

"Ha, like the thought hadn't crossed your mind."

"Not all of us think with our lady parts, you know. Some of us rational people like to think with our heads."

"Now, where's the fun in that?"

After we got off the phone, I stripped out of my bathing suit. The salt was crusting on my skin and I needed a hot shower to wash the day away. When I emerged, the mirrors were fogged with condensation, but I felt better. I rummaged through the suitcase and found a sundress. It was the most normal item of clothing in the entire bag, even though it was about five inches shorter than I would have normally worn and the black fabric was covered with tiny pink hearts. I pulled my wet hair into a high ponytail and headed toward the main house carrying the wet suit. I wasn't going to need it anymore, and it seemed only right to return it. Ken had his feet on the front desk when I got there. His olive skin was a hideous shade of crimson. "You!" he said when he saw me. "You and Lucas are so cruel. You left me sleeping in the midday sun. I'm burned to a crisp."

I cringed. "That looks pretty bad. Sorry."

He waved me off.

"I have something for that," I said. "Laurentina gave it to me."

"You got Laurentina's sunburn cream?" he asked. "She must have liked you."

"You know it?"

"It's famous. She grows everything herself."

"I'll share," I said. "But I need a favor. Can you take me on one more excursion tomorrow? I just need a few more pictures."

"Sure. No worries. It's my day off and I know a place." He scribbled a note. "I meant to ask you, how'd you guys get back? Tell me Lucas didn't make our VIP guest hitch."

"Why do you keep calling me VIP?" I asked. "I was supposed to be on the economy package."

"Oh, ah, I call all our guests VIP. You know, because you're all important."

"Gotcha. To answer your question, yes, we got a ride with someone named Elisabet," I said. "Maybe you know her?" I hated myself for it, but I wanted to see what he knew. I braced for the confirmation of my suspicions.

"How'd she look? Depressed?"

"Not really," I said. I eyed him. "Why would she . . ."

He gave me a look.

Wait a second, I thought. "You and Elisabet?" I said. "Hang on. Are you *Cheng-Han*?"

"She used my Taiwanese name?" He closed his eyes. "She looked good, didn't she? Scale of one to ten."

Threatening. "Just pretty good."

"Wait, she mentioned my name? She was talking about me. What'd she say?"

"She told Lucas not to tell you hello."

"Oh, that's good." He stood up and paced. "Do you mind, VIP? I'll meet you tomorrow at the villa, but I've got to make a call."

The appetite that had disappeared earlier in the afternoon returned with gusto and I hummed the entire way back to the villa. I ate room service that night wearing the robe that came with the room. I wolfed down two orders of some kind of giant lobster fritter that was like the best hush puppy I'd ever had, and a giant slice of chocolate cake called Decadence with a capital D. Sadie would've been kicking herself if she knew I was eating this, I thought. More for me. I ate every last morsel and then fell asleep in my new favorite robe on top of the comforter.

Twenty-Four

SADIE

HAVE YOU EVER SEEN people surfing those giant waves? I got to photograph some professional surfers in Praia do Norte in Nazaré, Portugal, a few years back. It was the wildest thing I've ever seen, like tiny insignificant specks of shadow and light charging skyscrapers made of water. One moment they're invincible, and the next a wall of water is devouring them and spitting them out in a mountain of froth. But for those few moments when they're careening down the water on their board at about one thousand miles per hour like a superhero, it's gotta be worth it, right? That's what I tell myself. Sometimes you're a boss, flying, charging a wave, and other times nature is smashing you to bits. Either way, it's sort of awesome.

I've been thinking a lot about that lately. About the ocean and those waves and the people out there on their boards hanging on for dear life.

Up until this trip, Marin never even saw the ocean. It was another thing she'd missed out on. On this trip, I hope she drinks it in. (Not literally, though. During the shoot in Portugal, I got so thirsty I resorted to gulping some seawater. It made me so sick Felix called me "the chummer" for a solid year afterward.)

Twenty-Five

MARIN

SADIE WAS PLAYING A drum. Bang, bang, bang! I put my hands over my ears. "Knock it off, Sadie," I grumbled. "I'm trying to sleep!"

Sadie ignored my pleas. Now she was hitting the bass drum. Bop, bop.

"Fine," I yelled. "I'm up! Are you happy, Sis?"

"Not really," a man's voice replied. "You're not a morning person, are you?"

I clenched my eyes closed against the lamplight. Something heavy pulled at my hair and then let go. Damp hair fell into my face. I forced my eyes open a little. Sadie and her drum set were nowhere to be seen. It was all coming back to me. I was on Saba at a luxury resort. And standing before me was Lucas Tsai.

I snatched at the edges of the robe I was wearing and pulled it closed. "What are you doing in here?"

"Yeah, sorry about that. I was knocking for a while."

Ah, the drumming. "Wait, where's Ken?"

"Occupied."

I thought back to the previous day. He had seemed pretty eager to make that phone call. "Elisabet?" I asked.

Lucas nodded.

"So you just bust in here instead?"

"I had a key. But point taken. Normally, I wouldn't break into a guest's room."

"That's comforting."

"I told Ken I would take you on this outing and I'm kind of in a hurry," he finished. He eyed a piece of cloth he was holding and then tossed it to me.

I lifted up the article of clothing, tiny jean shorts I would not be caught dead in, and shook my head. "These aren't mine," I said. "Remember? Wrong luggage?"

"Well, you'll need to put something on," he said. "A robe won't work for where we're going."

I stumbled out of bed. "It's fine. You have better things to do, other VIPs to take care of." My stomach protested the notion of a whole day with only the remnants of the bowl of tropical fruit. "I think I'll order some room service and you can go do more important things."

Lucas flashed me a disapproving look. Then he held up a travel cooler bag and lifted the lid. I couldn't help myself. I peeked inside. It was brimming with what looked like food he'd raided from a greasy spoon diner and a French patisserie. My mouth watered reflexively. I swallowed and reached out for the bag. He pulled it away from me.

"You can have this when we get there."

My shoulders sagged. "You're going to hold me hostage with food? That's just cruel."

"I'm very good at making deals," he said. "Get dressed and meet me in the parking lot and I'll give you a mini-muffin you can eat in the car."

I really liked mini-muffins. I didn't eat them, but I fantasized about eating them. Sadie always said that when she was traveling, she played by different rules. Maybe Saba Marin could eat mini-muffins. Saba Marin had already eaten the lobster fritter and the

Decadence chocolate cake. I shook my head. There was no Saba Marin. I was about to mind-over-matter and say no way to that smug, overly attractive man when my stomach growled at me.

"Fine," I said. "Just wait on the porch."

"Okay," he said.

"Ah, leave the muffin though, or there's no deal."

I devoured the muffin in two bites, the two most delicious bites I'd had in a long time. I'd expected a basic lemon-poppy-seed muffin, but I'd been wrong. This thing was chock-full of mango chunks and black sesame. It was exotic and delicious and practically buzzed on my tongue. I stuffed myself into the cut-off jeans and a paper-thin T-shirt that read, *Let's stay in bed*. My bra was clearly visible through the fabric. I caught sight of myself in the mirror and had to close my eyes for a second. It wasn't good. I returned to the bride's bag and rooted around. There wasn't anything better in there. She mustn't have planned on wearing a lot of clothes, because the bag's contents were essentially fifty percent lacy underwear, forty percent bold excuses for bikinis, two microscopic dresses, two blinged-out tracksuits, and a bunch of other items almost identical to the ones I was already wearing, along with a pair of strappy sandals and slip-on sneakers that looked new. I tried the sneakers and was relieved to find that they actually accommodated my entire foot, unlike the shorts that my butt was currently testing the limits of. I found a ponytail holder and some lip gloss in my purse and put them to use. The whole look was borderline hideous, but I didn't have much of a choice.

Lucas raised an eyebrow when I stepped out of the villa and pressed a fist to his mouth, presumably to trap a laugh. He cleared his throat.

"Yeah. I'm going to need another muffin," I said, gesturing to my outfit.

He started walking away, long purposeful strides, and I watched him for a moment, struck by the way he resembled some kind of runway model strutting in a casual wear show.

"Try to keep up," he called. I made a face at him that he couldn't see, but then he tossed a muffin over his shoulder, high into the air, and I scrambled off the porch and onto the path, hands stretched out, like an inebriated bridesmaid going after a bouquet. Everybody always thought Sadie was the athlete of the family, with all her rock climbing and mountaineering, but I caught that muffin without breaking stride and caught up with Lucas without so much as a stumble.

"All right, will you please tell me where we're going at dark o'clock in the morning?" I asked.

He kept right on walking, chin lifted. "Not a chance."

"I've already climbed the Ladder and dove in the ocean. What else is there to do?"

Later I was thinking that Lucas Tsai was pretty smart for not telling me where we were going, because I would have hightailed it back to the villa, bolted the doors, stripped out of Mrs. Right's clothes, and dove back under those eight-thousand-thread-count sheets. I was also thinking that I should start working out more. It started off innocently enough: a small wooden sign obscured by some tropical foliage and a set of stairs. If I hadn't known better, I might have thought that this was a replay of the Ladder.

"Let's go," Lucas said, slinging the holy grail of breakfast bags over his shoulder. I fell in beside him and started climbing the stairs, which he was taking two at a time. I took the stairs instead of the elevator all the time at work, so this wasn't going to be a problem for me, I thought as I hustled to stay beside him. It was hard to see, since the sun wasn't up and we were ascending into what seemed like a rain forest. Everywhere I looked around us were the outlines and shadows of leaves and different plants that seemed to grow below a canopy that enveloped us from above. The stairs gave way to a thin path worn in the dirt by all the other people who had likely climbed here at a normal hour; aka everyone else, because we were the only people around. The air grew moister, beading on my skin like dew on a plant. A cacophony of different birds calling and chirping to signal the imminent arrival of dawn filled my ears. It even smelled different here.

"Watch your step," Lucas said to me.

I stumbled over a stone that was sticking up in the middle of the path, but somehow, even in the dim light, Lucas grabbed my arm and righted me before I fell. I recovered my footing. We walked for a long time, rising higher and higher. The sounds of the birds intensified, as did the incline. My exposed thighs were screaming at me. I'd burned off the energy from the second muffin about five hundred feet of elevation ago.

"Can we stop for a minute?" I asked.

Lucas didn't respond, but he slowed and then halted on the path. He handed me a water.

"How much farther is this little mystery trip?" I asked.

"Not too far," he said.

I took a swig of water. "That means it's still a long way, doesn't it?"

He shrugged. "If I told you, you might turn back."

"I have no idea why I agreed to follow you, anyway," I shot back. Actually, I had a couple of ideas. One was the bizarre magnetism he radiated. Then there were the cheekbones. I wasn't a totally oblivious robot woman.

"You're mad at me," he said.

"I'm not." I pictured him smiling at Elisabet so easily, when I practically had to use a crowbar to get his lips to move. I made my face neutral. "I'm not mad." And I wasn't, really. I was hungry. My stomach had made quick work of my previous night's feast and was now gnawing away at itself. I put a hand over my abdomen.

Lucas must've noticed the gesture, because wordlessly he lifted the cooler and dangled it in front of me. God, he was such a bastard. A magnetic bastard, but still a bastard. My stomach reacted with an audible growl. I reached out, but he yanked the bag away.

"Not yet," he said. He looked around for a moment, searching for something in the negligible light. Then he pulled out his phone and used it as a flashlight.

"What are you looking for?" I asked, as he stepped off the trail and disappeared into the jungle.

I scanned the darkness. Where was he? My heartbeat accelerated. "Lucas?" I called. "Where are you?"

In response, there was only a rustling of leaves. I didn't like this. "C'mon, this isn't funny. Come back."

To my right and up ahead a little, across from where Lucas had disappeared into the rain forest, something moved. I took a step back. How could I have been so stupid . . . I'd let my hunger pull me into this stupid mystery hike and now I was in a dark jungle in a foreign country, alone with God knows what kind of snakes or criminals lurking around me. A strange sound came from the direction of the movement, low and mournful, like someone in pain. What the hell was that? "Lucas!" I hissed. "Is that you?" My breaths were coming fast now as I tried to decide whether to run or rush into the brush to save him. In the darkness, something furry brushed against my leg.

"Ahhh!" I shrieked, and jumped back, clamping my eyes shut and letting my arms flail wildly to ward off the attack. Then I froze. Someone was laughing, hard.

"Stop screaming, Marin. You're scaring the shit out of that poor little goat."

I opened my eyes and took in the scene. There was Lucas, holding what looked like a small ball in his hand. He was doubled over with laughter. About a foot in front of me stood a goat, knobby knees and floppy ears and all. The fur that I'd felt on my leg.

"Where the hell did you go?" I said, my voice coming out more shrill than I'd intended.

"I got you this," he said, still trying to catch his breath from laughing so hard. He held the small, football-shaped object up in front of me. I stared at it. "It's a mango. For you to eat."

I snatched it out of his hands without comment.

Later, I stood on the summit, tired and still hungry, the back of my borrowed shirt drenched in sweat. We'd climbed for what felt like hours and now I saw why Lucas had forced me to keep going. We were at the highest point on the island, blanketed in mist. I swept my hand through it in the gray-blue light that came before dawn turned the world pink and orange. I couldn't see much else yet, except for the leafy plants and ferns that blanketed the ground around me. Lucas waved me over to a large, flat rock, where he started setting out the contents of the cooler on a tablecloth.

"Take a seat," he said. "It's time for breakfast."

I picked up a small quiche and took a bite. "Thank you for bringing all this food. What is this place?"

"Mount Scenery. The highest peak on Saba. You can see the whole island from here, if the fog burns off."

"I like the fog," I said, and tucked my knees under me. The breeze was strong and had a slight chill left in it. "It's like sitting in a cloud."

Lucas pulled out a thermos, filled the lid, and handed it to me. "Coffee," he said. "It's still hot. It should warm you up."

"Thanks."

"You were upset about something yesterday," he said. He took a sip of coffee. "You didn't take the pearl."

"It's not important. I'm over it anyway," I said. "You seem so concerned with the pearl. Why does it matter?"

He was quiet for a long time. "My mom used to dive for pearls. She didn't even use a tank, just a snorkel Ba made for her out of a piece of bamboo. I used to watch her when I was a kid."

I rested my head on my knees and waited for him to go on.

"She was magical. I couldn't believe how long she could go without air. Sometimes I would sit on the rocks by the water and try to hold my breath while she was under. I never could hold it long enough. One day when I was ten, I'd been practicing and I held my breath for a full four and a half minutes. I thought for sure I would beat her. I held it so long that I passed out. When I woke up, Ba was holding me."

I knew what was coming. I'd had that same feeling the day I was standing in the principal's office. The world had started to tilt, like it wasn't a real world but a dream one, one that wasn't really happening, and it wasn't until my cheek slammed into the floor that I knew what was real.

"She never came up."

"I'm so sorry."

"It was a long time ago. After that it was just me and Ba. We left Saba. The only thing I had to remember her and this place for a long time were the pearls that she'd found. They were like my treasures." He looked at me. "It took time, but eventually I was fine. I had a great life with Ba, traveling the world and living in Taiwan. We spent most of our time together—except for those last few months when he was in Guangdong—until he passed away."

Guangdong. Why did that sound so familiar? Lucas must have noticed my confused expression, because he said, "I'm not saying it wasn't hard. But it's okay."

"Is it, though?" I asked. "I never knew my dad . . . he's sort of a giant question mark in my life. But my mom . . . I still miss her every day. Worse, I'm still mad at her. Not as much or as often, but the feelings are there. Like if she'd just stayed with us and done something safer, maybe I wouldn't have had to raise Sadie on my own."

He nodded. "That's one way of looking at it. If my mom hadn't been a pearl diver, she would have been safe . . . maybe. Or maybe she would have been miserable and died in her sleep. Who knows?"

"I guess you're right. I never really thought of it that way."

"And we wouldn't be here right now." He turned to look at me and his eyes were so sad and dark, like the deepest part of the ocean, the volcanic rock down there. So much that I couldn't understand, because I didn't know him well enough yet, but I wanted to . . . and so much that I *did* understand, as much as I wished I didn't.

The summit transformed around us. The grass turned the color of wheat, the cliffs transformed to liquid gold. We watched in silence. The rock where we'd perched for our picnic was not far from the edge, and the view I got glancing down over the edge made my heart pound. I could see the rain forest that we'd traveled through, the trees and the plants changing from ferns to larger-leafed palms. Below were the terra-cotta rooftops and white buildings, tiny specks against a thriving expanse of green. Beyond that, the sea stretched on forever. The sun was giant as it emerged from the ocean and took its place in the sky.

"I can't believe I never climbed a mountain before. If I'd known it would be like this . . ."

"What?"

I shrugged. "Maybe it would have changed things."

"I thought we covered that."

"Yeah, I know," I said. "It's just that Sadie and my mom were big climbers. It was sort of their thing. And then later on, my ex, Ted, always wanted me to go to the mountains with him, and I never went. I always had some excuse, but if I'm being honest, I think I was just scared."

"Of heights?"

"Maybe, a little. I'm scared right now. But I have to admit, this is not what I imagined a climb would be like. I guess I can't help wondering if things would have worked out with him if I hadn't been so afraid."

"Was it serious with this guy?"

I wrinkled my nose. "Ring-fell-out-of-his-pocket serious."

Lucas raised his eyebrows. "That *is* serious. What happened? It had to be more than your not going hiking."

"I don't know. Maybe I wasn't brave enough."

"I think you're brave," Lucas said. "But what others think isn't so important. What do you think?"

I couldn't put my feelings into words. I'd just told him things I'd never shared with anyone, and I didn't regret it. I was glad we were both here on this mountaintop. I stared into the distance with my arms snug around my knees. "I wish Sadie could see this," I said finally.

Lucas didn't respond. He was very serious. All of the pretension and the teasing, that bravado he'd radiated earlier, was gone. He met my eyes and then he nodded. We didn't say anything more.

He picked up my phone and snapped a picture.

Twenty-Six

I MET TED AT the start of my senior year at the University of Tennessee. Sadie was a freshman studying photography at Memphis College of Art. She came home on weekends, and I spent lonely weeknights in the library. Without her, the house gave me that same sense of unbearable quiet and loneliness that it had after Mom died. I couldn't take it. The change was good for my GPA, but not necessarily for my heart. Our house ran out of air without Sadie, and I felt like I was holding my breath with worry every time she didn't call me to check in when she said she would.

I didn't notice Ted at first. He was just some guy in a broken-in baseball cap who sat at the other end of the long wooden table where I sat most nights. He'd arrive, make a little too much noise slinging down his backpack on the table, scooching up his chair, but that was the extent to which I paid attention to him. Eventually, he sat closer and closer to me, until one day I looked up and there he was, dropping that backpack on the table directly across from me and sitting down.

"Hello, fellow library addict," he said, stretching out his hand. "I'm Ted."

I looked up from my notes. "Marin," I said, then went back to my notes.

"Cool name. You sail?"

I shook my head at him, and he held up a binder where a perfect hand-drawn rendition of Sailor Moon was surrounded by stickers—

Mountain Hardware, Save Tibet, Dang Sunglasses, Outward Bound, and *National Outdoor Leadership School.* "You even look a little like her," he said. He smiled then, the kind of bright, sunny, impish smile that I was desperately craving—a smile like Sadie's. I was hooked.

We sat like that across from each other at the library, and then the coffee shop, and then my kitchen table. That was how we fell in love. At least that was what I told myself. That it happened incrementally, carefully, responsibly over time, and not while he was pointing at his drawing of Sailor Moon, holding that dangerous-looking binder and smiling at me. I couldn't resist that smile. Ted knew that, that's why he wore it when he told me about the trip.

"It's one year in Nepal. God, can you believe it, Marin? It's the chance of a lifetime. A Fulbright! I never thought in a million years that I would win a Fulbright."

"It's amazing." I hugged him. "I'm so proud of you."

His eyes were bright as he started talking about the research that he was going to do, all the preparations and gear he needed to buy. Where he wanted to go climbing when he wasn't working. With every new detail, my stomach clenched a little tighter. I pushed the take-out box of pad thai away from me. I'd lost my appetite. In fact, I felt like I might vomit onto the coffee table.

"A year is a long time to be apart," I told him, "but it's doable."

"Apart?" He shook his head. "No, Marin. That's not what I meant. I want you to come with me. Imagine how great this would be for you. You could explore and get all sorts of inspiration and time for your writing. We could keep each other warm in a little house, just the two of us. Imagine the possibilities, being in another culture like that. Temples to visit, mountains to climb . . ."

I could picture it. Prayer flags fluttering in the wind. Ancient structures endowed with deep sacred meaning. Giant ice-covered peaks disappearing into the clouds. I could picture it because Mom had been there. She'd reported on a doomed Annapurna expedition a couple of years before she'd died in the Sudan. There'd been a long article in *Outdoors Magazine* with lots of glossy photographs, including one of Mom with the start of frostbite on her perfect freckled nose. Ted reached for my hand. "Come with me, Marin."

I pulled away. My heart was pounding and I didn't understand why. "A year? Nepal?" I shook my head. "I can't. It's too far and too long. Sadie needs me."

"No, she doesn't."

"How do you know?" I snapped.

"Because I already talked to her about this. She's all for it."

"You talked to her?"

"Yeah." His cheeks seemed to color a little. I guessed he was embarrassed that he'd admitted going behind my back to my sister to try to convince me to join in on his crazy scheme.

"She's hardly a reliable source. Sadie's always all for everything. Free-climbing in the Cumberland Plateau? Sure, why not? Hitchhiking to Raleigh-Durham to photograph some concert? Check. Breaking and entering some abandoned amusement park for a class project? No problem." I was on a roll now. "Sadie is just like Mom was. She doesn't think. She gets caught up in the excitement, in adventure, and her art, and next thing you know, she'll jump off a cliff if she thinks she'll get a good photo or a good rush. She needs me to keep her tethered to reality."

"I'm not asking for you to climb Everest, Marin. I just want us to be together. It'll be an adventure."

"It's not safe there."

"Is it so safe here? Someone was shot in downtown last week."

"It isn't the same."

"You always do this. Every time I want to have an adventure with you, you find some excuse, some reason not to go. Most of the time, it's Sadie."

"That's not true." But maybe it was.

"I've been presented with the opportunity of a lifetime, and I wanted to share it with you. Just this one time, I wanted you to be my partner and support my dreams."

"This isn't me, though, Ted. I'm not into adventure. It's not all fun and games. You knew that about me when we started dating."

"And you know me," he said. "I love the outdoors. I love new people and places and the feeling I get when I've seen something amazing from the top of a mountain."

"You sound like Sadie."

"Is that so bad? Did you ever think what it's like for her . . . that you use her as a shield?" The words rushed out of his mouth. He ran his hands back through his hair. Then out of nowhere, he grabbed my hands between his. "Please, Marin. Please come with me."

I shook my head slowly. "If you want to go to Nepal, I'm not going to stop you. But I can't go with you." I slid my hands out of his grip. "I'm sorry."

He stood up, knocking over his carton of noodles. They spilled all over the coffee table. He was agitated, pacing back and forth. I hadn't realized he'd be so upset. Ted was always so even tempered. We never fought.

I had to smooth things over. "Look, it'll be fine. We'll Skype. They have internet there somewhere, right? A year's a long time, but we could do it. I'll work here and you'll do your research, and then you'll come back to me and we'll pick up where we've left off." I said these things, but I couldn't help worrying that there'd be an avalanche, or Ted would end up in the bottom of some crevasse somewhere and never come back. He'd wander into the wrong area and end up on the receiving end of some sort of mortar shell.

"You don't really believe that," he said.

"Yes, I do."

"The look on your face says you don't."

"I don't understand why we're fighting. I just said you should go. I'm not holding you back."

"Jesus, Marin. It's not about holding me back. It's about us being partners." He grabbed his jacket off the arm of the sofa. Something flew out of it and landed on the floor. He scrambled for it and I turned to see what he'd dropped. It was a box. Small and square and velvet. The kind of box that basically screams *engagement ring*. He snatched it up without a word.

"I've gotta go."

I stood up. "You're leaving? Are you going to call me?"

He looked up. I thought he'd been mad, but now I saw my mistake. His eyes were red and shining. He opened his mouth. "Marin . . ." I waited for him to say something else. There were so many things he could have said that might have made me cave. I loved him that much. But he didn't say anything. He turned and walked out the door. He never called.

Later I learned from Sadie that the reason they'd "talked" was because he was planning on proposing as soon as I said yes to Nepal. He'd actually asked her permission, which was so adorable and backward that it made my heart throb with longing.

"You really jacked it up this time, Marin. Honestly, it's kind of refreshing. I'm usually the one making a mess out of things, but wow, you managed to make a complete disaster out of this situation."

"Hilarious, Sadie. I love that you can get a good laugh out of my pain."

"Somebody has to."

"Whatever. I don't think I messed it up, though."

"Seriously? How do you figure that?"

"Ted didn't get exactly what he wanted, so he left. I mean, imagine what would have happened if I married him. He's obviously unreliable. He just walked away from me."

Sadie looked thoughtful for a moment. "Maybe. Or maybe he's heartbroken."

I shrugged. "I guess. But I think I dodged a bullet."

"Keep telling yourself that, baby cakes. Hey, you know what this warrants?" Sadie said. "A giant Sadie special mega crunch ice cream sundae." She headed toward the kitchen. I started up the stairs.

"You want hot fudge?" she called. "You should call him, Marin. It's not too late."

I didn't answer. I closed my bedroom door and folded into myself the way I always did when life got to be too much for me. Only then did I let myself cry.

Since getting me to go rock climbing was totally out of the question, Sadie's backup solution to my heartbreak was to drag me along clubbing with her friends.

"You love dancing," she said, thrusting open my closet doors to rummage for a suitable outfit.

"In the living room, yeah. That's different. I don't want to go out."

"You've been moping for weeks about Teddy. A night out is exactly what you need."

If I was being honest with myself, Sadie was right, at least about the moping part. I had been shuffling around in my favorite sweatpants and one of Ted's old T-shirts more than was acceptable by normal standards. I'd also taken to eating just two food groups: gelato in a cup and instant noodles in a cup. "I can't keep eating like this," Sadie complained. "My stomach is killing me. I need you to be you again. I need regular food and conversation. So you need to dance."

"Nope." I shook my head. "I am not going clubbing with you."

"It's fun. There's good music and guys and so much dancing." She jumped up in the air and turned around and gave an over-the-top booty shake. "See! You know you can't resist my magic lady hips."

Sadie was relentless. She danced around the room, flinging my button-down shirts and slacks, my turtleneck sweaters and jeans over her shoulder while she went. I could only imagine how big the mess would get before she finally gave up.

"Oh, all right," I relented. "I'll go if it will make you stop trashing my room. But just to be clear, I have not been moping about Ted. We were too different. I stand by that. Things worked out for the best. The right decision is not always the easy decision."

"Okay, but the smart decision still sucks." Sadie dropped down on the foot of my bed. "You must miss him. He was here all the time and now he's on the other side of the world." Sadie looked wistful. After all these years with her, I could practically read her mind. It wished it was on the other side of the world too. I didn't think Sadie was as sad about Ted as she was that she wasn't having her own adventure. All of that insider knowledge may not have been entirely a result of our sisterly telepathic connection; my sister spent more time than anyone in the history of the universe looking at *National Geographic*. In fact, for the last four years, it was the only thing she'd asked for on her Christmas list.

I shrugged and sputtered out a whole bunch of bullshit I hoped she'd buy. "Sure. I miss Ted, I do. But it wouldn't have worked. We wouldn't have worked. Can you imagine me in Nepal?" In truth, I picked up the phone several times a day to call him but always hung up. Sadie was nodding but I ignored her. I was on a roll. "I'm too much of a homebody. I need someone more . . . secure. And besides, I don't actually need someone. I have you."

"Well, I am pretty awesome," Sadie said, and popped up to attack my dresser. "You must have something sexy somewhere in here."

"I'm not going for sexy. I'm going for mostly unwilling participant in this club outing."

She held up my favorite blouse with tiny dots and a sort of sash that tied at the neckline. "By the looks of this, you're going for repressed school principal."

"Hey, don't throw that one on the floor. I was planning on wearing it to my interview tomorrow."

She hung it reluctantly on the pull of my top drawer. "I'll just lend you something of mine," she said.

That was how I ended up inside of Code Blue, the loudest hip-hop club in all of Tennessee, in a pleather tube top and a pair of jeans that I kept yanking up so that my private areas wouldn't be on display, staring down at something called a Jägerbomb. I had to admit, the music was pretty good. The drink, not so much. After gagging down a few sips, much to Sadie's chagrin ("You're supposed to chug it, Marin!"), I gave up and sat at one of the high-top tables to the side of the room. Sadie was out on the dance floor grinding against a man I knew only as Hot Guy—as in Sadie said, "I'm going to go talk to that hot guy over there for a sec." That had been twenty minutes ago and she was still adhered to him, her blonde curls springing to the bass beat.

I kept count of the drinks she consumed while she and Hot Guy talked, then danced, then made out in the corner. It seemed like a lot. Despite her giant personality and seemingly boundless energy, my sister was a petite person. Built like one of those gymnasts who never quite seems to hit puberty.

"You've been nursing that drink for a while," a man's voice said. "Can I get you something different?"

I looked up at the guy who was speaking, clean-cut, tall, dark, and handsome, with a nice smile and a white button-down shirt on, untucked. He was very . . . not Ted. "I'm okay. Thanks." I'd lost sight of Sadie.

"You here with somebody?" he asked.

"My sister," I said. "But I can't seem to find her. I should probably go look for her."

"We could wait together," he suggested.

"I have a boyfriend. We're going to Nepal together."

I left him sitting at the table with my Jägerbomb. He was probably nice and maybe even the kind of guy who liked to stay in town, worked a steady job, and watched college basketball with friends for fun, but it didn't matter. I'd lost focus and I'd lost Sadie, who was probably off somewhere being incredibly irresponsible with Hot

Guy, who was likely not the kind of guy with a steady job, a college basketball habit, and a good, solid background.

I spotted Sadie's friend Kate at the bar. "Hey, have you seen Sadie?"

She shook her head and took a sip of a martini that was a shade of blue that probably belonged in a jet engine. "You've got to try this, Marin. It's so good." She held it out and slopped a little of the drink onto my top. It slid down the pleather and soaked the top of my jeans. I cringed. "Thanks, Kate," I told her. "I need to find Sadie, though."

Kate looked confused. "Why? She seemed like she and that hottie were having a great time. Sadie has all the luck. She always hooks up with the cutest guys."

I wanted to tell Kate that her drunk pouty face probably wasn't helping her attempts to catch the attention of the cute guys. I also wanted to ask her just what the hell she meant by "Sadie always hooks up with the cutest guys." Always hooks up? But all that would have to wait. The last time I'd seen my sister she'd been walking a little unsteadily toward the front of the club with that guy next to her. Sadie was already unpredictable; her drunken demeanor was a different proposition. And honestly, I wasn't in the right mindset to deal with another one of her crises. I headed toward the door.

The shortest path to the exit was through the dance floor, so I had to weave through the undulating crowd. I tried walking fast, but people kept bumping into me. It was as if they knew I wasn't dancing and were trying to get me off the dance floor. So I threw my hands up over my head, moved my hips, and let the beat move me all the way to the other side. A couple of people tried to dance up to me, but I kept going until my feet landed on carpet.

"Have you seen a blonde girl come through here?" I asked the bouncer. "Kinda small, super curly hair. Similar outfit?"

They guy eyed me for a moment. I watched him take it all in— the ridiculous tube top, the wet low-rise jeans (oh my God)—before he spoke. "Yeah, she left with some guy a couple minutes ago. I

offered to call 'em a cab, but they . . . how should I put it . . . de-
clined. You could probably still catch 'em, they were not particularly
coordinated."

"Thanks!" I said. I paused for a moment to yank off the ridiculous stilettos Sadie had insisted I wear.

"Hard-core, going barefoot. I like that," the bouncer said. "Go
get your girl."

I held my shoes up in a gesture of solidarity and took off running
down the street. After a block, I saw them. The guy had my sister
pressed up against a lamppost, and dammit if he wasn't trying to
pull her tube top down in the middle of downtown. As I neared, I
could see that Sadie was pushing at his hands, trying to get him to
stop.

"Pete, knock it off," she slurred.

"Hey!" I shouted. "Get your hands off my sister."

Pete turned his attention to me. "Mind your own business," he
snapped.

Sadie took the opportunity while he was distracted to bring her
heel down onto the top of his foot. He yowled with pain. Sadie
stepped forward and kneed him in the groin. She staggered a little
bit then, but I was there to put my arms around her and keep her
steady. She pointed a finger at him. "You. You need to learn about
consent, asshole."

We started to walk back toward my car. "Sadie—"

"What? He does need to learn about consent."

"I think you taught him pretty good."

"His nuts will remember even if his head doesn't," she said.

"Oh yeah?"

She stopped and looked at me. Her face was relaxed and unco-
ordinated, a look that unsettled me. She nodded emphatically.
"He'll be icing them for days." She laughed hard, and then she
threw up her instant noodles and, from the looks of it, several of
those colorful mixed drinks all over the sidewalk.

When we got home, I washed her face and helped her into her pajamas. I tucked her into my bed, and I climbed in next to her. We hadn't slept in the same bed since the week after Mom died. "You take too many chances," I whispered to her. "You scared me tonight. You were so reckless."

"I'm always reckless," she said. "That's what makes me fun."

I stayed awake for a long time, thinking about what could have happened if I hadn't been there. I twisted a lock of her hair around my finger and sang her to sleep like she was a little kid. Ted had said that I used Sadie as a shield. But I'd been right. There was no way I could go to the other side of the world. She wasn't careful; she was fun. She was also my whole world. And the thought of losing her was so much more than I could bear. I tried to shake the images of all the horrible outcomes from my mind, but once I'd let them in, I couldn't get rid of them. Before I knew it, I'd soaked the pillowcase beneath us with my tears.

Twenty-Seven

SADIE

I ONCE WATCHED A talk show where Will Smith, the actor, was sharing how he'd just gotten back from skydiving and he told the host, "Everything great is on the other side of fear." Now, I don't care what you think of the Fresh Prince or his qualifications for being an inspirational speaker—that shit is true. I would know. Even if skydiving isn't my particular brand of anxiety-producing awesomeness, Will Smith and I definitely drank from the same Kool-Aid fountain. I love a heart-in-your-stomach adventure. Like when I climbed Kangchenjunga in Nepal with a group of climbers from Austria. It's not famous because it's the third-tallest peak in the world, but because it is notoriously difficult. Locals say a man-devouring demon named *Dzö-nga* lives there, and I believe it. The face is so steep, snow simply slides off. You can't really use fixed ropes. It's just you versus the mountain and the weather. Versus yourself. Buddhists believe this mountain is a god, and while I've never subscribed to any particular religious system, the amazing feeling I got when our expedition stopped ten meters from the true summit, out of respect, made me think that maybe I was close to God then. It's something you think about only sometimes, when you are a climber, how close you are to dying up in that thin air, high above the earth with nothing except sheer will keeping your feet on the ground. I should've maybe seized that moment, asked for something, but as my sister also says, hindsight's always twenty-twenty. No matter how much I could use God now, I can't get back on that mountain. I'm not strong enough.

I could go on and on about all the things I've done that fulfilled my vow and my appetite for adventure, or the things that scared me and how they all turned out to be, as Will Smith said, great. I've lived lifetimes in twenty-six years. This time, though—well, it's different. The stakes have never been so high. And I've never had this kind of deadline before—can't be helped, I guess. So I do what I've always done. I carry the fear with me, hold it close, and keep putting one foot in front of the other. We all do that, in our own way. Marin missed that sunrise with me and Mom at the Tennessee Wall that last morning. She didn't go to Nepal and love Ted beneath fluttering prayer flags in the thin air up there. She needs to see the sun turn a mountain gold. She needs to feel the sensation of having conquered something hard, and that means she'll have to keep putting one foot in front of the other, even when she's tired, even when she's scared.

What a view.

Twenty-Eight

MARIN

THERE WAS A DISTINCT vibe of hangriness in the Jeep by the time we reached the bottom of the mountain and started back to the resort. As much as I'd enjoyed the view from the top of Mount Scenery and the fabulous dawn picnic, my stomach dissented, a little more loudly than I would have liked. Instead of driving faster on the way back, Lucas decided to take us on some sort of scenic detour. He pulled off the street and headed down a small dirt road—and calling it a road was a major stretch—toward what looked like a grove of trees. He stopped the Jeep in front of a small shack that was painted bright pink and flanked by lush banana plants. I was about to protest, when I noticed the woman on the porch wearing an apron. She was waving a wooden spoon at us.

"Lucas Tsai," she said. "I heard you were back, but I had to see with my own eyes."

"Hi, Mama B," he said, and gave a tiny bow of his head.

"You come to eat?" she asked, ducking into the dim shack. "Who's your friend?"

While they talked, I surveyed the space. It wasn't like any of the places back home, that was for sure. It had a dirt floor. In the back, there was some kind of propane tank–powered grill. I couldn't find a refrigerator, but there were a lot of buckets. It was a bout of travelers' diarrhea waiting to happen.

"I hope you're hungry, girl," the woman said. "I got johnnycakes and ribs today. I just need to grab 'em off the smoker out back."

My mouth watered.

Parasites, I countered.

My stomach growled.

Mama B flung open the smoker and the scent of the ribs—all spicy and smoky—tantalized its way straight into my nostrils.

My brain conceded and practically waved a napkin as a white flag.

Mama B was not stingy with her portions or her seasoning. The meal was a masterpiece. It was familiar (I'd had my fair share of amazing barbecue) but also tasted somehow completely unique. At first, we ate in silence. I sucked the tender meat from the bone and ate johnnycakes with my hands without paying much attention to Lucas. He was engrossed with his own refueling.

When we finished, Mama B brought out a strange-looking brown object covered with spikes.

"What's this?"

"Soursop," Lucas said. I waited for more of an explanation, but he didn't elaborate and instead turned his attention to peeling away the woody covering, revealing soft white flesh.

"What's soursop?" I pressed.

He tore off a chunk and held it out for me. I hesitated. Lucas popped the piece into his mouth. "Mama B, good soursop," he declared. She toweled off her hands on her apron and grabbed a piece for herself.

"You don't want to try it?" she asked me.

"What's it taste like?" I asked.

"Like soursop," she said with a chuckle.

The strange white stuff was disappearing at a rapid rate. Mama B and Lucas tore piece after piece off and ate them. They seemed to love soursop, whatever it was.

"I need to make a call," Lucas said. He stepped out of the shack and into the sunlight. I moved my hand toward the soursop. I didn't like eating strange foods. That was Sadie's deal, not mine. She was always coming home with stories about the bizarre things she and her production assistant, Felix, had eaten on their trips: chocolate-covered crickets, a spider burger, worms. I gagged a little recounting some of the things she admitted to not just trying but enjoying. But then I grasped a small sliver and tossed it into my mouth before I could think again. The flavor morphed in my mouth, starting out earthy and then blooming into something that wasn't quite strawberry or pineapple or citrus, but had the smoothness of a banana. It was the strangest thing I'd ever tasted. But it wasn't a spider burger, it was freaking transcendent. I grabbed another chunk.

Lucas settled back down in his seat at the table.

"I get it now," I said, and swallowed. "Why you didn't tell me what it was like."

"Mmm," he said.

"It's like every fruit and none of them at the same time."

"Do you like it?"

"Yes. It's amazing."

"I thought you didn't like trying new things."

"I don't."

"And yet . . ."

And yet. I picked up my phone in one hand and a piece of soursop in the other and opened my mouth as wide as it would go.

"That's a keeper," Mama B said.

Lucas set the plates he was helping her clear on the counter. "Yeah," he said. "It is."

"Fruit's good too," she said. Her hearty laugh filled the room, and I couldn't keep from smiling.

Twenty-Nine

LUCAS HAD TAKEN SADIE'S adventure mandate seriously, planning not one but two excursions for us that day. After lunch, he dropped me off at my villa with a promise that this evening's outing would be less death-defying than bungee jumping or skydiving but still adventurous enough to qualify as hard-core.

"What is it, then?" I asked.

He shook his head. "You'll just have to wait and see."

"You won't even give me a clue? How am I supposed to know what to wear?"

"Just dress like you're having a night out. I'm going to shower and do some work. I'll pick you up around seven. That's all I'm telling about it."

Whatever *it* was.

It was, in fact, Sabaoke, which Lucas explained to me later as I tried not to lose my lunch out the window of the Jeep during yet another episode of *Marin faces her fear of heights and speed and vehicles she isn't driving*. At least Ken wasn't behind the wheel.

"It's just what it sounds," he said. "Saba and karaoke together . . . Sabaoke."

"Seriously?" I grabbed the roll bar as we flew over a rut and slammed back down.

"Yeah. And it *is* serious. There's a tournament, and every year in November someone gets selected as the winner of Saba Idol. You can google it."

"Sounds like it will be fun to watch, then."

"Oh no, you're not going to watch. No, just think what an amazing picture that would make for your sister. You onstage, dramatic lighting, that dress . . ." His brows lifted. My hands went to the hem of the slinky black tank dress I was wearing. I'd been so relieved that I didn't need some kind of flight suit or harness when he'd said I should just dress for a night out that I hadn't cared that much about the dress's length, or lack thereof . . . until I sat down and realized it barely covered the underwear I was wearing, which was emblazoned across the back with lips made out of rows of red sequins. Lucas, in his usual fashion, was dressed in a pair of chinos and an Oxford shirt that somehow managed to look simultaneously perfect and as if he'd just thrown it on, like some kind of Ralph Lauren cologne ad.

"I hate to disappoint, but I don't sing," I said.

Lucas downshifted as the Jeep basically slid around a tight curve. "That's not entirely true, Marin. I've heard you."

"I'm calling bullshit."

"You're quite the vocalist when you've had a couple of drinks and have almost passed out."

Oh no. That smooth liquor from Taiwan with the red cap suddenly came to mind. My cheeks burned.

"Okay, I'll rephrase. I do not karaoke." I attempted to wrangle my hair, which was blowing everywhere. "Even if that were true, it doesn't equate with making a fool out of myself in front of a live audience, Lucas."

The start of a grin at the corner of his mouth told me that I was already losing this argument before it'd even begun. I was fairly certain Lucas got a kick out of my awkward protests. He whipped the Jeep into a parking lot in front of a white building with a red roof and shutters that looked a lot like Paradise Resort.

"Welcome to Scout's Place," Lucas said, opening the door for me. "Otherwise known as the best bar at the other resort on Saba."

Scout's Place wasn't a huge space, but it had a vibe that was both cozy and modern. There was a black bar that curved around and ran almost the length of the room. The rest of the fixtures were black except for the red lanterns that hung from the ceiling.

We got a table near the entrance and Lucas went to the bar to order us some beer and appetizers. While he chatted with the bartender, I eyed the room. It wasn't crowded, and the few people present were mostly chatting, sipping drinks, or eating. No one was singing. I pulled in a deep breath of relief. Maybe I'd finally caught a break and Sabaoke was canceled that night.

"Here you go," Lucas said, setting a beer in front of me. "One liquid courage for the lady, since it seemed to work so well last time."

"Let's not speak of that night," I said.

"Whatever you want. I wasn't sure if you were a 'get it over with' or 'put it off as long as possible,' so I signed you up for the third spot of the night."

"But no one's singing," I said. I took a tentative sip.

"Have patience, Marin. Sabaoke starts at eight p.m., and right now"—he glanced at his watch—"it's only seven nineteen. You'll have plenty of time to think about your song selection."

"It's not canceled, then?"

"Canceled?" Lucas laughed. "Not likely. We only cancel for acts of God . . . hurricanes, births, that sort of thing. Otherwise, Sabaoke happens. Plus, my friend Glen told me he heard the senator of Saba's singing tonight, so it's definitely happening." He leaned back in his chair, looking totally relaxed. He was always so at ease everywhere—how did he do that?

A crowd of people came in and a few of them waved. Lucas lifted his chin in greeting, smiling warmly.

"Why am I getting the impression you come to this a lot?"

"Okay, you got me. I try not to miss it when I'm here. Usually Ken comes with me, but I guess he's still bitter that he only got third runner-up last year. He sang a solid rendition of 'Livin' on a Prayer,' but if I'm being honest, it was a little pitchy."

"Pitchy?"

I swiveled around to find Ken standing behind me, hands on his hips. "Who's pitchy? Not all of us can be Jay Chou, bro."

I looked at Lucas quizzically.

Ken looked offended. "You don't know Jay Chou, Marin?" He dropped into the seat next to Lucas. "C'mon, international superstar? What about HuaHua?"

"Sorry." I shrugged. "No clue. Haven't you heard? I don't get out much."

Ken elbowed Lucas. "You were right, she *is* funny. Well, VIP, you're in for a real treat, then. Because my boy here is awe—" Lucas flung his arm around Ken and clamped his hand over Ken's mouth.

A server arrived with some kind of large fishbowl drink with a curling straw and flaming ring of pineapple. Ken wrestled away from Lucas and took a long pull from the straw. "Oh, I see," he said to Lucas. "It's a surprise. Or is that part of your plan . . . *nǐ xǐ huān tā, duì bú duì?*"

I frowned. Part of his plan? What was that all about?

Lucas shot Ken a look. He didn't look stern exactly, just serious. And kind of hot. I took a large gulp of my beer.

"Well, I've gotta make the rounds," Ken said. "My people are waiting."

We both watched Ken go. "His people?" I asked.

"I hate to admit I find him endearing."

I laughed. "Me too. Actually, he reminds me of my sister . . . she's a handful, but everyone adores her. Especially me . . . in spite of my better judgment sometimes. I think they'd get along."

"Well, maybe that's it. Ken *is* the closest thing I have to a sibling."

The server arrived then and set a large platter and two plates on the table. "Here you go," he said. "Enjoy."

"You like calamari?" Lucas asked. "If not, we can order something else from the menu. But Scout's calamari is awesome, I promise."

"Believe it or not, I like calamari. It was my mom's favorite. She always said that it got a bad rap and people always expect it to be the texture of rubber, but that's only if it's overcooked." I picked up a ring.

"What's the verdict?" Lucas asked.

The coating was crisp, salty, and the inside was perfectly tender. "Really good. Not at all overcooked." I took another one. "But I'm still not singing."

"I bet you'll change your tune."

"Cute."

"Oh, you got what I just did there?" He licked some salt from his thumb.

"Yeah, you're many things, Lucas Tsai, but subtle isn't one of them."

"I like to think I'm quite subtle," he said, turning his beer glass in a slow circle on the table. "Since you're so perceptive, tell me what else you've observed about me."

"Sure. I'll play." I snatched a ring of calamari he was about to pick up. "You're confident, that's for sure. Adventurous. Worldly and well-traveled. Obviously."

"Obviously. Anything else?"

"You're smart. People like you. You're like everyone's favorite big brother."

Lucas smiled. "As an only child, I like that. Being somebody's big brother is an honor. How'd you come to that conclusion?"

"You take care of people. The people who work at the resort. Ken. Even me. You're always doing something for someone."

He nodded. "I guess we have that in common, Ms. Big Sister. Is that it for your assessment of me? I was prepared for worse."

He'd rested his tanned arms on the table and the muscles in his forearms flexed as he leaned in. I must've been staring at his arms for longer than I thought as well, because when I looked up, his gaze was fixed on me. I gulped. "Nope. That's all I've got. I guess you're a little bit of a mystery."

I stared down at my beer for a moment before downing the rest. I could almost hear Sadie laughing at me. Lucas Tsai, mystery man. Liquid courage, my ass. Idiocy in a glass was more like it.

"My turn," Lucas said.

Oh dear Lord. "No pressure," I said.

"I'll be nice," he promised. But by the way he was looking at me again, I wasn't so sure. "You are intelligent, that's clear, and probably very successful at what you do. What is that again?"

"Advertising."

"So, are you good at advertising?"

"You could say that."

"You don't love it though."

Where did that come from? I took another gulp of beer.

"Am I right?"

"Do you love running hotels and airlines?" I asked, trying to deflect.

"To be honest, I never thought that much about it. My father built and ran our business, so that's what I do. I don't dislike it."

"Is that what you went to school for, business or hotel management, something like that?"

Lucas shook his head. "I went to school for engineering, actually."

"What kind?"

"We don't have to talk about this, Marin. I'm not that interesting, or mysterious. Besides, it was my turn to tell you what I'm learning about you. I think you're deflecting."

"If you want me to sing . . ."

"Well played." He swiped some sauce up with a ring of calamari. "I did go to business school for my MBA, but my undergrad was in architectural engineering."

"So you wanted to build bridges and skyrises and stuff?"

"Something like that."

I reached for another piece of calamari. "Do you miss it?"

He shook his head. "Not really. Running my father's business is fulfilling. I enjoy building on what he started. I like the challenge of keeping everything moving in the right direction. And it's not like I could walk away even if I didn't like it . . . We have a lot of employees who depend on us."

"When people need you, you make it work," I said. *Maybe it isn't your dream, but you can find contentment.*

"Ba was pretty open-minded. He just wanted me to be happy; he would have supported whatever I wanted to do. But honestly, I'm not sure what kind of architect I would have been. I wanted to be creative, but it was a lot of rulers and angle calculations for my taste. I prefer using my intuition. Fortunately, business is an outlet that lets me do that to solve problems."

"No offense, but that doesn't sound like a whole lot of fun." I reached for more calamari but found the plate empty. Lucas flagged down the waiter for another round of beers and more squid. "Got any hobbies?"

"We'll forget for the moment the fact that the woman who acted like a trip to the Caribbean was a torture tactic is basically accusing me of being a boring suit. I have hobbies. You should be familiar with them. Climbing. Diving. Other things." He smirked.

"Other things?"

"You're probably going to think this sounds ridiculous."

"More ridiculous than taking a strange, stranded, admittedly uptight American out for Sabaoke?"

"Point taken. Though I'm starting to doubt that you're as uptight as you think. But all that aside, I really think I'd like to design things."

"What kind of things? Resorts?"

He shrugged. "I don't know . . . possibly, or even something smaller, like jewelry. Does that sound crazy? It's probably just Saba rubbing off on me. Business and family matters kept me back in Taipei for most of last year, but now that I'm back I feel inspired."

"Laurentina *did* say everyone's an artist around here," I said. "Maybe you are too."

"Maybe." Lucas's eyes met mine. He smiled. "Are you excited about having dinner with her tomorrow?"

"Totally."

I was surprised at how much I was enjoying myself. The welcoming atmosphere of Scout's Place. The delicious food. The interesting conversation. Maybe Saba was rubbing off on me a little too. The lights dimmed. The bar had grown crowded while we were talking. A disco ball sent colored lights shimmering around the dark room. Someone tapped a microphone.

"Hey, Saba! Who's ready for Sabaoke?!"

Not this girl, that's who.

"Time to start warming up!" Lucas called to me over the cheering. He started to stand and without thinking I flung out a hand.

"Lucas, I can't do this. I'm not ready. There's so many people here . . . you didn't tell me there'd be this many people."

"No worries. It's not your turn, Marin." He took a step backward, smiling. "What kind of host would I be if I expected you to go first?"

The announcer's voice cut through the crowd's cheers. "We're starting off with a good one tonight, Saba! Let's hear it for our very own Lucas Tsai!"

Lucas flashed a devilish grin. "Just one of my many hobbies," he said. I opened my mouth to say something, but it took too long for the shock to dissipate enough for me to form actual words. He strode off toward the stage, rolling his sleeves up as he walked. The music started, the wild rainbow light show shifted to a spinning disco pattern, and Lucas gripped the microphone. He didn't give the appearance of being the least bit nervous. Instead, he looked like he belonged in front of a crowd.

I didn't recognize the song Lucas sang, but it wouldn't have mattered. He could've been singing the cat food jingle my team had rejected two weeks ago and I still would have turned into a pool of molten longing . . . he was *that* good. His voice was deep and rich; when he hit a high note, I got legitimate chills. I was so mesmerized by his singing that I barely noticed Ken taking a seat next to me. "I told you our boy was good, VIP," he said. "*Wéi!* Marin?"

I didn't mean to be rude, but I couldn't answer. Lucas was building up, raising an arm high as he hit a perfect last note, and I didn't want to miss any of it. He took a quick bow and the crowd went wild.

"Way to go, Tsai!" someone shouted. Several people high-fived him and clapped him on the back as he passed by on his way back to our table. He pulled his chair around and sat next to me.

"What'd you think?" he asked.

"You were really good."

"I think you're being kind," he said.

"No, not really," I said, recovering. "I actually find your prowess incredibly annoying. Is there anything you're *not* good at?"

He gave a slow shrug, but the look in his eyes read like a challenge. Suddenly, my mind raced with possibilities of other things he was probably quite good at. *He's a few levels above a pool boy, but he'll do,* I heard Sadie say. I shook my head to shut out the thoughts. What was wrong with me?

A young couple had replaced Lucas onstage and the DJ was introducing them. The familiar tune of "Love Shack" by the B-52's started up. Lucas smiled at me and leaned close.

"You're next," he said.

My heart accelerated, beating so fast it thrummed along with the drumbeat in my ears. It was sort of like panic, but different. Lucas was right, though I hated to admit it. I *did* like to sing. And even though the idea of doing it in front of a bunch of strangers in this bar was truly horrifying, it wasn't dangerous. There was no cliff to fall from. No one would get hurt. Still, why was my heart beating so fast?

"Just tell Glen what song you want when you get up there," Lucas said. His breath was warm and the skin on my neck tingled. "You're going to rock this, Marin."

I turned to him. "I don't know about that."

"It's going to be fine. You don't have to be good, you just have to have fun. It's that simple."

The "Love Shack" couple ended their duet with a gratuitous make-out session, which the half of Saba that now seemed to fill every available space in Scout's Place cheered on with gusto. I gulped and smoothed down my dress. Lucas gave me a reassuring nod. Ken threw his fist in the air.

"Jiā yóu!"

I didn't know what it meant, but it sounded good. I held up a tentative fist and tried to plaster a smile on my face while I approached the stage.

"Lucas's friend. What'll it be?" asked the DJ.

I stared at him. I'd been so busy being mesmerized by Lucas's amazing voice and hypothesizing about his other talents that I'd barely had time to freak out about my own performance, let alone think of a song. I glanced over my shoulder into the dark crowd. *Think, Marin. What would Sadie pick?* I pictured her getting ready for a night out, dancing around with her hairbrush, taking swigs from a bottle of champagne, singing off-key at the top of her lungs . . . Lady Gaga maybe? I bit my lip. I couldn't even think of anything recent.

"You're up," the guy said. "I need your song. Or do you wanna pass?"

I wanted to pass. I really wanted to pass. I glanced behind me. The light was spinning around the room, illuminating random faces in the crowd. It caught on Lucas for an instant. He was looking right at me and he nodded. I thought of what he'd said to me—just have fun.

"Do you have 'Dancing Queen'?"

The DJ scoffed. "Of course! I have everything ABBA ever wrote. Classic choice." He handed me the microphone. "Knock 'em dead."

I blew out a long breath as I stepped onto the stage clutching the microphone.

"Let's welcome our next singer, Marin, to the stage. I hear Marin is from Tennessee and is here on Saba having an island adventure. Anyway, put your hands together and get ready to sing along . . . I know you all know this one."

The familiar piano gliss rang out. Holy shit. I was doing this. People started screaming as soon as they recognized the intro. There was no backing out now. My voice wavered a little at first, but then the crowd joined in and something happened. My fear disappeared. I couldn't see all those faces staring at me, but I could hear them singing along. I fed off their energy. I saw myself sitting atop Mount Scenery and swimming in the ocean with Lucas. I had done those things. And now I was singing in front of a bar full of people and it felt amazing. I danced around to the music, jumping to the beat. The people in front of the stage were waving their arms back and forth. When the music finally faded out, I basked in the spotlight, out of breath. The room was quiet for a moment and I entertained the notion that while I'd been reveling in my musical out-of-body experience, I might have actually been truly awful. But then the crowd erupted with applause and cheers. People held out their arms and I jumped down from the stage like one of those crowd surfers. I completely forgot about my dress and my sequin-smooch undies. By the time I made it to the back of the bar, I was practically panting with exhilaration.

"Holy shit, VIP!" Ken shouted in my face. He gripped my shoulders and shook me a little. "You were awesome, you know that?!"

"Thanks!" Ken released me, and I whipped around. The music

was starting up again, "Clocks" by Coldplay. The spinning lights and the aftereffects of the adrenaline rush made me suddenly dizzy. I ran straight into Lucas's chest. I looked up at him, breathing hard.

"Did it feel as good as it looked?" he asked.

I covered my face in my hands for a moment, but there was no point trying to hide the huge grin on my face.

"Tell me you got a picture?" I asked.

He held his phone up and snapped one.

"But I'm not onstage anymore," I yelled over the chorus. "Sadie's never going to believe it."

Lucas leaned down and tucked a sweat-dampened tendril of hair behind my ear. He leaned in close and I sucked in a breath. "Believe me, Marin, I already got a bunch while you were up there having the time of your life. This one was for me."

Thirty

THE NEXT DAY, AFTER a stroll around the grounds, a leisurely afternoon at the pool, and an exorbitantly long (and well-deserved) nap, I pulled on the heart-covered sundress, donned a pair of sandals, slicked on some lip gloss, and headed to the main house, where I'd promised to meet Lucas to drive over to Ronaldo and Laurentina's for dinner.

He was standing out front next to a large bird of paradise in a pot. I smoothed my hands over my dress, which suddenly felt a little bit too cutesy. Lucas, on the other hand, was radiating that kind of effortless style that neither I nor Mrs. Right could come close to accomplishing. He had on a pair of suede loafers, tailored black pants that most closely resembled clam diggers, a black V-neck T-shirt, and a fitted linen jacket the color of sand. He was probably the only man I'd ever come across who could not only pull off clam diggers but made those short pants look good. He wore his black hair slicked back away from his face and there was just enough of a golden tan from the sun to highlight his sharp jawline and high cheekbones. It just wasn't right for a man to be that good-looking when I was stuck with lip gloss and a dress that came from the juniors section.

"You look nice," he said.

I held out the sides of the skirt and let them drop. "This is the dress of a fourteen-year-old . . . or a very strange Tennessee newlywed."

He flashed me a lopsided grin. "Not sure about that," he said. "I think it suits you." He opened the door to the Jeep for me. I climbed inside and we headed out through the gates. I'd purposely worn a ponytail to avoid having to wrangle my hair for the entire trip, but someone had put the top back on the truck. *So much for being prepared,* I thought, and pulled the elastic out of my hair.

Ronaldo was waiting on the front steps of the cottage when we arrived. He ushered us inside and we joined in the chaos of shelling beans and stirring things. Laurentina was at the stove frying fish. She waved over her shoulder when we came in. The baby was in a wooden high chair; he popped peas into his mouth one by one, picking them up between two fingers and mashing them with his fist when he got too many. Two small children dressed in athletic T-shirts and shorts ran around the kitchen and then out into the driveway.

"Ken coming?" Ronaldo asked. "We haven't seen him in a while."

"He's taking care of things at the resort tonight."

"He's hiding, is what he's doing," Laurentina said. She used a wooden spatula to turn a piece of fish in the oil, and it hissed at her. "Probably thought I'd grill him about Elisabet."

"Wouldn't you?" Ronaldo said. He chuckled.

"Yeah. You bet your ass I would. She's a nice lady and he messed that up good. Crashed the plane before it even got off the runway."

Ronaldo handed Lucas a bottle of beer and snapped off the top. "She's feisty, but she's a smart woman, my wife. What happened there?"

Lucas shook his head. He took a sip of his beer. "I don't know. Ken doesn't know how to be happy."

Laurentina set out a salad in a big wooden bowl and a small round loaf of bread that was still hot. "What about you? You do?"

"Probably not."

"Fish is 'bout ready. Ronaldo, call those boys in, will you?"

The boys clamored in, and after much noise and a bit of running around, they washed their hands and took their seats at the table. Ronaldo gestured for me to sit down next to Lucas and then went to help Laurentina with the fish.

Confession. I am not a fan of fish or unknown green liquids. The only fish I ever eat is salmon, and even when it's covered with maple glaze, I have to choke it down. I eyed the spread. The bowl of green stew reminded me of my green smoothies that I drink for my health but have to pinch my nose shut to get down or I gag. What had I gotten myself into? I reminded myself of the delicious soursop I'd enjoyed at Mama B's. Surely I could handle some soup and a bit of fish.

Laurentina grasped Ronaldo's hand and mine and bowed her head. "Oh, Gracious Lord," she said, "thank you for the bounty that we are about to receive. Amen."

"Amen," said the little boys.

What ensued was a sort of beautiful melee that only mealtime with a baby, two small boys, and four adults could be. Everyone was scooping food, eating, chewing, talking.

"Who wants callaloo soup?" Laurentina asked.

She filled our bowls for us and I watched the others lap their portions up like ravenous puppies before I tasted a small amount from the end of my spoon. It was interesting, spicy and creamy, a little bitter, but mostly nutty. Like spinach but not. I took another spoonful. Before I knew it, my bowl was empty. I ripped off a hunk of bread and used it to wipe the leftover soup from my bowl like the little boys.

"You like it?" Laurentina asked.

"It's great," I said, and I meant it.

I took a bite of the fried fish. I didn't know what kind of fish it was—only that the white flesh was flaky and tender. It practically melted in my mouth, and when it did, the flavor was mild and delicious. At home, I hated fish. I did not hate this fish. Before long, everyone had started to get full and the serving and eating slowed down. The boys retired to the room they shared to do homework. Laurentina served some kind of papaya pudding that was quite possibly the most delicious thing I had ever consumed in my life and mugs with warm Saba rum, a spicy concoction that set my cheeks aflame and made me feel friendly and relaxed. "Eat more, Lucas," Laurentina said. "You're all bony edges."

"D'you know, Marin, this guy over here," Ronaldo said, using his spoon to gesture at Lucas, "got busted when he was eight years old for trying to start a goat racing gambling ring."

Laurentina wiped tears from her eyes. "I'll never forget the sight of him hanging on for dear life when that goat took off with him down The Road on Windwardside. The police were chasing him on their bikes and couldn't keep up."

"You've all known each other a long time," I said.

"We were all so happy when he came back after college. We were hoping to keep him, but it seems he's always jetting off to some big city somewhere for work."

Lucas held up his hands. "Guilty. I admit it."

"Stop trying to settle him down, Laurentina," Ronaldo teased.

She gave him a look. "That's right, Ro. You tsk at me like you haven't been trying to do the same thing. The tales I could tell. Don't get me started."

"How long have you two been married?" I asked.

"Ha," Laurentina said. "Too long, some days. Not long enough, others."

"Wise woman," Ronaldo said. "She's right too. I tell my friend here, and Ken, find yourself a nice, smart woman like my Laurentina, and you'll have a good life like me. But they don't listen for shit."

Lucas raised his eyebrows. "I don't remember you telling me that, ever. I thought you said—"

"Let's not go on about what I said." Ronaldo gestured at him with his mug. "I'm telling you now. Those fancy looks will fade, Mr. Tsai. Strike while the frying pan is hot." He cocked his head toward me. I hid behind my own mug of rum.

"I think you're mixing your sayings," Laurentina said. "I'll let you have your man talk, I promised Marin over here I'd show her how I do my lace."

Over in the corner, Laurentina picked up one of the pieces of fabric from the table and got out a wooden box that was full of needles and thread. "Have a seat," she said. "We can talk while I work."

Laurentina explained the process, the patterns she and other lace artisans knew by heart, how each person had her own special style. I watched her hands move in some choreographed dance that I couldn't quite understand.

"Lots of tourists come to see our lace, but you're different," she said. "You remind me of those researchers that came a while back. They were creating a book of patterns. Even promised to bring us all copies when they come back around. Why is this so fascinating?"

"I like learning about the amazing things people do in the places they were born. When I was younger, I used to write about it. Back in high school, I wrote an essay about a group of women who wove fabric in Nicaragua. They were artists, but they also were entrepreneurs. Their art paid for their food, gave other people jobs . . . it empowered them. To them, and maybe to other people too, it seemed like a small thing, something basic, but it was such a powerful thing."

She rocked back and forth in her chair a few times. "I never thought of it like that," she said. "This is just something that I do, I've always done. My mama did it before me and hers before her. So you're a writer?"

"Not now. I was then. Well, kind of."

"Were you any good?"

I shrugged. "I won an award."

"Seriously?"

"It was kind of a big award. I had to turn my essay into a full-length piece and a publishing house was going to make it into a book."

"Amazing," Laurentina said. She smoothed her hand over the lace she'd completed so far and tied off the thread. "What's your book called?"

"Nothing," I said. "I didn't finish it. After that, I didn't write anymore, at least not like that. I work in advertising now."

"Why'd you stop?"

"Things happened. I had to take care of my little sister. I didn't have time for frivolous things."

"Who says it's frivolous?" she asked. She set down her lace and went to get Jonathan, who was fussing in his high chair. She put him on her hip and offered him her breast. "Did you like it?"

I thought back to when I wrote real things, not just slogans. I'd loved it. I nodded.

"I love making lace. It's who I am. When I make something beautiful, I feel good, like only I could have made that thing. I wouldn't let anything keep me from doing what I love." She smoothed a hand over Jonathan's head. He'd almost finished nursing and now his little long-lashed eyelids struggled to stay open. "You want to hold him?"

Before I could refuse—I had no experience with babies—she handed him off to me like a little package. I cradled him in my arms. He was so perfect. He had the same dark skin as his father, his mother's big eyes and coal-black lashes. I ran the back of my index finger over his soft cheeks. I looked up and saw Lucas holding my phone up. The flash went off.

Thirty-One

IT'S AMAZING HOW MUCH a distance can stretch when you want something on the other end. A few steps might as well be a thousand miles when it separates you from your dream. Back then, it shouldn't have surprised me that the walk from our house to the mailbox—those few steps from the front door to the street where the clematis, resilient as ever, was already snaking up the post—seemed to take an hour to traverse. It might as well have been the Appalachian Trail or the Cumberland Gap that Mom and Sadie always climbed without me. But there might have been a letter from the admissions department at Columbia University in there, and I'd wanted the fat envelope, the kind with the congratulations and all the information about housing and meal plans and major advisors, for as long as I could hold a pen.

It's a place for serious writers and journalists, Mom had said when we planned a visit sophomore year. *New York is*—she'd taken a long breath here—*bursting with life and lights. You'll love it, Marin, just like I did.* She'd gone there, and the work she'd done had catapulted her into the job that led her to being one of the best international correspondents in the whole country. It's where she'd met my dad, a man who seemed more like a myth than a person. I had a few blurry memories of a rich voice, a tall figure with dark hair, but I had been too small when he'd left to remember much more. Sadie hadn't even been born when he disappeared from our lives. Mom rarely spoke of him, and when she did, it was with this strange kind of distant admiration that kept me and Sadie up all night hypothesizing about how our dad was probably some kind of secret agent or royal recluse. Eventually, we stopped trying to figure out his identity. Whoever he was, legend or not, he wasn't there, and that was what mattered.

I'm not sure why I filled out the application after she died. Maybe it was that she'd already organized all the admissions materials in a neat folder with my name scrawled across the top in thick Sharpie and set it on top of the red folder that contained all of her important documents like her will and the station's insurance policy. The thick black letters of my name and the location felt a bit like a mandate, even though mandates weren't really Mom's thing. Later, if I really thought about it, I probably sent in that information because I thought that being at the same school where she'd become an adult, come into her own, met my dad, fallen in love . . . all of those things of hers . . . would make me closer to her somehow. Or maybe there was a tiny thread of hope inside me that thought I might be able to track my dad down, and that it wouldn't be just me and Sadie against the world anymore.

Mom had been gone for months. Sadie and I'd spent a whole unbearable, hot summer without her. I turned eighteen that June and became Sadie's legal guardian. Sadie dropped my cake taking it out of the oven and insisted we eat it with spoons off the kitchen floor.

Fall came and we went back to school and fell into a routine that felt like a pair of shoes someone else had worn for a long time. It pinched in places and went concave in others. We were living someone else's life now. It didn't fit right. I couldn't even write about it.

The adults around us, teachers and staff at the high school, tried. We still were forced to meet with the counselor once a week and talk about our feelings, or in Sadie's case why she felt the need to skip school to go bouldering in Stone Fort every Friday. Mrs. Overbeck, my language arts teacher, helped me with my college applications. She must've read my Columbia application about ten times. She kept saying it was a great choice for me. I applied to other places. Safety schools that were less competitive. In-state schools that weren't all the way across the country and were less expensive. I'd already heard from the University of Tennessee at Chattanooga. But in my heart, Columbia was the only place I'd ever considered going, the only place I wanted to go.

It took me a minute before I finally broke down and opened the mailbox. Sadie had been standing in the open doorway watching me, and she'd shouted, "Jeez, Marin, you'd think there was a tiger inside waiting to bite you. Just open it up already!"

So I did. I took the little metal piece between my fingers and pulled. Then I reached inside the hollow space and pulled out a stack of envelopes. Half the pile was the usual bills. A couple of cards rounded the bulk of the mail—we were still getting condolences from people in far-off places, people our mother had touched in some small way during her career. Sadie had run up beside me and she snatched the pile out of my hand, sending our electric bill into a puddle. She held up an envelope triumphantly over her head.

"What is it?" I asked, jumping up to try to get it from her.

"Your eyes work," she teased. "You tell me."

I squinted at the return address. Columbia University Department of Admissions. Oh my God. It was fat. It was a fat envelope. Sadie danced a jig in the street, whooping with joy. "This thing is so heavy," she said. "You must have gotten in! You got in. You got in." Left foot, right foot. I finally managed to wrest the thing away from her. The light mist had turned to a full downpour, which Sadie did not seem to notice. She was still wrapped up in a full-on victory dance in the street.

"We're getting soaked," I said. "C'mon." I jogged to the safety of our covered porch. But Sadie didn't follow me. She was kicking up water from puddles, stretching her arms out, turning her face skyward. Her hair was saturated. The tight spirals had spun out straight as water dripped off the ends. "Sadie," I yelled. The sky was getting darker. "Come inside. It's pouring!"

She stopped spinning and looked at me. Even in the dim gray light, she was glowing. "I know," she called back to me. "Isn't it amazing?" At that moment a bright white streak of lightning sizzled across the sky. The fine hair on my arms stood on end. Sadie didn't move. She was reveling. That was what she called it, when she got wrapped up in how awesome the world was and didn't notice anything else. I dropped the envelope on the rocking chair and ran out into the rain. As I took hold of her arm, a loud rumble of thunder seemed to shake the ground. An instant later the sky lit up as a bolt of lightning struck a tree a few hundred yards down the street. I pulled Sadie behind me back toward the safety of our house, our mother's house.

Later, after we'd both had hot showers and eaten, I cleaned up the dishes and went up to my room. I still hadn't opened the Columbia envelope. The other admissions offer letters from the regional schools were in a neat stack in the corner of my desk. On top of them, the Columbia envelope sat. It had gotten drenched and left a damp rectangle on the stack. Some of the ink on the UT letter had smeared. Sadie had stuck a Post-it on top of the envelope that read, *Pick Me!* I took a deep breath and started to tear at the flap. I felt a twinge in my stomach. We'd eaten too much homemade pizza, I decided, twisting a little in my chair. It didn't help. The twinge didn't go away, it just turned into a strange heaviness. My heart was beating fast. I shook the sensations off and returned my attention to the envelope. Why were my hands shaking? Finally, I got the envelope open and pulled out the cover sheet.

Dear Marin, We are delighted. . . .

It was everything I'd ever wanted, but somehow instead of seeing the rest of the words on that fancy letterhead, all I saw was Sadie, spinning in the rain, in the dark street, and that shard of lightning sizzling down and splitting the Newmans' ancient oak tree right down the middle. It could have been her. God, she was so reckless. If it hadn't been for me dragging her inside, who knows what might have happened? I glanced up at the map of the United States that we used to use to mark our adventures as a family when Mom was alive. There were pins all over—Joshua Tree, Chicago, Québec, and all the way up from our town of Sweetwater, just outside Chattanooga, to New York City. I'd planned on having my own map someday, all my adventures marked out like I was conquering the world. But that was before. How was I supposed to be brave without Mom? Now I counted the seconds it took my finger to travel there and looked back at Sadie's Post-it note. In classic Sadie style, she had used four different colored markers and had filled each bubble letter with a unique pattern—stripes in the P, swirls in the I. I stared at it for a minute until it blurred, then I looked at the letter from Columbia, the distance on the map. *Pick me.* I picked up the letter from Columbia and dropped it into the trash can. Then I stuck Sadie's Post-it note to the top corner of my computer screen. I navigated to UT at Chattanooga's online admissions portal and moved the cursor to the button that read, *Accept offer.*

Mom and I had talked so many times about my going to Columbia. For as long as I could remember, I'd wanted to follow in her footsteps. Be a writer. Travel the world and do important things. Be fearless. Live on words and adrenaline, just like she did. But she wasn't here. Where had words and adrenaline got her? Where had they gotten me . . . and Sadie? We were on our own, living lives that looked the same but didn't fit anymore. And maybe Columbia didn't fit me anymore either. It was so far away from Sadie—a plane trip far. Who was going to pull her out of the street when it stormed? Who was going to make sure she showed up at school often enough to graduate? I looked over at Sadie's message one last time. *Pick me.*

I clicked the button. I wasn't irresponsible or risky. I would make sure that our little family of two would be safe and sound and in one piece. Even if it meant staying here and letting go of my dream of sitting where Mom had once sat and learned, walking the same bustling streets Mom had walked. I let go of my dream of graduating with a degree in English from Columbia. No, I wasn't going anywhere, ever again.

The following fall I enrolled at UT at C. I lived at home and commuted back and forth to class. No one said anything. I guess a lot of people just assumed that I didn't get into Columbia. People were still afraid to bring things up to me. It's like they thought I was some fragile incendiary device that might explode at the slightest provocation. Only Mrs. Overbeck seemed to sniff out the truth and wasn't afraid to mention it. "I just don't understand," she said. "I talked to a friend who is in the English department and she said you were one of the best applicants they saw this year. They adored your essay. Plus, you won the Graywolf Nonfiction Prize. UT is fine, Marin, it is. But why would you pass up Columbia? It's the dream." I'd shrugged, said something about New York being a bit too big and wild for me. "At least tell me you're working on finishing the book. Having your creative nonfiction manuscript published is a once-in-a-lifetime thing."

"I'm working on it," I lied. I wasn't willing to tell her the truth; I was barely able to admit it to myself. I'd packed up all my notebooks and put them away. They were just words, made-up stories and fantasy, tales of people I didn't really know, who I'd never meet. To me, they were not real, not important. Stories were what had gotten my mother killed; they'd left me and Sadie on our own.

Thirty-Two

AFTER ALL THE RUM was drunk and the dishes put away, Lucas and I took The Road home on foot. Neither of us was in any shape to drive.

"Be careful, you two," Laurentina called from the doorway.

"Not too careful," Ronaldo said. Laurentina gave him a playful whack and then they disappeared inside.

"Well, that was wonderful," I said. "The rum. The food. The conversation. Laurentina and Ronaldo. The rum." The rum had been wonderful, perhaps a little too wonderful. I wobbled and my arm bumped against Lucas's side.

He smiled down at me. "I'm glad you enjoyed yourself. You and Laurentina seemed to hit it off."

"We did," I said, trying to focus on walking in a straight line. "So, what were you and Ronaldo talking about half the night?" I asked Lucas as we walked along the side of the road.

"What were you and Laurentina discussing?" Lucas asked.

"Lace and regret," I said, trying not to slur.

"Same." His hand brushed against mine.

"Right."

"Okay, if you must know, we were talking about you," he said. I made a face. "Was it bad?"

Lucas shook his head. "Let's just say you light up when you're interested in something." He staggered a little bit and I grabbed on to his elbow. "You're worse than I am," he said. "Don't try to help me and get hurt yourself."

"Oh, shut up," I said. "Stop being so handsome." I clapped a hand over my mouth.

To his credit, Lucas did not say anything. For a full minute. He just stood there looking at me, getting more attractive with each second that passed. His lips parted in slow motion.

He said, *"Suǒ yǐ nǐ jué de wǒ hěn shuài."*

There it was. I didn't know what he was saying, but the smirk on his face said it all. I stepped up to him, swaying just a little. My face was very close to his, glaring up at him. "I know you do that on purpose."

"What?" he asked. I started to tip. "Listen, Marin Cole. It's not my problem if not knowing what I'm saying drives you wild."

"That's what you think, Lucas Tsai."

He gave me a bemused smile and then I leaned forward and kissed that smile right off his face. I suppose I should mention that I also kissed us off the edge of the road. We tumbled down a short, thankfully grassy embankment and ended up splayed out on the rocky beach. Lucas groaned, and I scrambled off him. When I stood up, I took in the scene. The good news was, we hadn't rolled off a cliff and were alive and in one piece. This was also the bad news. Because the incident had shaken the alcohol out of my system or something and now I felt remarkably sober and mortified enough that I wanted to die and have someone dig a hole to Taiwan to get away from Lucas Tsai and his gorgeous lip gloss–covered face.

"What was that?" he asked, sitting up.

"A car almost hit us," I shrieked. "Didn't you see it? It came flying around the curve."

"Something hit me," he said. He was on his feet now. He took a step toward me and I took one back. "But I'm pretty sure it was human."

"Every time I get on a beach with you something humiliating happens."

"Your English makes less sense than my Mandarin."

"Remember, last time, I lost my sheet. And—"

"I didn't find that humiliating."

"I did!"

He was closing the distance, stepping forward faster than I could retreat. His hand slipped around my waist. He looked down at my stupid dress and smiled. Why was I breathing so fast? "You really shouldn't."

His hand fit perfectly in the small of my back and my heart was pounding in my chest.

"We should go," I mumbled.

He leaned very close to me and grasped my chin gently between his fingers.

And then Lucas Tsai, hotelier, secret Sabaoke superstar, and jet-setting international hottie, kissed me. The moon was shimmering on the ocean, waves flowed in over the volcanic rock beach, seabirds swooped and dove in the sky, and I noticed exactly zero percent of that. I was too busy noticing Lucas's hands in my hair, on my waist—oh, and up under my too-short-thank-you-Mrs.-Right dress, his lips tender and firm—and by the way, if you're hypothesizing that a guy who can speak eight different languages fluently can do amazing things with his mouth, you'd be right. At that moment, he was speaking the language of *Get that dress off you and get these pants off me and let's go reenact our little post-massage mishap with a mature-content rating.* Who was I? I was like a woman who'd lived with amnesia for years, amnesia that made me forget that I had needs and wants until this very moment. My memory was back, baby. I was needing and wanting all over this beach. I grabbed fistfuls of Lucas's shirt and leaned into him.

"We should go back to the resort," Lucas said, pulling back.

"Oh." I failed to keep the disappointment out of my voice.

He ran the soft part of his thumb over my cheek and shook his head. "It's not quite this public at our resort."

Ohhhh.

We headed back up to the road. Lucas went first and I followed. He reached back to help me over several stones at the edge of the beach, but even after we'd made it safely to the road, he held on to my hand. It felt so natural, walking like that, our fingers intertwined.

It was a long walk back to the resort. As much as I was all for not driving under the influence and against riding with strangers, my feet were starting to protest wearing someone else's strappy sandals for a trek without the numbing aid of a lot of mugs of spiced Saba rum. I stopped.

"What are you doing?"

I crouched down and undid the shoes' buckles. Then I picked them up in my hands, looking at them for a moment (they really were very pretty shoes), before I hurled them over a makeshift guardrail into the dark sea. "I'm sorry, Mrs. Right," I said. "You have good taste in underwear, but your shoes suck."

Lucas raised an eyebrow. "How do you plan on walking the rest of the way without shoes?"

I shrugged. "I don't have experience with being spontaneous . . . I'm winging it," I said.

He sighed and stepped in front of me. Then he crouched down. "Get on," he said.

I'll admit it. I had to resist the urge to snap a picture of myself, still slightly drunk and shoeless, high on kissing endorphins, getting a piggyback ride from Lucas, and sending it to Sadie. That would have earned me an instant passport, I figured. But I was more concerned with the smell of his skin and the feeling of his strong arms holding on to me and trying to figure out exactly what he'd meant about things being more "private" at the resort. I rested my head on his shoulder as he carried me. He didn't seem to grow tired. Even when we reached the gates, he didn't set me down. Instead, Lucas took us down a path behind the main house, one I hadn't been down before.

"Where are we going?" I asked.

"I have my own beach. Not exactly a beach, but it's as beachy as you can get on Saba, and it's mine."

Lucas stopped. He set me down on a flat black rock that made me the same height as him. The ocean was in front of us, but the rest of the world seemed to disappear into the darkness except for a dim yellow light that bled out of a small cottage.

"What about guests?" I asked.

He slid his hands around my waist. "Not even guests can come here."

"I'm a guest."

"Not tonight." His mouth met mine in the darkness. It had been so long, but somehow, my body knew what to do as soon as Lucas touched me. He threaded his fingers into my hair and I melted into him. A few days on a volcanic island with Lucas and now I was molten lava, liquid, powerful, burning hot.

When we broke apart, our chests heaving for lack of oxygen and unbridled arousal, I thought to myself, *I shouldn't do this.* But I wanted to. So. Freaking. Bad. Sadie'd told me to be adventurous. She would definitely approve of this. In fact, she'd probably be proud. I told the little voice in the back of my head that was telling me to go back to my room to shut up, and then I went for it. I took hold of the hem of the sundress and pulled it over my head. Mrs. Right had left some very nice underwear and my own conservative, full-coverage undies were currently drying after a good hand-washing in the sink. I'd had no choice. Sometimes the universe strands you on an island and other times it gives you the luggage of a Victoria's Secret platinum card holder and puts you on a beach with a freaking fantasy of a man. Call it fate.

I'm normally a self-conscious person. But in that moment on the dark beach with the silvery moon our only illumination, the way Lucas was looking at me, I felt beautiful and alive. When he ran his fingertips over my collarbone, something inside me woke up, something bold and hungry and *awake*. I took off his jacket and flung it up in the air behind us. Then I pushed his shirt up over his head. His lips found mine again and I reached for his pants.

Moments later, Lucas grabbed my hand, wove his fingers between mine, and then he started toward the water. I followed behind him, trying my best to find my footing on the uneven surface.

"What are we doing?"

"Having a do-over," he said.

The water was warm and luminescent in the moonlight. The crests of the waves shimmered like the pearl we'd found diving. We went deeper and deeper into the water, until it was up to our ribs. I reached down and unclasped the red lace bra and flung it into the waves. Then I wrapped my arms around Lucas's neck. My bare skin pressed to his. I let my head fall back against the water, knowing that Lucas would hold me to him, that I could just let go, because he was there.

"Are you sure?" he whispered.

"I've never been more certain of anything," I said.

Lucas's fingertips brushed over my hips. If I could have captioned this one, I would have said: *The skinny-dipping was transcendent.*

Thirty-Three

I WOKE UP TANGLED in silk sheets and awash in a swath of rich papaya-colored light seeping through the shutters. A terry cloth robe was hanging over a wingback chair next to the nightstand. I pulled in a relieved breath. Lucas wasn't around. I climbed out of bed and into the robe. The sundress I'd been wearing the previous evening was hanging from a coat hanger in the bathroom. It was still damp. My skin was crusted with salt and my hair was a mass of dark tangles.

For a moment, I considered sneaking back to my villa. The trouble was, I hadn't exactly been paying careful attention to the route we took last night to get here. I'd been too preoccupied with lust. I recalled with equal parts blissful delight and total mortification that Lucas had carried me home after I'd attacked him on the road and thrown my shoes into the ocean. That part was a little foggy. The rest of the evening's events were quite clear. Without the haze of alcohol, I remembered the taste of his mouth, each path his fingertips traced along my bare skin, the deep ache in my chest when he looked at me. I knew one thing for certain: I did not want him to see me like this. I jumped into the shower and used some of his shampoo to wash my hair. Afterward, wrapped in a towel, I squeezed the excess moisture from my hair and breathed in the familiar scent of him.

"Good morning," he said.

I jumped. Fortunately, I had the good sense to hang on to my towel. "Hi," I said.

"There's coffee on the patio if you want some," he said. "I also brought you clean clothes."

"You found something in that bag?"

He shook his head. "I went over to Windwardside and bought you something. My friend Brigette owns a boutique over there." I followed him back into the bedroom, where he produced a small shopping bag that held a guava-colored tank dress made from fuzzy cotton. It was long, with beautiful lace embroidery around the neckline that reminded me of Laurentina's creations.

"I almost forgot, there's shoes too. Since you, ah, lost yours last night."

I bit my lip. "Thank you."

"Get dressed and come outside for breakfast," he said.

I let my towel fall to the floor and pulled the new dress over my head. The fabric was so soft against my skin, and the fit was perfect. It had a laid-back island feel and was more colorful than something I would have picked for myself, but I appreciated the more modest cut compared with the rest of Mrs. Right's options. I wove my hair into a damp braid and joined Lucas on the patio.

The table was piled high with fruit, crisp bacon, and pastries. Two steaming mugs of coffee sat at the center of the table. I sat across from Lucas and started eating. Even after the huge feast Laurentina and Ronaldo had prepared last night, and all the drinking, I was starving. I scarfed down an almond croissant and half my cup of coffee before I realized Lucas wasn't eating.

"You're just watching me eat?" I asked. "Aren't you hungry?"

"I ate earlier," he said. "This isn't my normal breakfast menu."

"What'd you eat?" I asked, picking up a long slice of mango.

"Our chef lets me make *dàn bǐng* and *mántou* in the kitchen for breakfast most days. That's like a crispy version of an egg crepe and a steamed bun. I've been eating it since I was a kid. It reminds me of home."

"Sounds nice."

"Mmm. Have you talked to your sister yet, about the passport?"

I had barely remembered my phone. I'd been too occupied reliving the events of the night before. A flush crept up my neck and into my cheeks. "Tell me I didn't throw my phone in the sea," I said.

He laughed. "You did not. I took it from you when we left Laurentina and Ronaldo's for safekeeping."

"You knew me that well."

He took a sip of coffee. "Some things aren't meant for Instagram." He extracted my phone from his pocket and slid it across the table.

I didn't pick it up right away. I was waiting for him to say something more. What, exactly, I wasn't sure, but something.

"So last night . . . ," I began.

"Last night . . ."

"Do you do that often, I mean with guests, or . . ."

"Was pretty amazing—" he said at the same time. "Wait, what? No. I don't bring resort guests to my home, ever. I thought I told you that."

"I was distracted."

"I'm surprised you'd think that. Maybe you are more adventurous than *you* let on," he said.

"I am not."

"You jumped me on the road."

I buried my head in my hands. "I seem to remember something like that."

"It's kind of hard to forget," he said.

I peeked over my arm. *Please let him not mean that in a bad way. Please.*

He reached across the table and traced each of my knuckles. "I wouldn't want to."

My phone was still sitting between us on the linen tablecloth. It buzzed. We both looked at it. I hesitated. When I'd been lying in bed earlier, the thought had crossed my mind that Sadie would never believe this. For a brief moment, I'd wondered if I should send her a picture of me in those silk sheets with the caption *#NotMy-Room*. But now that she was actually calling, I didn't want to answer. Because what happened last night was only part of the story. And Sadie was very good at reading me like a book. I was supposed to be going a little wild, having a little fun . . . Falling for my island host was not part of the plan. I looked up at Lucas.

I said, "I'll get it later." Then I took his hand and led him back inside, where I let him take off the dress he'd bought me.

Thirty-Four

SADIE

THERE'S A HILL OUTSIDE the city that dusk turns to fire. I sit there on winter evenings, my breath around me in clouds like a dragon, waiting. The blackbirds come, then swirl around me, charcoal against the jeweled sky, swooping and swirling, chaotic and controlled, thousands of pieces, a whole. They beckon me to join their dance. I long to leap, to unbind my wings and let the wind carry me on its whim, but I am too afraid. I can only stand and spread my arms and pretend to fly. I'm not a bird, or a dragon, but I still revel in the cool breeze on my face and my skin set ablaze by the setting sun as the tiny world I call home below me blinks on, one light at a time, as if it were the sky.

You've been reading my letters for a while, Lucas. And your dad told me how smart you are, so I'm sure as hell you know that's not my writing. I'm not poetic, and quite frankly, I'd be covered in scales and filling the sky with my fire if I were a dragon on a hill, but that's not the point. I didn't write it. Marin did. I found this when I was going through some of Mom's notebooks after the fire. Mom had written *Marin, Age 11* on the back. It's just one of probably hundreds of short bits of writing, scribbled on scrap paper and in random spiral notebooks, that Marin packed up in cardboard boxes with all of Mom's belongings after she passed away. I never understood why she did that. Why she put the most important, treasured things out of sight. Was she trying to forget? When Mom died, I wanted reminders of her everywhere. Being able to see her and remember made me feel brave, but it wasn't like that for Marin. Looking back, I think she was actually angry. Here she was, not even in college, and Mom had left her holding the bag, holding me, the house, the responsibility, all of it.

Do you think she'll be mad at me too?

Maybe this wasn't the right way to do this. I mean, I never wanted to lie to her, even though I always have. We each have our ways of protecting each other. She tries to control me, to mitigate risk, and I lie to her. I lie about my assignments, about the risks. I lied when I started to get sick and didn't tell her. I lie and lie and lie. Don't get me wrong, Marin lies too. Like when she and Ted broke up and she said she was better off and then she cried in her room when she thought I couldn't hear her. I blamed myself for that one.

That's why I'm sending Ted to Saba. I told you there'd be a surprise appearance, remember? Ta-da! This brain tumor has made me smart, I think. Is that possible? Cancer made me a genius . . . now there's a news story for you. Anyway, all I know is that once you love someone, like really love them, that doesn't just disappear. They can go to the Himalayas and you can stay home doing jack shit, but those feelings are still there. Like muscle memory in your heart. Maybe Ted and Marin just need to remember. Or move on. It's put-up-or-shut-up time.

You know, I racked my brain the whole time I was in China. I just couldn't see another way—Marin had made me her whole world. What was she gonna do when I was gone? She always jokes about how I'm her sun and she's just orbiting around me. I tell her it's bullshit, but in a way, it's true. I was always kind of a shitty student, but I do remember what would happen to Earth if the sun died. I just wanted her to be okay without me. But now I'm wondering if I've made a mistake. Not really about Ted—well, maybe—but about this whole thing.

At Fuda, the doctors tried a lot of different things to heal me. Some painful things. I told myself that the pain was worth it, if it helped. If it saved me. And I guess maybe I told myself the same thing about Marin.

Am I wrong? Am I lying to myself now?

I thought the hurt would be worth it, but I'm still dying.

Thirty-Five

MARIN

I DIDN'T TAKE ANY pictures that day. Or maybe I took some pictures, but they weren't for public consumption. At any rate, Lucas and I spent most of the day on various surfaces in and around his villa indulging our more hedonistic tendencies and now we were refueling at a candlelit table at the resort's five-star restaurant. The restaurant was full of other guests, couples mostly, laughing and smiling, talking in low voices. I wondered if we looked like them.

We were halfway through a surf and turf course when Lucas slid something across the table toward me.

"What's this?" I said. "I'm starting to feel like the Spoiled Queen on the Unspoiled Island. I haven't gotten you anything, *and* you already got me a dress and this?"

"Open the bag," he said. "It's something small."

I unfolded the shopping bag and pulled out a leather-bound notebook. I looked up at him.

"I overheard you and Laurentina talking after dinner about how you used to write. I thought maybe you'd like to have a notebook in case you felt like writing something."

I turned the book over in my hand. The leather had been dyed the color of the ocean at Torrens Point on a sunny day. Subtle waves had been hand-tooled across the bottom third. It was a beautiful notebook. I just didn't have anything to write in it.

"Thank you," I said, and tucked it back into the bag. "I'm really out of practice though. These days, all I write are slogans. Maybe I could write some for your resort."

"Tsai Group's always looking for talent," said Lucas. "But it seems to me that you have your own ideas about what you really want to write. Should we get more wine?"

I looked over his shoulder to see if I could spot our waiter while I downed the last of my merlot. "Excuse me," Lucas said, trying to get our server's attention. A man standing a few feet behind Lucas turned around.

"Sorry?" he said, stepping toward our table. "Were you talking to me?"

My glass slipped out of my hand. It bounced on the table and splattered a few spots of bright red on the linen. Lucas righted it. He was used to guests interacting with him; in my brief time at the resort, people had stopped him multiple times to rave about their stay, praising his beautiful grounds or the staff's excellent service—but this wasn't an ordinary guest.

"Ted?" I said, blinking. "What are you doing here?"

"It's crazy, right?" He sat down in the open chair next to Lucas. "I saw your Project Paradise stuff on Instagram. Anyway, I could barely believe my eyes. Marin Cole, on a tropical island, climbing mountains and, I mean, scuba diving? I couldn't believe it. I had to come see for myself."

"Ted?" Lucas said to me, his voice low. "The Ted?"

I widened my eyes so he'd know I was as surprised as he was and nodded. I turned my attention back to Ted. "So you came to Saba . . . That's a pretty big trip from . . . I'm sorry, I have no idea where you've been all these years. Are you still in Nepal?"

"No. I left there a while ago. I've been all over the place. Canada,

New Zealand for a stretch, Wyoming. I've actually been back in Tennessee."

"You're back in Tennessee? Since when?" The irony wasn't lost on me.

"Last fall. I'm working with a professor at UT on a project." I reached across the table and grabbed Lucas's wineglass. I gulped the entire contents down in one long swig. Lucas flagged the waiter down for another.

The waiter, God bless him, returned in a flash. "Leave the bottle, I have a feeling we might need it," Lucas muttered.

"Of course, Mr. Tsai," the server said. "Can I get you anything else? Some dessert, perhaps?"

"Do you want dessert, Marin?" Lucas asked. He held my gaze. I wasn't hungry anymore, but I found myself nodding.

"What would you like, ma'am? The passion fruit crème brûlée is excellent."

"Oh, that would be g—"

"Do you like crème brûlée?" Ted asked. "I thought you only ate Ben and Jerry's Chunky Monkey."

"Just bring us everything," Lucas said. "She can decide what she wants." He poured himself a large glass of wine and drained it. Then he topped it off again.

Ted eyed him. "I like this guy. 'Bring everything.' He laughed. "That's the best kind of guest at these places. Awesome. I'm in. I'm starving."

"He's not a guest, Ted."

Lucas smiled and blinked at Ted. I almost spit out my wine. Then, in the most dashing move I have ever seen in my life, he rose from his chair and gave a quarter bow. He extended his hand. "Apologies. We haven't been formally introduced," he said. "I'm Lucas Tsai, the proprietor."

Ted tried his best to mimic Lucas's strangely easy formality, but he ended up looking awkward and robotic. "Theodore Hurston the Third," he said. Seriously. "So how do you and Marin know each other?"

Lucas thumbed the stem of his wineglass. I swallowed. He looked like he was about to say something that would either send me into flashbacks of our night together or into the corner trying to rock my way out of mortification. But he simply said, "She's my special guest. I've had the pleasure of working on her photo project with her."

The server returned with the dessert tray then and we were all distracted for a moment by the display of dessert artwork. I picked up the small ramekin with the crème brûlée I'd wanted and cracked the sugar crust with a spoon. I could feel both men's eyes on me as I took my first bite and savored it.

"Hey, let's take a picture," Ted said. He handed his phone to Lucas. "Will you take one of the two of us, bud?"

Lucas's expression didn't change. I wondered if he was annoyed.

"C'mon, Marin," Ted said, leaning toward me and putting an arm around me. "I've been following the Paradise Project since you started it. We can post this one on there."

The flash made me blink. "Here you go," Lucas said, setting the phone between us on the table. "You both look great." He sat back down. "So, Theodore, Marin tells me that you two are old friends."

"Really?" Ted looked at me. "She's a funny one. We weren't exactly friends. One generally doesn't propose to friends."

A hard piece of sugar lodged in the back of my throat. I coughed. "You didn't propose to me, Ted."

"I was going to."

Lucas picked up his phone and glanced at the screen. "If you'll excuse me, I need to attend to some business, and you two seem to have a lot to discuss. I'll leave you to it."

I grasped the cuff of his shirtsleeve. "You don't have to go."

He pulled his jacket off the back of his chair and started to put it on. I let go of his sleeve.

"It's fine," he said. "I have some acquisitions paperwork I need to review for an early meeting. Enjoy your dessert."

He fixed his jacket and nodded before he walked off. Ken stopped near him and said something, but Lucas was already on his phone. He kept walking.

When he'd gone, I pointed my spoon at Ted. "I don't get you," I said. "I haven't seen you in forever. And then you see a picture of me on vacation and you think, what, you'll just show up and pretend nothing happened?"

"What did happen, Mar? You tell me. Because I spent years trying to figure it out."

"Seriously? You left me, Ted," I said. "It's not a mystery you need to unravel."

"You're different than before, not just the freewheeling on a tropical island. The Marin I knew wouldn't talk to me like that. C'mon, you and I both know I didn't leave you. Marin, I loved you. You chose to stay home instead of coming with me. And before you start explaining all your reasons, please don't. That's not what I'm looking for here. I get it. How important your sister is to you was one of the things I loved most about you, even if it drove a wedge between us. Besides, I think we both know it wasn't all about her. I might have been the one who left the country, but you were the one who left our relationship." He let out a long sigh and ran his hands through his wavy blond hair. "This wasn't how I envisioned this going."

"What did you expect?" I said. "I've never been one for surprises."

"I guess I didn't really think it through. I'm not great at planning things out in advance. I just knew I had to see you . . . and then it seemed like you were on a date just now, and it threw me off."

"I'm not." We hadn't officially called it a date, but it'd certainly felt like one—a really amazing one, if I was being honest. And then there was all the time we'd spent together before that. The scuba diving. The singing at Scout's. Dinner with friends. What had those things been? Stops on a very elaborate tour with a guide who made my heart race whenever he leaned in to say something to me? Was that all?

Ted was still rattling along. "I mean, I knew I still had feelings for you, but I didn't think I would be so jealous that I'd come off like a prick."

I folded my napkin to hide my trembling hands. Ted still loved me. Ted, the man I'd wanted to spend forever with in Tennessee. He'd come all the way here and now he was confessing his feelings. What was going on? I'd tucked all my feelings away and piled things on top of them so long ago, I wasn't even sure if they existed anymore. So I panicked. "You know what," I said, "it's fine. We all acted badly. It's an awkward situation. Let's see how the picture turned out."

I picked up the phone and stared at the screen where Lucas had left the photo open.

"I just told you I still have feelings for you," he said. He lifted Lucas's still full wineglass and took a long drink from it.

"I heard you." I'd gotten his message loud and clear. I wasn't confused about where Ted stood, although how he'd gotten to that point was baffling. My problem was, I didn't know my own feelings. I was also busy studying the image.

"And?"

I looked up from my dessert and met Ted's gaze. I'd forgotten how blue his eyes were, like the Caribbean Sea. He'd aged since we'd been apart. The mountain sun had etched fine lines at the corners of his eyes. I glanced back at the image. To say it wasn't the best picture I'd ever seen of Ted would have been the understatement of the century. His lips were in a weird shape, as if he'd just eaten a piece of spoiled fish, and he was in mid-blink, the whites of one eye showing. He'd taken off his hat and there was a visible ring in his hair where it had been. I almost felt sorry for him.

"Say something, Marin," he said.

I plunged my spoon into the custard and filled my mouth with the rich sweetness. After I swallowed, I said, "This crème brûlée is amazing."

Thirty-Six

SADIE

TED. TEDDY. THEODORE HURSTON III. He's not as much of a dude bro as he seems, even though his favorite accessory is the infamous baseball hat. All anyone needs to know is that back when they coupled up in college, he and Marin were good together, and then I made a giant mess out of it. I know I made him sound like he sucks earlier, but he made Marin happy until he left. You'll have to take my word for it when I tell you that listening to your sister crying herself to sleep at night is nearly as brutal an experience as facing your own mortality. And when it's your fault, well, then it's worse. I don't know what will happen this time. Maybe this is the romance novel–style second chance they both deserve or maybe Marin will finally get the closure she needs to move on. Either way, this one I'm leaving up to her.

Thirty-Seven

MARIN

I STAYED AT THE table in the resort restaurant, in front of the spread of desserts that Lucas had ordered, for a long time after Ted had left. Initially, I'd planned on eating my feelings, but since I didn't really know what the hell those feelings were and I was rather full from the lobster and the steak and all the other delicious things I'd already eaten, I just sat there like a confused zombie.

"Are you going to finish all this?" Ken asked. He dropped into the chair across from me. "We have a photographer coming tomorrow for a promotional campaign shoot and I've been running around all day trying to make sure that everything is set; I've hardly had time to eat."

"Help yourself," I said.

I held my wineglass in my hand and swirled the liquid around, watching it drip down the side. "I'm more of a beer drinker," Ken said. He picked up a piece of chocolate cake and popped it into his mouth. He frowned. "Elisabet's is better than this. That's annoying."

He flagged down the waiter and ordered a beer. "You know what, Wallace? Just bring me a whole six-pack. Mr. Tsai is on a tear with this promo. Then I couldn't find him all day."

I sipped my wine.

Wallace returned with the beer and Ken held his out. *"Gānbēi,"* he said.

"Gānbēi?" I said back and tipped my wineglass to my lips. Ken swallowed the gulp of beer he'd taken and set the bottle down.

"Miss VIP, you wouldn't know anything about my boss being MIA all day, would you?"

I shrugged.

"I checked your hashtag this morning and the latest post was you holding Laurentina and Ronaldo's baby at nine o'clock last night. I'm guessing Lucas put that one up." He took another drink of beer. "But today, *nothing*. No more scuba diving. No sailing. No 'Dancing Queen.' No zip-li—"

"I will zip-line over my dead body."

"I think you know what I'm getting at here."

I tipped my head to the side. It was a habit I'd picked up from Sadie, a kind of power move she used when she wanted to control a situation. "If what you're hinting at was true, don't you think he'd be here?"

That wasn't a lie. He'd walked away from the table and left me to face Ted and all those murky feelings. It reminded me of when we dove through those tunnels, where you never knew what you'd find through the silt and the darkness, something amazing or something sharp that could cut you.

"I'm sure he had his reasons."

I shook my head. "It's fine. He's an enigma. Warm and funny one moment, distant and cold the next. It's not like I'm his girlfriend or something . . . I'm just a short-term guest."

Ken set his beer down too hard and sent a splatter of suds all over the tablecloth. "Wait, I was right? I was just messing with you! You guys really hooked up? Wow. I can't believe it."

"Seems like he can't believe it either," I muttered.

Ken shook his head. "Marin, I don't know what you're thinking right now, but for what it's worth, Lucas Tsai is the nicest guy you'll ever meet. I should know. He basically adopted me as a brother when we were kids. He's about the farthest thing from an asshole possible. There's no way he'd casually hook up with you and then blow you off."

"I don't know, Ken. It kind of seemed exactly like that. Maybe it's just me?"

Ken was pulling at the bottle label. He tore a long strip before he answered. "It's not you. He's not himself right now. Because of his Ba."

I thought back to Lucas telling me about how his father had died. "Oh. I didn't think about that. I guess I didn't realize it would still affect him so much."

"Still? It was only a few weeks ago."

"I didn't know that. I guess I don't know anything. He only said his dad had died a while back."

Ken shook his head in disbelief. "Not a while back. Lucas just got back from mourning in Taiwan the same time that you arrived . . . so you can imagine he's not in the best place emotionally. Try not to take it personally."

"I feel awful," I said. "Was his dad sick for a long time?"

Ken shook his head. "Probably. Like Lucas, he worked too much, except he didn't take great care of himself, I don't think. Whenever Tsai Bóbo was sick and Lucas tried to get him to go to the doctor, he'd just say he would drink fish soup instead. By the time he went to the doctor, the cancer had already spread to a couple places. There wasn't much that could be done at that point."

I didn't know what to say. I poked at the crushed ice in my water glass with a straw.

"I think Lucas feels bad about that. Like maybe he should've pushed him to go to the doctor sooner. But I don't know if it would've made a difference, you know? We can't force people to change their nature. And Lucas tried so hard to help when he got the diagnosis. He even found this place in Guangdong province, on the southeast coast, not too far from Hong Kong. I guess this obscure cancer hospital has oncologists who are supposed to be miracle workers or something. A lot of people with terminal cancer go there. Maybe you've heard of it?"

I shook my head. Ken's words were still rattling around inside my head. Guangdong—I had that strange feeling again. Only this time, I was sure I'd heard it before. From Sadie.

"Wait," I said. "What did you just say?"

"Huh?"

"About the miracles? The G thing?"

"You mean the cancer hospital? The one in Guangdong?"

He was waiting for me to respond, but I was too busy chasing thoughts as they spun around my head, like threads of a spiderweb, memories, tiny fragments of conversations. Conversations with Sadie. She'd been there.

"I think I have heard of it. Or at least the place. There's a temple there, right?"

Ken looked thoughtful. "There's lots of temples. Did you have one you were thinking of?"

I pressed a fist to my forehead, trying to think of the name. What was it? "Fu something? Fuda, maybe. And another part that started with a G too?"

"Guangzhou Fuda?" Ken said. His brow was furrowed.

Goose bumps prickled on my skin. I nodded. "That's it."

"That's not a temple. That's the hospital."

I shook my head. That couldn't be right. I remembered the whole conversation now. Sadie told me she'd been visiting a temple called Guangzhou Fuda.

"Marin?"

I blinked. My eyes came back into focus and there was Lucas standing next to Ken.

"What'd you do to her, Ken? She looks like she saw a ghost. Sorry I bailed on you earlier," Lucas said, pulling up a chair to sit beside me. "I didn't think it was appropriate for me to take part in that conversation . . . under the circumstances."

I scrambled out of my chair, knocking over Ken's beer in the process. "I'm sorry," I muttered, and took off running toward the villa.

"Marin!" Lucas called after me. "Where are you going?" I didn't turn around. I'd always had a knack for sussing out worst-case scenarios. In any situation, I could pick them out almost instantly, like a word search. Sadie had called it my curse. I'd comforted myself with the knowledge that at least I'd never be unprepared for disaster again, like I'd been that day in the principal's office when they gave me the news about Mom. That's what I'd told myself. Knowing what could go wrong would keep us safe. I couldn't have missed something. I wouldn't have. But I'd known something wasn't right with Sadie when she got back from China. She'd been off. Tired and thin. She'd barely eaten. She'd told me she'd been at a sacred site . . . Guangzhou Fuda. And now Ken was saying that there was no temple. Had Sadie lied to me?

As soon as his words had sunk in I'd pieced together the most horrible worst-case scenario imaginable. And as my feet sped over the cobbled path through the trees toward my villa, I prayed that I was wrong about this one. I couldn't bear to be right. I couldn't bear for this to be true. Because if it was . . . my precious twenty-six-year-old sister, my heart, my sun and stars, had been at that hospital. And there was only one reason a person would go to an obscure cancer hospital and lie to their family about it.

No. Sadie must have had her reasons. She couldn't be sick.

When I got back to my room, I couldn't find my phone. I searched frantically: the nightstand, the bathroom, under the bed. Then I remembered I'd left my phone at Lucas's place. It was cooler when I stepped back outside. I crossed my arms and rubbed the bare, goose-bumped flesh as I ran down the narrow path to the outskirts of the resort, where Lucas lived.

He'd left the door unlocked, so I went in and headed straight for the bed where we'd spent the night before. My head throbbed with fear about what could be true about Sadie, with visions of earlier, me and Lucas tangled together, smiling, a sheen of sweat on our skin. I could hardly discern what was real and what wasn't. I found my phone on the nightstand. Lucas must've plugged it in for me.

I picked it up and looked at the lock screen. It was a picture of me and Sadie, taken before she'd left for China. She was kissing my cheek, squeezing my neck too tight with her arm. She looked like herself. Happy. Giant neon-green sunglasses on her face. That wasn't what a sick person looked like, I tried to tell myself. Except I knew better. I sat on the edge of the bed and tried to call Sadie. I couldn't get through.

"Sadie, call me as soon as you get this," I said. "I'm freaking out a little here. And I need you to call me back, okay?"

I tried Sadie's boss, Jessica, after that. She hadn't seen Sadie. "I'm worried," I confessed. "Is there something I should know about Sadie's assignment in China?"

Jessica was quiet for a moment. "You girls should talk. If I talk to her, I promise I'll tell her to call you."

I hung up and stared at the phone in my hands for a moment. What was I going to do? I thought back to what Ken had told me. Lucas's dad had been a patient at that hospital. Maybe he knew Sadie. Maybe they'd met while she was doing her assignment. Because that's all she was doing there. Lucas had left on his desk lamp. I walked toward it. I knew I shouldn't. But I couldn't help myself. I needed answers. I needed relief from this kind of fear. It was totally different than the fear I'd felt with Lucas when I'd climbed the Ladder or gone skinny-dipping. That fear made my heart race, my pupils expand to take it all in. This fear was constricting, squeezing me. I could barely breathe. There were some papers on the desk, official-looking documents on Tsai Group letterhead, some written in traditional Chinese characters that I couldn't read. I paused. What was I doing? Only hours earlier I'd wrapped myself in his arms, and now I was going to do what, exactly? Invade his privacy?

I didn't even know what I was looking for. But I couldn't stop myself. I yanked open the desk drawer and riffled through the contents. My hand caught on something—a big manila envelope, its paper worn thin from use. It was held shut with a red cord wrapped around a cardboard circle. Just an ordinary envelope. We used the same kind at work to pass documents between different departments. But I could tell that Lucas had spent a lot of time handling it. It was important to him somehow. I turned it upside down over the desk and watched folded pieces of paper, postcards, smaller thin airmail envelopes torn open all spill down like giant snowflakes. I picked up a single rectangle of smooth white paper with a single world—*Ba*—scrawled on the back. I turned it over slowly to reveal a photograph of a smiling man. The same man I'd seen on Sadie's laptop the night I'd brought her home from the airport. Ba. I lowered myself into the chair and reached for an envelope. I didn't even have to read it to know. The handwriting was Sadie's.

"Marin."

The sound of Lucas's voice sent a chill across my skin. I swiveled around slowly, not sure what I would find. He stood in the doorway, clutching the wooden doorframe.

"What is all this?" I demanded. I scooped the letters into my hands and held them up.

He shoved his hands into his pockets and walked toward me. I pushed back in the chair to keep the distance between us.

"You'd better tell me right now why you have a bunch of letters from my sister."

He crouched down in front of me, taking hold of the arms of the chair so I couldn't roll away from him. When he looked up at me, his face was drawn.

"I think you know why . . ."

It was getting difficult to breathe. *Calm down, Marin,* I tried to tell myself. *You're overreacting.* But then why did Lucas look so troubled? There was a deep furrow between his brows and I could see the muscles of his jaw working, like he was chewing the words to soften them before he spat them at me.

I shook my head. "I don't."

"Ken told you about Guangzhou Fuda; he just told me."

"So Sadie knew your dad?" I asked. That didn't mean anything. "Did she take this picture of him? Was she writing letters for him?"

Lucas put his hand on my arm and shook his head gently. "They were there at the same time. They became friends."

I said nothing. I was shaking my head back and forth.

"Ba gave me this envelope before he died. He asked me to keep a promise he'd made to Sadie. I—"

"No."

"I promised. I know this doesn't make sense right now. But you have to know, I didn't have a choice. I had to honor him. I took the letters and I did what I promised. At least I've been trying to."

"Tell me about the promise, Lucas." I couldn't look at him. My eyes were fixed on the letters.

"She wanted me to take care of you while you were here and to keep all of it secret."

"So everything that's happened to me, that was what? Some part of a secret plan? Is that what you're telling me?" I swallowed hard and fought back the tears that were stinging my eyes.

"It was supposed to be this simple thing—showing you the island, taking you on a few adventures—I didn't think I wou—"

"Why would Sadie do that? Why would she make some secret plan to give to a stranger?"

Lucas flinched a little at my words. His chest rose as he pulled in a slow breath. The silence stretched out between us. We'd been so close earlier, my skin on his skin, his lips on my lips, and now . . . we were a million miles apart.

"There's something else you're not telling me," I said. "What else have you been keeping from me?"

I tried to tell myself that my irrational fears were just that, irrational. "Say it," I whispered, my voice taut. "I have to hear you say it."

He shook his head slowly. "I can't. I promised them, Marin."

"What about me?"

He closed his eyes and breathed out a sigh. "You're right. You should know the truth." He stepped over to the desk and selected an envelope. Then he placed it gently in my open palms. "But it can't come from me. You should hear it from Sadie."

She hadn't written much, but it was enough. It was too much. The paper left a million tiny paper cuts all over my heart. I hemorrhaged. I let the letter fall from my fingertips.

"So," I said slowly, "what you didn't have the decency to tell me yourself is that none of this is real. Nothing . . . except this: while I've been running around on this godforsaken volcano in the middle of the ocean snapping pictures of myself doing stupid stunts and snuggling up to a *liar*, Sadie's running out of time."

I turned and ran out the door without saying another word. Lucas didn't call out after me this time. He didn't chase after me. It was just as well. There was no way to go back to the way things had been, not after this. Besides, there wasn't anything to go back to. All those things I thought I'd felt . . . it'd all just been an illusion, a mirage, like an oasis in the desert. If Sadie was sick, then there wasn't even a desert to begin with. Nothing else mattered.

Out in the night, I stopped at the start of the path. I didn't know where to go. Every option seemed wrong. I turned back, just for an instant. I wanted to turn around. I wanted to ask him if everything had just been part of the plan. If he was just really good at keeping promises or if maybe I wasn't a complete fool and he actually felt something toward me. Worst of all, I wanted him to wrap me in his arms and tell me that he really would take care of me. My whole world had just exploded into bits and I wanted to cling to him. It's a special kind of torture when the one person you want when you're lost in a black ocean is the very person who just blew up your boat. Through the window, I could make out Lucas inside, even blurred through my tears. He turned to his desk and the pile of postcards and letters Sadie had written and swept his arm across the desk in one quick, arcing motion. The cards went flying in all directions, like an explosion of paper.

I felt the impact like he'd hit me. I ran.

Thirty-Eight

SADIE

YOU DON'T THINK YOU'LL get colon cancer when you're twenty-five. Not when your stomach hurts and you start to lose weight. Not when you see blood in the toilet. Not even when you google it and every website puts it on a short list of options for your symptoms. You don't even believe it when the doctor tells you. I didn't. I was healthy. If I'd been a dude, people would have called me strapping. I looked freaking amazing in a tank top. I was globe-trotting with my camera, kayaking class fours and climbing mountains and living the literal high life. Sure, looking back, maybe there were a few tiny things—I got nauseated sometimes or went to the bathroom more often than most people I knew, but who doesn't have GI issues? And anyway, I chalked that up to the shit food Felix made when we were on assignment. Felix is amazing, by the way, which is why we've basically been together for the last two years—another secret I've been keeping from Marin—but his cooking sucks and he always wants to eat local specialties that are all well and good until you realize what you're actually eating and by then it's too late. By the time I started to feel tired and sick, I really was sick.

I tried to make a joke about my doctor's grave expression being a little too on the nose. Nobody laughed. By then, the cancer had spread to my abdominal lymph nodes and my liver. The oncologist gave me eighteen months. I gave him the finger.

The trip I took to Peru this past year was actually a stint at Hopkins. Felix took me there for surgery, where they took out everything they could and put me on some kind of clinical-trial chemo that rocked my world, but didn't make my hair fall out. And I was so glad, because Marin loves my curls, and she would have known in the weird way that sisters just know things, like they feel it instead of thinking it. I wasn't ready for her to know. I wasn't ready for the very surreal thing I'd been struggling with to be fully real. The chemo didn't kill my hair; it also didn't get rid of my cancer. We tried other things. Immunotherapy. Failed. Everything. Failed. Eighteen months became six just like that.

You already know about China. I guess your dad and I were the exceptions to the miracle hospital legend. I hope you know that we are, we were, okay with that. As okay as we could be. He told me. He'd done everything he ever wanted—he had you, a legacy to leave you, the time with your mom, the resort, paradise. And you know, my life has already been pretty miraculous. Who gets to climb mountains and take pictures for a living? It doesn't get any better than that. And I have the world's greatest sister. I got to meet your Ba . . . I mean, game over. Probably the wrong thing to say. I would blame it on the drugs, but honestly at this point I'm just on a lot of really good weed, and that's probably not affecting my mind as much as the new malignancy the doctor here in Tennessee just found in my brain.

I wish I could have gone to his funeral. I know he wanted the works, crying crowd and all. Tell me they really wailed, Lucas. I would have. I would have cried the Sacred Three Rivers' worth of tears. Maybe we'll get reincarnated together. Maybe I'll see Mom again. The three of us all shimmering like pearls in the sky, I can see that.

I don't know what will happen. I don't know how much time I'll get. I don't know how to tell Marin that I have to go again and this time I won't be coming back. When we lost Mom, Marin broke a little inside. It's like fear seeped in and took root, and tangled her up in those vines, in a careful, quiet little life. And part of that is because of me. Someone had to keep things stable, tether me to reality, give me a soft place to land. She did that for me. I don't want to break her again. I want her to have a chance to see what she could be without that fear, without me, before I have to leave her. Marin always says that I'm her sun—bright and warm—and she's just orbiting around me. Maybe I already told you that; my memory is a fickle witch these days. Trust me when I say telling Marin the truth about my diagnosis is like handing her a stick of the world's most powerful dynamite. I guess when I started all this I hoped that if she got a glimpse of the wonderful world, how beautiful and brave she can be, then maybe she'd have something to hold on to after I blow our world apart.

Marin thinks I'm so strong; she never told me, but I think sometimes she wanted to be like me and Mom, and maybe she even thought she was weak compared to us. It's not true. Look at me. I can stare down a bottomless crevasse, but I can't even face my sister to tell her the truth. I stared in the mirror this morning and still had a hard time admitting it to myself, to be honest. Chances are, I'll never set foot on another mountain, or have the sensation of sun and wind and sea spray on my face, adrenaline coursing through my veins. It really sucks. But missing all that, it's nothing compared to breaking my big sister's heart. I love her so much. So much that I need to pretend for a little longer that us being apart is just another trip. Some trivial temporary thing. A little project. I promised her that I would never leave her. I'd go do my wilding out and then come home. I'd never leave her like Mom did.

The ultimate promise. I can't break it.

So I sent her away instead.

Thirty-Nine

MARIN

I'M NOT A RUNNER, never have been, don't particularly want to be. Even hiking up Mount Scenery at a slow pace had left my legs sore and tight. Sadie's the athlete in the family, but that, along with everything I thought I knew about her and our life, had changed in an instant. After I fled Lucas's house, I found myself on a narrow, unmarked path fighting my way through a thick tangle of banana plants and elephant ears. My chest heaved and I stumbled over the uneven terrain, which I couldn't make out in the darkness. Under any other circumstances, I would have probably been freaking out about being lost in the jungle, but it never crossed my mind. My only concern was putting one foot in front of the other as fast and for as long as I possibly could. I couldn't think. Every time I tried, the smeared words from Sadie's letter pounded in my head: *cancer, too late, metastases, brain.* I ran with my hands out in front of me, fighting the giant leaves that slapped at my skin. Then I slammed into something hard. There was a deep grunt and I stumbled backward and pitched into the dirt.

My first thought was Lucas. I didn't want to see him. I couldn't see him, not right now, not like this, not after what he'd done. All he had to do was tell me the truth, and I could have been at home, doing what I do best, making a plan to help my sister, taking care of her. Oh God. Who was taking care of Sadie? I'd been gallivanting all over Saba, swimming naked and having drunken one-night stands like some kind of idiot on spring break, and she was . . . I couldn't bear the thought.

"Marin?" The voice coming from the figure that I'd just bounced off of wasn't Lucas's, but it was one I knew well. Ted took a step toward me. "Jesus, you came out of nowhere. You run now?"

I wiped my wet face with the back of my hand, but I didn't attempt to get up.

Ted extended a hand. "Are you okay?"

I couldn't get off the ground. I didn't even have the energy to take his hand. I shook my head. "No," I said, voice quavering. "I'm the opposite of okay. I'm not okay. Nothing is okay."

"Whoa, all right," Ted said. He lowered himself down to the ground beside me. "What's going on?"

"I can't," I managed between sobs.

"That's okay. You don't have to talk." He put his arm around me. I let my head fall on his shoulder. It felt so heavy all of a sudden, like every particle of energy had drained out of me at once. We stayed like that for a long time, my tears soaking his T-shirt, neither of us saying anything. When I finally caught my breath and managed to stave off the tears, I pulled away from him.

"Do you want to talk about it?" he asked. "Is it that guy? The resort owner one from dinner? I knew he was an asshole the moment I laid eyes on him."

I shook my head.

"No to the guy, or no to talking?"

"It's Sadie." My voice cracked. "I just, I—" The suffocating feeling returned. I sucked in air, but I couldn't get enough. I put my head between my knees.

"She's okay, it's okay," Ted said. "I just talked to her yesterday."

"You talked to her?"

"She sent me down here. No," he said, shaking his head. "I wanted to come here. I wanted you, but she told me where you were."

"She's okay?" I stifled a ragged sob.

"Yeah. Felix was there and she was chilling on the couch. She had your Instagram page open and was showing me all the pictures. God, you looked so beautiful on that mountain."

I was drowning. Back in that murky sea where nothing made sense. I couldn't get enough air. I pressed my hands to my chest.

"Slow down, Marin," Ted said. "You're going to hyperventilate. Try to breathe through your nose."

But I couldn't slow down. I was spinning out of control, hurtling through the darkness with no home, no light, nothing. I curled into a ball and wept. I heard muffled voices, but they sounded so far from me, as if we were on different planets. Then a pair of strong arms gripped me and I was floating back through the jungle.

When I woke later, through swollen-lidded eyes, I saw I was back in my room. I had one moment of peace before I remembered the night before—the letter, running from Lucas, Ted's voice, and the feel of the cool jungle floor. He must've carried me back, I thought.

My phone was sitting on the bedside table. I picked it up and dialed Sadie. *Please answer. Please.*

"Marin?" Her voice was raspy.

"I'm coming home, Sadie."

"Lucas told you."

"No. But that's not important. I'm coming back, Sadie. I don't care what the doctors told you. We can fight this together, just wait for me. I'll figure something out."

She was quiet for a minute. I could hear her breaths, steady rattles, through the line. "Don't," she said finally.

"I am," I said, defiant.

"Marin," she began. I waited for her to say something else, but heard nothing except for a shuffling on the other end.

"Sadie," I said. "Are you there?"

"It's Felix."

"Oh."

"Listen, Marin, Sadie's not having a great day."

My chest hurt so much that I felt like I must be having a heart attack. The world froze. Even the dust motes seemed to stop moving. They hung suspended in front of me.

"What does that mean?" I asked, trying to make my voice calm.

"She's hurting," he said. "It's not just her body." He sighed. "She didn't want this to happen. You were supposed to have a great trip and then she was going to tell you when you and Ted got back to Tennessee."

"I don't understand."

"You know your sister," Felix said. "She's one of a kind." I could almost hear the sad smile in his voice. "She made me order a cake for the day after tomorrow from that bakery downtown, the one you guys like. She wanted lemon strawberry, you know the one with the lemon curd and the jam—she's been very obsessed with *The Great British Bake Off* lately. It had to be a Victoria sandwich cake, she said, and on the top she wanted tons of rainbow-colored roses and for them to write *Surprise, I'm dying* on it. Of course, they refused. I'm probably banned from that bakery forever."

I forced myself to swallow. "What does the cake say?"

"*We had a good run.*" His voice cracked. "I'm sure you know, Marin, just how much she loves you. But she has a lot of regret when it comes to you too. I think she feels like she held you back and she doesn't want to go out being a burden."

That strange ache bloomed in my chest again. I could feel the start of another panic attack. Already, my cheeks were wet with tears. "Sadie is my everything, Felix. She's not a burden. Put her back on."

"Give her a little more time. She's not ready yet," he said. "I'll call you."

After we both hung up, I picked up the room phone and dialed the front desk. Ken answered.

"Concierge services, this is Ken. How may I assist you?"

"It's Marin," I said.

"Marin." From the way he said my name, carefully, like it might explode on his lips when he spoke it aloud, I could tell Lucas must've told him what had happened after dinner.

"Did you know?" I asked.

"I didn't. Lucas only told the staff that you were a VIP guest. That's it. None of us had any idea about what was going on. He carried it all himself."

I said nothing.

"I'm not defending him. But remember, he just lost his dad. You have to believe that if it weren't for that, for him wanting to honor his Ba's last request, Lucas would have never hurt you like this."

"He told you that?"

"I know him. But no, we didn't get a chance to talk . . . He left before I had a chance."

"He left? For where?"

"I don't know, Marin. If I did, I would say."

"You know what? It doesn't matter anyway." I thought about asking him to drive me to the airport, but I hadn't decided what to do. I just wanted to talk to Sadie again.

There was a knock on the door. I looked up just as Ted was stepping into the villa, and I hung up the phone. "It wasn't locked," he said. "I hope it's okay."

I shrugged.

"We didn't get a chance to really talk last night. You were in rough shape."

"Thanks for helping me get back," I said.

His forehead wrinkled for an instant, but he shrugged. "I'm glad I could be there for you. Do you want to talk about it now? Something's going on with Sadie?"

I nodded. "She's sick, Ted. Really sick." I told him what I'd understood from her letter. "She has colon cancer."

"I had no idea. But that's not that serious, right? Can't they just remove it, or do chemo or something?"

"I don't know. I think she's done treatments, but they haven't worked. It's spread."

His eyes widened. "Where?"

"Her brain." I had to close my eyes then. I couldn't watch him react.

"Marin," he whispered, "I'm sorry." He was crossing the room, reaching out for me, cupping my face in his hands. "No wonder you were so upset last night."

"What am I supposed to do? What can I do? She told me not to come home. Of course I'm going home. I have to be with her."

He pulled me into him. I let him hug me. He was like an old sweatshirt, comfortable and broken-in, familiar. He even smelled the same as all those years ago when we spent nights in the library stealing glances over the tops of textbooks. When I pulled back, he tucked my hair behind my ears and gave me a tight smile, the awkward pity smile I recognized from the people at Mom's funeral. All those people who hadn't really known her, so sad to see her gone so young. A thoughtless tragedy, they said, though I knew they secretly thought it was her own fault. Over the years, I'd blamed her too. Didn't she know that we needed her? Why couldn't she have been like the other mothers, who stayed home, stayed safe, and watched their children grow old? Only the good die young, some random mourner had said. Mom had been forty-six. Twenty years older than Sadie was now. I let my eyes close so I wouldn't have to see that pitiful smile, the one that told me there was no hope left anymore. They say if the sun ever dies, life on Earth would end, and even though I knew nothing about science, I knew this was true. Sadie was dying. She didn't want me to come home. Lucas was gone. How was I supposed to go on?

Ted kissed me then, pressed his dry lips to my salty ones, and I let him. I was too broken to stop him.

"Let me be there for you, Marin," he whispered into my mouth. "Let me take care of you."

I pulled away. "What are you saying?"

Ted reached down and unzipped the pocket of his cargo shorts. I'd always hated those things. He put a small booklet into my hands. I ran my palm over the top of it. It was my new passport.

"Sadie's friend had this issued to replace the one that you lost. She gave it to me to bring it to you."

I looked at him questioningly. I still didn't understand all of this.

"A new passport and a fresh start," Ted said. "What do you think?"

I flipped through the booklet. It had the same picture as my original passport. It might as well have been the one I lost. It *was* the one I'd lost. There was the stamp I'd gotten in Anegada, right where it'd been days earlier, smeared ink and all. No Saba stamp, though. I hadn't needed one. It was almost as if I'd never been here at all.

Forty

IT IS A TRUTH almost universally acknowledged by survivors that you will ask yourself if you missed something. If you should have known. If you just weren't paying enough attention, or worse. Maybe Lucas thought this too, with Ba or his mom when she was diving that day.

For me, I wondered the same thoughts on endless repeat.

If I was oblivious.

If I was selfish.

If this was my fault.

If only I'd caught it sooner. If only I'd done more.

If. If. If.

And maybe these "survivors," a word that is such bullshit I can't even wrap my head around it, do what I did, and go back through every interaction, every moment, like flipping through a catalog, looking for evidence, to see if there was something they missed.

Should I have known something was up when I found Sadie packing? She didn't look the way she normally did when getting ready for an assignment. She wasn't bouncing with enthusiasm, flinging shirts and underwear, camera gear all over her bed, constantly on the phone. Pure frenetic chaos. This was quiet. A little too calm. Resigned.

I'd looked at the open suitcase at the foot of the bed and then back to Sadie. There was a stack of soft sweaters, one I'd given her for her most recent birthday on top, next to other cold-weather clothes; the latest issue of *National Geographic*, which had that stunning photo from her trip to Puerto Rico inside; her favorite book, *Einstein's Dreams.*

"You're leaving again?" I'd asked from the doorway.

She had looked up from her packing. "Yeah."

"But you just got back."

"Marin, don't start, okay? I—" She sat on the edge of the bed.

"You can turn down assignments, you know. Weren't you just saying the other day how tired you were after your last expedition? I think your exact words were, 'If Kangchenjunga's home to a man-devouring demon, the compressor route up Cerro Torre without the bolts is definitely a demon hotel.' You broke four ribs and could barely get out of bed. Pass this one to some other budding photo-journalist and take the next one. I could take a few days off, we could plan some R&R together? We haven't had a rom-com marathon in forever. What do you think?"

She closed her eyes for a moment before she answered. "It isn't that kind of trip. I have to go." She stood up again and laid the shirt she'd been folding in her suitcase. "But I love the idea of some sister time when I get back."

When Sadie gets excited about something, her face sort of lights up from inside, turning her into an adorable version of a twinkle light. It's virtually impossible to say no to a human twinkle light. I sighed. "All right. So, what exciting and dangerous destination are you off to this time?"

"China."

I stared my little sister down. "China." My mind had jumped to a newsreel of recent headlines that featured China. "Is it safe there?"

"Jesus, Marin. It's fine. I'll be fine there."

"You have a guide or a host or something? You don't speak Chinese—"

"Chinese isn't a language," Sadie said.

"What do they speak, then? Where exactly are you headed, anyway?"

Sadie took a deep breath. She never enjoyed my pre-trip questions, but seemed less tolerant than usual. "It's the Guangdong
province and they mostly speak Cantonese there, among other languages, of which there are many." She was emptying her underwear
drawer rather aggressively. She added something under her breath,
which sounded a lot like "You might know that if you ever went
anywhere," but I couldn't be sure. I didn't want to fight with Sadie.
I didn't want her to leave. Every time she left, I felt like I was holding my breath the entire time. My phone, my email, the TV were
all possible sources of devastating bad news. I couldn't look at them,
I couldn't stop checking them. And if I happened to see a sheriff
coming toward me, it was over. I was lucky if I stayed upright, because usually something like that would send me into a corner, with
a raging panic attack and flashbacks. I never told Sadie this, because
I didn't want to burden her. I figured she just needed to get this sort
of lust for adventure, this wildness, out of her, like a college coed
sowing their wild oats, and that eventually she'd decide that life was
sweetest at home, safe, with me. But now, she'd only been home for
two weeks and she was already flying to the other side of the world,
a place people literally joked about digging through the center of
the earth to reach.

"Okay, I guess I'll let you finish packing, then." I paused in the
doorway. "I was thinking of making a lasagna. How about we have
dinner together before you head out?"

"That's sweet, Marin. But I've got a lot to do and I'm not really
that hungry."

"This is because I was pestering you too much, isn't it? I'm sorry.
I just worry about you, you know that, right? You seem . . . I don't
know, stressed. If it's work, I'm sure there's something for you at
Astute . . . They're always talking about how great it would be to
have an in-house photographer for ad shoots."

Sadie flashed me a pleading look, the kind that said, *Please,
Marin, shut up before I lose it.* I held my hands up. "Okay, I get it.

I'll let you be. But the offer still stands. Lasagna, stress-free local job; you want it, I'll make it happen, little sister."

In the morning, I offered to drive Sadie to the airport and she took me up on it for once. "The magazine isn't sending a car for you?" I asked. "What about Felix? Isn't he going?"

"Not this time," she said. "It's all good. It will be nice to spend the extra time together. I'll need it to apologize for being so short with you last night."

I shook my head. "It was my fault. I was surprised, that's all. So I went all overbearing parent on you."

She smiled. "At least you can admit it. They say that's half the battle."

I loaded her suitcase into the trunk of the car and we set off. It was a beautiful day, the kind that skiers call a bluebird day. Perfect. I put the Indigo Girls on my phone and blasted it through the car's sound system. By now, we had the harmonies to "Power of Two" perfected. Sadie looked out the window while we drove. When the song was over, I asked, "So what's the story in—what's it called—Guangdo?"

"Guangdong," she offered, tracing her finger along the glass. "There's a place of miracles there."

It sounded alluring and mysterious, and to my glee, not particularly dangerous. "So you won't be climbing any mountains or meeting any scary political leaders?"

"Nothing like that." Sadie reached out and squeezed my hand.

I pulled up in front of the terminal. We hugged for so long that a security guy came over and rapped on my window.

"I guess I should get in there," Sadie said. She hopped out and took her things from the trunk.

I had this strange feeling that she'd left something at home, but I couldn't think what. "Have you got everything?" I asked through the open passenger-side window. She grabbed her purse and her suitcase and nodded. "Yup."

"Passport?" I said. "Boarding pass?"

"Check and check," she said, patting her bag. "I'm good. Bye, Marin. I love you!"

"I love you too. Be safe!" I called.

She blew me a kiss and then she disappeared into the crowd. I tried to blow a kiss back to her, but the traffic patrol had gotten irritated and blew his whistle at me. I pulled out into traffic and a taxi driver blared his horn at me.

"Okay," I said into my rearview, wiping the tears from my eyes with my sleeve. "She's my little sister, all right? I'm going. Jeez."

Forty-One

I BARELY SLEPT THAT night. The next day, Ken drove me to the airport, alone. I didn't have the energy to process the situation with Ted or to answer what he'd asked me about starting over, and Lucas was gone on some kind of emergency business. And even though I was worried, I didn't have the mental space to think about him. I was angry and hurt and heartbroken, but I didn't have time for any of that. I was too busy trying to get more information from Felix, who had been responding to the stream of texts that I'd been sending since the day before. He still hadn't managed to overrule the no-fly zone Sadie had enacted for me. But I had a passport now, and a very helpful concierge named Ken.

"I've got you booked on the first outbound flight from St. Maarten to Miami to Chattanooga. You should be there around eight or so. Someone will meet you at arrivals and drive you home," he said. The gates to Paradise opened and Ken eased the Jeep out onto the main road.

"Thank you. For everything. I mean it . . . You are a really good person. I'm glad I met you."

We passed the rest of the ride to the tiny airport in silence, neither of us knowing what to say. I stared out the open window at the sea, the green hills that rolled down to the coast, at this beautiful place I was just starting to know. But now I was leaving. Before long, the open clearing where the airfield was marked with strips of runway loomed ahead of us. Ken slowed the truck and parked on the side of the road. "You don't want to talk to him before you go?" he asked. "I could call him."

I shook my head slowly. "What would I say?"

He examined me. Then he shook his head. "I don't know. Elisabet always said I was an idiot when it came to matters of the heart. She's probably right. She usually is. Me? Well, it wouldn't be the first time I've read something wrong."

"I only care about Sadie. That's it."

He nodded slowly. He looked like he was about to say something more, but instead he only said, "Makes sense."

"I know what you're thinking . . . you probably were under the mistaken impression that we were falling for each other or something, but we're not. And when I say that, you probably want to tell me that even so, I shouldn't leave things like this, but I didn't leave. He did. I mean, he was never really here in the first place, right? He was just an actor in a plan. I was another deal to him."

Ken's gaze was fixed on something in the distance beyond the windshield. "Right. I got it."

I squinted to try and see what he was so interested in. It was just an ordinary day. Sun-drenched and warm. Cloud-dotted blue sky. A deep rocky-gray coast that I'd grown to love. Brilliant green grass like in the pictures I'd seen of Ireland. The airport with the famously short runway. Ahead of us, a small plane was coming in for a landing. We both watched as it closed the distance between the sky and the ground, touched down, did a gentle turn before the end of the runway, and came to a stop about twenty yards in front of us. The propeller stopped, and then the door opened, releasing a set of stairs. Ken cut the Jeep's engine. He turned back to me.

"Are you sure about everything you just said?"

Before I could answer, Ken was out of the truck, jogging across the field toward the plane. I sat in the passenger seat, seat belt still fastened, transfixed, as Lucas emerged from the doorway of the airplane with my sister in his arms. I ripped my seat belt off and flung the car door open. I couldn't feel my legs beneath me as I sprinted through the grass. My tears turned the scene to a Monet, dots of paint, washes of color, my sunshine's arms wrapped around Lucas's neck. Behind them, Felix carried bags, Sadie's sticker-covered suitcase, and a small oxygen tank.

I pressed my forehead against hers when I reached her. "Sadie," I said. "Sadie."

She smiled and nodded. "The one and only," she said in a raw voice. "You're here."

"You know I love a dramatic entrance."

"This qualifies." I smoothed my hand over her forehead. "You should have told me," I said.

"I know."

"I could've helped, could've taken care of you. You don't have to do this by yourself."

"I know that too. But I wasn't alone. I have Felix." She turned to wink at him. How had I never noticed the love there? It was all over their faces, like one-hundred-point font. "I just wanted to take care of you for once, while I still could. You had to give me that."

Lucas cleared his throat. "Ken will take you all back to the resort in the Jeep. I need to get the plane back to the hangar."

"What about you?" I asked. I still couldn't meet his eyes.

"It's Saba," he said. "I'll catch a ride with someone."

Thank you, Sadie mouthed. Lucas set her into the back seat beside me. Then he gave her the slightest of bows and walked away. I reached over and buckled her seat belt.

"He is not what I was expecting at all," Sadie said when he was out of earshot. "I didn't realize I was conspiring with an Asian su-permodel when I made this plan. I mean, he was kind of brooding on the plane, like a little bit Mr. Darcy–esque; not that I'm com-plaining. Maybe I should have left you at home and come on this adventure on my own."

"Hey!" Felix called over his shoulder from the passenger seat.

"Seriously, Sades," I said, "you're talking about how hot Lucas is at a time like this?"

"You're right, Marin. If there's anything good about being sick, other than everyone has to do what you want, it's that it definitely puts things into perspective, helps you see what's really important. And hot Lucas is very important. I mean, wow, he's *important*."

"You are shameless," I told her.

She turned to Felix. "You know, I should have done more research. A Google search, something. I went to all the trouble to have Ted deliver the passport. I had no idea that the perfect guy for you was already in the picture. Go figure."

"I thought you were Team Ted, though," he said.

"Not completely. The jury is still out on good old Teddy. But I feel like you're missing the fact that Lucas is not only accommodating and beautiful but he's a *pilot*," Sadie said. "He literally flew us here."

"You make a good point. I may have been converted to Team Lucas myself," Felix said.

"I hate to interrupt," I said. "But don't you think we have more meaningful things to talk about?"

Sadie waggled her eyebrows at me. "Definitely," she said. "It means nothing what we think. The real question is, which team are you on, Mar? Or are you playing both sides? Please tell me you're playing both sides."

Sadie was still Sadie. Still radiant, despite the dark hollows in her cheeks and beneath her eyes. I scooted closer, and she rested her head on my shoulder.

Ken took The Road slowly, trying to make the sharp turns into gentle curves. I took several minutes to work up the courage to speak. "How bad is it, Sadie?"

She closed her eyes for a moment, like a child making a birthday wish, but instead of blowing out the candles, she sighed. "I've had better days. And I've had more of them." Her eyes filled with tears, but she smiled through them. Without missing a beat, she added, "God, this place really is paradise. Tsai wasn't kidding about that."

Forty-Two

KEN AND TWO OF the female staff helped Sadie get settled into the master bedroom in my villa. She swore she didn't want it, but it was more open and offered more space for Felix and all of her medical equipment.

I cuddled with her in bed for a long time and then she sent me out. A doctor who taught at the medical school on the island was coming out to check on her medications and make sure she had everything she needed before a nurse took over her routine care. Lucas had arranged everything.

"I'll stay," I said. "I want to hear what the doctor has to say."

"No, you don't," Sadie said. "Go get some breakfast and come back in a little while. We can spend the whole day together."

"Sadie . . ."

She cast a look at Felix, who stepped over. "It's not that kind of visit, Marin, not the kind with news."

"Can you get me some guava jelly?" Sadie asked. "Ken told me someone he knows makes some that is really good."

I gave in. "If you want guava jelly, my dear, I will get you guava jelly."

I looked through my clothes and sighed. The only clean thing was the dress that Lucas had bought me.

"I brought some of your things," Sadie said. "Felix took care of it, so who knows what he packed, but they're clean . . . and they aren't bedazzled."

I turned to her. "The suitcase was you?"

She grinned. "Of course. I am truly a master. I was buying some weed from Jeremy Conklin, you know, the pizza delivery guy from Rubino's, and I overheard his older sister talking about a trip to St. Maarten. I dropped the C word and she was only too happy to help ensure you had a more appropriate tropical wardrobe. Apparently, she covets Banana Republic, so she's enjoying the clothes you meant to bring on the trip."

"Sadie."

"The underwear is new. In case you were worried."

I put on a calf-length seersucker sundress that I hadn't worn in years and pulled my hair back into a tight ponytail. Felix hadn't done too badly, I thought as I checked myself in the mirror.

"Don't forget," Sadie said.

"I know, guava jelly and lots of presents," I said, and kissed her on the forehead. Then I set off to locate Ken.

I found him by the pool, sleeping beneath a towel and an oversize pair of Armani sunglasses. He jumped when I tapped his shoulder. "Elisabet," he groaned.

"You should just apologize," I said. "Guava jelly?"

"Huh?"

"Where do I get the special guava jelly? Sadie wants some."

"Oh, there's a place on the Windwardside. Bingo's market. They sell all homemade stuff there. You want the kind with the red-and-white cap." He folded his arms across his chest. "Do you need a ride?"

I shook my head. "I think I'll walk over."

"It's kind of a hike," he said, stifling a yawn. "Lucas was going to head that way soon. I know he'd take you."

I couldn't believe Lucas was up after he'd flown to Tennessee and straight back without sleeping. Ken hadn't done that and he was barely conscious.

"My sister brought my shoes," I said.

"Okay."

"If I get tired, I can always hitch, right?"

"Who *are* you?" Ken smiled sleepily at me and then pulled the towel back up over his head.

I slung my purse over my shoulder and started toward the gates. Guests were starting to head toward the pool, and a small tour bus with linen-clad passengers was heading toward Ladder Bay and Mount Scenery. As I walked, I took in the sights. The birds were singing, soaring against the blue sky into the cloud forest that rose up beside me. The ocean shimmered in the distance below. I stopped at one vista and looked down at the beach. It was still early, a few boats bobbed in the water, but the stony shore was deserted. There was something glinting in the sun down below. I stepped carefully down the embankment toward the beach to get a closer look. There were the sandals I'd thrown the other night, wedged between two black boulders and tangled with kelp. I ran my finger over the silver straps but decided to leave them there. I didn't need strappy sandals anymore, and those had hurt my feet.

After about half an hour on the narrow road, I began to regret my pride and found myself wishing that I had asked Ken to arrange a ride to the Windwardside of the island for me. The only time I'd ever ridden with a stranger was when Lucas was with me, and everyone knew him. Except maybe me. At the rate I was going, I'd be gone all day. I stopped and sat on a large rock beside the road and stuck out my thumb. Ten minutes passed and not one car went by. I kept looking in the direction of the resort, half expecting to see the Jeep with Lucas behind the wheel. I didn't know if I was hoping I would or dreading it. Finally, a small green pickup truck passed me. The driver slowed the vehicle and pulled off to the edge. I jogged to the driver's side.

"Thanks for stopping," I said.

A familiar face peered back at me. "Where you headed, Marin?" Laurentina asked.

It turned out that Laurentina was also headed over to Wind-wardside with a fresh delivery of table linens and blouses for a shop that carried her lace. I slid onto the bench seat on the passenger side and we took off.

"Thank you for dinner the other night. I hope I didn't get too rowdy," I said.

"Why do you say that?"

"I think Lucas and I both overindulged in the rum," I said.

"Oh, you sure did. But Ronaldo and I enjoyed it. That's how it is when you've been married a long time like us. You get a kick out of watching people drink too much and fall in love."

"Falling maybe," I said. "But not love."

Laurentina took her eyes off the road to give me a look. "Mm-hmm."

"Really." I picked at a loose thread on the hem of my skirt. "What do you know about guava jelly?" I asked.

"I don't know much about guava jelly, but I do know what it looks like when two people like each other."

"Let's not talk about it."

We were quiet for what seemed like a few extraordinarily long seconds. I thought about holding my breath.

"You're in the market for guava jelly, huh? You know about the kind with the red-and-white lid?"

"I've heard that's the one I should be looking for."

"You like guava?"

"It's for my sister," I said. "She just got here."

"How come she's not shopping for jelly with you? I'd like to meet this sister of yours."

I pinched the thread between my fingers and yanked. "She's sick."

Laurentina pulled the truck off the road and into a small gravel parking lot in front of a barbecue restaurant that, according to the sign, didn't open until five p.m. She turned to me. "What do you mean, sick? You're saying she's not-up-for-visitors sick?"

I nodded.

"You didn't mention that at dinner. Isn't that kind of a big thing to leave out?"

It was. A huge error of omission. The kind of omission that made dream-filled houses crumble to the ground and wash away with the rising tide. "I didn't know then," I said. My mouth turned sour. For a moment, I thought I might vomit in Laurentina's truck. I flung the door open and staggered out.

Laurentina was out of the truck and next to me in an instant. She rubbed her hand over my back, the way she'd soothed baby Jonathan when he'd cried before bedtime. "Okay," she said. "Let it out."

In between breaths, I said, "Lucas knew. This whole time, he knew. He knew she was dying. He knew that I had no idea. He knew that I was starting to like him and that he was just playing along. And he kept all of it from me." I turned to her. "What am I supposed to do? Tell me. What do you think I should do?"

"Oh, baby," she said. "What makes you think any of us knows what the hell we're supposed to do? Most of the time, I don't have a clue. None of us do, not even Lucas Tsai—for all the credit you give him in that department. We're all just trying to do our best with what we've got."

"But I have to do something. I can't let this just happen. Sadie is my little sister. We only have each other in this world. It's *my* job to take care of her."

"I thought your sister was grown. You don't have to take care of her. Just be there for her, that's what people really need mostly, except for babies. You know my Jonathan needs his milk. So, get her guava jelly. Listen to her. Hold on to her hand when she's in pain."

When Laurentina said it like that, it seemed so simple. "Let's get back in the truck," she said. "I just need to drop off this load of lace and then I can help you find the jelly and take you back to the resort."

We drove a few more miles down the road and then parked in front of a small set of shops. I helped her carry a large woven bag filled with folded lace into a boutique. An older woman with white-blonde hair and a thick Dutch accent took the stacks of fabric. She unfolded an embroidered peasant blouse and held it up.

"Laurentina," she said, "you've outdone yourself. These are beautiful."

"Sadie would love that," I said. I pulled out my wallet. "I know you haven't put them out yet, but I'd like to buy one."

The woman wrapped the blouse in tissue paper and took my money. Afterward, Laurentina took me to the market next door, where they had shelves of guava jelly and other local food. I didn't know what Sadie would want to eat now. I picked a few items I thought she might like—some postcards, a coconut oil lip balm, some kind of salve that came in a little tin, the jelly with the red-and-white lid, and a piece of driftwood that was painted with the intricate pattern of monarch's wings. We packed them in the back of the truck next to the bag with the shirt Laurentina had made and headed back to the resort.

"When will you leave Saba?"

I shook my head. "I don't know . . . Used to be that I couldn't wait to get out of here. But it burrowed under my skin. I'm different here, I feel it. And now that Sadie's here, I can't leave. I won't leave until she's ready to."

Laurentina nodded. "This place does something to people. I think it's good that you can share it with your sister," she said. She didn't say what we were both thinking. That it was good that I could share it with Sadie while she was still with me.

Forty-Three

WHEN I GOT BACK to the villa, Sadie and Felix were both asleep on the loveseat. She was curled up, her head on his thigh. I paused and got out my phone to take a picture of the perfect quiet moment. He had a book falling out of one hand. I gently transferred the book, a worn copy of Sadie's favorite, *Einstein's Dreams*, to the side table. That book had been everywhere with her, a constant companion—like Felix. He hadn't shaved, and his scruff was coming in like a dark, chaotic shadow, just like the ones under his eyes. I'd never really looked at him before. We'd met a few times, but I hadn't seen him. Not like this.

There was a time after Mom died when Sadie and I slept in Mom's bed. I think we needed to know the other one was there. She always curled up, knees to chest, like now. And I would run my fingers through her soft curls until I fell asleep. Somehow I knew that as long as we were together, everything would be okay.

Would everything be okay? I wondered. I couldn't see how it was possible. And yet . . . we were still here.

Sadie sighed in her sleep and Felix shifted his hand to her back. They both seemed so vulnerable, so intimate, and I found myself feeling like an intruder on some moment I wasn't meant to witness. I thought about going to the main house to sit in the garden or check out the pool, but I was too afraid to run into Lucas, or even Ted. Had I ever fallen asleep on him like that, with him reading to me and stroking my back? I couldn't remember.

I stepped out onto the patio and headed toward the water to sit. Sadie had always said that there was something healing about the ocean. Then again, Sadie also believed that neon-yellow turmeric paste would get rid of all diseases, bad moods, and evil spirits, and that sleeping with a book under your pillow could substitute for studying—mental osmosis, she called it. The day had turned gray. I couldn't see Mount Scenery rising up behind me, but I could feel its presence, likely covered in thick clouds of fog. The gentle warm breeze from earlier had turned stiff. My skin prickled with goose bumps and I had to wrap my arms around my knees for warmth. It didn't help that the rock I chose to sit on was slightly damp.

I'm not sure how long I sat there. If I measured my time in pages, I'd filled eight of the lined pages of the leather book Lucas had given me with scrawled notes from my conversation the other night with Laurentina about how she got into lace making, the history of lace on Saba, her own history. They were just phrases, strings of words from my memory, but I could see them melding together into the promise of something. My hand cramped, but I kept writing. When I finally stopped to look up from my work, the horizon was changing behind the clouds. Turning copper and salmon-colored, the sky looked beautiful and sad. The sea was dark gray and covered with whitecaps. The tide had come in and soaked the toes of my sneakers. Surely Sadie and Felix were up from their nap now.

I heard voices from the jungle path. Straining to hear over the sounds of the birds that chattered back and forth among the bushes, I made out Sadie's voice and Felix . . . no, that wasn't Felix. I drew closer, making sure to stay out of sight on the side of the villa. A few feet away from me, Lucas and Sadie were sitting next to each other on the patio.

"I didn't manage the entire list. I'm sorry. I couldn't find a dictator on such short notice."

"No worries."

"You've really met a dictator? Who was it? Trump?"

"Oh, God no," Sadie said. "Paul Kagame. A man of many contradictions. He's done many things to improve Rwanda and yet he's one of the most repressive leaders in the world."

"You are just as Marin described you," Lucas said. "I'm suddenly feeling more than a little inadequate."

From my spot on the side of the villa, I could see Sadie smile. "Please. I could have kept a running list of all the things that my sister doesn't handle well . . . danger, climbing shit, mystery foods, you know, basically all the fun stuff. But you got her to climb a mountain, and eat soursop—I haven't even had that one—and wear a wet suit. Those are miraculous feats."

"She did them. I just provided the transport."

"You're not giving yourself enough credit. Honestly, I'm impressed. Your dad told me that you were amazing, but I figured that was just parental pride talking."

Lucas leaned back a little. He did that thing, the one he did when he was caught off guard, smoothing his hands back through his hair. Two days ago, he'd done that after I'd kissed him so hard I'd sent us tumbling down an embankment.

"You're surprised?" she said. "You must know he thought the world of you."

"I know he wanted me to be happy. I hoped that I made him proud. Things are different now, I think, with families. Where I'm from it's not really the norm to tell your children that you love them. Unlike you Americans who go around telling everybody. He showed it, in his way, but he was a man of few words."

"Not with me." She took a sip of water. "Maybe he was saying all the words he'd been saving? It just occurred to me that maybe that's what I was doing with the letters. You think?" she said. "He bragged about you to everyone at the clinic. He was so proud of you, of how much you had accomplished. He might not have told you, but I'm positive he loved you very much. We talked all the time . . . about how he regretted having to leave so much on your shoulders but knew he could entrust you with it all and it would be fine. He spoke of how capable you were, how smart and good. When I decided to do something about Marin, I knew that you would be the right person to help me. I felt it."

"But I messed everything up. I didn't help her at all. I hurt her."

"*I* hurt her, Lucas. You didn't do anything wrong. You were keeping my secret and the promise you made to your dad to help me. I know it doesn't seem like this, but I swear on every picture I've ever taken, Marin isn't mad at you. She's angry with me; she feels like she can't be mad at me right now, so she's blaming you. That's just how it works. She'll get over it if you give her a chance to."

I opened my mouth to debate her. I was not mad at her. How could I be? I was mad at the world. I was mad at fate or God or whatever it was that felt it could just take everyone away from me on a whim. And I was mad at Lucas for breathing me to life just in time to rip me to pieces.

He said, "I don't know, Sadie. I think it's best if I step aside. I helped Marin have a few adventures, and anyway, you're here now. You're who she needs. I'm just an outsider."

"That isn't true. Seriously, you should talk to her. Don't leave things between the two of you like this."

Lucas shook his head. "There's no point in trying to explain. It wouldn't do any good. Besides, this was only ever going to be a temporary thing. The board won't wait for me forever. I'm going to have to go back to Taipei soon to handle the rest of the businesses."

"You're really pulling the work card?"

"It's my father's empire. I can't just abandon it."

"This place, you, your family—that's what was most important to him. No way would he want you running away from this for a board meeting. I think you know that." Sadie fixed him in her gaze. "I may have cancer in my brain, but I'm not stupid, Lucas. I can tell there's something between you and my sister."

"It's nothing serious," he said. I pressed myself against the wooden siding and let my head tip back. I squeezed my eyes shut. "Maybe it seemed that way. We did have some intense experiences together these past few days."

"Do you really buy that bullshit?" Sadie asked. "Because I don't."

"We hardly know each other. But from what I *do* know of your sister . . . even if there was something starting between us, she doesn't need me. She needs you. And now that you're together, it's only natural for me to get back to my other responsibilities. I have all the other hotels to manage and a new solar glass plant opening next month. I don't really have any time available for a romance. I'm sorry. And it doesn't matter anyway, right? Ted's back."

Sadie nodded slowly. "That's my fault too. When I asked you to get on that plane and look out for Marin, I didn't know you well enough to think that you would be such a good match for each other. And honestly, I thought maybe there could still be feelings between her and Ted. She never moved on after him. At the very least, I thought if they didn't get back together, Marin might get some closure. But you're right. I get it. I knew when I came up with this scheme that it wouldn't go on forever. Life goes on." With that, she turned her attention to the napkin on the table. A thread was coming loose and she grasped it between her fingers. "Mostly."

After a long stretch of silence, Sadie finally snapped off the tail of the loose thread. "You know, I'm actually not feeling that great. I think I'll head back to my room now."

Lucas stood up with her. "Are you all right?"

She stopped him with a pat on his forearm. "I'm just tired. Traveling took more out of me than I expected."

Felix appeared in the villa doorway. "Calm down, you," she said. "I can handle walking a couple of feet."

"Indulge me," Felix said, swooping in beside her. "Besides, if I carry you, I can look down your shirt."

"See why I love him?" Sadie said. She reached up and cupped his cheek in her hand.

Lucas smiled, but even from my hiding place I could see the sadness in his expression. "Well, if there's anything you need, don't hes—"

"I won't. You're on my speed dial now, Lucas Tsai." She turned to Felix and whispered, "It's your lucky day, manservant, because your mistress isn't wearing a bra."

They disappeared into the villa. I waited until Lucas had headed off in the other direction toward his own house before I walked across the patio toward the French doors.

"Marin," he said.

I dropped the notebook.

"I didn't mean to startle you," Lucas said. He stooped down and picked up the notebook. He turned it over in his hand and brushed the sand from the cover before handing it back to me. "I forgot my phone."

"Oh." I couldn't come up with anything else to say. I pressed the notebook to my chest, like armor.

He reached past me and picked up his phone from a metal side table. He tucked it into his jacket pocket. "Got it." He patted the pocket. "Well, ah, good night."

"Hey," I called after him. "Thank you for bringing Sadie here."

He nodded. "Of course. It was nothing." He put his hands in his pockets; he appeared to be studying something on the ground for a moment, contemplating his words before he spoke. "I am deeply sorry for how this turned out . . . I never expected . . ." I watched him extract one of his hands from his pocket and reach toward me. I stopped breathing. He was reaching for my hand, but then he paused and redirected the gesture back through his hair. He shook his head, confused.

I hadn't expected all this either. I could feel the tears threatening to spill. I turned away to hide them.

"Good night," he said.

I turned back to watch him walk away. He was moving slowly away from me. Beneath the book, a strange sensation bloomed in my chest. I tore my gaze from him. The porch light clicked on and Sadie and Felix came outside.

"Time for my medicine," she said. She extracted a blunt from the pocket of the romper she was wearing. "Ken got this for me this afternoon. Isn't it sexy?"

I forced a smile and nodded. "Super sexy, Sadie. If you could sleep with weed, we'd all want to be sleeping with that weed."

"Who said anything about sleeping with . . ." She craned her neck to look at Felix. "Is it just me, Feel, or did Marin make a sex joke?"

"I think it qualifies."

"Oh my God," Sadie said. "You slept with someone down here."

I looked away, which was a stupid move because Sadie and I both did that whenever we were busted. She'd perfected the look-away over the years. It was her tell. I hardly had anything to tell . . . until now. Sadie was looking at me like a hopped-up female version of Sherlock Holmes.

"Was it Teddy? Your ass from the past?" She turned to Felix. "See what I did there?"

"You're a wonder, that's for sure," he said.

Sadie was quiet for a moment and then she gasped. Felix and I both startled. But she was okay. Her eyes were wide and she pointed her finger at me. "Not Teddy. I'd bet a million dollars. I've got it. I mean, it makes perfect sense. He *was* acting like a dejected puppy! You guys did it."

"Who?"

"Do people still call it that—*did it*?" Felix asked.

I didn't say anything. Sadie held out the joint.

"Sorry, Felix, I think Marin needs this more than we do."

"I'm so confused. Is this like sister telepathy or something?"

"Ugh, men. So oblivious." She produced a lighter from her pocket and sparked the joint. She took a long pull and held it. Exhaling, she said, "I mean, Marin, I applaud you. He's super fly."

"You are so retro tonight," Felix said. "I'm freaking loving it. But I still don't know who the hell you are talking about."

Sadie passed Felix the joint. "'I wish my pants wore me like that'—your words. Does that ring any bells for you?"

Felix offered the weed to me. "You sly fox. You tapped Lucas Tsai. I always knew you had it in you. Didn't I say that, Sadie—"

"She had it in her. She *really* did." Sadie dissolved into giggles.

"I can't take her anywhere. But kudos to you . . ."

"You guys are the worst," I said. But they weren't. Sadie was still trying futilely to suppress her laughter at her own stupid double entendre and Felix was looking at her like his heart was going to burst out of his chest. They were the best. I'd never seen Sadie in love. I'd never seen her like this. She was so alive. And yet.

The pre-crying sting was starting in my nose. I was not going to ruin this moment, even if it was at my expense. I was going to laugh with Sadie and the love of her life. I was going to laugh like I wasn't going to lose her. Pretending to ignore Sadie's and Felix's shocked expressions, I took the joint from his hand and brought it to my lips.

"What did you *do* to her?" Felix said. "I think you broke your sister."

He was trying to be funny, I thought as I inhaled the smoke into my lungs, but he was absolutely right. I *was* broken.

At least my heart was.

Forty-Four

SADIE WOKE UP RARING to go. True to form, she had a top-five list of things she wanted to do on Saba. I wanted to call them bad ideas and Felix winced at some of them, but who were we kidding? We were her personal genies.

"Don't you want to rest in the hammock?" I asked. "The breeze is incredible."

"Zip-lining," she said. "I want to go zip-lining."

"I don't think that's the best—"

She made a face and I shut up. "Sounds like somebody is too scared. Doesn't Marin sound scared, Felix?"

From the other room, Felix said, "Petrified."

"I was thinking of you, actually. Wouldn't that be too much for your body right now?"

"So I'm supposed to just sit around? When have you ever known me to do that?"

She was right. Never. She might have been frail and weak, but Sadie was still Sadie. She couldn't just sit still.

"It's dangerous," I said.

"Maybe. But what a way to go, you know, compared to the other one." She reached out and squeezed my hand. "You know you can't say no to me. I'll make the face. Don't make me make the face, Marin."

I took a deep breath. "You win. I admit, I'm defeated. I never could say no to you; I'm not about to start now."

"Yay." She smiled. "Hey, Felix, we're going zip-lining. Can you help me get changed?"

Felix appeared in the doorway. His eyes were red, but he was grinning. "I would *love* nothing more than to take your clothes off."

"You're going to tell me about this at some point, right?" I asked.

"Every last dirty detail," she said, "but only as a trade."

"Huh?"

"Don't play dumb with me, Sis. Did you think I was going to let that little revelation go without a debrief? Besides, I'm so right. In this mangolicious morning light, I can see you've got *I slept with Lucas Tsai* written all over your neck."

Reflexively, I touched my neck. Felix passed by with a stack of clothes in his arms. They exchanged a look. I pulled my hand away. "That's crazy," I covered. "What does that even mean . . . written on my neck? Isn't the saying 'written all over your face'?"

"I think it's a very good thing that enormous hickey isn't on your face," Sadie said.

"I'm going to go now."

I closed the door behind me gently, waiting for the click. I heard Sadie's voice, muffled. "Get over here," she told Felix. It was the strangest thing to see her this happy, so at peace, in this situation. It was surreal. She had cancer. She had a boyfriend. All this new information, the good, the bad, the heart imploding, overwhelmed me. I had so much I wanted to say and so many questions that I needed answers to, but I wasn't about to get them now because we were going to attach ourselves to ropes and go careening down a mountain. The very thought of zip-lining; the word itself gave me goose bumps, but I'd done a lot of things that practically gave me palpitations in the last few days—scuba diving, mountain climbing, skinny-dipping, Sabaoke . . . other stuff, and I'd survived. I was maybe a little emotionally battered, but at the same time I somehow felt more like myself than I had in years. Sadie wanted us to go zip-lining, so the only acceptable response was "Where's the harness?"

I was sitting on the couch in my favorite pair of gray shorts and a striped boatneck T-shirt courtesy of Felix, when he and Sadie emerged from the bedroom. They both looked a little flushed. Felix helped Sadie over to the couch.

"I'll get your bag," he said, and disappeared back into the bedroom.

"Where's Lucas?" Sadie asked me.

I shrugged. "I haven't seen him."

"But you told him to come, right?" She leaned toward me.

"No . . . ," I admitted. "Ken can drive us."

"So there's not going to be a round two?"

I didn't answer.

"I want Lucas to come. For me," she said.

"I don—"

She put her hand out, palm up. "If you won't call him—"

"All right. I'll call him."

I picked up the phone and dialed his villa. The phone rang a few times before he answered.

"*Wéi?*"

"Lucas, hi."

"Marin. Is everything okay?"

"Oh, yeah, we're, um, all right. I just, well, Sadie wanted me to invite you to come zip-lining with us this morning."

"You're okay with that?"

"Of course."

"Then I'll come. Give me a few minutes to get changed."

I hung up and turned back to Sadie. "He'll be here soon. Satisfied?"

Sadie narrowed her eyes at me, but before she could answer, there was a knock on the door. "That was quick," I said, and headed over to open the door. I still hadn't talked to Lucas about what had happened, and I didn't want to. My heart beat faster as I twisted the doorknob. I wasn't ready to be stared down by those dark, knowing eyes of his or to see that little smile, the one with the small dimple in the left corner of his mouth. But I didn't have to, because Lucas wasn't at the door, Ted was. He was wearing the same old University of Tennessee baseball hat he'd worn when we were dating.

"Hey, Marin," he said.

"Hi."

"Sadie." He lifted his hand in a little wave.

"Hey, stranger," she said. "Don't just stand in the doorway. Get in here."

He took a seat in an armchair across from her. "So how's life been treating you, Teddy? You look the same as the last time I saw you. Hat and all," Sadie said.

"I told her about the passport," he said. "We don't have to pretend."

"Oops. I guess I was being a little bit of a schemer. I suppose I figured she was single, you were single. Why were you still single again?"

He shrugged. "Marin was a tough act to follow, I guess."

Sadie raised an eyebrow. "You can't just throw that out there and not follow up. C'mon, Teddy. I'm dying to hear more about how you never got over my sister."

There was a fraught silence. Ted looked at me and I shifted uncomfortably in my seat. Felix came out of the bedroom with a duffel bag. "You're all packed," he said. "Jeez, what happened in here? You guys look weird."

"They didn't appreciate my cancer humor."

Felix perched on the arm of the sofa next to Sadie and kissed her cheek. "Babe, how many times have I told you—no one appreciates your cancer humor except for me. I dig it."

"That's why I keep you around." She smiled.

"And here I was thinking you were after me for my fantastic ass."

"That too," she said.

"I heard this is where the zip-lining excursion was meeting," a voice said. My body tensed. Beside me, Ted's expression changed. Lucas had arrived.

Back in the States, there would have been questions and forms, medical warnings and liability waivers in order to zip-line, but not on Saba. Lucas drove us over narrow, winding roads around the edge of the island, and then at some unmarked point he turned the Jeep onto a dirt path that seemed to disappear into the vegetation. For several minutes, we proceeded slowly through the lower layer of the jungle. Giant glossy leaves slapped against the side of the vehicle, and Lucas steered carefully around rocks and trees in the Jeep's path. Finally, the plant life thinned out, and we emerged on top of a hill. I didn't see a sign or anything, like I expected with this kind of tourist attraction, but one thing I had learned in my short time on Saba was that my expectations were often defied. A man with short black hair and dark brown skin waved when he saw us. He was wearing a bright white shirt that matched his smile.

If the man had any reaction to our strange group, or about the fact that one of us was clearly sick and had to be carried on her boyfriend's back to the place where we would get our harnesses, he didn't show it. He slung the equipment over his shoulder and talked to Lucas while he led the way past a small cottage and up a short trail to the zip line.

"Is this okay?" I asked Lucas.

"Of course."

"I mean, is it safe? There's no one else here. It doesn't seem legit."

"This is Eviton, Laurentina's cousin. He'll take good care of you all."

"Who's going first?" Eviton asked. "I've got two lines, so two of you can go at the same time if you want."

"Me," Sadie said. "Marin, go with me?"

I looked at her and then made the mistake of following the cable down the hillside with my gaze.

"Felix and I can go first and catch the ladies at the bottom," Lucas suggested.

"Good idea," Felix agreed. "I should wait for Sadie at the bottom."

"Fine by me," Ted said. "I'll stay and help the girls get into their gear."

Lucas looked him over. "Eviton will do that. It has to be done a certain way. But you can go last. That suits you."

"That's settled, then," Sadie said.

Lucas came over to me. "I can take a picture of you and Sadie coming down the zip line if you want," he whispered. I looked at him and nodded. I hadn't thought of that. I wanted every picture of her, of us together, that I could get. "That would be perfect. Thank you."

Our fingers touched for an instant when he took the phone from my hand, but we both pulled our hands away.

I watched Eviton's hands as he adjusted the harnesses for Felix and Lucas and attached safety lines with giant metal carabiners. He gave each rigging a firm tug. He seemed thorough enough, and the fact that he was related to Laurentina was reassuring, but that didn't stop my heart from pounding. And it wasn't even my turn yet. I looked away.

Sadie tugged on my sleeve. "Aren't you going to watch?"

I shook my head. I couldn't bear watching Lucas jump off a cliff, dangling from a metal wire, and go careening through the air. I was being ridiculous. I knew this. After what he'd done, I should have shoved him off that cliff myself. He'd lied to me, over and over. He'd had sex with me under false pretenses. And, worst of all, I'd liked it. My stupid hand was still tingling where he'd touched it. I was an absolute idiot.

"Go!" Eviton shouted.

I waited for the whooshing sound to end, for Felix's hollering to stop, as I held my breath. "You can turn around now, you wussy," Sadie said.

"You ready?" Ted asked.

"Yup," I said. I stepped into the harness and he helped me pull it up. *I can't do this,* I thought, and squeezed my eyes shut. A carabiner clicked into place. "You can do this, Marin." His hand rested on the small of my back. I didn't want him to push me. I wanted to go on my own, when I was prepared, when I felt ready.

"Ted, don't," I said. "I'm not ready."

Then Sadie yelled, "No one's ever ready, Marin! You just do it anyway. GO!"

Ted's hands gripped my waist and then he pushed. Wind whipped at my face. Sadie was screaming, whooping with delight. I opened my eyes. We weren't far apart, maybe a couple of feet; I could see the sheer joy in her face. She let her head hang back and howled. We were picking up speed. Below me, the jungle gave way to rocks, and I could see the ocean shimmering in the distance. When I looked up, the sky was a brilliant blue. We were birds, soaring through the air, trilling at each other. I stared at Sadie. My beautiful bird.

The brake kicked in and I bounced a little at the end before Lucas grabbed me. I hadn't been this close to him since the night we'd spent together. He was very proper about the whole thing. He didn't look into my eyes, like I'd feared. He only touched the rigging. As soon as my feet were safely on the platform, he let go. On the other platform, Felix and Sadie were making out. Lucas looked away.

"What?" she said when she noticed me staring. "Adrenaline's an aphrodisiac. You guys know, right?"

Felix laughed. "You are so bad."

"Do you want to see the picture?" Lucas asked. I checked the screen. God, we looked so brilliantly happy—me and Sadie—flying through the air.

"Ooh, let me see," Sadie said. "Marin, we look like freaking majestic beasts. I love it!"

We did look like majestic beasts, Sadie and I. The sun filtering through the canopy had bathed us in light and I was beaming. Sadie was perfect. My heart was still pounding. "You're right, Sadie. This is pretty awesome . . . the picture, all of it."

Ted arrived at the platform then, gave an enthusiastic whoop. "Good call on the zip-linging, Sadie. That was a total rush. Who's up for another run?"

Sadie raised her hand, and we started back up. It took a little while to get to the top. The hill was steep and we tried to let Felix set the pace since he was carrying Sadie on his back.

When we got to the top, she said, "I'll go first. Babe, let's go together."

Felix sat down. I thought he needed to catch his breath, but he gently took my sister's wrist in his hand. He said something to her that I couldn't hear.

"It's not that high," she said.

"Just rest for a few minutes, okay, babe? The doctor warned you about doing too much."

"Fuck the doctor."

"I'm afraid I'm madly in love with the most phenomenal woman on earth, so I'll have to pass on Dr. Reed. I get the appeal though. He's smart and fit. Maybe I'll keep him on the bench." He was still holding on to her hand. *Just a little rest,* he mouthed.

She sagged a little bit, but she acquiesced, settling onto his lap. "Someone else go," Sadie said. "I've had enough excitement. We're taking a cuddle break." She'd paled in the last few minutes, I thought.

"Everything okay?" Lucas asked.

"Fine. Sadie's overdoing it, I think."

He nodded. "This must be a lot."

"Try telling her that. You won't get far. Sadie always does things her own way."

"I meant for you," he said.

I shrugged. "I'm fine."

"That's a lot of *fines*."

"Marin always did like to keep her cards close to her chest." Lucas and I both turned. Ted had spun his hat around so it was backward. "It's funny watching it from the outside. I mean, jeez, I was a jackass back then." He held his hands out in front of him. "No hard feelings, man. It took me a long time to realize that she was worth every bit of extra effort."

I thought Lucas would say something. People didn't talk to him like that. They revered him or treated him like family; they respected him. They did not challenge him. He put his hands in his pockets and gave a subtle nod. Then he walked away.

Ted took a step toward me; his lips started to move. I could feel the pull of Lucas, of my eyes wanting to follow him. A few feet behind him, Felix was holding a juice box for Sadie; she took small sips from the straw. Lucas had been right. This was hard. Too hard.

I stepped over to the platform and gave Eviton a nod. He hooked my harness into the rigging and spun the carabiner safely into place. Then I leapt off all on my own.

Forty-Five

WHEN WE GOT BACK to the villa, Sadie took a long nap. Felix and I sat outside while she slept, drinking cold beers and eating pizza that Ken brought by. We ate and drank in silence for a while. I was still trying to process everything that had happened.

"This is good pizza," Felix said. "Not exactly what I pictured eating when Sadie said we were going to the Caribbean, but it's good."

I set my napkin down. "I don't get it, Felix. How can you pretend everything is normal? I mean, you and Sadie act like you're on your honeymoon or something. She's sick."

Felix wiped some condensation off his beer with his thumb. "I'm aware of that," he said, his voice low. He looked up at me. "What should we be doing, Marin? Closing up shop?"

"I didn't mean—"

"Did you ever think that *this* is why she didn't tell you?"

I let his words sting for a moment. What could I say? She hadn't told me. But she'd said she didn't know how. Felix shook his head. "Sorry," he mumbled. He pressed his fist against his forehead. "I'm angry. It's not your fault; I shouldn't take it out on you. Jesus, she's only twenty-six. Twenty-six. We were supposed to have everything ahead of us. I didn't even know she wasn't feeling well. If I'd known, I would've made her go to the doctor sooner. Maybe . . . I don't know. Maybe it would have made a difference."

I squeezed my eyes shut.

"If I could go back, I'd change that. I'd pay more attention. But I wouldn't change *this*. None of it. I'm going to love her as much as I can as long as I can." He twisted his glass on the table. "And besides, who says this can't be our honeymoon?"

I nodded hard, swiping tears from my cheeks. I gave him a huge hug, dear Felix. He wasn't who I'd pictured for Sadie, but then again, I hadn't pictured her ever settling down with anyone.

"I have a warm-up suit that says *Just Married* on the ass in Swarovski crystals," I offered. "You guys can totally borrow it."

Sadie wandered out then. She stopped to lean against the doorway.

"Are you making a move on my man?" Sadie teased. "Jeez, Mar, a little skinny-dipping and you turn into a nympho."

Felix jumped out of his chair to help her, but she waved him off. She moved slowly toward the open chair near us.

"So for real, what were you guys talking about?" she asked.

"You," I said.

Felix was still standing. "You want something to drink?" he asked. "I saw some coconut water in the fridge."

She nodded.

When he'd gone, Sadie turned to me. "Thank you for today. I know it's not your thing."

"You're my thing," I said. She took my hand in hers. It was cold. "Besides," I said. "Maybe your little plan worked. I'm starting to realize that not all risk is bad. A little adventure can be a good thing."

"Just a little," she said.

I held my thumb and index finger close. "Just a bit."

"A smidgen." She smiled. "I know I haven't made things easy on you, Mar. I take chances and I don't listen. And then I fall, or get arrested, or come home from Peru sick as a dog."

"Was that when you knew?"

Sadie twisted her fingers together. "Felix had tried to cook guinea pig over a campfire . . . you know, it's considered a delicacy. Remember? You turned four shades of green when I told you—but that wasn't the reason I was so sick. It's funny. Lucas's dad loved that story. You probably can't imagine this, but it wasn't all doom and gloom and deep conversations there; we had quite a time talking about all the things we loved to eat that other people found gross. The live drunken shrimp and scorpions on a stick. The tuna eye. I think he especially liked freaking out the two food-snob Americans who were there." She looked thoughtful. "He wasn't just funny, but kind and generous. He was the best."

There was a time I'd thought those things about Lucas too. Now, I wasn't sure about him. I wasn't sure of anything anymore. My whole world had turned upside down. Sadie must've read my mind the way only she could, because she reached for my hand and gave it a weak squeeze. "When Lucas showed up in Tennessee, I knew I'd messed this all up. You have to know that I never wanted to hurt you, Sissy. This sucks. It's like no matter what I do, I'm going to hurt you. I just wanted to help you."

I sniffed. "You did, Sadie. You did help me."

"Don't be sad," she said. "I can handle this, the cancer, all of it, but I can't bear that. I hate it when you cry."

"I'm not." I looked up at the sky and blinked back my tears. Felix reappeared in the doorway with the coconut water.

"I think," he said, setting the drink in front of Sadie, "what your sister is trying to say is that she's overwhelmed with emotion about the proposal?"

"Huh?" said Sadie. "Did you guys smoke the rest of my weed while I was napping?"

Felix's gaze settled on the coconut water. It was perfectly normal. The little carton. The straw. Oh my God, the ring around the straw. There was a ring around the straw. Sadie must've seen it then too, because she gasped. She looked at Felix.

"We didn't smoke your weed, baby." He was getting down on

one knee. "Your sister was pointing out that you and I have been acting like we were on our honeymoon down here. And it got me thinking, why shouldn't we be on our honeymoon?"

He reached out and took Sadie's hand.

"Sadie, you and I have traveled the world together. We've seen each other at our best, and our worst."

A tear slid down Sadie's cheek.

"We've seen amazingly beautiful things, faced terrifying things, and at the end of the day, I wouldn't want to go anywhere or do any of those things with anyone but you. You are the bravest, most brilliant, talented, funny, caring, crazy person I've ever met. No other photographer or person holds a candle to you."

Sadie was full-on crying now. I was a wreck. Felix's eyes were full of tears, but he was hanging in there. He said, "Working with you, whether it's carrying your gear or cooking your food, has been the greatest honor of my life. And so, I was wondering if you could do me one more honor. If you'll have me, I'd love to be your husband. I'd love to say that I am yours. Sadie, will you marry me?"

I looked at Sadie. She was staring at Felix. She glanced down at the coconut water. He reached out and slid the ring off the straw. "I've had this for a while," he said.

"How long?"

"Since K. But then you got sick and I thought . . . I don't know what I thought."

She cupped his face in her hands. "Felix Gabriel Hernandez, you are a dumbass . . . You're my dumbass though."

"Does that mean—"

"Yes," Sadie said. "Since we're already here, I guess, why not?"

She stuck out her hand and he slid the ring on. It was a little loose on her finger, but she closed her hand into a fist and held it to her heart. He wrapped his arms around her.

I brushed a rogue tear away from my face. "I'll call Ken and have someone send over champagne."

As I walked toward the villa, I heard Sadie say, "I'm only kidding, Feel. This was my last dream. You."

I stepped inside and picked up the phone and dialed the front desk. Tears were flowing freely now and I was in the middle of a sniff when the phone stopped ringing.

"Concierge."

"Ken, it's Marin."

"Ken is out. This is Lucas."

I should've recognized his voice. I just didn't expect that the hotel owner would be working the front desk of his own hotel. "Isn't that a little below your pay grade?" I said, trying to cover my shock.

"He had a date, and Marlena, our other concierge, teaches choir on Wednesdays, so it's me. How can I help?"

The businesslike tone stung a little.

"Oh, I was hoping to get some champagne delivered."

"Sure. I'll have someone bring it over."

I deflated. He hadn't even asked what we were celebrating.

"Sadie and Felix just got engaged. So, um, that sort of leads to my next question. Do you guys do impromptu weddings at Paradise Resort?"

Forty-Six

LUCAS CAME IN THE morning with breakfast for us and Laurentina, who'd come to measure Sadie for her wedding dress. The villa was going to be wedding-planning central for the next few days at least. Felix and Sadie and I had stayed up the evening before, drinking the complimentary champagne Lucas had sent over and talking about what they wanted for their wedding. No one said it, but we were all thinking that time was of the essence.

Sadie wanted a dress. Beautiful, white, nontraditional, the only one of its kind. Something uniquely Saban. She wanted steel drums and gardenias and to send off those paper lanterns with candles inside. I rattled these requests off to Lucas, thinking that he might not be able to satisfy them all on such short notice, but he simply took notes, quick, beautiful notes that I couldn't read, and nodded along. Asking Laurentina to make a lace dress for Sadie had been my idea.

I greeted Lucas at the door. "Sadie's still sleeping. Come on in though."

Lucas set the food basket on the table. "Call Ken and someone will come pick this up when you're finished. I need to make some calls about the flowers," Lucas said, turning toward the door.

"I can ask her for something else," I said. "Sadie's always been flexible."

He shook his head. "I'll find them."

I followed him out. "Thank you for all this." I crossed my arms across my chest.

"It's nothing," he said. His hand went to his hair.

"We haven't really talked," I said.

"Don't worry about it," he said. "You don't owe me conversation."

"But I want to—"

Felix poked his head out the door. "Hey, I thought I heard you, Lucas. Can someone take me into town later? Sadie wants me to wear something special, so she's sending me shopping."

"I can take you, or Ken, probably. He should be in any time now."

"That's right," I said. "He had a date last night."

"Elisabet," Lucas said. "I guess he did realize what he was missing."

"That's good."

We'd almost slipped back into that rhythm, the easy conversations from before things had split open, but he was already stepping back.

"Call me when you're ready to go, Felix," Lucas said. He turned and headed back to the jungle path.

When Lucas was totally out of sight, Felix gave me a look. "You're really going to leave it like that?" he said.

"I tried."

"If Sadie saw your version of 'trying,' she'd kick your ass."

"Good thing she's still sleeping, then."

He shook his head. "You're not completely off the hook. She's awake. She's having a chat with your friend Laurentina over eggs Benedict as we speak."

"Since when does Sadie like eggs?"

Felix's hand flexed on the door. "They're easy to swallow. And she really needs the calories."

And there it was, just like that, the reminder of the terrible truth. We'd been so caught up in proposals and dresses and island challenges that we'd almost forgotten. And maybe that was the point. Were we all just wrapping something awful and heartbreaking in white satin?

Felix went back inside. Through the open door, I heard him greet Sadie, asking what he'd missed. She sent him away so he wouldn't know the dress details. He passed by me a few moments later with a croissant in his hand.

"Keep an eye on her, will you?" he asked me. "She takes her steroid as soon as she's eaten. It's in the pill sorter on the dresser. The other one is in the bottle with the red cap. You shouldn't need it."

Felix had filled me in on all of Sadie's meds when they arrived. Steroids to keep the swelling in her brain down. Anti-seizure medication in case of emergency. Pain medication. I hadn't wanted to look at them, the pill sorter, the orange bottles, the one with the red cap—they were tangible reminders of just how sick my sister was. I hoped we wouldn't need them today. Today had to be all about white satin and lace.

I joined Laurentina and my sister at the table. Sadie was spooning tiny bites of egg into her mouth. Her hands trembled a little, causing her to lose the morsel more than once. I resisted the urge to help feed her. Laurentina was sketching on a sheet of paper while she asked Sadie questions. What kind of shape did she like best for dresses? Did she want straps? How fancy did she want the dress to be? She'd brought some samples of some of her different lace embroidery patterns.

Sadie flipped through them slowly. Now and then she'd lose focus. "What's that bird?" she asked.

"What bird, Sadie?" I asked.

"The colorful one. It was sitting on the back of the chair."

"If it was multicolored it was probably a rainbow macaw, we have some around here. Not as many as before, but some."

"I want birds in my lace," Sadie said.

"Can you do that?" I asked. It seemed like an impossible task given the time frame we were going for.

Laurentina looked at the sketch she'd been making, an empire-waisted gown with a princess neckline and a lace overlay. She didn't say anything, but she drew tiny birds, wings outstretched on the lace. When she'd finished, she held it up. "How's this?" she said.

I stared at the sketch and then I watched Sadie. She set her spoon down and ran a finger over the pencil lines. "That's it," she said. "That's exactly the dress I dreamed of."

I glanced at Sadie's plate. It looked as if she hadn't eaten at all. Lucas had included some fresh-pressed juices in glass bottles with straws. "Want a smoothie?" I asked her.

"I'm not that hungry," she said. "Maybe later."

"Could I take your measurements now?" Laurentina asked. "Then I can get started right away. Lucas said you're hoping to have the wedding soon."

Sadie slowly rose out of her chair. She had to use her hands on the table to push herself to a standing position. I wanted to help her, but I knew better. Laurentina worked quickly, moving the tape measure about Sadie's frail body with deft and careful fingers. I wrote the numbers down for her on the sketch.

"If it's okay, I want to ask my friend Esmeralda to help me," Laurentina said when she'd finished. "She's a very gifted seamstress. She can make the bodice and I'll do the lace. Together we can be done faster. Every bride is impatient. I remember I was . . . I couldn't wait to be with Ronaldo. I wanted to run down the aisle."

We smiled at her. "Of course, whatever you need to do is fine," I told her, walking her to the door. "Please let me know how much to pay you both."

She put her hand on mine. "Keep your money. This is my gift to my new friend. I will make your sister a beautiful dress."

"Everyone is being so wonderful, I don't know what to say."

"Say nothing. This is simply our way."

"What is?" I asked, hoping for Laurentina to give me some sort of sage advice, the kind someone who had three children a husband and practiced a historic art might give. She wasn't much older than me, but she was the only mother I knew.

"We help people who need it. That's it. Nothing more than that."

I considered this for a moment. From the moment I'd set foot on Saba, everyone I met had been so helpful, so generous. Offering rides, food, conversation, a sort of easy kindness that I hadn't experienced at home. Sure, people in Tennessee were nice, friendly. But this was different. Here, they made a strange woman stranded on a forced holiday feel like family. And maybe that was the mark of a truly special place. I could understand why Sadie had called it paradise. It was.

"I'll bring the dress as soon as it's ready," Laurentina said.

I nodded. "Thank you."

From the open doorway, I turned to look back at Sadie, who had curled up on the couch, her head resting on one arm. She'd gotten so small, she reminded me of when we were little girls. Sadie would go so hard on all of her climbing and troublemaking that at night she'd crash on our overstuffed sofa, always like this, her head on her outstretched arm, while we watched reruns of *Who's the Boss?* During the day Sadie liked to wear our mother's rabbit fur stole—the white one she'd worn to prom back when it wasn't the worst thing ever to wear fur—and a pair of neon-green sunglasses with gold lenses and pretend she was Mona. Mona always made Mom laugh. It had never occurred to me that was the whole reason Sadie played Mona so much when Mom would come home . . . even after she'd lost interest in *Who's the Boss?* and couldn't stand the sight of that fur. She saw the pain Mom brought home with her, the shadow of the bad things she'd seen on assignment, the fear that nipped at her heels even in the safety of our own home, the regret that she'd leave us again soon, sadness over what she'd missed—the plays, my first period, Sadie's chipped tooth, my Graywolf prize. Even then, Sadie had wanted to help. She might as well have been from Saba. She was wasting away, and instead of taking care of herself, she was trying to help me. Some people were like that—helpers. They put other people before themselves, took risks to help people, did the dangerous things, the hard things, just to help. Like Mom. Like Sadie. She'd done all this—the trip, the bag, sending Ted, even getting Lucas involved, just to help me. Lucas. I thought back to the pained look on his face when I'd found the letters. Maybe helping was all Lucas had been trying to do too.

I closed the door behind me gently, taking care not to make a sound. Then I sat next to Sadie on the couch and smoothed what was left of her hair. When we were little, Mom used to do this at bedtime every night. It was all I had to give.

"You did this that day," Sadie said.

"I thought you were asleep," I said. I didn't have to ask the day she meant. It was the one we'd learned we'd lost our mother. Another day that turned our world upside down. A day you don't get over.

"Even all these years later," Sadie said, "I get this weird feeling, like a black box deep inside me lifts open for a second and all the missing Mom, that pain, just leaks out—it hurts so much I can't breathe."

I squeezed my eyes shut.

"There's something I need to tell you, Sissy. When I remember the hard part, I don't remember the day that we found out. That's what you were thinking, right? No. I remember the day she left for that trip. She and I got up early for a climb at the Tennessee Wall. You were sleeping. You'd been up late every night for weeks working on that essay that Mom had promised she was going to send to some of her contacts as soon as she got back. You wanted it to be perfect." Sadie paused for a raspy breath. I held mine. "Mom and I did a quick ascent, making it to the top of Golden Locks before the sun set the sandstone on fire. I lay my head in her lap for a long time and she ran her fingers through my curls. Anyway, Mom and I got home too late. It was time for school and her flight, and you'd spent the morning eating cereal alone while I'd been with her in those glittering hills. I'm sorry. I'm so sorry about that."

"Sadie, don't do that. Please. We both had our ways of bonding with Mom. I never blamed you." I traced along the crown of her head.

"You know something, Sissy? I can't remember what Mom said that day at Golden Locks. Even now, I can't picture her face clearly. But I can sometimes feel her fingers sliding through my hair. You do it just the same, you know."

"I thought I'd be like her," I admitted. "That's as close as I got."

"You should be yourself. That's more than enough." I was about to say I wasn't so sure, but even now Sadie beat me to it. "You know, Sissy, Mom never sang when she smoothed my hair. She was wonderful and I miss her. But that part's just you, and I love it."

Forty-Seven

SOMETHING I HAVE LEARNED is this: there's only so much sadness your soul can handle at one time. We have a maximum. And we'd reached it, every single one of us in our bizarre little family. When we weren't putting together the paper lanterns or arranging the gardenias that Lucas had flown somewhere overnight to pick up, the dread crept in. We kept busy.

The wedding dress took four days. Four days in which Sadie stopped eating the food that the resort staff brought and Felix had to ply her with shakes that reminded me of the SlimFasts I'd drank in high school every spring. Sadie, on the other hand, had turned up her nose.

You realize this is the bullshit patriarchy that makes you think you need to lose weight to fit an unrealistic idealistic female body type that is perpetuated by the mass media, right? Step away from the liquid misogyny, Marin!

Now she took sips through a straw. Sometimes she choked. Her cheekbones became more pronounced. She slept more. Felix developed a crevasse between his brows. He paced while she slept. The day Laurentina showed up with the finished dress, Felix and I were debating whether we should call the doctor and have him come out.

"Her oncologist told us this would happen," Felix said.

"There must be something that they can do, though. Something to help her with the swallowing at least? Fluids or some kind of nutrition?"

"She didn't want that, Marin."

I sagged. I knew that. Sadie had made her wishes very clear. No nutrition. No fluids. No extraordinary measures. She wanted two things. To marry Felix surrounded by the scent of white gardenias and jasmine on a rocky black beach in a beautiful dress and to die in her own way in her own time.

"I know," I said. "It still feels awful."

"Believe me, kid," he said. "I'm feeling it too."

We hugged each other tight. "You know I'm older than you, right?" I said.

Behind us, someone knocked on the glass of the French door. I recognized Laurentina right away. She was wearing a beautiful yellow print dress and her arms were full with a white garment bag.

"It's done," she said.

I pulled in a relieved breath. "Thank goodness," I told her. "Let's go show Sadie."

Felix and I exchanged a look. I think he and I must've been thinking the same thing, because he said he was going to let Lucas know, and then he took the hanger where his linen pants and embroidered shirt had been hanging.

Sadie brightened when she saw Laurentina and what she was holding. She pushed herself up a little in bed. "Oh, you wonder," she said, "how'd you get it done so quickly?"

Laurentina unzipped the garment bag. "Island magic. Our secret," she said.

"My lips are sealed," Sadie said.

Laurentina handed the dress to me and I brought it over to Sadie. She spent a long time looking at it, running her fingertips over the pattern. It looked just like the picture, from the silky strapless bodice to the lace overlay.

"I'm afraid it may be too big," Sadie said. "I've lost my appetite."

Laurentina shook her head and held up her bag. "Nothing a needle and thread can't fix."

Sadie looked at me, her eyes brighter than they'd been in days. "Where's Felix?" she asked.

"I think he went to put on his wedding clothes," I told her.

She looked like she might shatter into tiny perfect pieces. "Really? Now?"

I nodded. "Let's get you in your dress."

Sadie sat up slowly. Then she put her arms in the air, like a child waiting for their mom to dress them. I had to squeeze my eyes shut, like that time I looked down at Ladder Bay. I could feel the rocks below waiting to shatter us both upon them. I let out a slow breath and opened my eyes.

Laurentina stepped forward. She lifted the dress up. "Here we go," she said. I carefully took hold of the other side. Once it was over her shoulders, Sadie grabbed on to my arm and slowly got to her feet. I tried not to think how cold her hand felt against my skin. Her own skin was mottled and pale. The half moons beneath her eyes were the same gray as the pebbles on the beach where Lucas and Ken were putting out the flowers. It took a great deal of thread to make the dress fit Sadie's shrunken body, but the lace overlay with its beautiful soaring birds of paradise softened her sharp edges. With the extra layers of fabric and some of my makeup, she almost looked like the old Sadie. We made ourselves forget.

"I can't believe I'm getting married before you," Sadie said, staring at our reflection in the mirror. She was still leaning on my arm. "You must be pissed."

"I'm livid."

"This could have been you and Teddy if you hadn't boinked Saba's finest."

"You are the worst."

"In your whole life, you'll never find someone worse than me."

Well, that did it. I started to cry. Ugly, face-squinching, body-shaking sobs. "Oh, Sissy, don't do that. Don't do that. Today is a happy day. And I really need this makeup to stay put so Felix doesn't think he's marrying a White Walker from *Game of Thrones*."

"Okay," I said, swiping at my face. "I've had my moment. I'm done now. Your makeup is safe. Let's get you hitched."

"Magnificent."

There was the little problem of getting to the ceremony site, since Sadie insisted on being traditional for the first time in her entire existence and said there was no way she was going to let Felix see her before the wedding.

"It's bad luck," she said.

"Um . . ." There was a little piece of me that was pretty certain Sadie was fucking with me. She wanted me to point out the irony so she could have a laugh. But mostly I just wanted to cry. Did luck get any worse than hers? It seemed to me that fate had been particularly cruel in Sadie's case. But if she felt that way, she'd never said.

Fortunately, Ken showed up with a dirt bike, which, from the look on Sadie's face when she climbed on, was the exact form of transportation she always envisioned for her wedding.

I pulled on the dress that I'd found in the same shop where I'd bought the blouse for Sadie the other day. Sadie had liked a white one, but I had objected. "Yes!" she'd said. "It's very Pippa Middleton."

"I guess that makes you Princess Kate?"

"Hey, if the crown fits . . ."

In the end, we found a pale peach dress that looked like something a ballerina would wear on a night out after a performance and Sadie said it was perfect for my winter coloring, whatever that meant. "Plus, your lackluster boobs look ah-maz-ing," she'd said.

I'd shushed her, but that had only egged her on. She raised the volume. "Does that thing have a corset? If not, there's some kind of magic happening there because . . . Unless there's something you want to tell me. Was your night with Mr. Tsai unusually productive?"

"Oh my God, Sadie. No," I'd said. "I'll get the dress, okay?"

I zipped up the dress and hightailed it out of the villa and down the path that led to Lucas's house. He'd offered his private beach for the ceremony and Felix and Sadie thought it was perfect. The path through the jungle was too rough for the dirt bike with Sadie on it, so I beat Ken and Sadie to the site. Felix was waiting by the water. He looked handsome. He'd shaved and slicked his hair back. I couldn't help but wonder if Lucas had been involved in the positive change in Felix's grooming. A single gardenia was pinned to the lapel of Felix's embroidered shirt. Lucas stood beside him. He was looking at the ground, waiting. *Any second now,* I thought, *he's going to look up and see me . . . At least my lackluster boobs look amazing.* Not that it mattered. It didn't. The rumbling sound of the dirt bike's engine in the cove announced Sadie before she arrived. Everyone's eyes fixed on the spot where she'd appear in a few moments, riding in like some kind of glorious badass. It was the perfect Sadie entrance. Ted came up beside me.

"You look incredible," he said, his voice barely a whisper. He brushed his lips over my cheek.

"Wait 'til you see Sadie," I said.

He nodded. "There she is," he said. "Wow."

Forty-Eight

LUCAS WORKED A MIRACLE on that beach. There was an altar made out of driftwood and different-colored strips of fabric and a non-denominational minister who looked a bit like Taye Diggs and sounded a lot like him. Somehow, Lucas had even found a steel drum band that knew how to play Bob Dylan's "Wedding Song." Sadie's gardenias and jasmine were everywhere, like perfect white clouds of seafoam on the dark rocky shoreline. Their scent filled the air. But none of it compared to my sister. She was thin and frail, but she was radiating light. It hurt a little to look at her—she was too beautiful, my bright sun—but I couldn't look away.

Sadie moved slowly along the beach, escorted by Ken. In one hand, she clasped a small bouquet of gardenias; the other she wrapped tightly around Ken's forearm. I turned to glance at Felix. He looked as if he'd forgotten how to breathe until she took his hand and stood in front of him.

"Hi," she said.

Felix smiled. "Wow."

The officiant stepped forward. "We're all here today to witness the marriage of two extraordinary people, Sadie and Felix. They are not halves of a whole, but two complete individuals who have chosen to twine their lives together. Like the island trees that twist around each other and grow along the rough shore, Sadie and Felix, you are independent, but stronger together. Through this union you will face joy and hardship, you will weather the sunshine and the storms, in unity and love, together."

I closed my eyes for a moment. Did the officiant know the storm they were already facing? Even together, they couldn't withstand it. I couldn't. And yet, Sadie was smiling up at Felix as if nothing were wrong. This was the happiest day of her life.

Sadie said, "Anyone who knows my family knows I'm not the writer here." Behind Felix, Lucas shook his head. Sadie continued. "But, Felix, you've convinced me that there's pretty much nothing I can't do as long as you're by my side, so I gave it a shot. When you lose your mom like I did, it can make you think that you can't hold on too tight—to people, to life—because it all might end without warning. I never wanted to love anyone or depend on anyone before you. I know I said I was hallucinating from seawater when I kissed you that first time in Portugal, but I wasn't; I'd wanted to kiss you for a while. I did it on purpose. Falling for you was completely by accident. You took care of me and made me truly happy, and I changed. You accept me in all my glory and at my absolute worst. You're always truthful, except when you're keeping my secrets and covering up my crimes. You let me make mistakes, and you even come along for the ride. You are tender and fierce and you always hold on to my hand for as long as I want. I know the minister isn't going to say the sickness and health, 'til death do us part thing because that would be a real downer, but we've already kept those promises. You've been there whenever I needed you, wherever I needed you. I'd say that I vow to love you for the rest of my life . . . but we all know that's nowhere near long enough. So I'll promise you forever instead." Her voice cracked a little at the end, while the rest of us broke into bits.

Felix had been holding it together pretty well, but he lost it in that moment. We all did. Both Lucas and Ken bowed their heads. Ken took a swipe at his eyes with the back of his hand. A sob racked

Felix's body, but he managed to hold his head high. Sadie reached up and wiped the tears from his cheeks. His whole jaw trembled as he put on a smile.

Ted leaned over to me and whispered, "This could be us, Mar. Can you see it?"

I had seen it, years ago. The old Marin and the old Ted. Was I that girl anymore? And truth be told, I'd also seen it five minutes earlier during one of those stolen glances at Lucas across the make-shift driftwood altar when I'd been thinking about how he'd flown a plane just to get the flowers my sister wanted. But I couldn't see any of that right now. This was a day about Sadie and Felix. Only them.

Felix said, "Sadie, you are a force. You're gravity. Before we even met, you pulled me to you. I never told you this, but I saw a photograph you took during art school. It was on display at the arts center in Memphis. You shared your soul in that picture. It was a bird taking off, something simple and pure, but I felt like crying when I saw it. I couldn't get it out of my head. So when you came to the magazine, I asked to be assigned to you. I thought it would be an honor to work with someone so talented. But then I met you and you were . . . you. Singular. And after that I always wanted to be right by your side, no matter what was happening. And I still do. The good, the bad, the ugly. Since I've known you, you've kept me grounded and you've made me fly. We've been all over the world together, seen such amazing things . . . and yet none of them are even in the same universe as you. You are funny and wild, kind and beautiful, you are open and powerful and sexy, and so much stronger than the rest of us little people. I can't believe my luck, that I get to love and support you each day. That yours is the face I fall asleep and wake up to. You are the wonder of my world." He cleared his throat. "I love you so much. You will always be everywhere and everything to me."

I planned to remember every word my sister and Felix said to each other, and at the same time, I heard nothing. I was transfixed by how happy they looked. Sadie had the kind of expression that seemed to shout her joy, like she was about to burst at any moment from sheer bliss. I was glad to gain a brother, another planet orbiting around Sadie, our bright sun. I was also too busy trying to hold back a monsoon of tears that threatened to flood my face any second.

Felix and Sadie clasped each other's hands and exchanged rings and laughed and cried, while the true sun sank lower and flamed red in the sky behind them. The moon rose and turned Sadie to silver. Lucas and Ken lit lamps and built a small bonfire. The steel drummers played, but Sadie only managed a gentle swaying to the rhythm, supported by the arms of her husband. Her husband. It all seemed like a fantasy. But then again, my whole world, everything I knew and didn't know, had turned upside down. Sadie had a husband. She was wearing a ring. It spun loose on her finger when I held her hand and helped her over to a seat at a small table set for her and Felix.

There was callaloo soup in hollowed-out coconuts, which Sadie ate slowly. "I can see why you like this so much," she told me. "It might be my new favorite thing." A waiter brought lobster and clams that had been cooked in a pit covered with hot stones on the beach. Felix fed Sadie a few tiny pieces. Elisabet had made a beautiful cake. It was two tiers, separated by a thin layer of Sadie's beloved guava jelly. The whole thing was covered in sunset-colored buttercream and giant tropical blooms made from sugar paste.

"Isn't she talented?" Ken whispered to me when Elisabet set the cake down in front of everyone. He wasn't looking at me when he said it, I noticed. Sadie and Felix's love was contagious, it seemed.

Felix and Sadie cut the cake together. She couldn't swallow it, but that didn't stop her from smearing most of her slice on Felix's face anyway. She even licked the frosting off while we all cheered her on.

Laurentina and Ronaldo stopped by to say good night.

"You are a stunning bride," Ronaldo said.

"It was one hundred percent the dress," Sadie said. "Thank you."

Laurentina shook her head. "No. It's you. The both of you. What you have together is special. Take care of it, and each other. We both wish you so much happiness."

Laurentina touched my cheek and smiled. "Good night, darling," she said. She turned to Ronaldo. "There's just something about weddings, isn't there? Makes you want to tell people you love them."

"We better not," Ronaldo said, giving her a squeeze. "If I recall, the last time we went to a wedding we ended up with Jonathon nine months later. Our house is already at capacity."

After the rest of the handful of guests had left, Lucas and Ken brought out the paper lanterns. Lucas handed one to me. I wanted to tell him just how grateful I was for everything he'd done to pull this wedding off, but I only managed a "Thanks," a quiet one at that. He nodded.

Our small group stood around with pens writing our wishes on the paper. Ted stood next to me, so I saw his: *A second chance.* I wrote *A miracle* on mine. I couldn't see anyone else's lantern well enough to make out what they'd written. I did wonder what Lucas's said, if he'd written something at all. He walked around, lighting the candles with a long match. We held on to them for a moment while the air inside them grew warm, and then they lifted out of our hands up into the star-speckled sky. I walked over to where Sadie was standing and wrapped my arms around her.

"What did your lantern say?" I asked her.

"That's for me to know and you to find out," she said.

"You're married," I said. I leaned the side of my head against hers.

"I'm married. Definitely another item to put on this list of things I did not see happening." She sighed. "He's pretty rad though, my Felix."

Felix was dancing to the steel drums alone. Some sort of horrific rump-shaking to a tune called "Big Bamboo," which Sadie had specifically requested. "Shake it, baby," Sadie called.

"Yup," I said, "He's totally rad."

So was she. They were a perfect match. Felix was right, Sadie was a force. She was gravity. Without her, we all might as well have been those wish lanterns floating away in the night sky. It was such a beautiful day, but I couldn't quiet the thought that kept spinning around in my mind: what would we do without her?

Forty-Nine

I STAYED ON THE beach for a long time after Felix took an exhausted Sadie home. He'd carried her down the pathway toward the villa like he was crossing some very long threshold. The steel drummers left too, taking some of the cake with them. I sat next to the small bonfire Lucas had made earlier, while he fed it with pieces of driftwood he found stuck between rocks on the beach. Ken disappeared and returned with a guitar.

"This reminds me of old times," Ted said.

"You guys knew each other in school?" Ken asked.

"Yeah, we dated in college," Ted said, before I had a chance to answer. "I even bought this girl a ring at one point."

Ken strummed his guitar. Next to him, Lucas perched on a rock. He leaned back, resting his weight on his hands, and looked up at the sky.

"I messed it up, though. I had this amazing opportunity to go to Nepal. And, well, I'm sure you both know how Marin is—she didn't want to go. I could've made it work. I should have. But I was young and dumb. I didn't realize it then, but being with her was the real opportunity of a lifetime."

I looked over at him. It wasn't an act. This was the Ted I remembered, the one I'd met in the library. The person, back then, who had made me feel whole for the first time since my mother had died. He really meant what he was saying. The flames reflected on his face turned his eyes a striking green. Lucas got up and found more wood to feed the fire. He set a large piece on top and sent red sparks into the inky sky. He hadn't said a word.

Ken ran out of songs and called it a night. "One last piece of cake for the road," he said, picking up a chunk in his hand. He took a bite. "God, it tastes like love and longing. Every time. How does she do that?"

"It's a mystery," Lucas said.

"Sweet torture, is what it is," Ken said. "Good night, all."

"Good night, Ken," I added.

There was a chill in the night air that made me shiver. My bare arms prickled with goose bumps. Ted took off his jacket and put it over my shoulders. Lucas scoured the other side of the beach for more firewood.

"Can we talk?" Ted asked.

I was staring out at the ocean, watching the waves turn white in the moonlight for a moment before they dissolved into the darkness again.

"Not right now," I said. "I don't even know what to think right now. I mean, I *can't* think right now. I'm going to need some time."

Ted exhaled. "I get it."

"Do you?" How could he?

"I'm willing to wait, Marin. I'm not going to rush you."

I didn't realize he meant it literally. What felt like hours passed and Ted did not move. Lucas kept the fire and his silence going, stoking them both. Our eyes met once or twice over the flame, but that was all. Ted yawned loudly. I was tired too, and sore from sitting on the pebbled beach.

"Aren't you going to turn in soon?" Ted asked.

"I thought I'd leave the newlyweds alone tonight. Kind of a buzzkill having your big sis around on your honeymoon."

Ted cleared his throat. "You can stay with me. I've got a room in the main house."

I rested my chin on my knee. "I don't think that's a good idea," I said. "But you should get some sleep."

"I can hang out with you," he said.

I shook my head. "We'll talk tomorrow."

Ted glanced at Lucas, who was too busy poking the logs with a stick to notice. He stood up and brushed his hands on his pants. "Are you sure? It doesn't feel right leaving you out here . . ." I could tell he wanted to say "with him," but to Ted's credit, he did not finish his sentence.

"I'll be fine," I said. "I like it here. Besides, Saba is super safe."

"You really *have* changed," he said. Then he turned and started to walk away.

"Ted, wait," I called after him. I pulled his coat off my shoulders. "You forgot your jacket."

"Keep it," he said. "At least I know you won't be cold."

I watched him walk away. Today had been a very confusing day. Wonderful, bittersweet, but confusing. The wedding party was down to the final two. Me in my dress on one side of the fire, holding Ted's jacket, and Lucas, who had barely spoken a word the entire day, on the other. I tried to think of something to say. I tried channeling Sadie, who always had the perfect irreverent comment to start any conversation. I couldn't think of anything. My rage had cooled slightly, but I was still angry. And then there were other feelings I couldn't quite categorize. I found myself craving another piece of the cake Elisabet had made.

Lucas stepped around the fire and stood beside me. *"Zǒu ba,"* he said.

"I'm good."

He extended his hand to me. "Let's go."

I looked up at him; he was silhouetted against the night sky, outlined in silver moonbeams. In the distance, I could make out the shape of his house. And suddenly I was back there, lying in his bed, and on this beach, the water sloshing around us. My hand in his.

My hand in his? When had I grabbed on to his hand? I had no clue, but our fingers were laced together and he was leading me toward his house. Fast-moving clouds eclipsed the moon and rain began to pour down. Lucas picked up his pace and I ran along behind him, struggling to keep my footing over the uneven surface. My heart thundered in my chest.

We made it inside before a bolt of lightning seared across the sky. Our clothes were saturated with rain and my chest was heaving from the sprint from the beach. Lucas was standing too close to me again. He was soaked too. A dark slice of hair cut across his forehead and hung in his eyes, water dripping from the ends. My skin tingled with the electricity between us. There was a roar of thunder so loud that it shook the house and then another bolt of lightning, closer this time. I started to shiver.

"I'll get you some dry clothes," he said. He stepped out of reach. I couldn't move. He returned with a large towel and a T-shirt and sweatpants for me to put on, but he set them on a nearby chair. On the other side of the room, he stripped out of his soaked clothes and pulled on a pair of gym shorts. My dress was dripping. A pool formed on the floor around my feet. I tried the zipper, but my fingers were trembling too badly. Lucas stepped forward and slid the zipper down for me. His index finger traced down my spine. I held my breath.

"Where should I hang the dress?" I asked.

"Just leave it on the chair," he said, already on the other side of the room. "I'll have it cleaned for you in the morning."

I pulled on the shirt and pants. "It's okay. I can take care of it. And please let me know how much everything was, for today. I want to pay for it."

He shook his head. "You don't need to do that."

"You've been so generous, and I really appreciate it. But you've done so much more than enough. Please let me pay for the villa and the wedding expenses."

"I gave those things to you because I wanted to. Let's leave it at that."

I didn't know what to say. "Um, do you have a blanket that I could use on the couch?" I asked.

"I'm taking the couch," he said.

"I don't mind," I said. But he was already adjusting a throw pillow under his neck.

I wanted to protest, but I was too drained. I was worried about Sadie, even though I knew Felix was with her. I was feeling guilty. In fleeing the storm, I'd left Ted's jacket on the rocks in the rain. Between the storm and the tide, it probably wouldn't be there in the morning. And then there was that tiny little sliver of me that had hoped Lucas wouldn't have taken the couch so easily. It was that piece that wanted him to curl himself around me in the bed we'd shared, the piece that would have forgiven him if he'd said anything instead of being silent the whole night. He'd said nothing, but I'd gotten the message, loud and clear. He'd gotten me out of the storm because he was a good person. He'd thrown a wedding for Sadie and let us stay here and even refused payment. Because he wanted to. Because, to him, it was the right thing to do. Lucas honored people; he kept his promises. But he hadn't made me any, and he wasn't going to, because at the end of the day, he didn't have real feelings for me.

"Good night," I said. I went into the bedroom and lay down on his pillow. It was going to be a long night. Back at home, I used to listen to the rain effect on my sleep sound machine. It was a one hundred percent foolproof method to make me pass out, even when my mind was running through a list of worst-case scenarios or lines of copy. I had my own personal rain machine happening here, and I wasn't even close to dozing off. I rolled over, adjusted the covers, refluffed the pillow.

In the living room, a light clicked on and I heard Lucas's slippers shuffling across the tile floor. I stared at the doorway. In the span of thirty seconds, I played an entire conversation in my mind. *Say something,* I thought. *Tell me my fears are wrong. Tell me I don't need to worry. Tell me what I thought we were feeling was real after all. And maybe I won't be all alone.* The shuffling sound was closer. The door gave a muffled groan. I closed my eyes and pretended to sleep. I pictured Lucas climbing in next to me, whispering these reassurances in my ear.

The light in the living room clicked off.

Fifty

BY THE TIME I woke in the morning, mercifully, Lucas had already left. I skulked down to the beach and picked up Ted's jacket. It was soaking wet and had some crusted seafoam and a garnish of kelp around a button, but it was intact. I tucked it on the same hanger as my dress and headed back to my villa, hoping to sneak in before Sadie and Felix woke from some love-drunk slumber.

"Looks like somebody's doing a walk of shame," Sadie said. I jumped. Not only was she awake, she was sitting in one of the chairs on the patio, sipping some kind of smoothie. "At least my wedding day was a banner one for the Cole sisters. Felix didn't want me to overexert myself so he spent the night be—"

I held up a hand and shook my head. "Nope. Not listening. Nothing happened last night. Not for me and not for you."

Sadie pressed her lips together. "Sure. Just one question for ya, Sis. If, like you said, 'nothing happened,' why are you wearing Lucas's clothes?"

"Who says I'm wearing his clothes?"

She pointed a finger. "My eyesight's not perfect, but I'm pretty sure that says *Light up Taiwan* and then there's a bunch of traditional Chinese logograms next to that circle."

I glanced down. Yes, there it was just as Sadie described. I crossed my arms over the logo. It was as if Lucas had picked that shirt on purpose so everyone would know. But that was illogical because nothing had happened. Lucas was a lot of things (insert pathetic sigh), but illogical was not one of them.

"I guess I do owe you fifty bucks," Felix said. He was carrying two steaming mugs of coffee. "Looks like somebody needs a coffee. Up late, were we, Marin?"

"I'm going to shower," I said. "But I will take the coffee."

"Don't take too long," Sadie said. "We're going to spend the day in Ladder Bay."

I opened my mouth to object. I'd been to the Ladder, and I didn't want to ruin Sadie's plan, but there was no way she was climbing it, even on Felix's back.

"Stop worrying. Ken's going to take us on the boat. I have a whole plan. I want to go swimming and lie in the sun like a seal. The guys are going to bring a picnic."

Her face was still wan and pale, but her eyes were shining with excitement.

"Is this a good idea?" I asked Felix. "Yesterday was a lot. We don't want to push her too hard."

"I haven't seen her this energetic in a long time," he said. He shrugged. "It couldn't hurt." Then louder, so Sadie could hear, he said, "What my wife wants, she gets."

He took off to get things squared away with Ken. While he was gone, I helped Sadie tie a string bikini that was covered with lipstick kisses as tight as it would go. It still hung off her body. I had to look away. "Hand me the sweat suit," she said. I helped her into the white velour warm-up suit with *Just Married* in shimmering embroidery on the butt. It was loose, but I couldn't see the outline of her bones beneath her skin with it on. "This thing is so toasty. I've been so cold," she said. She'd been struggling to regulate her temperature. Ken had brought extra blankets, soft ones that felt like velvet, and we piled them over her while she slept.

"I wish I'd tried this on earlier. Juicy Couture, where have you been all my life?" she said, and smiled. "It's funny—I'd pictured you wearing this stuff. I mean, back when Trudy showed it to me, I practically fell off my chair."

"Let me guess, Trudy is the fake bride who stole my bag and left me this monstrosity of a wardrobe?"

"Yeah, Jeremy's sister, remember? But she's not a fake bride. She really got married. She just wouldn't be caught dead in these clothes. And we prefer the term *accomplice*."

"Oh, okay, then."

"She stole your passport too, after you landed. An old-fashioned bump and lift. Sorry about that."

"So, then your State Department 'friend'—let me guess, he doesn't exist?"

"Oh, he's real. I didn't call him, though. Good thing too. He can get a little clingy." Sadie rubbed her velour-covered arms. "I wish I had one of these in every color or one for each day of the week. I'd probably want something different on the ass though. *Just Married* seems a little blah for me, don't you think, and time-limited . . . kind of a one-trick pony? What about *Super-cali-frass-alistic*? Now, that has staying power."

"I don't think you've got enough real estate back there for that one, Sades. Better keep brainstorming."

I stared at the contents of the closet, trying to pick something to wear. Not that it mattered.

"You should wear that dress," Sadie said, pointing to the one Lucas had bought me.

"I don't think so," I told her. "It's too fancy."

"It's not one of the ones that Felix packed for you," she said. "Dish."

"There's nothing to dish."

"Where'd you get that perfect dress, Mar?"

"Lucas bought it," I mumbled.

"Thought so." She lifted the hanger. "What? Thought I wouldn't hear you? I'm going to give you two options, tell me about you and

Lucas or put the dress on. I saw you guys at the wedding. The way you were and weren't looking at each other the whole time . . . There's more to that story than just a night of fun and some cute pictures. He looked like he wanted to roast Ted on a spit over that bonfire he made."

"No, he didn't." I shook my head. "I don't know what to say, Sadie. There's no scoop, and even if there were, I wouldn't know what to tell you that you don't already know. We had dinner at Laurentina and Ronaldo's house and had a lot of rum. I kissed him first, I think." I sighed. "I know, rookie mistake."

Sadie made a face. "Why is that a mistake? I kissed Felix first in Portugal. I've kissed a lot of people first. I'm all about kissing first. And, it's not usually a mistake. I mean, maybe that one time with the guy at that club in Chattanooga. But for the most part, I'm pro–kissing first. At least then there's no confusion."

"But there is confusion. So much confusion."

"How's that?"

"I guess I thought that the kiss was like attraction."

"Can't blame ya there."

"And a bit too much Saba spiced rum with some feelings stirred into the mix."

Sadie waited for me to finish.

"It wasn't for real. We both just got caught up, I think."

"And . . ."

"And it's different now. The spell broke or something. It's not important anyway." I turned to her. "I'll wear the dress if you really want me to."

She shook her head. "Wear what you want, Sissy. I'm done meddling."

"So no more secret letters?" I asked, thinking of the ones I'd dumped onto Lucas's desk. The ones he'd sent flying with a sweep of his arm when I ran off. I slipped the dress from the hanger.

"Scout's honor," Sadie said.

"You have your fingers crossed, don't you?" I wriggled out of Lucas's shirt and pants and slid the dress over my head. It was just as soft and perfect as I remembered it being. As if it had been made for me. As if it'd been picked by someone who cared about me, who knew the real me.

"Wouldn't you like to know?" She flashed one of her trademark devilish grins.

Felix came in then and asked, "Ready to go?" He leaned over to scoop up Sadie, but she waved him off.

"I feel like walking myself," she said. "Okay?"

He grinned at her. Wordlessly, he extended an arm and she twined hers through his. "To the boat!" she said.

I took the bags and followed along behind.

When we anchored in the bay, we saw what the boys had been up to while Sadie and I were drinking coffee at the villa and talking about Lucas and his stupid shirt and our stance on who should kiss first. There beyond the tide line was a small stretch of actual smooth sand in a crescent shape. Lucas was arranging several lounge chairs and bright yellow umbrellas in a line. I took off the dress and put it into a dry bag that Ken set out for us. Then I jumped off the side of the boat in my bathing suit. Sadie'd brought along the one-piece I liked for swimming laps at the Y, but I opted for a bright green bikini with a halter top that I'd seen at the resort shop two days earlier. I swam to shore. Behind me, Felix carried Sadie through the water and helped her get settled into one of the chairs. He dried her with a towel and helped her back into the warm-up suit. Lucas handed me a towel.

"Thanks for this," I said. "It's amazing. I can't believe you got sand out here. It must have been a lot of work."

"It was worth it." He gave me a slight nod. "She said you would like it. I'm realizing Sadie's quite the mastermind."

I had to smile at that. He smiled back. "You and me both," I told him.

A bottle of wine. Fresh fruit, cut thin and icy cold. She wanted a day at the beach, like a real honeymoon. We gave it to her. We floated in the gentle waves, faces turned up to the sun. I dove with Lucas and tried to find another pearl. I did end up with a beautiful conch shell, its inside sunset-colored and smooth. Sadie pressed it to her ear, while I stood dripping before her. Why hadn't we done this kind of thing sooner? There were so many trips, so many adventures we could have had. I'd missed out on so much of her.

Since I'd learned the truth about Sadie's prognosis, I'd devoured blogs and research about patients who were dying of cancer. A lot of websites said that people usually want to die at home, in a familiar, comfortable place. But she wasn't dying, not yet. We lay on the beach and let the sun sprinkle our skin with freckles. She looked healthier, I thought. Better.

"I love this place," she said, squinting into the sun.

"Do you think you'll want to go home, Sadie?" I asked. "If the time comes?"

She laced her fingers through mine. "You are my home. And besides, I feel pretty good here. Maybe it's the island air, I don't know. Maybe being married suits me . . . imagine that." Today, for the first time, I felt hope swelling up in my chest, like one of those supermoon tides. Maybe Sadie would be one of the miracles from Guangzhou Fuda. Maybe her miracle was just a little slow.

We napped through the afternoon and woke up hungry. Lucas and Ken caught fish and cooked them over the fire. Sadie leaned against Felix while she scraped strips of juicy mango clean with her teeth. She nibbled on the fish skewers.

At night, we had fireworks. Bright red and white, blue, whistlers and loud booms. They exploded against the night sky and on the water's surface. I watched the colors reflected on Sadie's face.

I love you, Sadie mouthed to me.

Not as much as I love you.

On the boat ride home, Sadie leaned on my shoulder. "How are you feeling?" I asked.

"Mmm . . ." she said.

"You ate today."

"You wore the dress," she said. "It was a perfect day."

I tucked an arm behind her head and she nestled into me, the way she had when we were little and Mom was away. She smelled of sea salt and sweet fruit. Felix blew her a kiss from where he stood, tying the boat off at the pier for Ken.

"I'll take the couch tonight so you can have some sister time," he said. "I somehow managed to sunburn my ass, so no frisky business for me, love."

Sadie had already fallen asleep and had to be carried to bed and tucked in, like a child who'd played so hard, with such joy and abandon, that she'd used every last drop of energy.

She never woke up.

Fifty-One

SADIE

FOR THE SAKE OF full disclosure, I was giving it one last shot in China. Your dad got me into that clinic, did he tell you that, Lucas? We'd talked on those message boards for so many months, but how well do you ever know a stranger, right? He was a remarkable man. God, I fucking hate that. I hate when people say trite things like that. People will probably say things like that at my funeral. If it comes to that, can you please tell Marin I don't want one? Unless it's a Viking funeral. I wouldn't mind something like that, except maybe without all the fire. I'm not sure I'd want to be shot with flaming arrows. But I like the idea of wearing something beautiful and being surrounded by flowers and set adrift on some sort of simple wooden boat. I don't like to think about what would happen eventually—the horrified tourists who would stumble upon the craft and be permanently traumatized by the sight of my leathered body or the eventual decay of the boat and subsequent consumption of my corpse by sea creatures—who wants to think about eventuality? Especially when you're dying. Still, maybe you could make something like that happen, something beautiful and freeing, with some floating lanterns or wish paper thrown in for good measure? I shouldn't ask all this of you. I know I shouldn't. It isn't fair. You don't know me, you don't know my sister . . . yet. But just believe me when I tell you that we're worth it.

Fifty-Two

MARIN

WE LATER LEARNED THAT health professionals in palliative care have a name for Sadie's amazing day. They call it an "end-of-life rally," a revival of energy and appetite, a trick. Every doctor and nurse seems to have a story of a patient who perked up enough to have those last great conversations with loved ones, to eat a few bites of a favorite sandwich when they hadn't eaten solid food in weeks, one last big burst of beautiful energy before they slip away. They say it's a gift, but it felt like the cruelest trick of all.

I'd lain next to her, curled against her bony frame, smoothing the soft, fragile skin on her cheek, counting her breaths, until I fell asleep, hopeful. I woke in the morning. Sadie didn't. Her body had held on, hovering in that state between life and death, for twenty-four hours. The most excruciating twenty-four hours, during which I pressed cotton balls damp with coconut oil to her lips, held her hand, prayed.

The nurses assured me she wasn't in pain. That the labored breathing wasn't distressing to her, like it was to us. She was peaceful. This was how it happened. Her body shut down, rattling breath by rattling breath, and I told her all my favorite stories, her trouble-making from when she was probably too young to remember, memories of Mom, and new stories too. I told her about my time on the island, about this great gift she had given me. How I hadn't even noticed how much I'd walled myself in these years in a prison of my own making. I'd been bored and lonely and stuck. I hadn't seen it, but Sadie had. She'd set me free. And all I could do was thank her, and hold her hand until it was time to let go.

Sadie stopped breathing just after noon the next day.

Ken and Lucas brought armfuls of ferns, brightly colored hibiscus, and wild begonia. They made a bed of flora, soft and technicolor, bold and defiant against the simple wood raft. Laurentina had her mom watch the boys and she came and helped me dress Sadie in the wedding dress she'd created, the one that was covered with perfect white birds, flying, wings wide in the intricate lace she'd made. When the time came and the sun was fiery orange in the sky, Felix carried Sadie to the raft and laid her atop the flowers. His face was shining with tears. Sadie looked so beautiful, even drained of color. She looked like an alabaster angel. My perfect sister. My throat ached from the sobs I withheld. I had no energy left to cry. I still couldn't believe all this, that Sadie being gone was real. But I wanted the world to know what it had lost. I wanted someone's voice to fill the air with sorrow, for the wind to carry cries everywhere.

When a seabird flew overhead, its shriek came close to the sound of my own heart. I'd read Sadie's wishes. The illegal, outrageous wishes. The Viking funeral at sea that was meant for kings. She was a king to me, to all of us. But I had left the details to the guys who were still functioning, and Ken promised me that Lucas had friends in high places and no one would disrupt Sadie's send-off. And even after everything that had happened between us, I knew I could trust Lucas with this. He stood next to Ken, staring out at the horizon. I wondered if he was remembering his Ba right now. If he and Sadie were together somewhere else at this moment. If she was already that bird, swooping in the sky above herself.

Felix hit the hard beach on his knees. The air rushed out of my lungs. I ran to the water's edge. A mournful scream filled the air; it vibrated through my body and into the ocean like the haunting song of some humpback whale. Someone's hands were on my shoulders. The sound hurt my ears. I was being lifted off the ground. I looked up and saw Lucas above me. He was looking ahead, away from the beach, moving in slow motion. Taking me away from Sadie and the raft and the vast ocean and shrieking birds.

"Make it stop," I said. And it did. There were no more horrible cries, because they'd been coming from me all along. I hadn't even known. My throat was raw. I soaked Lucas's shirt while he carried me back to his villa. Mine was still full of all the signs of Sadie. Her clothes. The pill bottles and oxygen tank. The smell of weed and gardenias. I could picture her lying in the bed looking so peaceful in the morning when I opened my eyes. I hadn't known she was already gone.

He opened the door to his house and brought me inside. The last time I'd stood here, I was soaking wet, shivering from the rain that blessed Sadie and Felix's wedding. I'd wanted things back the way they were, and at that time, I stupidly thought that was possible. But it wasn't. There was no going back. Sadie was gone. I couldn't bring her back. It hurt to breathe without her, like there was a gaping, Sadie-size hole in my chest that nothing would ever fill.

Lucas set me on the couch and put a blanket over me. Then he brought out a bottle, the same red one we'd drunk that first day on Saba, and poured me a large glass.

"It will help."

Lucas wrapped my trembling hands around the glass and I drained it obediently. I felt so tired all of a sudden. "It's okay to sleep," he said, smoothing the damp hair from my cheek.

"Nothing is okay."

He was quiet for a long time. Then he said, *"Wǒ zhēn dẹ hěn yí hàn. Dāng wǒ wò zhù nǐ dẹ shǒu, wǒ gǎn jué chu nǐ dẹ xīn suì."*

"What does that mean?" I sniffed.

"It means, I'm so sorry. When I hold your hand, I can feel your heartbreak."

I nodded and tucked my hand under my cheek. "I think I'll sleep now."

"I'm going to check on Felix. I'll be back."

I wanted to grab his hand. Tell him not to go. I didn't want to be alone. But instead, I gripped the bottle and poured myself another drink. I needed to be numb.

The cruel thing about death is that you forget it happened. So you get the torturous experience of relearning that your someone is gone again and again. It's like being stabbed in the heart with a blunt object every time you think to tell them something, or reach for them, or dial their number by accident, and then you remember. Or when you wake up on the couch of a man you could have loved if your world hadn't imploded and your figurative heart was not currently being stabbed over and over by a blunt implement.

I don't know how long I slept. It could have been days, it could have been a mere moment. When I woke, the sun was low on the horizon and my very first thought was what kind of wisecrack Sadie was going to hit me with about yet another sexless sleepover at Lucas's place. At least I wasn't wearing his clothes this time. Stab. There was a glass of water and a bottle of ibuprofen on the coffee table next to me along with an extra set of my own clothes, washed and neatly folded in a stack. My eyes were swollen and my head throbbed. I took the medicine and drank all the water.

There was no sign of Lucas, so I scribbled a note, thanking him for letting me stay there, and then I left. I needed to find Felix. When I remembered, worrying about him took over all of my mental space. I thought back to the day before, when he had fallen onto the rocky beach on his knees. I checked the villa first. He was packing his suitcase when I opened the French doors and stepped inside.

He'd grown a few days' worth of stubble and his hair was disheveled. He had to push it back out of his eyes to see me, bloodshot eyes that looked like they'd been rimmed with red eyeliner—he was either more stoned than anyone in the history of the world, or he'd been crying nonstop. He tried to smile, but only his lips moved.

"Hey, Felix," I said. "I'm sorry I deserted you."

"You were gone a long time," he said. "I would've worried, but I wasn't exactly with it myself."

"Same. I've been asleep. Lucas brought me to his place and I crashed on the couch."

He nodded and folded a shirt.

"So you're going," I said.

He set the shirt down in the suitcase. "I can't be here right now. She's everywhere I look. I keep wanting to talk to her, to go into our room and see her there, to wake up and realize this was just a terrible fucking nightmare, but it's not."

My eyes filled with tears. "Me too."

"Yesterday, I called Jessica and she said she had an assignment for me if I wanted something. It's a couple of months in Kuala Lumpur. I think it will be good for me to have something useful to do. And I think Sadie would like it, you know, because our work was so important to us. She wouldn't want me sitting here crying, wishing her back to life. She'd want me to go out, you know, go big or go home."

I nodded. He knew her so well. "You should. You guys were all about adventure. She always said those assignments gave her life. Seeing a new place, learning the people, climbing stuff. All of it. She'd want you to go." I perched on the edge of the bed. "I guess maybe it's time I should go home. That was always my thing."

Felix picked up the velour tracksuit jacket Sadie had worn on the beach and held it up. "Was it?"

"I don't even know anymore. If you asked me two weeks ago, I would have had an answer. Now?" I shrugged. "I guess I'm lost."

Felix forced his arms into the tracksuit and zipped it up. The crystals in the word *Bride* caught the setting sun and lit the room with rainbows that danced on the walls. "Without her—we're all lost, Marin."

I'd been trying not to cry, but the surface tension broke and my sorrow poured out. It took me a few moments to catch my breath and stave stem the flow of tears. "Yeah," I said. "Yeah."

He put his arms around me and squeezed tight. We stayed like that for several raspy breaths. When we pulled away, he wiped his face with the velour sleeve.

"You look really good in that jacket," I said.

"You think? Maybe I should keep it." He patted me on the head. "There's something else I should do."

"What's that?" I said, folding the matching pants and dropping them into his suitcase.

"On behalf of your sister," he said, "I forbid you to go home. She would be so pissed if she knew you were even thinking about it. So I'm saying no."

I sniffed hard and fought the tears that were trying to start again. "Is that so? You do realize she also said 'Stick it to the man' on the regular."

"I'm pretty confident that she didn't mean me."

"Keep telling yourself that, Felix."

"How about you tell me what you're really going to do?"

I searched the room for some kind of sign, something Sadie might have left, instructions or even another scheme, anything that would tell me what I should do next, how I might recover, if I possibly could. I didn't see anything. Someone had straightened up.

I shrugged. "I got nothing. All this time, she was the one who had everything all figured out. Leave it to Sadie to know what I needed better than I did. The hikes, the scuba . . . even Sabaoke . . . she knew."

"Sabaoke?"

"You know, it's Saba's version of karaoke. She had Lucas take me last Friday."

Felix shook his head, chuckling. "No freaking way. If there was anything Sadie would not have tortured you with, it's karaoke. She detested it with every fiber of her being."

"Really?"

"One hundred percent."

How odd. I'd loved every minute of it. My gaze landed on the blue notebook. Felix turned to see what I was looking at.

"Oh yeah, I found that under the bed when I was getting my stuff together. It isn't Sadie's."

I stepped over and picked it up.

"It's mine." I turned the book in my hand, smoothed my fingertips over the soft leather. A piece of paper fell and drifted down to the floor. I crouched to pick it up. Someone had tucked Laurentina's sketch of the wedding dress inside the book. There were the measurements I had taken down. The tiny drawings of birds. The beautiful script of Laurentina's hand, with *Sadie's Wedding Gown* written across the top. It was between the pages I'd written about the art of making lace on Saba, about Laurentina and her family, the story I'd thought of starting but decided not to finish. I ran my hand over the sketch. There was a something there, I thought, about love, and sisters, about women and art and grief, about the tiny details that make the fabric of our lives. If only I were brave enough to tell it.

"I have to go," I told Felix.

"Make bad choices," he said.

"Don't leave without saying goodbye."

Fifty-Three

WHEN MY MOM DIED, some well-meaning person brought me a casserole and a book about grief. It had a diagram with the stages and I remembered staying up all night poring over the chart, trying to figure out exactly how long it would take for me to feel like I wasn't drowning. There was one phase that talked about energy-wasting behaviors. From what little I remembered, it was like you get super busy so that you don't have to process something that you're not ready to deal with.

I was not ready to deal with the reality of Sadie's being dead. I can say she's dead now. It still hurts like a bitch, but I can admit it. Then, not so much. Then, I ran around doing errands and research. I spent hours scrubbing Ted's ruined sport coat with shampoo and a toothbrush and delivered it to him at his room in the main house like a resort employee. He looked a little perplexed at first, but then he quickly ushered me inside.

The room he was staying in was attractive, with a terra-cotta tile floor and a dark wood four-poster bed and gauzy mosquito netting hanging down, but it was so small compared to the villa, that I felt claustrophobic sitting in there with him.

"How've you been holding up?" he asked.

I shrugged. "Probably about what you'd expect. Not great."

He nodded. "Have you thought about what you're going to do?" he asked. "I mean, you can't realistically stay here forever."

I didn't need the reminder. When I wasn't filling my mind with menial tasks, it was the only thing there. Since Sadie was gone, I had no reason to stay. Work wouldn't wait for me forever, no matter how understanding they'd been about my "family situation." And I couldn't afford this place. Lucas had held up his end of the bargain he'd made with Sadie and his dad. I couldn't stay here for free anymore. My stomach started to hurt. Sadie had taken my appetite with her; I hadn't eaten in days. "I don't know."

"Do you want to know what I think?" Ted asked.

"Yes? No? I'm not sure." I was afraid of what he might say, and at that point, feeling the way I did, I wasn't sure I could bear to hear it. "Don't tell me. Not right now, okay?"

"You're not sure what to do because of him."

I shook my head.

"It's Lucas. He's holding you back."

"No. He's not." I sighed. "*I'm* holding me back. I've been holding me back for a long time. That's why Sadie did all this, right? She must've told you something."

"She said you were asleep, something like that. You knew your sister. I didn't get it exactly."

The way he'd put her in the past tense so easily smarted. I bit the inside of my lip.

"I figured she meant you hadn't done much. You'd never moved, you were still at that same job. Did you even like working there?"

"What about you? I thought you wanted to do research in Nepal? Now you're back in Tennessee."

"Yeah, well, it was harder than I thought it would be. I hadn't counted on going alone. It's not like I gave up. I was there for two years before I came back, and the offer from Dr. Metcalfe was amazing. It was definitely my area of interest, and those kinds of positions don't come along very often. But, if you're asking if you were part of the equation when I came back, then yeah. You were."

"You never reached out to me."

"I thought about it. The timing never seemed right. Plus, there was a piece of me that figured you would've moved on. I pictured you married, a kid on the way or something. And then Sadie reached out to me. It's funny. I thought she wasn't a huge fan."

"She wasn't."

"She still called me though. For you."

I stayed quiet.

"I don't get it, Marin," Ted said. "What we had was so great. And we could have it again. I want that. I thought you would want it too."

I examined his face, the blond stubble that was starting to come in on his jaw. His complexion had tanned to a golden brown, but he looked haggard.

"Why'd you come here, Ted?" I asked. I needed to know.

He gave me a look. "I thought I made that pretty clear."

"Did you?"

"I told you about how I felt."

"You said I was different now. You saw my pictures?" I shrugged. "I don't know if I'm really different than before. I mean, yeah, I had a few adventures and took some photos, but I'm still the same person. I'm still scared shitless most of the time. And look at me, I've spent a good part of my life afraid of losing the people that I care about . . . Now I have."

Ted leaned back in his chair. "You haven't." He squeezed the bill of his baseball cap in his hands. "Unless . . . you don't care about me anymore." There wasn't any malice in his voice. He hadn't said it to hurt me. He didn't even sound wounded. Maybe that was the worst part. "Do you not care about me anymore?"

I waited a long time before answering him. I counted my heartbeats, slow and steady, thunking in my chest. "That's not it. I don't know if I can give you what you want. Maybe I'm the same as before. Maybe I'm just not the right person for you."

He shook his head. "Or maybe this wasn't the best time to talk about this. Sadie just passed away—"

I held my hand out to stop his words.

"Sorry," he said. "I just mean . . . Fuck." He pulled his hat off his head and crushed it in his hands. "The thing is, I love you, Marin. I'm pretty certain that I will always love you. And I'm going back to Tennessee tomorrow. Come with me. Don't give me an answer now. Just meet me at the airport at noon if you're coming."

"I'll think about it," I said.

He reached out and took my hand. "I mean it," he said. "When you get home, you won't have to be alone."

I looked at him looking at me with those big blue eyes that had once made my heart rate rise. Would it be so hard to go back to the way things were? I'd loved him so much. I still did, in a way. I knew how my hand fit in his. I liked the clean smell of his soap and the way he was steady and smart and caring. He'd made me laugh once. Made me feel safe. Could he still?

"I should go," I said.

Fifty-Four

I RAN INTO KEN on my way through the lobby, as in I slammed into him because I was too busy replaying the conversation with Ted to notice that he was standing in front of the stairwell, wiping a ring of water left by the flower arrangement on an antique table.

"Marin," he said, regaining his balance. "I didn't expect to see you out. You're stronger than me."

"Sorry," I said. "I'm distracted."

"I didn't mean like you're the Incredible Hulk. I meant as in you're out and about after such a massive trauma. That kind of strong."

I shrugged and then dropped onto the couch. "Honestly, I'm not."

"I'm probably saying all the wrong stuff. I can only imagine what you're going through. I think about it and it would be like me losing Lucas." He shook his head. "I wouldn't be vertical, that's for sure."

"Yeah. It really sucks," I said. "And I suck."

Ken was looking at me with that earnest, gentle expression. His face so open that I just split apart. "I feel awful, I am awful. I still can't really believe it's real. I keep thinking she's just off somewhere taking a nap or getting a massage, like what kind of idiot forgets their sister is dead? And then when I do remember, all I want to do is cry until I dehydrate and shrivel up and turn to dust and disappear." The words spilled out of my mouth before I could stop them.

It was like I was a bystander to my own confession. I could hear my voice shaking and I hated it, but I was powerless to shut it down.

Ken put a hand on my shoulder. "I'm sorry," he said, "I didn't mean to make it worse. But don't be so hard on yourself. Your world has shifted. It's got to take a long time to adjust. That's not you being awful, that's the way it is."

I thought about that. This was another experience I couldn't control. Like zip-lining, except that in this version I kept smashing into the same tree over and over. It was unbearable.

"Not to change the subject," Ken said, "but Lucas has been looking for you. He's in his office. If you have a few minutes, I can take you there."

There it was. Lucas was going to tell me that it was time for me to go. I'd known it was coming. A luxury resort couldn't be a holding area for some weird American in mourning who wasn't footing her own bill. I thought about Ted's offer.

Lucas was sitting at his desk, signing some papers, when Ken led me in. "Lǎobǎn," he said.

Lucas looked up. All of the oxygen was sucked out of the room when his eyes met mine. The furniture, the floor, everything disappeared. I was floating in front of him, suffocating.

"Hi," I said, my voice caught in my throat.

"Marin."

"I'll pack my stuff," I said.

He looked surprised. "There's no need for that."

I closed my eyes in relief. "So you didn't want to see me to tell me that I need to check out?"

"Not at all. That wasn't my intent." He rocked back in his desk chair. "I promised to take care of you; that means you may stay as long as you need."

I sank into the chair in front of him. The panic I'd been holding back suddenly whirred through my veins. I could hear my heartbeat.

Lucas said, "I've been wondering when is the right time to give this to you." He held the object up, and now I saw that he'd been holding an envelope. It wasn't the manila one I'd seen before. It was smaller, like a birthday card, and bright blue.

The tears filled my eyes before it even registered. "Is that from Sadie?" I said, though it came out as a sob.

"She gave it to me a few days ago and told me that I should give it to you after she'd gone. She said I would know when. Your sister gives me too much credit. Ba would have known the exact moment, but not me. I thought . . . maybe it's too soon, but I don't want to keep things from you anymore." He held it out. I leaned over and snatched it out of his hand like a greedy child.

"You should read it alone, I think," he said. "I'm going down to the docks for a bit if you need me. It's a nice day—I thought maybe I'd take the boat out."

As soon as he left, I sat back with the envelope in my hands. I studied it for a few minutes. Sadie had written my name on the front, the way she always had, bubble letters filled with patterns: waves in the M, palm trees meeting for the A, the R had tiny birds, the I, fireworks, and the N was filled with hearts. The writing wasn't faint, so she must've written it a while ago, when she still had some strength in her hands. The last week, she wouldn't have been able to write like this. I traced the letters with my finger, treasuring the effort and the care in each line. I could almost see my hand touching hers as she moved the pen to make the shapes and the designs. I pictured her look of concentration, the slightly furrowed brow, the way she sort of bit her tongue when she was focusing hard on something.

I took a deep breath and pulled the flap open. She hadn't sealed the envelope. Sadie never did. She always thought it was such a shame when people ripped envelopes open and ruined them; "They're half the fun of mail" was one of her classic lines. She had a drawerful of envelopes at home, perfectly intact ones that Mom had sent us when she was on assignment. I didn't get it until now. I wondered what else I had missed that Sadie had known instinctively.

I pulled the card out and held it up. On the front there was a photograph of a dog with his head out a car window. The wind had pushed his loose skin back so it looked like he was smiling a great big smile. I shook my head. Classic Sadie. Weird on the outside, profound on the inside. My heart paced a little faster as I prepared to read what kind of lovely parting message she'd written me. She must've known there'd be decisions I'd have to make. I closed my eyes for a moment like I was making a birthday wish—*Tell me what I should do, Sadie*—and slowly opened the card. I turned it over. It couldn't be. This couldn't be my sister's final message to me. Lucas must've made a mistake, grabbed the wrong card and stuck it in the wrong envelope. I looked again. I burst through his office door and through the lobby the way I'd come, past Ken, who shouted something after me, and then down the drive, through the gate, down the hill to the dock.

"Lucas," I yelled, in between heaving breaths.

"Marin?" Lucas called back from the deck. "Is everything okay?"

"No." I shook my head.

"What's going on?" he asked. I couldn't answer. I was clutching the card in my hand, still not able to catch my breath. "Hang on," he said. He moved quickly, crossing the deck, hopping back onto the pier.

He was by my side, his hand on my arm. "What's wrong?"

I tried to steady my voice. "This couldn't have been for me," I said. "She sent you all those letters. I saw them. Pages and pages of them on your desk that day. This can't be mine."

"I'm not following," Lucas said. "What she wrote upset you?"

"How could you give this to me?" I held it up.

"A dog? Marin, I'm sorry. I didn't look at it. Sadie gave me the envelope and asked me to give it to you. Should we call Felix? Maybe he knows something."

I blew out a long breath of air. "There's no point."

"Why? What did it say?" he asked.

"It didn't say anything," I said. I squeezed my eyes hard to staunch the flow of tears. "She didn't write anything. She spent an hour drawing designs in bubble letters on the envelope and then she didn't write a goddamn thing to me."

Lucas flinched. "It was blank?"

"Yeah. Except for the printed part."

"What was that?"

"You saw the dog on the front, right; head out the window, skin smashed back like he was in a wind tunnel. And then inside . . . inside . . ." I could barely make the words come out. "Inside it read, 'Bixby didn't want his owner to know it was he who had farted.'"

"Your sister left you a card with a fart joke?" he asked. The corner of his mouth twitched.

"I thought Sadie was writing me this meaningful message about life and what it meant, what she hoped for me. I thought she was going to tell me what I should do, or even just that she loved me . . . but instead, she gave me this . . . this . . ."

"Fart joke." He rubbed the corner of his mouth.

"I'm glad someone thinks it's funny."

"I'm sorry. It's not. It's a little funny. Keep in mind, your sister has been writing to me for a while. To me, it seems a very Sadie thing to do. But I am sorry. I don't think she would've wanted to hurt you. I feel responsible. I wish I hadn't gotten your hopes up about it."

"It's not your fault. You're not the person who . . ." My voice trailed off. I was so angry at her, I'd forgotten to feel awful for a moment.

"Do you want to come out on the water with me?" Lucas asked, squinting into the sun.

I stared at the card, the single line of typed text. Lucas was right, the card was classic Sadie. She'd pissed me off on purpose, probably, been lighthearted in the face of the darkest, hardest thing. Made a joke when I was heartbroken. She'd made me want to laugh and punch her at the same time. I'd forgotten for just a moment that I was shattered. *Was that the point?* I wanted to ask her. *You really had nothing to say to me? You put me through this whole Marin Life Makeover challenge and then left me hanging.*

I thought of all the things I'd done because of Sadie. I'd faced my fears of travel and adventure and flying. I'd sung for a roomful of people. I'd let go with a man who I knew was all kinds of wrong for me. I'd seen and done scary and amazing things, and not only had the world not ended, it had been awesome. I felt more alive than I had in a very long time, thanks to Sadie and her scheming. I felt more alive . . . and she was dead. It wasn't fair. And then now when I needed her most to tell me what to do, she was gone.

"Thanks for everything, Sadie," I whispered into the breeze. I had to face it. There were no more notes, no more projects. No more schemes. Sadie wasn't on the next flight, or tricking me, or fashionably late. She was dead. I was going to have to do this next part on my own.

I held the card in my hands. What did I want? A decision would need to be made sooner or later. Would I get on the boat with Lucas, who was looking at me with those dark eyes that seemed to have so much to say, or go back to Sweetwater, back to work that was secure and not entirely soul-sucking, and give it another shot with Ted? Or something else entirely on my own? My head and heart were such a jumble of emotions, I wasn't sure what I was feeling. I had all these decisions to make and I was in the worst possible mental place to make them. I wasn't ready. Didn't Sadie get that? She'd given me nothing. The next step was entirely on me. Safe little boring life or something else?

I'm not ready! I wanted to shout into the wind loud enough that she could hear me wherever she was. Her reply came in a memory, the two of us, me and her, strapped to the zip-line. *No one's ever ready, you just do it anyway.*

I turned my back to the boat and walked away. With every step, something inside me tore, piece by piece. A stiff breeze kicked up and I wondered if I would blow away like confetti, like the dandelion wishes Sadie and I made when we were kids.

Fifty-Five

I DIDN'T EXPECT TO see Lucas again after that. I figured the image of him standing on the boat deck, hand outstretched, was going to be the end of it. But here he was, only a few hours later, coming out of the jungle path by the villa. He was wearing casual clothes; I recognized them as the ones he'd lent me that day. The *Light up Taiwan* T-shirt Sadie had teased me about. Thin gray sweatpants. Slides. His hair was wet and hung straight down to his eyes. There was something brown tucked beneath one of his arms.

The sun had dipped below the horizon and the lights hanging from the trees had blinked on. I loved those lights, like fireflies caught in the trees. I was still reeling from Sadie's final message to me. I just couldn't understand how she would think that it was anything but a little cruel. The strange thing was that Sadie was never cruel. She was free-spirited and even slightly strange, but she'd never hurt anyone, especially me—just like Lucas had said. It'd occurred to me that maybe she hadn't had a chance to write the message she'd wanted. Maybe if she'd just had one more day, she would have been able to say the things she'd wanted to say to me. Maybe she'd been confused. Brain cancer and all that. Copious amounts of weed.

It was very lonely at the villa without Sadie and Felix riffing off each other. It was enough to fuel hours of crying according to my watch. I sat alone on the porch, dressed in my new uniform of a resort robe. Just me in my robe and my friend, a giant glass of wine, hanging out under the stars, crying the night away. Lucas looked how Lucas always looked. Too good. At the sight of him, I swiped my cheeks with the sleeve of my robe. He sat down across from me.

"Welcome to my crying porch," I said. "Come for the wine, stay for the crying." I tried to smile.

Lucas stared at me for a long moment. I got so uncomfortable, I had to look away. "These robes are fantastic," I said. "Super absorbant."

"I told you about when Ba died," he said, "I'd cried so much, I hired a troupe of professional criers for the funeral."

"That's a thing?"

"Yeah, some people think it is good to have a lot of tears shed for you."

"Huh." I could understand now why a person would have professional criers at a funeral. No amount of crying seemed sufficient for Sadie. I took a gulp of wine. "Maybe I should go pro. I mean, this"—I gestured to myself—"is becoming more than a hobby for me. And I don't think I want to write advertising copy anymore, so, you know, I could use a new career path. Professional crier could totally be it. It's only in Taiwan though? 'Cause I only speak English."

Lucas produced the thing he'd been carrying, a large manila envelope that I knew by heart. He seemed to weigh it in his hands, like he wasn't quite sure what he should do with it, before he held it out. "I was insensitive about the card. I'm sorry. Maybe Sadie didn't mean for it to be delivered like that. She probably didn't get the chance to write her message. I never meant to upset you by giving it to you." He cleared his throat and put the envelope into my hands. "I know I've upset you a lot, not just about the card. And I don't know if you feel like you can trust me now, but I need to at least say the words. Hurting you is the last thing I wanted to do, Marin. I know this won't fix anything, but I want to try."

The weight of all the letters and postcards Sadie had written was almost unbearable. I set it on my lap.

Lucas said, "It's all of them. Every letter Sadie wrote. I tried to put them in order, but she wasn't always reliable about dating them. I know you saw one that time in my office, but I think you should read them all. It's like her whole history and the greatest love letter ever written, all wrapped up in one, and it's not mine . . . it's yours. It was for you."

He stood up. "I just came by to give you that."

"I'm sorry I didn't get on the boat."

He shook his head and gave me a sad smile. "Probably for the best," he said. "All things considered."

"Can I ask you something?" I said.

"Anything," he said.

"The singing . . . it was your idea, wasn't it?"

He pushed at something on the ground with his shoe. "You have a nice voice. Again, I'm so sorry. I thought you'd like it." He turned and left.

It was my favorite, I couldn't bring myself to say.

After he'd gone, I ran my hands over the envelope. It felt familiar in my hand, even in the dim light. I retreated to the smaller bedroom I'd taken over when Sadie came to the island, and turned on the bedside lamp. Then I began to read.

Dear Lucas,

My name is Sadie Cole, and I am a friend of your dad. Or I was. By the time you're reading these letters, I could be dead. Cancer keeps its own schedule . . . but by now you already know that too. You probably think it's strange that a twenty-six-year-old woman would call your Ba her friend, but we had more in common than just our prognoses. Your dad said that you are the best man he knows. That you are honorable and brave, that anyone could trust you with her life. So I'm entrusting my sister to you. I am guessing you probably are thinking of setting this letter down and stepping away from it, like it's a firework about to go off in your hand. Here's the thing: fireworks, if handled properly, are just about the best thing to ever happen to the night sky since the stars and whatever asteroid is pummeling toward Earth right now.

Fifty-Six

YOU'RE LEAVING?" LUCAS ASKED.

I twisted my hands around the handle of my bag. To anyone else, it must've looked like I was smiling, but Lucas knew my real smile and this wasn't it.

"Are you going back to Tennessee?"

"It was a tough choice. I thought about Italy."

"Those two are night and day. Why Italy?"

"I think I've always wanted to go there. I'm nervous about going somewhere I've never been, but even that seems like a better option than going home to our house and Sadie not being there."

"I could see you there. It's a beautiful place," Lucas said, nodding. "I have a little house in Conca dei Marini." He shoved his hands in his pockets.

"Maybe," I said. "I guess I'll have to find out for myself someday."

Lucas met my eyes, finally. He'd been avoiding them, I could tell. Still, I broke eye contact first, taking a quick glance at my watch. "I should probably head in before I miss my flight home."

He nodded. Behind him I could see Ted; he swung his giant backpack onto one shoulder.

"Thank you for everything," I told Lucas. "I'm glad I got to meet you." Was I? This ache did not feel like gladness, it felt decidedly worse.

"Despite the circumstances."

"Yeah. Despite the worst of circumstances."

We stood together in silence for a moment. It was a perfect day, the kind that brides and grooms dream of, the kind of bluebird day that mountaineers like Sadie revered. Sadie would have loved a day like this. She would've been trying to figure out exactly how to squeeze the most out of it. A little breeze ruffled through my hair and blew it into my face. Lucas stepped forward and reached out, like he was going to smooth it back for me, but he stopped. What had I expected? He'd satisfied his promise. His work was done. I was no longer the scaredy-cat who overanalyzed everything and put myself and my desires last. But that didn't change the way things were. I wanted to go to Italy, but I needed to go home.

I fixed my own hair, tucking it behind my ears. I looked around at the ocean, the sky, and took a deep breath.

"Marin—"

"Lucas—"

"I hope you have a happy life."

"Anything is possible," I said. "At least, that's what I've been told."

I started to walk toward the hangar, but turned back. "You should make a new sun-powered resort or make jewelry," I called. "You should do whatever makes you happy." I wasn't sure if he heard me over the wind. I told myself it didn't matter and strode off toward the small airport, where I'd get on a plane that would barrel down the world's shortest runway on the first leg of the journey back to Tennessee. I tried to keep my breathing steady. No reason to panic. I'd climbed, dived, zipped, lost, and I'd survived it all. I told myself these things while I wiped tears away with the back of my hand.

"Okay, Mar?" Ted asked me.

I nodded. "Just a little nervous about the flight."

"Eh, it's not so bad," he said. "Try riding a helicopter above twenty-thousand feet. Now, that's dicey."

"I can imagine." I could imagine. In fact, I was imagining at that moment. I hadn't thought about helicopters in a long time. My stomach swirled. I glanced over my shoulder. I did not want the parting shot that Lucas got of me to be me throwing up outside the Saba airport.

"You don't look so hot, kid," Ted said.

I shook my head. "I'm fine. I'm just ready to get this trip over with."

"Same," he said. "Don't get me wrong . . . it's crazy beautiful here, but it's the kind of place that I wouldn't want to stay more than a day or two."

He'd been there a week and a half.

"An island this small—after forty-eight hours, it kind of starts to feel like a prison, with nowhere to go and nothing left to do."

We walked through the tiny airport and out to the tarmac, where a handful of people who looked a little motion sick and rattled, to be honest, were picking up their luggage. We gave an attendant our tickets and climbed the stairs into the tiny plane. Ted's bag got caught on the door. I had to give him a little push inside to get him back upright.

We found our seats next to each other by the wing. I'd read this was the most dangerous place to sit, but the plane was full. Ted smiled at me reassuringly and pulled out an e-reader. His free hand, that I knew mine fit perfectly inside, rested on my thigh. I took a breath. The plane pulled away from the airport and turned toward the runway.

"What are you reading?" I asked.

"*Ulysses,*" Ted said. "Remember, I gave you that copy senior year? Did you ever finish it?"

I could picture the book, its pages dog-eared, soft cover coming apart, sitting on the table in the villa where I'd left it. I shook my head.

"I'm glad you came here, Ted," I said. "I know it wasn't easy."

He looked up from his reading. "Me too." He gave my thigh a gentle squeeze.

I looked down at his hand. "I don't know how you do it, but somehow you seem to appear in my life when everything is falling apart, when I need you. I've thought a lot about what you said. And you're right . . . we were great when we were together. I'll admit the thought of trying again is really tempting. I'm so comfortable with you and I know I'd be happy and safe."

Ted grinned at me. "We'd both be those things, Marin. It would be great."

"The thing is, I'm not the person I was when we were together, and I'm guessing neither are you. Do you really only want safe and comfortable? Because I'm not sure I do. I think we both deserve more than that."

The plane picked up speed. Ted pulled his hand away. He nodded. After a long pause, he said, "Obviously that's not the answer I was hoping for, but I understand. I gave it a shot, right?"

I nodded and tried to smile, but we were barreling down the world's shortest runway.

"He was a tough act to follow."

I held my breath during the terrifying takeoff. I leaned toward the window and watched the ground disappear beneath us. The plane banked around and Saba appeared again, a big dot in the vast sea. She was rugged rock and green, terra-cotta roofed, and magnificent, and I wondered for a moment if I hadn't left my heart there on the runway.

Fifty-Seven

FOR YEARS, SADIE HAD been on me about selling the house. "Why don't you buy one of those places downtown, the cute little condos? You don't need all this space, do you? I'm here less and less."

I'd looked at her. "Don't get me started on that. I'd like you here more. The last thing I'm going to do is give you an excuse not to come home."

"It's too big. Too much. It's vying for the Smithsonian of Tennessee. You probably have twenty-five years of crap in your closet, no joke. Mine's worse. You know what I found the other day? Three of my old retainers. Like the one I broke making out with Matt Carpenter in ninth grade."

Matt Carpenter had been my year. I'd conveniently forgotten about Sadie's foray into retainer-breaking sessions with a guy who was already managing the Pizza Shack and had a mustache. The moving part I'd shrugged off by saying it'd be too much work. Of course that hadn't been the real reason. The house was what tied us together, I thought. Where we'd grown up, where we'd been a family. I couldn't let that go.

I had been totally right about moving being too much work, though. For the last week, I'd spent most of my time on the floor of one of the seemingly endless number of closets in our home, surrounded by papers and moth-bitten sweaters and a shoebox full of several broken retainers. I'm not even sure all of them were hers. I smiled at that.

I slept in Sadie's bed for two nights, trying to breathe in what tiny molecules of her scent remained before I gave in and stuffed the entire bedding set into a large donation bag.

I'd culled our life down to a couple of boxes that I planned to put into storage for the time being. They were the important things: a book of Mom's prizewinning articles that a publisher had put together a few years after she died; Sadie's first print from art school; a handful of family photos. I donated Sadie's photography gear to a local art student. Most of the clothes went to a charity shop down the street that had a truck that provided meals and books and fed kids' hungry stomachs and minds. The only thing I had left to sort through was my own room. I'd saved it for last.

My room hadn't changed much since I was a teenager. I even had the same comforter. Laura Ashley wasn't messing around with quality. It had faded a little over the years, but otherwise it looked new. I pulled it off and stuffed it into a trash bag of donations. It didn't suit me anymore. My desk was a trove of papers that should have been thrown out forever ago. College essays and literary analyses. Little blue test booklets. I opened the bottom drawer of the desk. I had a couple of diaries from when I was really young that I thought I might want to look through later. I tossed them into a "keep" box. There was a manila envelope at the bottom.

My fingers trembled. In addition to fearing the normal unsettling things like heights, I'd developed a complex about manila envelopes. No one could blame me, really, after I'd read all of Sadie's letters to Lucas. If you opened a manila envelope and found a heart, a full beating heart, inside it, you'd get a complex too. I pulled it out anyway and opened it. Sometimes it's better just to get it over with. I already knew what was inside this manila envelope, even without seeing the Graywolf return address stamp on the outside. The postmark was a few weeks after Mom had died. I slid the paper out. It was good quality, some kind of woven linen blend. Heavier than normal paper. I traced the letterhead. I knew the words by heart, the ones written to tell me that my essay had won the creative nonfiction prize, and that came with money and the opportunity to turn my essay into a full-length manuscript that they would publish. I was not quite eighteen years old then. My essay had been the one about the women in Nicaragua—the weavers. Unbeknownst to me at the time, my mom had sent it in. I thought she hadn't read it. This was the kind of thing that could launch a young writer's career. But I was a child. I'd lost my mother. My sister was hanging from church rafters and breaking retainers with grown men. I'd put it in a drawer and never looked at it again, until this moment.

I stared at it for a long time. Then I folded it in half and tucked it inside the blue leather notebook Lucas had given me on Saba. I surveyed the room and decided everything else, except for some of my clothes, could go. My phone buzzed then. Ted. He'd settled for friendship and we'd even hung out a few times.

"Hi," I said.

"Hey, Mar. How's the packing going?"

"I think I've reached the my-back-hurts-just-toss-everything threshold."

"Sucks," he said. "I picked up tacos. You want to come over and watch *Jeopardy!*?"

It turned out Ted liked rituals. Takeout and evening TV—they were like me, he said, things he missed while he was away.

I spun around in my desk chair. "I don't know. I'm almost done here . . . I think I should probably just try to finish."

"That's cool, I'm pretty hungry anyway. More tacos for me."

"Okay. Have a good night."

After I hung up, I ran my hand over the leather notebook. The prize letter was hanging out a little, so I used my palm to push the papers back in. The letter formed a neat line with Laurentina's sketch. I had that feeling, the effervescent one I'd had in Saba, when I'd thought there was something to the lace and the weavers and sisters and life. I pulled out my laptop and began to write.

Fifty-Eight

SADIE

I KNOW I SAID I was done with these. You should know by now, I'm full of surprises.

Go after her, you dummy.

Fifty-Nine

MARIN

MY BOSS FOLDED THE piece of paper in half and tossed it back across the desk. "What the hell is this?"

"I'm resigning," I said, pushing the paper back toward her.

"You don't have to do that, Marin," she said. "You need more time? Take it. But don't resign. We need you; you're the best writer we have."

"That's really kind of you, but I think *I* need me more."

She shook her head and took the letter. "Okay. I can't say I'm happy, but I also can't argue with that. You've been through a lot. Do you have something in mind?"

I bit my lip.

"You have so many options," she said. "The world is your oyster."

The thing is that *so many options* sounds great, but in truth it's overwhelming as hell, and oysters reminded me of Lucas and the pearl that I should have treasured but left behind like some kind of imbecile.

"I have an idea," I told her. "But it's just a seed of an idea, really. I think I'd like to travel a little before I make any big changes."

"Well, I wish you the very best of luck, Marin. You'll always have a place here if you decide to come back."

A week later, the Realtor I'd hired hammered a FOR SALE sign into my front lawn with a mallet. I could say that it didn't feel like someone was driving a very large stake into my heart, but that would be a lie. Sadie would have wanted this, I told myself. But that didn't make it any easier. I shook the Realtor's hand and crossed the driveway to the car where Ted was waiting with the engine running. I slid into the passenger seat. Before I buckled my seat belt, I took a deep breath and blew it out.

"You ready?" he asked.

"Probably not," I said. I checked my purse. Yup, there was my passport, the notorious stolen and returned passport, with its one stamp. I set it on my lap.

"I can't believe you're doing this," Ted said. "You weren't kidding when you told me that you aren't the same girl you were back in the day."

"Well, you went on a blind date last week, so I guess we're both having new adventures. How'd that go, by the way?"

He put the car in gear, wordlessly, but the sly grin said enough.

"That good, huh?"

"I'm seeing her again on Friday."

I was happy for him. He was just as wonderful as I remembered. Kind, thoughtful, adorable in that worn-out-baseball-cap way. But I was different. I'd changed. And I realized that even though love—like the kind Sadie and Felix had—can be everything, not every love is like that. And if it's not an everything love, the kind that keeps you tethered to earth and makes you fly at the same time, it's better to be free.

On the drive to the Nashville airport, Ted listened to country music on the radio, sad songs about heartache and drinking, and I didn't complain like I did when we were in college. I felt a kinship with those broken people now.

Ted pulled the car up in front of the departure sign at the airport terminal. He popped the trunk and I extracted my bag.

"Thanks for the ride," I said through the passenger-side window.

"This is surreal," he said. "Are you sure you want to do this?"

I nodded. "I gotta go," I told him.

"Do you even have a plan?" he asked.

"I have a ticket," I said. I gripped my plane ticket and my passport in my hand and walked away before I had the chance to question myself.

"Take care of yourself, Marin," he said.

"I will."

I strolled through the terminal with its sea of travelers, boarded an international flight, and flew to Italy. I managed to make it through the flight without vomiting or spilling my underwear all over the plane, so I figured that was a sign from the universe that I'd made the right choice.

There was no Lucas Tsai shepherding me around this time, no Sadie behind the curtain. I stood in the airport and tried to take deep breaths. *What would Sadie do?* I wondered. Whatever the hell she wanted. I started in Venice, slowly. I did the typical things all tourists are expected to do. Rode on a gondola, visited St. Mark's Basilica and cried at the beauty of it, ate pasta until I thought I might burst and all the linguini would fly out like streamers. From there, I took a water bus to Burano, a place known for two things: rainbow-colored buildings lining the canals and lace. When I was doing research for my book, I discovered that lace had been born on Burano in the 1500s. The jewel of the island is the Museo del Merletto and I knew as soon as I read about it that I *had* to go there.

The man running the water taxi gave me directions I didn't quite understand, but I found the museum on my own anyway. I walked past the lace displays there—the travel websites hadn't done it justice—and I took copious notes in my blue notebook; it was practically bursting now. There was a parasol made entirely out of intricate lace. A tapestry that ran the length of a hallway. And then, an entire roomful of embroidered satin and lace wedding gowns. I pressed my hand over my chest where the deep ache was. I wish I could've seen Sadie's dress here.

On the other side of the room, I spotted a small group of elderly women working. I walked over to them.

"May I watch, *signora*?" I asked.

The one in the middle nodded.

"I'm Marin," I said. "*La merletto è bello*," I added in embarrassingly bad, halting Italian.

She laughed. "Good try. I am glad you like my lace. I am Sofia," she said. "Come. Look." She showed me her technique. I was amazed at the speed of her fingers.

"How do you do that?" I asked.

"I been making lace since I'm a girl and I go on making it until I drop. Practice. Much practice."

"We are all this way," another woman added. She told me that there is a local legend about how the lace came about, a love story, of course. A sailor gave his wife a perfect piece of seaweed before he left her behind for a voyage. She immortalized the gift with a needle and thread to remember him.

"Horseshit," another woman, this one named Francesca, said. According to her view of history, the lace was just another project that women did when they finished mending the men's fishing nets.

"I like the other story better," Sofia said.

"I hope you stick yourself with your needle," said Francesca. "Everything is love to you. Love. Love." She pretended to spit. "Something beautiful from ugliness is good too."

"What do you think?" Sofia said. "Love or beauty from ugliness?"

I smiled. "I think maybe both have their place."

Francesca turned to Sofia. "She's smart. I like her."

"I'd like to buy some Burano lace. Do you know a good place?" I asked.

Francesca snorted. "Good luck, everything in the shops is made in China now." She gestured for me to come closer. In a low voice she added, "On machines."

The other ladies made the sign of the cross and went back to their work.

"May I show you something?" I asked them. I opened my notebook and took out Laurentina's sketch, the lace with the bird pattern she'd drawn for Sadie's wedding gown.

Sofia peered at it. She ran her gnarled fingers over the paper. "Hmmm . . ."

"Can you make this?"

She shook her head. "Not me. It's very special. Francesca maybe."

Francesca scrunched her face with annoyance, but she leaned over and looked at the drawing anyway. She gave a short nod. "It's difficult. But I think I can do it. Where did you get this drawing? Not around here?"

I shook my head. "Somewhere far away. Another island, called Saba in the Caribbean Sea. It's very special to me."

"Mmm. You want me to make it?"

I thought about it for a moment. "Would you?"

"How much?"

"Just one bird. A small amount." I planned to carry it with me wherever I went. "But I'll pay whatever you want."

The house in Tennessee had sold in two days. I was suddenly flush with cash.

Francesca considered this for a moment. She squinted at my face and then back at the sketch. "I think your lace has its own story. No money. I make it for you as a gift."

I waited several hours for Francesca to make my lace, Sadie's lace, Laurentina's lace. Her needle worked and stitched us all together in a circle. It was the perfect closure.

She squeezed my hands when she placed the piece of lace into them. "Be good," she said.

I tucked the lace into my book.

"May I take your picture before I go?" I asked.

The women obliged me, looking up from their needlework for

the several moments it took for me to snap a few shots on my phone. Then I said farewell and headed back to Venice, posting the pictures online on the ferry ride.

I loved Venice, but I had heard it was sinking and I felt it. With each passing day, I grew lonelier. My heart grew heavy even with Sadie's lace in my pocket. I started to think I was making a mistake. So I left.

I found what Sadie would have called my "Marin Mojo" wandering the streets of Positano like Diane Lane in *Under the Tuscan Sun* while birds swooped overhead. I bought a big hat that looked ridiculous and wore it everywhere, not giving one single fuck. Sadie and I had always loved that movie. I'd loved the weird postcards that she'd written about grapes while she was on her trip. Sadie had loved how Diane Lane's character just bought a house, without a second thought, and made her own family. I thought maybe I'd buy a villa in Tuscany, just like her, but then I thought, my Sandra Oh was Sadie and I couldn't call her, and that just seemed too sad. That's how I started writing the postcards. I traveled down the coast and back up, seeing every sight I'd ever wanted to see and ones I didn't know existed until local people told me about them. Around every turn there seemed to be something to marvel at, something I wished I could share with Sadie. It was ugly and beautiful all at once. Bitter like the olive I naïvely picked from a tree and ate, oil dripping down my fingers, pit spit into the rich soil.

"Excuse me, *signora*," I said to a woman sweeping a porch with a sign that read DA AFFITTARE posted in the window. "Is this a hotel?"

"You want to rent the apartment?" she asked.

I looked at the small white building nestled into a mountainside. The sea breeze was strong here. It reminded me of Saba. I nodded. "Yes."

She took a key out of her apron and helped me carry in my suitcase. Later, I sat on the veranda of the tiny apartment I was renting, drinking a bottle of limoncello she'd brought me and writing it all down. Every luscious detail, the smells and tastes and sounds, the color palette, the feeling of the air. The kind of music it made me think of. The limoncello was sweet and tart and deceptively powerful. My cheeks grew hot and I found myself thinking of Lucas and Saba rum and writing postcards. *Dear Lucas, I'm sorry I left.* No. That wasn't right. I flung the postcard over the railing. I picked another blank postcard from my stack. This one had a picture of the famous Smeraldo cave, which is bathed in an emerald-green light. *Dear Lucas, Wish you were here.* Ugh, fling. Did I wish he was here? I wished Sadie was, I was sure of that. I pulled out my phone and dialed Laurentina.

"Marin!" she answered. "I had a feeling you were going to call."

"You know everything."

"See, Ronaldo, Marin says I know everything. I'm always telling him that."

"How are you? How's the baby?"

"I'm craving guava jelly something awful, but otherwise we're both doing just fine. Unlike some people, who are drunk. It's not good to drink by yourself, you know. Or do you have company?"

"No company."

"Are you okay?"

"I'm fine. I just wanted to hear the news from Saba, that's all."

"Let's see, there's some researchers here making another book of lace patterns on Saba. They're not as fun to have dinner with as you. Ken and Elisabet are on the outs again. We're taking bets on who's gonna cave first. You want in? I'll front you some money. You can pay me when you come back."

"I don't know when I'll be back," I said.

"He's working too much," she said. "We haven't seen much of him." I didn't have to ask who she meant. I'd littered the piazza with postcards to him that I wasn't going to send. "Don't stay away too long, Marin."

The truth was, the longer I stayed in Italy, the more pictures

I posted online, the more I loved it here. But that didn't stop me from missing Saba and its people with every fiber of my heart. Turns out that since the heart is a muscle, it's composed of bundles of fibers, not so different from lace, but stronger. So much stronger. Mine ached, but it was still beating.

Sixty

Dear Sadie,

You'll be happy to know that I rented a convertible. I always wondered how you felt climbing those mountains—maybe I was a little jealous—but now I think I know. It's driving you crazy, isn't it?

Barreling down the Amalfi Coast with the wind in my hair, I can feel you. You're in the bright sun warm on my face, in the limoncello and that sparkling brightness I feel when I taste it. The air here is different, but the cliffs, the ocean below, the white buildings and terra-cotta roofs nestled into the hills remind me of Saba.

Tonight the lights blinked on one by one and I strolled along the beach barefoot, enjoying the feel of the wet sand gently giving way beneath my feet, and I can almost feel you. That's something this place has on Saba—sand. It reminds me of our last day together and the sand the guys brought in to make you your very own beach.

It's taken me a while to get here. At first, I didn't write you because it was too hard. It made me miss you. And then when I started I only wanted to tell you the good stuff. Stupid, I know. You always saw right though me. So here it is. I was angry when I got your card. I've been angry about a lot of things. I was angry at you, for sending me away. For not telling me the truth. I was mad at the world, at Lucas, at cancer. I'm still mad at cancer, if I'm being honest. I can't meditate my way out of it. Cancer sucks. But I was angry long before cancer called. I've been angry with Mom for so long I almost can't remember a time when I wasn't.

I didn't know that anger and fear could be so coiled together that I couldn't even distinguish between them anymore. So I was pretty pissed when I opened that stupid card and you hadn't written anything. But I think I get it now. The student has become the teacher, right?

I'm writing again. Not just this letter, but a book. It turns out that the editor who read my essay back in high school and gave me the Graywolf prize still works there. I sent her my new story and she hooked me up with this agent that she knows and it's going to be a book. You probably know what it's about already. You know everything, you always did, even before you became some sort of all-knowing magical bird-dragon. The book is about you and me and Mom, about the women who wove in Nicaragua and changed their destiny, about the essay I didn't finish, and our destiny, and about Laurentina and Saba and the women who make lace, and your wedding dress, and it ends here on another island called Burano, with a bunch of little old ladies, who I think would've been us if we'd been able to grow old together. I know that's the worst pitch ever, but you would love it.

I read your letters. I know this one doesn't even come close to yours. I'm not as funny or irreverent as you. I'm not as brave. But I am, finally, after all this time, myself. I'm not all the way there yet, but every day I spend out here on my own in places I've never been, the closer I get. I still wake up sometimes expecting to hear your voice. I try to call you, forgetting that you aren't going to answer the phone. Sometimes it hurts so much that I don't know how my heart keeps beating. Other times, I can't believe this wild, wonderful world we live in that I get to experience.

You should know I'm still taking pictures and posting in Project Paradise. I've got followers, which is ridiculous. You should have had followers, not me. But still, it's nice to know that people know us, they care about our journey. It's yours too. Yours and mine. Because you're always with me. Don't get me wrong. There is no silver lining. This isn't God doing things for her reasons. I will miss you until someone sends my body out to sea on a raft surrounded by flowers and yards of lace. But I'm okay.

We never know how things are going to turn out. Like you said that day when we flew together on Saba, no one's ever ready. You just do it anyway. I wasn't ready to be without you. But I'm doing it.

Sixty-One

THE AIR WAS FULL of music and the scent of basil and lemon. I closed my notebook and took a deep breath.

"What are you writing?" the woman who owned the trattoria asked.

I was trying to come up with the words to explain these letters I'd been writing to Sadie since I'd gotten to Italy. I was thinking they might be my next project. My Italian was not good enough yet. "A book," I said. An answer that came from my limited vocabulary, and yet, saying the actual word felt like it was the perfect answer. I smiled.

"A book," she repeated, refilling my wine. "How exciting!"

She set a platter of antipasti in front of me and I picked at the offerings, sucking the salt from my fingers. A string of small bulbs overhead swayed in the cool night breeze. I pulled my pashmina around my shoulders.

"*Signora*, if it's not too much trouble, could you prepare a small breakfast I could take with me in the morning? I'm going to hike the Path of the Gods."

"By yourself? It can be quite strenuous at places, especially at Vallone Grarelle."

I nodded. "I don't mind."

I rose before the sun and got dressed in the gray predawn light and made my way to the trail. The pathway was narrow and worn down by tourists and locals alike, and before that by the mules that carried supplies between the towns the path connected.

Since I'd arrived at the Amalfi Coast, everyone I met had told me that the Sentiero degli Dei was an experience I needed to have. It sounded beautiful, transcendent even, until I found out it was basically an eight kilometer hike on a cliff's edge. Super. I'd planned to take the journey as a time to enjoy the history and the unrivaled surroundings that seemed to be everywhere on the Italian coast, and to honor Sadie, since this was exactly the type of thing that she'd love to see me doing. Now, I figured instead of observing me with pride, she'd be having a great freaking laugh as I tried not to look down at my impending doom.

The Path of the Gods linked a little village called Agerola with Nocelle, near the base of Monte Peruso. It wasn't supposed to be too hard, and in the distance, I was supposed to be able to see Capri. It was the best way to take in the area.

I found the trail head in Agerola and set off. I had the recommended meal for the trail, water, practical shoes. Since the theme of amusing Sadie was at the forefront of my mind, I pulled out the one shirt I'd kept from my time on Saba—a hot pink one with *Mrs. Right* across the chest—and put it on. There was a chill in the air, so I put a sweatshirt over it before I set off. Not that it mattered; I didn't expect to see anyone. The tourist season wasn't at its peak yet, and it was so early, most people would be sleeping off their endless pasta dinners and rivers of wine for hours.

The hike started off easily enough. It wound up the hillside, past little bushes and a patchwork of fields. *This isn't so bad*, I thought. For some time, I walked like this, over the gentle graded trail, wondering how far I'd gone. When was I supposed to feel God? It was pretty, but it wasn't soul-shaking. And then suddenly the Mediterranean Sea revealed herself before me in the dim, pinky, pre-sunrise light. The trail dumped me out on the side of a cliff; I could see the beach and the ocean below. The air rushed out of my lungs. Exhilaration, petrification? Maybe it was both. Fear and wonder aren't mutually exclusive—Sadie had taught me that.

I pushed on, putting one foot carefully in front of the other. I tried not to look over the side.

I must have reached Vallone Grarelle, I thought, because the *signora* had called it challenging, and holy hell, was I being challenged. With every step, my foot seemed to slip or displace some loose pebbles that then bounced down the steep face beside me. I focused on my breathing and crouched down to steady myself with my hands. I finally took a break. My butt on the ground seemed like a safe alternative to this scrambling that I was currently failing at, and besides, I was missing the view. I got out my water and the meal the *signora* had packed, and ate while I enjoyed the sight of the islands in the distance. The mist had burned off and now there was a warm breeze, perfumed with bougainvillea and lavender that grew on the hillsides like weeds.

The air was turning warmer. I knew the sun was on its way. It had cut a slice of copper along the horizon. I stuffed my sweatshirt into my backpack and tucked my breakfast away. Then I leaned back on my arms, closed my eyes, and lifted my face to prepare for the sun's appearance.

"I made it," I said aloud, hoping Sadie would hear me.

"Nice shirt."

It couldn't be. I opened my eyes. There was Lucas, squinting down at me. He looked exactly the same as the day I'd left.

It took me a moment to pull myself together enough to speak. "I couldn't bear to part with it."

Lucas crouched down slowly. I reminded myself to breathe. It seemed to take him forever to reach me. He set his hands on my shoulders and leaned down farther until he was face-to-face with me. The sun was just starting to peek over the horizon. Around us the remaining mist turned to gold.

"Me either," Lucas said.

"Is that the truth?"

He nodded. "I couldn't bear to part with *you*, Marin."

"Is that why you're here?"

Lucas pressed his hand to my cheek and I leaned into it.

"Yes," he said. "Well, that and I got your note."

"My . . . Wait, how did you know?"

"What are the odds that she would give us both that random dog card? And besides, your handwriting is much neater than your sister's."

"She never was a good student," I said. "She was a great teacher, though. She taught me so much. She helped me remember who I truly am."

He sat down beside me. "Who is that?"

"I'm a sister who misses her sister every day. I'm a writer. I'm a person who hasn't seen the whole world yet and desperately wants to. I'm someone who is terrified of heights but loves standing on a mountaintop and enjoying the view. I'm a girl who is afraid of the ocean and still found a pearl in an oyster while diving off a tropical island. I love to sing. I'm braver than I think."

Lucas nodded, but he stayed quiet. I wasn't done. "I'm not perfect. I get scared and I hide. I don't know much about the world. I only speak English. I mean, I don't understand a lick of Mandarin, but I could listen to Lucas Tsai speak it all day long. Because I love him."

"Do you want to know who I am?" he asked. His hands were folded in his lap. His voice was tight.

I nodded. I was a little afraid of what he might say, but he was here, and that was major. Sadie always said that getting there was the hardest part. And Mom told us taking the first step was always the scariest one. How many steps had Lucas taken to reach me?

He said, "I'm a son who misses his father every day. I'm a businessman. I'm someone who has seen the whole world and didn't truly find home until I met you. I'm fluent in eight languages, and passable in twelve, but I only want to speak Mandarin around you on the off chance that you'll get frustrated and tackle-kiss me like that night on The Road. I'm a guy who told myself I wasn't afraid of anything, and I wasn't, until I thought I was going to lose you. Because I'm in love with you, Marin Cole. I'm totally, completely in love with you."

He held his fist up in front of me and opened it. There in his palm was a perfect pearl, white and lustrous like bridal silk, but it was set in the middle of a simple golden disc hanging from a delicate chain. I picked it up between my fingers. "Is this what I think it is?"

"Well, you can't find treasure," he said, running a hand through his hair, "and leave it behind."

Lucas fastened the necklace's clasp for me and then slid his hand into the hair at the nape of my neck and kissed me. We did not fall off the cliff this time. We stayed up there in the sky while the sun washed over us, warm and resplendent, like a blessing from above. He took my hand and started to lead me down the mountain.

"Hey, tell me something," I said.

"What?"

"If you knew I wrote that last card myself, what took you so long? Were you not sure?"

He smiled and shook his head. "Actually, I would've found you anyway. But I wanted to finish my first project for you—"

"It's beautiful."

"Thank you. But that's not it. I sold the airline and some of the other businesses. I decided to make a line of eco-friendly resorts that are also free retreats for artists and people who need healing or inspiration."

I swiped at a tear. "That was your project?"

"It's not done, but yeah. You're the one who gave me the idea, really. I wanted to honor Ba, and I hoped it would honor Sadie too."

"No wonder you took so long," I said through my tears.

"Well, there's also the fact that you're a hard one to pin down, Marin Cole. By the time I got to Tennessee, you were already gone, and let's just say Ted wasn't exactly a helpful source of information."

I cringed.

"It's fine. He's like an overprotective Labrador. I finally wore him down. He's at least leaning Team Lucas now. He has a girlfriend who seems very nice, a veterinarian. Anyway, Ted said you were in Venice, I went to Venice. But then I saw the picture of you online, the one from Burano. I went to Burano, you came down to Amalfi. Honestly, I'm a little tired. I thought you were a homebody. I did not expect to be chasing you around this much."

"I thought you were kind of a sexy international man of intrigue and badassery. Was I wrong?"

"Let's get down this mountain and I'll let you decide. For now, let's talk about where we should go next. What destination is top on your list? Ken is taking over some more business operations stuff and the retreats are just starting construction, so I have some time on my hands. And I've got my own transportation. I'll take you wherever you want to go."

"Ken is running things?"

"With the baby on the way he needed a raise, so I promoted him. Elisabet has made him quite responsible. I think he's going to make a great CEO. I'm not sure about his diaper-changing abilities, but Ronaldo is supposed to be training him."

I tried to process everything Lucas was telling me. "Wait, I thought they were on the outs. What's going on? Is everyone having babies on Saba?"

"Some things are fate," he said. He kissed me again. "Have you decided?" he asked when we finally separated.

"I can't," I said.

Lucas stood perfectly still. He didn't say anything, he just eyed me.

I grabbed his arm and pulled him toward me. "No. It's just that I'm finishing the manuscript with this." I pulled out the tiny piece of lace Francesca had made for me from the notebook.

"Nice notebook," he said. "Where'd you get it?"

Smiling, I wrapped my arms around him. "I'm so inspired here. And then of course, I'll need to send it to my editor, and probably make lots of edits under tight deadlines, and then there's book tours, and—"

"Message received. Sadie did tell me that you like to be in control."

I pressed my cheek to his chest. It was hard to believe I could be so happy, that in the midst of my sorrow, I'd found joy.

"Marin?"

"Yeah?"

"Would this be a bad time to tell you that we have to go down fifteen hundred steps on the side of a cliff to finish the trail?"

"Maybe we should talk this through," I said. "Why rush? Like I said, I feel inspired here. Like *right* here."

"You win," he said. He patted the ground next to him on the first stair. I sat down and leaned into him. "We'll stay. I'm feeling inspired myself. And besides," he said, brushing his lips over my hair. "I could always let you just kiss us over the edge."

"Ha," I said, pulling him toward me by the front of his hooded sweatshirt. "Lucas Tsai, *nǐ shì wǒ de.*"

His eyes widened. "I'm yours, huh?" He was losing a battle to hold back a grin. "It would seem you've been busy while we've been apart."

"True on both counts," I said, leaning closer. "I guess I won't have to rage kiss you anymore when you're speaking Mandarin."

He looked thoughtful. "How's your Italian? Did I mention that mine is impeccable?" He was so close that his lips brushed over mine when he spoke. *"Ti farò impazzire dal desiderio." I'm going to drive you wild with desire.*

I turned toward him. In one fluid motion, he managed to snatch my phone and pull me toward him. He kissed me. The flash went off.

Acknowledgments

I am indebted to so many wonderful, generous people without whom this story wouldn't exist. To start, I have to thank my phenomenal agent, Sharon Pelletier, who has believed in me from the beginning and championed all of my work tirelessly over the years! You've been a constant source of encouragement and helped me grow so much as a writer. Making you cry in a bar was one of the highlights of my writing career. Thank you also to Lauren Abramo and Kemi Faderin at Dystel, Goderich, & Bourret. To my fantastic editor at Berkley, Kerry Donovan, I am so grateful for you. I couldn't have asked for a more insightful and supportive partner in this process! You immediately got the heart of this story and have been instrumental in making it the best it could be. Thank you also to Vikki Chu for designing the cover of my dreams, and to the rest of the amazing Berkley dream team, especially Mary Geren, Megha Jain, Bridget O'Toole, and Brittanie Black. I am beyond lucky to work with all of you.

A number of wonderfully smart and generous people contributed to the Mandarin dialogue, including my dear friend Wei-Chun Huangfu, who helped me refine my original pinyin translation (even though she's busy being a superstar scientist in Taipei), Tianyi Feng, who copyedited the pinyin, and Yinqian Renxiao, who generously answered all my texts when I couldn't quite make up my mind about how I wanted to express the word *heartbreak*.

I'm blessed with a group of friends who have been there for me through every triumph and low point—Lindsay, Alyson, Kate, and Ginger, thank you! To the Bitches Who Book, never have I known a group of more caring, vulnerable, smart, and supportive women. Thank you for taking me in and letting me be a part of the world's most special book club.

I also have to thank Molly Pascal, my brilliantly talented friend and writing partner, who read every page of this book, was always up for brainstorming, fostered many a breakthrough, and continues to be both an inspiration and the best cheerleader. Thank you also to my writing support crew: Amy Clarke, Anna Newallo, Denise Williams, and Jen DeLuca—this journey is amazing, but not always easy, and it truly takes a village. Thank you for being my village.

Last, but not least, I would not be where I am today without the support of my family. Mom, you've read every story I've ever written and supported me unconditionally my entire life. Sal, I would know nothing of protective and careful big sisters if it wasn't for you. Dad, you always know just what to say to make me feel better. To my husband, Tom, you are the inspiration for every love story I ever write (even if I don't let you read them before they're done), and never begrudge me writing time or pets. To my sweet children, Greta and Elliot, you show me every single day that there is no limit to how much a person can love or laugh. You always say you love me more, but that is impossible.

KEEP READING FOR A SPECIAL
PREVIEW OF LIBBY HUBSCHER'S
NEXT ROMANCE,
IF YOU ASK ME
COMING IN SPRING 2022
FROM BERKLEY JOVE!

MY MOTHER ALWAYS SAID people who work in helping professions are the ones most in need of professional help themselves. She's usually right about most things. After all, I became an advice columnist. Imagine the irony . . . who needs more help than that?

When things started to go awry, I was sitting in a staff meeting at 2 p.m., politely nibbling on a stale Girl Scout cookie courtesy of the real estate columnist's daughter, waiting for the *Raleigh Times* owner to arrive and the other shoe to drop. The last time Ed Hastings had been here, half our staff had been let go . . . low subscription numbers, lost ad revenue, and all that. Today, he whooshed into the room and the air whooshed out—everyone fell silent. I brushed a crumb from my notepad, straightened up, and squared my shoulders. If I was getting the axe, the least I could do was sit up straight.

"Afternoon, folks," Ed said. "I'll keep this brief."

"The online edition has been doing well," Tyler, the Out and About columnist interjected. "We've had great ad commitment for next quarter."

"Let's not get ahead of ourselves." Ed straightened his lavender tie. He can pull that color off. It would've washed me out. "I'm not here for layoffs. Tyler's right, we're faring fine, for now. Out and About, of course, has been one of our top features. Actually, I'm here to announce a few pieces of good news. First, as you likely already know, our brilliant managing editor received the Hillman

Award for her series on corruption in the North Carolina general assembly—kudos again, Kyra. Second, we've got a columnist who, if everything goes according to plan, is about to go national."

He surveyed the room, appraising us, while we all wondered who was about to get lucky. Had his gaze lingered on Ashleigh? She wrote the society pages on top of meaty public interest pieces and looked like a princess in pearls, her natural blonde waves cascading over her shoulders. Or maybe Javier? His coverage of the evolution of the education system had been insightful and thoroughly researched, with crisp writing to boot. They were the real journalists. I smiled preemptively, preparing to show a gracious response.

Hastings extended his arms. "Our very own Dear Sweetie!"

The small room exploded with applause. Javier whistled. "Way to go, Violet!" Tyler said in a tone that sounded as much of an indictment as it did a congratulations.

"Alright, everybody," Kyra said, saving me from the attention, "it is wonderful news, and absolutely well deserved, but the syndication's not a done deal yet. There are a few columnists in the running—all talented. The next three months will determine what happens. Okay, that's it, great job, you superstars. Back to work."

A couple of people congratulated me as they trickled out of the room. I thanked them, but I stayed put, processing. Kyra raised an eyebrow. I'd thought my face had been neutral, pleasantly surprised; truth be told, I was flummoxed. And despite years of practice controlling my expressions, curating them for each situation, she read me like a book, just as she always had when we were college roommates at State.

"You're not excited?" she asked.

"No . . . of course I am. Who wouldn't be excited? I'm just shocked, I guess. You are sneaky. I had no idea."

She shrugged. "I always tell Rox that I would've made a great spy. Keeping secrets, digging up dirty ones, whatever . . . it's one of my many gifts."

"Right, well don't look at me. I've got no secrets. I'm just a happily married advice columnist."

"Yeah, yeah. How about a kick-ass soon-to-be-nationally-syndicated advice columnist? It sounds more exciting and less smug married."

"It does have a ring to it," I admitted, finally standing up slowly. My legs still felt like rubber after an unusually brutal boot camp class this morning.

"Why do you look like my grandma getting out of her Barca-Lounger? Tell me you're not still doing that awful fitness class at the crack of dawn."

I ignored her and smoothed down my skirt. "Do you mind if I head home early? I was thinking I'd finally break out that sushi-making kit Sam got me for our anniversary and surprise him with my news at dinner."

"Raw fish . . . how sexy. You're not planning on placing the rolls all over yourself like Samantha in *Sex and the City*, are you?"

I recoiled. "That's an option, thanks to all those sessions at that awful fitness class you keep teasing me about. But no, I was not planning on turning myself into a naked human platter." Although, it had been a while since Sam and I had had anything other than the standard ten-minute, two-position, perfectly fine sex. I pictured a piece of sashimi on my décolletage. *No.*

"Good. Cause if I recall, that did not end well for Smith and Samantha. Didn't they break up in that episode?"

"Unlike some people, I haven't watched that show since we binged it in college. Not to worry. I definitely will not be wearing a California roll tonight, so I guess my marriage is safe."

"In that case, I suppose strategizing how to get your column on top can wait till tomorrow."

"Thanks, Boss." I grinned at her, collected my leather folio, and power walked out of the office. I couldn't wait to see the look on Sam's face when I surprised him with my big news.

. . .

Sam and I moved to Apex ten years earlier when the few subdivisions being built were mixed in among horse farms like some kind of utopia. It was so charming and perfect; we'd loved it right away, just like how we'd fallen for each other. It wasn't like that anymore. The tiny historic downtown still stood, as picturesque as ever, but there were more communities, and fewer trees.

On my way home, I stopped at the newest addition—a high-end grocery store—to buy some sushi-grade tuna and salmon and a bottle of prosecco, then headed toward the year-old firehouse, where the crew was polishing the fire truck to a high shine, and finally hung a left before pulling into my neighborhood. It had been the first one Sam and I had looked at when we decided to buy. The only one.

We lived in a sky blue Victorian on a cul-de-sac where I made up for our childlessness by baking Ritz cracker chocolate toffee bark every Christmas, throwing the Labor Day cookout with an honest-to-god bouncy castle, and bringing flowers and, not one, but *two* bottles of wine—red and white—to the community book club each month. It was idyllic. Sam mowed the zoysia lawn in perfectly parallel lines and I planted clematis and azaleas that burst with color along our picket fence every spring. It was the kind of life I'd pictured when I was a girl, watching my mother plan all those fancy weddings for her clients and dreaming about my own happily ever after.

I parked in the driveway next to Sam's car—he'd taken an interest in the environment recently and carpooled with one of our neighbors who worked for the same firm most days—and grabbed the mail. I bounced up the steps, wrangling the giant stack of mail, the grocery bag, and my keys. Inside, I left my shoes beside the door before heading into the kitchen. I dropped the mail on the table. Some of my readers' letters always ended up here, so we got more mail than most people. I ran a hand over the envelopes, debating whether I should open them, start the sushi rice, or get changed. I was dying to get out of my constricting work clothes and into a pair of nice jeans and a tank top, and unwind my hair out of the high bun that had become a uniform over the years, but I wanted to make sure I had everything ready by the time Sam came home.

I cooked the short-grain rice until it was tender, fanning it precisely the way the directions specified, added the rice vinegar, placed it on the cling wrap on the little mat, and then filled it with the fish and cucumber sliced into tiny sticks, before I tucked it into the fridge next to the chilling bubbly. Sam wasn't due back for another two hours, which gave me plenty of time to shave, wash my hair with that coconut shampoo he liked, do my hair and makeup, and greet him at the front door.

I went straight to the bathroom and turned on the shower. I hated to be wasteful, but the water took forever to get hot—the water heater was old like the linoleum. Maybe we could use the extra income from the syndication to finally redo the bathroom. Even better, Sam could stop working so hard to get promoted, all those early mornings and late nights, and—I dared to dream—his mother might even stop calling my column a "little hobby."

I was on my way to put my skirt in the bag for dry cleaning when I froze. Among my mother's many mantras I followed to a T was "messy bed, messy head." Sam must've been in a hurry this morning: he'd pulled the covers up, but he'd left the blanket I used to block the blasting air conditioner he liked at night all wadded and lumpy beneath the duvet. He also hadn't opened the curtains. I left them—with any luck, we'd want them closed later anyway—but the bed had to be fixed. I flung the comforter back so I could grab the blanket and smooth the whole tangled mess out.

I admit it, I screamed when I saw them. At first, I only registered people in my supposed-to-be-empty house. A moment passed—my scream hanging in the air—before the people flailed about searching for cover and I was able to finally process what I was seeing. The tangled mess. *Blankets*, I'd thought. Not Sam. Not my husband. Not my husband Sam intertwined with a woman.

Seeing is believing, my mother said that too.

I saw. Sam's pale skin, naked, his face like an Edvard Munch paining, his blonde curls a mess, and the woman, her hair blonder than his, her skin a shade tanner, but precisely as nude. She buried her face in his chest.

"Oh my God," Sam said. "Violet. Oh God."

None of us moved. I didn't take a breath for several seconds; I was too busy wondering if I was having some sort of episode or near-death experience that was causing me to hallucinate. Had I actually tripped and hit my head on the footboard? The woman's hand clutched for the covers. She wasn't wearing a wedding ring, I noted.

"What is this?" I managed to squeak.

Sam squirmed. "What are you doing home so early?"

I stepped back. My lip was starting to tremble, so I bit it. I realized that I was standing in a wrinkled blouse and my shapewear and I just *couldn't*. There's only so much humiliation a person can bear; certainly I had exceeded the all-time limit. I skulked back to the bathroom and shut the door. The shower was steaming, so I stepped beneath it, letting the water rush over me. It soaked through my stupid clothing and scalded my skin. Mascara dripped down my cheeks and onto my hands when I wiped my cheeks. I pressed my back against the wall of the shower and slid down to the floor.

That couldn't have been real, could it? Sam with another woman, in our bed? But I'd seen them with my own eyes. All that skin. A perfectly toned ass. The platinum blonde hair with the telltale post-coital matting. *Idiot*, I thought. I'd jinxed myself with the sushi. And after being the victim of the worst possible kind of surprise, Sam had tried to protect her. *Her.* Like she was the one who stood to be harmed in the situation. A sob rose up in my throat, but I clapped my hands over my mouth. The ability to cry, really cry, without making a sound was a skill I'd perfected over a lifetime, and I was thankful for it now. My perfect world had just imploded while I stood there in my Spanx. No way was I letting the perpetrators hear me have a breakdown in the bathroom.

I stayed in the shower until the water ran ice cold. Surely they weren't still lying there? The mirror was covered with a sheen of condensation, but I could make out my reflection, blurred, like a ghost. A drowned raccoon ghost with the mascara smeared around both eyes. That wouldn't do, I told myself. I washed my face and reapplied my makeup. Then I got out my volumizing blow-drying brush and did my hair. I once saw a quote on Pinterest that said, "If my hair looks good, I can deal with anything." I guess this was a test of that adage. I opened the bathroom door. The bedroom was dark, the bed made so tightly you could bounce a quarter off of it. Sam cleared his throat from the doorway.

"We should talk," he said. I opened and closed dresser drawers in succession, pulling out my nicest underwear, jeans, a black T-shirt. "Violet."

I shook my head. "It's not a good time," I said.

"I need to explain."

I turned to face him. His button-down was off by a button; I resisted the urge to fix it. "I think you should go. I need to get changed." He looked at me. An hour ago, the eye contact alone would've melted me into a puddle, but now I felt I might spontaneously combust and be reduced to a pile of ash on our carpet, something to be sucked up by our robot vacuum.

I listened to Sam's footsteps on the stairs. The creak of the front door. The turn of the deadbolt as he locked it from the outside. His car started and then it was quiet again. Even with the bed made and Sam and whomever that was gone, and my hair voluminous as all get out, I could still see them. I retreated to the kitchen, to cold sushi and the pile of my mail. There's nothing better for avoiding your own devastation than a mountain of other people's problems.

I choked down a mouthful of tuna—the gelatinous rice sticking in my throat—and chased it with a generous gulp of prosecco I'd planned on using to toast my big news, while I tore open the first envelope, a pink one with loopy cursive on the front. *Dear Sweetie,* it read, *I don't know what to do. I feel like my whole world is falling apart.*

You and me both, Pink Envelope.

You and me both.

Libby Hubscher is an author and scientist. She studied biology at Bowdoin College in Brunswick, Maine, and holds a doctor of philosophy in molecular toxicology from North Carolina State University. Her work has appeared online and in textbooks, scientific journals, and literary journals. Her short story "The Unwelcome Guest" was long-listed for the Wigleaf Top 50 in 2018. She lives in North Carolina with her husband, two young children, and a menagerie of pets.

CONNECT ONLINE

LibbyHubscher.com
🐦 EMHubscher
📷 LibbyHubscher
f LibbyHubscher

Ready to find
your next great read?

Let us help.

Visit prh.com/nextread